T0267044

WATER'S BREAK

WATER'S BREAK

SOPHIA L. HANSEN

In the beginning was the Word . . . and the Word became flesh.

This book is dedicated to my mother,

Hyun Sook Lee Beidel,

who instilled in me her love of story.

And to you, dear reader.

It is my fervent hope that these words take on

their unique form as you read,

and this story comes to life in your heart.

In the beginning was the Deep.
The Deep was whole and covered all.
The Deep was whole and supported all.
In the Deep was life and peace.
The Deep was complete.

We loved and lived in the Deep.
Giving and receiving,
sharing space, sharing life.
Inhabiting the shallows and the depths,
loving the surface light and the colder climes.

We were farmers, teachers, and explorers,
but more than anything, we were lovers,
knowing and being known.
Without fear, without hesitation.
We dwelt in communion.

Until the Water broke.

from the Song of Endings
Jonnat's Verse

1

NICA shrank into the kelp forest, thankful for the camouflage its dappled greens provided. Trusting the massive plants' grasp on the ocean floor, she wrapped her legs around a towering stalk, ignoring the prickles that grabbed at her skin. A frond brushed the welts on her hand and she winced, squinting with dismay at the angry streak, bright red and stark against her green webbing. Fire corals should be left alone, as the Deep intended, not braided into a trellis. Why did she ever agree to lead Rissa's nuptial pod?

Hold fast.

Her heart thumped, threatening to expose her. *Slow.* She forced it to calm, quieting the thuds until they barely sent a ripple through the forest.

Her sister's mood rode the currents well ahead of her presence. Even at this distance, Nica could feel Rissa's blood pressure rise.

"You can't hide forever."

She fought the urge to dart as Rissa drew closer. She was still not near enough to detect her. *Unless I do something stupid.* Nica dared not move, even to maintain her position amidst the swaying kelp.

Temperature. Focus, Nica. She closed her eyes. *Decrease heat output.* Constricting pores would regulate her body temperature so she could blend in with the ambient waters.

Her chest ached from the mad dash for cover, but she resisted the urge to gulp. Instead, she extended her jaw into a wide gape. The waters drifted freely across her fluttering lung linings, steeping them with the gasses needed, carrying away what was not.

"Show yourself," Rissa demanded.

Nica's sensory pores ached from the tension in Rissa's words—so compressed, squeezed through tightened lips.

No one can see me in this kelp, so there's no need to panic. Threading one arm along the wafting blades, she wrapped the other around her radiating curls, moving with care, trying not to disturb the surrounding currents. *If only my hair were green, as well.* She would have bound it after firstmeal, but hiding had not been on the agenda when she'd left the cavern.

Where are those magmas when I need them? The bright orange guardfish were one of the few denizens that matched her lava-colored mane. Without a decoy, anyone within sight-distance could notice the glint of her straying tendrils, even at this depth's light. Not that there was much to see by. The breaking sun's light was more shadow than shine. The unseasonable chill sent a shudder down her dorsals.

Rissa's voice washed against her, tinged with frustration. "You know I'll find you. I always do."

Nica quelled her alarm. Signals of panic would give her away, even if her hair didn't.

She tasted the streams winding around her, sifting through particles in the kelp and brine. Currents were propelling matter from the ocean floor. She glanced up at the canopy of waves. A rising current this early? It wasn't even close to sunpeak. *Shells!* How did she miss that? She scanned for better cover.

A face as green as hers shot into view, grinning with triumph. "She's here."

"Kel. You eel." Nica launched off the kelp stalk, barreling headfirst at her brother.

Kel dodged her with practiced ease. "You really want every Olomi in the Deep to know you're such a larva?" He swished by and tugged at the bright yellow and black braided cords that hung from her tunic with a scoff. "These don't mean much if you act like a fry."

"You've had Guardian cords for three cycles," Nica retorted, "and you still spend every free ripple competing on that jump team."

"He's right, you know." Rissa's signal arrived just before she floated into sight. "You're an Olomi Guardian, not a flathead. Stop hiding just because I want you to lead my nuptial pod when I bond with Jonnat."

"You mean weed-dragon," Nica murmured into the stream.

"Excuse me?" Rissa closed the distance between them, her rosette-lined eyebrows raising with her tone. Even in her ire, her sister's pink elegance shimmered as Nica's greens never would.

"Flatheads hide in the sand. Weed-dragons use kelp. So technically—"

Heat radiated from Rissa.

Nica changed course, descending in hasty deference to their eldest. "I mean, I'm honored to be at your side when you make your vows. You just didn't warn me that being your prime attendant meant party planning and making decorations. Look"—she lifted her hands—"coral burns. You know I'm no good with braids." She grimaced.

"Oh swish, don't be a minnow." Rissa sniffed. "You can't feel anything on webbing."

"But that wrap," Nica persisted, "I can't take in a decent draught, let alone swim straight wearing that dress."

"I'm in Jonnat's nuptial pod and you don't see me darting for cover." Kel whisked behind, pulling at her hair.

"Eel." Nica whirled to face him, trying to suppress the rise he'd successfully provoked. "All you have to do is show up in a formal tunic. You have no real responsibilities." *As usual.*

"What's that? Can't hear you." Kel tweaked her hair again as he slipped past.

"Kel!" Rissa's rebuke resonated with overtones of their mother. "Stop harassing Nica. You should be an example. You're older, and you're a higher ranked Guardian."

She scolded Kel without shifting her stance, unmoved by the currents. Even her braids, thick and black as Ìyá's, draped perfectly down her dorsal, accenting her pale pink skin and the dark red rosettes that graced her sensory lines.

"And Nica, do you think being my prime attendant means the

tide is about you? It's my bonding. It will be as *I* want it. When you make your bonding vows, you can make your own decisions."

"Don't you mean if, Sisi?" Kel darted past with another jab.

"Kel!"

He shrugged. "Did my job. You wanted to find her. Didn't sign on for a lecture."

With a swish, he was gone.

Nica watched his wake, wishing she could follow. *Even if he is an eel.*

"Now can we please do something about this tangle?" Rissa sighed and removed a starfish from Nica's hair.

"Ow!" A snort of bubbles erupted. "I'm a Guardian. Not a showpiece."

"I'm not saying that. It's just, you should try to act more mature, like, well, like . . . "

"I don't need to act like you." She blew a thin stream at a tendril dangling from her forehead. "I'm a—"

"I know, I know. Honestly, Nica, you've been saying the same thing since you were eight. '*I want to be a Guardian, just like Bàbá.*' It's been ten cycles and you've earned your cords. Mission accomplished. Would it kill you to stop acting like an urchin?"

Nica wriggled out of her sister's reach. "Not all of us can get paid to be pretty. So what if I'm not perfect like you? Maybe I want to actually make a difference."

She regretted the words as soon as she said them, but it was too late. The barb had struck its mark.

The rosettes marking Rissa's sensory lines flushed dark red, but Nica clung to her glare, refusing to yield.

"Sisę." Rissa rested her hands on Nica's shoulders. "You don't have to be a Guardian to help people. You could be a healer or a teacher."

Nica shrugged her sister off, clenching onto her cords. "I could also be a—"

Flashes of blue flitted throughout the unusually dark kelp forest. Nica frowned, rotating slowly. *Morning shadows should have given way to the sun by now.*

"Why are the night fish rising?"

Arrival

We hang, motionless. Appearing lifeless, though life is the objective. But first, destruction. We have traveled far, and long, without life to interrupt our synchronized approach.

We hang, motionless. Designed neither for beauty nor speed, but survival. Blinking, silent, against the void. Anticipation without desire. Expectation without hope. We wait.

We hang, motionless. Tracking with the womb that will receive our charges. The home to replace that which was spent. But before implantation, this world must be conformed.

Medical Officer's Journal:
upon entering orbit planet Aquan

2

GRIT and seaweed buffeted Nica in the briny turbulence. Thrashing against churning eddies, she fought to reach the ocean's inky canopy. Night fish, glowing blue against the darkness, darted between her legs, flashing as they swarmed through tangled greens. Cete and squid hunted in the chaos, chasing their nocturnal feast as they did every night.

Except it was sunpeak.

Her sister's call cut through the roiling currents. "Get back down to the reef."

"Can't . . ." Nica paused amid the rising shoals of limbed and finned creatures. "Something's wrong up top. It shouldn't be this dark."

Teeth clamped against the whirling sediment, she flushed her lungs with water and launched with a scissor kick. She breached the waves, then gasped, but not from the unusual chill.

Rissa lunged out of the foam by her side. "What do you mean, it shouldn't be . . ." her voice faded.

The sisters floundered, speechless, at the veil filling the sky. Never before had the view of the heavens been blocked. Sunpeak's light was banished. Darkness blanketed the Deep.

Winds lashed the water's surface, the waves hurling peaks at them and the other Olomi who emerged from the protection of the sea. Brightly colored Olomi—yellows, oranges, and pinks—bobbed in sharp contrast to the murky waves. The darker blues, grays, and greens were harder to distinguish against the ocean's shrouded face. All battled the tempest as gloom engulfed the horizon.

"Nica?" Rissa grabbed her arm. Flecks of seafoam scattered from the delicate webbing between her trembling fingers and her rosettes paled to ash as she pointed.

Nica tracked her sister's point to a break in the unnatural cover. The darkness had spawned a host of shades. Great columns, black as orcas and twice as large, plummeted toward the surface like spears launched from the sky. Shadows took on substance, form, and force, piercing the water's surface.

The Deep has been violated.

Her Guardian training kicked in. Even a rookie didn't need to understand a threat's nature to recognize danger.

"Dive!" she screamed at the surfaced Olomi before she plunged below.

Shock waves thrust her back like a piece of debris. Pulses concussed all around, leaving her sore and spent. She tried to take a reading, to gather any information on the attack that fell from above.

Solid. Smooth. No limbs or fins. No life signs. But—vibrations?

Heat followed, emanating in waves as the closest projectile streaked to the depths.

She jerked back. It was boiling the water!

"Rissa. Avoid the wake." Nica pushed her message as far as she could. "The water-trail burns."

There was no response.

"Rissa? . . . *Rissa!*"

A deep rumble reverberated through her pores and down to her bones. She clamped her hands over her ears, but could not block all her receptors. The seabed trembled and its waters vibrated as the skies above the surface darkened once again.

Powerful swells sent her tumbling as a mass wider than a seamount descended into the churning surf. Helpless, she tucked into a ball until a surge slammed her against a rock wall.

Sea green faded to black.

REPORT

   STASIS REGENERATIVE
   CYCLE COMPLETE

   INITIATE NUTRITIVE BATH . . .

   INITIATE MUSCLE STIMULATION . . .

   INITIATE GRAVITATIONAL
   ADJUSTMENT . . .

   RESTORATIVE PROCESS COMPLETE

   EOR

3

DARKNESS. Nica writhed, only to find her limbs restrained by tether-like tentacles, squeezing and biting into her flesh. She squinted, opening her eyes just a crack. Black spots swarmed all around, but shaking her head to clear them was a mistake. Waves of nausea battered her, further blurring her vision.

Focus . . . on something. Anything.

Her head throbbed, with spikes of pain reverberating against her skull. Hints of blood wafted past and put every receptor on alert. She tasted the water as her heart began to pound.

Old blood. Not fresh. Not mine. Dilating the pores along her sensory lines, she sifted the streams for threat indicators. *No predators, at least.*

She struggled to tear free of the prickly float-weed and hair moss tangled in the kelp, but her efforts were futile.

She bit down on the brambles with a shudder. The bitter leaves set her teeth on edge, stinging her lips, but its mild toxin failed to numb her taste buds. Accumulated bits of rot spread from the spines onto her tongue. Her stomach threatened to revolt. *In through the nose. Out through the mouth.* The leathery fronds gave way and Nica broke from the seaweeds.

Taking in a large gulp to steady herself, she studied her surroundings. Nothing was familiar.

Where am I? What happened? And where's Rissa?

Fragmented images trickled into her consciousness. The shadow. The splashdowns. Of all the storms she'd seasoned, none ever displayed this kind of violence from the heavens.

With the increase in clarity, even her pain took on a pattern. The hammering in her head wasn't an attack, but a percussive sending—widespread and long-ranged signals to broadcast a communiqué across many waters.

ALL GUARDIANS: REPORT

Nica searched for something hard to beat out a message. Her message might need to travel far. There was nothing.

ALL GUARDIANS: STATUS REPORT

She spat out bits of weed and fiber, hoping her clicks could reach a relay.

"Guardian Relay, Nica, reporting."

NICA: REPORT LOCATION.

Then, "Nica. Report location." Her father's sounding replaced the relay's staccato broadcast, firm but insistent.

More sob than sound emerged as she whispered, "Bàbá, I don't know."

REPORT

DELPH 5 REPORT

CONCUSSION CHARGES ACTIVATED

SAMPLES ACQUIRED

INITIATE CONDITIONING

TECHNOLOGY RECLAMATION ENGINEER:
CRYOGENIC HUSBANDRY

EOR

4

HURRICANES and maelstroms warred above and below the face of the Deep. Olomi who sought safety in the depths met destruction when lava erupted from the fractured core. Relentless need surrounded Nica and desperate cries flooded her. The clamor of panic and despair competed with her father's transmission, almost drowning it out.

She closed her eyes to the vortex of chaos and focused on his signal. Enhanced by their blood bonds, family ties forged by time and heritage reinforced the connection all shared in the Deep—communion. Bàbá's message prevailed, resonating along the receptors under her dark green striations, relaying her mother's position. A draught escaped her lips as the tension slipped away.

Nica pivoted to dive as her father's signal reverberated through the tumult again. "Kel. Jonnat. With me."

Heat rose in her chest and her cheeks greened with envy. *He always chooses Kel.* Breathing deeply to quell her own storm, she kicked off, hoping no one would pick up on the hardening knot of resentment.

Bàbá flashed through the waters, maintaining the lead. His darker green was the only indication of the decades separating him from Kel and Jonnat. Hard-pressed to match their senior in strength or speed, the bright green and blue streaks of the younger Olomi pursued, but could not flank him. Schooling with precision, they sped to evacuate the next lava flow. Nica tracked them as long as she could, but as she neared her assignment, any trace of their presence had been swallowed by the Deep.

Turbulent emotions roiled through the currents as Nica approached her ìyá's work site, but the physical devastation before her was beyond anything she could have imagined. Obsidian totems that had graced the entrances to these spacious caverns lay askew, haphazardly strewn across the seascape as if a gam of whales had swum amok. Intricately carved columns, once documenting the legacy of the residents, now threatened their lives. The seabed had heaved, and structures built on it could not withstand the storm.

It was more than Nica could bear. Unwilling to add her voice to the chaos, she searched for Ìyá, scanning for her braid, glossy and black against her vibrant scarlet markings. *There!* Joy shot through her. She swooped down to her mother's side. *Ìyá will know what to do.*

"Bàbá sent me."

"Oh, good." Ìyá smiled briefly and passed Nica a struggling fry. "Take him to the healer's station."

"Ìyáaaaaaaaaaaaa!" The child howled for his mother, the translucent wash of his cheeks flushing bright yellow, then paused mid-wail to take in another draught. Nica winced as piercing shrieks flew from his orange-banded lips. His waves of distress assaulted her, furiously buzzing her receptors and threatening to crash her sensory canals. She held him at arm's length, frozen at the auditory and emotional onslaught. Her gaze lifted from the fry to the devastated homes surrounding them. *Too much. Can't–*

"Nica." Ìyá's voice pushed through the surge of panic. "Breathe with me."

She closed her eyes and matched her mother's deliberate breaths, slowly cycling water until the pressure in her head receded and her heartbeat slowed to a less frantic pace.

"Now, have the healers check him," Ìyá said, then turned back to pry another large stone from the pile.

Nica swam the hysterical child over to the healer's shelter. She drew him in close, like Ìyá did, but her charge pushed with all his might against the embrace. She whispered words of comfort in his ears. He shrieked louder. She tried distracting him with swooping and bouncing, then somersaults and rolls, but nothing worked. No matter what she tried, she couldn't get him to stop. How was it so easy for her mother to soothe him? *And me.* The world was falling apart, and Ìyá could bring peace in a breath.

Relief washed over Nica when the healer station came in sight. She handed the child, no calmer for her efforts, to the first Olomi displaying green and blue Healer cords, then scooted back as fast as she could. His cries followed her, roiling the waves, as she hurried back to her ìyá, still working to excavate the wreckage that was once a home. Stacked rocks and slabs had once supported the cavern, their decorative carvings enhancing the dwelling. But neither the natural nor Olomi-made structures could withstand the quaking beneath the Deep.

Grit from the crumbling entry arch drifted onto her mother as the excavation continued. Nica ducked under and braced the archway with her back. Straining against the weight despite the stones that dug into her dorsals, she maintained her position until the last section trapping an Olomi woman was removed.

Ìyá pulled the dazed mother free and slipped an arm under her. "Now let me get you to the healer station. A little one there will be very happy to see you."

Nica shifted to extricate herself, but an echo of a sob drifted from deeper within the cavern. She ducked her head under the arch, leaning in. Though the structure was unstable, she cast a gentle signal. "Is anyone in here?"

Not daring to breathe, she waited for a response. Any response.

"I . . . I'm stuck." A tremor dislodged portions of the building and sent them tumbling. "Bàbá can't—"

"Can you move?" Nica strained to receive the answer.

"—little." The tremulous vibrations pulled at her heart.

A host of possible reasons preventing the father from sounding his call darted through Nica's thoughts. None were reassuring.

She scanned the area for help, but Ìyá was out of sight and any nearby rescue workers were occupied. Her back was the only thing holding the opening right now, and the last thing she wanted was to end up trapped and needing rescue herself.

There—a pod of juveniles milled about, gawking from the edges. "Hey! Some help here!"

The juvies, vibrant in their adolescent blues, greens, and oranges, streamed toward her, bravado and curiosity jostling in the waters surrounding them. A yellow whose markings were just turning opaque trailed behind, emanating uncertainty in all directions.

"Yes. All of you!" she told the pod. "I need you two biggest to take over for me here. Brace the arch." She squeezed through the opening. "You three support them. Be ready to help when I signal."

Her young volunteers' faces were sober as they nodded.

Nica swam through the partially collapsed chambers, testing the current as it snaked around obstacles. She eyed the debris floating down from higher instabilities, studying the supports throughout the structure.

"Where are you?" She cast her call forward, clicking gently, not wanting to cause any further disturbance. This situation was volatile enough as it stood. "I need you to show me."

Another tremor shuddered through the structure.

". . . back . . ."

It wasn't much, faint and disjointed, but the fry was able to project enough for Nica to navigate through the chambers. Careful not to sweep her wake against unstable supports, she wove through fallen beams and leaning slabs until she reached the back of the cavern. This was where the signal had originated.

Nica's chest tightened as she entered the chamber. The back section had been reduced to a heap of rubble. In the turmoil, the child and father had sought shelter in the place they considered most secure. Rocked to its foundation, their sanctuary could become their tomb.

"Hello?" she called softly into the room. "I'm Nica." She wedged a beam in the doorway as she searched for the occupants. "What's your name?"

"Ah—Ahnay."

The voice drifted out from the pile of shelving against the back wall. She spied an arm, too dark to be a child's, protruding awkwardly amid the ruins. Nica checked the orange limb for a pulse and was relieved to discover one, despite the lack of any other response.

"Ahnay—that's a pretty name." She grunted a little as she pushed her shoulder against the slabs resting on the adult's body. She would not be able to free him without help.

She called out to the juvies at the entrance, trying to avoid unnecessary reverberations in what remained of the structure. "I need two of you—back storeroom." Nica projected the path she'd taken in. "Stay away from the walls—watch out for falling ceilings."

Silent whimpering drifted over to her from the pile.

"Don't worry, Ahnay. We have some extra help coming." She pulled on a slab of stone wide as her handspan and twice her length. "How old are you?"

"F-four." The fry's voice shook a little as Nica shifted some of the weight above her.

"Such a big girl!" The shelf moved a bit, and Nica expelled a deep breath and widened her stance. "Ahnay, can you show me your hand?"

A translucent hand, orange-tinted and webbed, emerged from under the adult's arm. Nica grasped it as far past the elbow as she could, and pulled. A little Olomi with orange highlighting along her dorsal line wriggled out and attached herself firmly to her rescuer's arm.

"Let's see how you are doing." Nica leaned against the debris and pulled Ahnay close, settling her slight form on her hip.

Despite some surface abrasions and bruising, she appeared unhurt, but her lips and cheeks were paling at an alarming rate. Nica brushed aside the sun-white hair and felt her forehead. *Too cold. But the father . . . The roof won't last much longer. Need to get them both out fast.*

"Ahnay, I need you to be brave for a moment."

The fry nodded, trying to still her trembling lip. Her gaze flicked up to the ceiling, trailing down as another section of stone slid from its mooring and tumbled to the floor, landing as a cloud of debris rose to obscure its presence.

Nica moved her to the center of the room, clear of falling debris. "I need to check on your bàbá. Can you stay still while I do that?"

The little head bobbed again, fine white hairs pulsing against the current. Wrapping her arms around her knees, Ahnay stuck her thumb in her mouth, eyes fixed on her father's arm.

Nica braced her shoulder against the layered slabs of stone and pushed. They were too heavy to move. Flipping upside down, she planted her hands on the floor and shoved up against the load with her feet. The inverted position allowed her to reach further under his body to get a better grip, but she still couldn't budge Ahnay's father.

She exhaled as the pod streamed in, nodding at the yellow Olomi. "This is Ahnay. Watch over her."

The young yellow swooped to Ahnay's side with a barrel roll finish, teasing a faint smile out of the fry. "Hi, Ahnay, I'm Lia."

With Ahnay engaged, Nica beckoned for the older, blue-tinged male to adopt the same inverted position as she was in. "Latch on."

With a flex, they activated the hair-like barbs that lined their palms to get a firm grip on the Olomi's sleek hide. Together, they pried him out from under the load as the weight of the wreckage slid off. The blue tumbled into Lia and Ahnay, setting off a round of giggles.

Their laughter died out as the father's orange form drifted with the current.

"Hey, he's not moving." Lia pulled Ahnay close, turning the child away from her father's inert form. "He's not . . ."

"No, he's unconscious. I don't know how bad his injuries are, but without your help, I couldn't have gotten him. You are official heroes! But now—" Another tremor went through the cavern. "We need to get out."

"Ahnay, honey." More debris tumbled from the ceiling. "Let's bring your bàbá to the healer."

The child nodded, but her orange eyes remained locked onto her father's still form.

"The waters are a little wild out there, so Lia is going to carry you out while, um—" she cocked her head at the bright-hued blue.

"Jamen." The juvie grunted as he adjusted his grip on the older Olomi's legs.

"—while Jamen and I help your bàbá." Nica and the blue juvie hefted the unconscious father. "Your job is to hold on tight."

"Yes, Miss Nica." Ahnay nodded and hugged Lia's neck.

Last moon, I was still in training, too young to help anyone. Now I'm a 'Miss' and directing juvies in a rescue.

"Hey, Miss Nica."

"Yes?"

"You're a girl."

"That's right." Nica managed a grin as her smallest charge peered at her over Lia's shoulder.

"And you're a Guardian."

"Right again."

"But Ìyá said there aren't any girl Guardians." Ahnay's head bobbed up and down as her young escort wove through the obstacle course of rubble.

Nica laughed. "That's what my brother said when I was little, but guess what?"

"What?"

"There are now."

The ocean floor quaked again as they reached the archway. Nica signaled the pod to hold until the trembling stilled. Lia ducked under with the fry, then Jamen and Nica maneuvered Ahnay's father through the tight opening.

"You all did great."

"Miss Nica?"

"Yes?"

"I'm glad you're a Guardian."

"So am I, Ahnay. But this sun, we are all Guardians."

REPORT

DELPH 5 REPORT

GEOLOGICAL STABILITY
PRECLUDES USE OF
CONCUSSION CHARGES

MANUAL TRACKING AND SAMPLE
ACQUISITION REQUIRED

INITIATE CONDITIONING

SEISMIC ANALYST: CARTOGRAPHY
AND GEOLOGY

EOR

5

ANGER and frustration rode the streams flowing Nica's way, and she wasn't sure why, but she was the target. A corpulent Olomi plowed through the crowds like a whale attacking a sardine baitball. Fleshy layers of mottled brown and gray flowed around him, stacked in rings upon each other like so many octopus carcasses, interrupted only by deeply inset eyes and a bristly moustache.

Nica backpaddled, trying to look busy. His tunic—*how much kelp did they have to weave to net him?*—was draped with multiple ranking cords. She didn't need trouble from someone this high up the food chain. She cast about for cover, but none could be found. Everything was leveled.

Traces of rheumy pink pulsated between his dark folds as he launched at her. "Rookie! What were you thinking?"

She racked her brain. What had she done? "I . . . I . . . don't know what you're talking—"

"Your little extraction expedition was unassigned, unsanctioned, and unapproved."

This was what had him so upset? Nica's nostrils flared. "I was thinking someone needed to help that little girl."

"And, of course, that someone had to be you. Alone. Would it kill you go through appropriate channels?"

"It might have killed her. What if the entrance had collapsed while I was waiting for approval?"

"What if it had collapsed while you were inside? What if no one knew you were in there?"

"But I got help—"

His face flushed even more and the veins on his neck looked like they were about to burst. "Juveniles! You got juvies."

Nica was speechless.

"I don't care if you are the Head Guardian's daughter. This was completely reckless." He loomed over and grabbed hold of her new Guardian cords. "You don't deserve these. You clearly aren't prepared for these situations and you don't have enough experience."

Nica snapped her cords back, refusing to cower. "Who has been trained for this? Who's got experience in earthquakes and lava eruptions and explosions from above—all at the same time? No one. But sometimes, someone has to do something, and I'm not gonna wait for permission to save a life."

Without warning, her mother inserted herself between the two and into the conversation. "And I know of several Olomi who are thankful that this Guardian did not hesitate to do what was necessary to preserve their family."

The old Olomi sputtered. "Oh. Excuse me, Laina. I didn't realize . . ."

"My daughter realizes that there are still lessons to be learned, but I will not have her berated for doing everything within her power to safeguard the lives of others. It's what she has sworn to do. Furthermore, it's what she was made to do."

"I was only saying—"

"I think enough has been said, and we all have more work to do. Thank you, Councillian." With this dismissal, her mother turned and herded Nica away.

"Councillian?" Nica mouthed the question to her mother when they were out of voice range. "That's why all the cords."

Ìyá nodded. "You do know how to pick your fights."

"I didn't start this one, Ìyá. Really."

"I know dear, but the Councillian did have a point. You could have been trapped, and who would know? I . . . I don't think I could take losing you too."

"Still no word from Rissa?"

"Nothing." Her mother shook her head. "It's been three suns, and Jonnat hasn't heard from her either."

"Don't worry. I'm sure she's fine," Nica tried to reassure her. "You know communication has been scrambled ever since the Breaking. Remember, Rissa's the responsible one. She'll be careful."

As the words left her lips, the attempt at humor felt more like a scoff. Had she spoken out of turn? Would the water betray her? Truth was always revealed. The Deep made sure of it.

REPORT

DELPH 2 REPORT

MASS SAMPLE ACQUISITION
RESULTS VARIED

UNACCEPTABLE PERCENTAGE OF
SAMPLE DAMAGED

MEDICAL OFFICER: AQUA SAPIEN
HYBRID EMBRYOLOGY

EOR

6

·· BROKEN ··

NOT ALL the families were as lucky as Ahnay's. Mothers lost children, husbands lost wives, and grandparents were called upon to serve as parents for their children's children. Suns were full of heartbreak, and eves overflowed with grief. With each turn of sorrow, Nica watched the grief etched into her mother deepen. Rissa was still missing, and her father's team was assigned to evacuation efforts at volcanic sites.

On the sixth moon of rescue and recovery, Jonnat sent word to her mother using an official relay.

LAINA. COME QUICKLY.

The coordinates indicated were near a deep canyon. One where a major lava flow had broken through.

BRING NICA.

Nica's heart dropped. The formal method of communication was a portent of misfortune. No nuance, affect, or emotion. Nothing more communicated than the sender's words and that the circumstances warranted using the relay.

"We can't wait for a group transport," her mother fretted.

"How about a porpoise-booster?" Nica offered.

"Make it a twin."

"It's Daevu. I know it." Ìyá's words squeezed through compressed lips as her fingers dug into the carriage grips.

The seascape sped by in a blur of kelp forests and deep coral reefs as Nica searched for words to allay her mother's fears, but she had none. If her father were able, he would have responded to Ìyá's incessant calls. Jonnat had not reached out to them with any further information. Even Kel was silent.

Jonnat met them when they arrived, his face dark with misery. Ìyá kicked off the transport before it came to a halt and streamed to him.

"Where is Daevu?"

"Our best healer is with him now. I tried to convince him to leave, Laina. It was too hot, even for me. But there were still people missing . . ."

"Of course there were." Ìyá's words launched like spears.

"I'm so sorry, I should have stayed with him after we evacuated the last group."

"Why didn't you make him go, Jonnat?"

"Me? Make Daevu?" Jonnat's voice was shaky. "He ordered us out."

He took in a deep draught of water, holding it as his lungs absorbed the oxygen. Then, he constricted the exhale to a tight, small stream before continuing with a steadier voice.

"Daevu did the last check. He was making sure no one was left behind when the roof collapsed. We got him out, but . . ."

"Take me to him."

Nica trailed behind her mother and Jonnat. Every bit of scarlet had drained from Ìyá's rosettes, leaving her paler than dead coral. She'd never seen her mother so grim, nor sound so bitter. As a Guardian, Nica had sworn to protect her people. Now her own family was in crisis, and there was nothing she could do to help.

As they drifted toward the cave designated for the injured, emanating streams met them with traces of blood and decay. Guardians hovered above, patrolling the sea-space, protecting the cavern's vulnerable occupants from creatures who might be drawn by its aura. The necessity sent a shiver across Nica's dorsals. And now Bàbá was one of their charges.

Jonnat approached an older Olomi wearing Healers Guild colors, but not any cords of mastery. *Odd for one this dark to not have gained his cords.* She tilted toward her mother to get her read, but Ìyá revealed as much as a glacier, moving only when the Olomi in blue and green beckoned for them to follow.

Deep inside the grotto, the strongest man she knew rested on feathery kelp, almost unrecognizable under the dressings. Her bàbá's eyes were filled with pain, and his skin was so seared that there was no green visible—only red and black blistering revealed where the coverings gapped. Ìyá hovered at his side, unable to even hold his hand, but clasping hers together so tightly the knuckles threatened to burst through their webbing. Kel was nowhere to be seen, and suddenly Nica couldn't bear to stay.

She kicked off, surging out of the cavern, and almost collided with Jonnat.

"Oh, Master Jonnat, I couldn't . . . I mean, I'm sorry. I can't . . ." She could feel the embarrassment spilling off her in a million directions, but the long-limbed, blue Guardian's pain was palpable as well. *Time to channel it, Nica.*

"Nica." Jonnat exhaled slowly, restraining the water and his emotions to a slow and steady release. "You don't have to use my title outside of the classroom. We're family. Or we were going to be . . ."

With that, his pain began to seep again.

Nica could not contain herself.

"What are we doing here? We're supposed to be Guardians—but my bàbá, the Head Guardian, is . . ." She gestured wildly at the cavern, unable to voice her worst fears. "And why is some no-cord running the clinic? And why these caverns? Who thinks they're safe anymore? They've proved to be anything but!" Nica's tirade dissolved into hiccoughing tears. "Everything's collapsing. How am I supposed to help anyone? And when I do . . . it . . . comes out all wrong."

"I'm sorry, Nica," Jonnat said quietly. "It's not just you. We're all doing the best we can with what we have."

He turned her to face the entrance. "Teemok, the older Olomi who greeted you here? He's not cordless. He's got Mastery Cords in literature and philosophy. He just doesn't think they're helpful right now. His daughter used to work this clinic. She gave her life protecting her patients. Her bàbá wanted to help in whatever way he could, so he directs family members to their loved ones, and sits with those who have no one."

Nica's green deepened in a flush of shame. "Bu-but I have to do something." Her voice cracked. "Bàbá is so bad. Rissa's still missing, and we've looked everywhere. Everything is broken. Even the water."

"That's it!" Jonnat looked up to the surface. "We've looked everywhere in the Deep. But what if Rissa is on the other side of these water-breaks? We're going to have to go over them if we can't pass here."

"But rookies aren't cleared for abovewater training."

Jonnat leveled a sober gaze at her. "Well, that's about to change."

REPORT

DELPH-2

Preliminary findings concur with data assumptions.

Resource acquisition proceeding according to plan.

Expedition Commander:
Terraformation/Agriculture/Labor

EOR

7

JONNAT circled the freshly grounded pod of Guardians. All had volunteered for field training, but most had no idea what they were in for and floundered in the unfamiliar currents. A few adapted their stances and donned their gear with ease.

Nica planted her hands firmly on her knees, as if pushing against the air bearing down on her. She gasped, then wheezed in the arid atmosphere.

"You really shouldn't pant like that," Kel said with a smirk. "It dries out your lung linings faster."

Jonnat saw the glare Nica leveled at her brother. He tossed a flask at Kel, who stumbled back from the unexpected lob. "Then show her how to avoid that."

He addressed the rest of the pod. "If you've had abovewater training, pair up with a rookie and show them how to acclimate."

Inspection complete, he returned to the equipment net. Holding up another flask, he addressed the group. "This contains your water. If you dispense some onto your facemask, it adds moisture to the air you take in, but that's a temporary solution. Slow, shallow breaths will also delay evaporation from the mucus lining your lungs. If your lining needs to adapt, it can, but it's a painful process. Don't stay exposed above too long, and don't forget to blink.

"You think you're invincible. You're young, you're fast, and you're strong. But," he paused, waiting until he had everyone's attention, "you are of the water, and need to return to that water before desiccation sets in. Protect your moisture."

One of the Guardians interrupted. "Master Jonnat, what's the longest you've stayed abovewater?"

Another chimed in. "How many kinds of air-breathers are there?"

"Is it true you've seen sky-swimmers?"

"Are the creatures intelligent?"

"Are they edible?"

The questions, full of admiration and curiosity, darted in the wind as whispered reports of his exploits were shared.

"This isn't an adventure!" He took in a slow, measured, breath—mindful to give time for his body to humidify the gas before it hit his lung linings.

"My abovewater expeditions before the Breaking were under much different circumstances. These breaches and eruptions have drastically altered our surface atmosphere. It would be unwise to make assumptions regarding your survival based on my previous experiences. Exercise wisdom and caution and you may resubmerge unscathed."

Jonnat wrapped the braided kelp, deftly nestling the loops in his palm. "If these cords get kinked or knotted, it causes tiny breaks in the fibers. That can lead to equipment failure when someone's life is on the line."

Tossing it on a stack with the other loops of cabled kelp, he surveyed the equipment set aside for the team. "You'll need an etching pad, stylus, head protection, face wrap, blade with strap, bladder, small spade, and rake."

He ignored the skepticism in their raised eyebrows. They were trained Guardians, but inexperienced in abovewater expeditions. Jonnat was the acknowledged expert on the communities of life inhabiting the tree islands, or he had been until the Breaking.

He hoped they could learn from his experience, but pain had taught him his most valuable lessons, and it would be their best educator, as well.

"Gear up. Time for land-laps. I'm looking for endurance, not speed. Go!"

REPORT

DELPH-2

Conditioning proceeding
according to plan.

Expedition Commander:
Terraformation/Agriculture/Labor

EOR

8

·· HOPE ··

IT STARTED like an itch. A trace of nothing, teasing at the base of her skull. Vibrations falling into place, becoming pieces of rhythm. Triggered memory filled in the spaces as the tones, even delayed and fragmented, invoked the song. Nica froze. The music resonated within her core before the notes could reach her ears.

Rissa! Her heart leapt with hope. It had to be her!

No one else knew Ìyágba's song, written with and for her first granddaughter. And no one else could sing it. Only Rissa had inherited that vocal gift, the ability to produce tritones. It had to be her.

Nica dashed back and forth along the barricade. The sound came from beyond. Behind the barrier. She'd already investigated this section, but sounded against it again and again. She must have missed an opening. Somewhere. But she found nothing, no passage through, as far as her signal could reach. The Breaking had divided not only the water, but also its people.

She streamed to the surface, not knowing what she would find. Would Jonnat's training be sufficient? Massive swells threatened to slam her against the wall, forcing her further and further out to sea. The water-break was unapproachable, standing firm against the Deep.

An ache billowed within her chest. Moons had come, and gone, and come again. The unnatural storm had lasted less than a week, but its wake . . .

Searching, and hoping, she persisted until frustration drove her mad. To be this close but have nothing.

No. It wasn't nothing. I'll get past these barriers, find Rissa, and bring her home.

Nica sped home, hitching on to a dolphin-booster, urging it faster the entire distance. Vaulting off the ride, she barreled through the archway.

"Ìyá!"

She streamed to the entry, dismissing familiar turbulence in the courtyard. *When Ìyá hears—*

The turbulence tackled her.

Chesnae and Pilto, the family fry, tumbled into her from both sides of the stream that divided Ìyá's gardens. Swirling to a stop, she grabbed both younger siblings by the scruff and suspended them in front of her. Born less than a year apart, "the littles" as the older three insisted on calling them, were often mistaken for twins. This delighted little Chesnae, but irked her slightly older brother.

"You littles are supposed to be helping Ìyá in the garden."

They wriggled in her grasp, trying to free themselves and reach each other.

"She started it."

"Did not."

"Did so."

"Let go! You're not Ìyá!"

"Hey!" Nica glared at them. "If you don't cut it out, you're going to wish I was Ìyá."

Pilto gulped as the color drained from his face. Chesnae's lip began to tremble, and she began to suck water rapidly.

Shells. She hadn't been the most patient babysitter. The last thing she needed was for Chessie to start bawling.

"I hope you haven't been giving Ìyá this much trouble."

The littles stopped struggling and hung from Nica's fists, subdued in defeat. Relaxing her grip, she looked from Pil's silvery curls to the black tendrils sprouting like an anemone from Chessie's head, and then to the urchin-infested garden beds. Shaking her head at the sorry state of it all, she launched each fry toward plots on opposite sides of the stream.

"Net the most urchins and you get to pick dessert. Go!"

Nica watched them scurry to outdo each other. They were still translucent, showing only the slightest hint of color along their lateral lines. They needed more . . . more discipline, more guidance, more care. It wasn't fair. But nothing was through these tides. She allowed a sigh, composing herself to find her mother.

"Ìyá?"

There was no response, but that wasn't unusual. Each sun since the tortoise litter brought Bàbá home, Ìyá seemed to drift a little further. This tide, Nica found her hovering over a bed of dulse. Her graceful movements could have been mistaken for harvesting, but she did little more than stroke the dark red fronds. She approached her mother gently. The kelp blades wafted in the currents, displaying as much purpose as their gardener's hands. *Maybe hearing about her firstborn . . .*

Nica held her mother's hands, trying to catch her gaze. "Ìyá, Rissa is alive."

She shook her gently, trying to reach through her mother's stupor. "I heard Ìyágba's song by the great barrier. It was Rissa. I'm sure of it!"

Would this news break through?

"Ìyá?"

Nothing. Just an empty gaze staring past her.

You need her right now, don't you? You need Rissa, not me. Rissa would have the words. She would know what to say. She could make you listen. But Rissa's not here, and you're stuck with me. And right now—that's not enough.

She took her mother's hands in her own, massaging the porcelain knuckles and light pink web base. "Don't worry, Ìyá. I know Rissa is out there, and I promise, I'll bring her back to you."

Nica fled to her father's chamber, bursting through the curtain of seagrass. "Bàbá! I heard Rissa!"

"Is this the rest your father is getting?" The gray-bearded healer attending her bàbá leveled a stern gaze at her, his pale eyes piercing through a bushy mantle of blue-green brows. The reprimand restrained Nica's headway, but not the currents that followed and unsettled the healing kelp draped over his patient.

"Yeah, Nica." Kel rearranged the disturbed dressings with grand, exacting motions as Bàbá turned his head to her. "Why can't you be more careful?"

Suspended at the entrance, Nica flushed even greener with chagrin. Her heart ached at the sight. Her father was reduced to a shell of the man he once was. Spreading the alert to the deeper caverns of the dangerous lava and gasses emanating had saved scores of lives, but it had nearly cost him his own.

Bàbá smiled despite his injuries, waving his third-born in. "Your remedies are good for the body, old friend, but my dear daughter is good for my soul."

Gliding past the healer, Nica settled next to her father's seaweed bed, careful to not cause any further disturbance.

"Bàbá, I think Rissa is alive."

Kel rolled his eyes.

The healer shook his head. "It's been moons since the breaking of the water. Your father does not need to be disturbed by idle rumors and false hope."

Frustrated at his skepticism, Nica tried to explain. "I think I heard Rissa's voice past the great reef. She was singing Ìyá'gba's song."

"Have you told your ìyá?"

"I tried Bàbá, but she still . . . drifts."

Her bàbá sighed, resting his hand on his daughter's. "I know it's been difficult on you and your brother while we are recovering. Know that even though your ìyá is not herself, she appreciates all you do." He looked from Nica to Kel. "As do I. This is just a squall that has blown in and stirred up sand. But it will pass. Storms always do."

Ignoring her brother's noiseless snort, Nica turned to her father. "I swear, Bàbá. I will find Rissa. Nothing will stop me."

"I believe you will, Nica. Go see Jonnat."

"Bẹẹni. Yes, Bàbá, I'll go at once."

Throwing a glare at Kel, Nica whisked out of the room before he could say a word.

I'll find you, Rissa. For Ìyá. For Bàbá. No matter what it takes. I'll find you and bring you home.

REPORT

DELPH-2

COMPATIBILITY TRIALS INITIATED.

MEDICAL OFFICER: AQUA SAPIEN
HYBRID EMBRYOLOGY

EOR

9

J ONNAT picked up Nica's turbulence long before she entered the cavern. Brash and headstrong, she was Rissa's opposite in every way, but she was also his fiancé's sister, and her pain, untempered by age or experience, echoed his own.

They had searched for Rissa, as well as the many others who were missing, but to no avail. In the wake of so many peers and elders succumbing to disability or death from the breaking of the water, responsibility lay with Jonnat to prepare new teams of explorers. Moon after moon, the ache persisted. But his was not the only loss, and loss was not his only responsibility. Life demanded attention.

Jonnat pored over surface reports, old and new, as well as his journals from previous expeditions. Useless for navigation since the upheaval, there was still knowledge to be shared regarding survival out of their element.

> The Breaking, as the people refer to the incident that razed our world, has not only shattered our physical reality, but has also ravaged the Olomi spirit. Where hearts and thoughts have been held in communion, shared freely along the currents of the Deep, the devastating onslaught has introduced barriers that have not previously been encountered in our history.
>
> Eruptions from the pierced core producing

violent streams of lava drove our people into isolation as they fled this secondary invasion.

Olomi who refused to school with their panicked neighbors were overcome by waves of heat emanating from the molten flow.

The destruction is both widespread and unimaginable.

"Master Jonnat," she finally broke in.

He looked up from the report. "Nica, my students have been dismissed. As I have mentioned before, there's no need for formality outside of class."

The green along her sensory lines deepened, along with emanations of heat as her embarrassment obscured the preceding impatience and anxiety.

He gave an inward sigh. He never knew what would throw her mood into a maelstrom. "I'm sorry, Nica. I didn't mean for it to sound like an admonition."

"It's just that you've been an instructor for as long as I can remember. You only became a future brother a few moons before the Break—" Her mouth clamped shut and brows furrowed as she tread water nervously.

Was there any other reckoning of existence aside from before or after the Breaking? Would future life and tides forever be defined by it? "Why don't you let me know what's on your mind?" he said.

Nica took in a large draught of water, and then blew it out slowly. "I was exploring near the new barrier . . ."

"Were you with a partner? That area hasn't been cleared yet."

"Yes, I mean, no. I mean—I know it's not cleared for civilians, but I'm a Guardian, and that's why I've been training with you. And no, I didn't take a partner, because I wasn't planning to go close, but . . ." She hesitated.

"You 'weren't planning to go close to the barrier, but' what?" Jonnat kept his tone calm, though his focus was intent upon her.

"I wanted to see if I could find anything that could help me find out what happened to Rissa. And I did. I think I heard the echo of Rissa's voice from the other side."

Jonnat remained silent, but his thoughts raced as fast as his heart. Losing Rissa had wrenched his soul. Could he allow hope to rise above the backwash? He'd never expected that his skill as an explorer would be his only lifeline.

Nica fidgeted, still suspended in the entrance.

Jonnat began to count out supplies.

"Two loops cable. Two flasks. Neck wraps, one, two." He glanced up at her. "Do you have your own blade? Or are you going to need one from inventory?"

Noticing her perplexed state, Jonnat replied to the question she hadn't voiced.

"We leave at first light."

10

·· TAKEN ··

THEY APPROACHED the land mass punctuating their sea, skirting its edges with caution. It was not the first time Jonnat had investigated exposed surfaces on their world, but this mount above the sea was entirely different. Cliffs towered around them, unmoving despite the crashing waves. All the power of the Deep threw itself against the intruding wall, but to no avail. The unnatural mountain, planted deep into the seabed, would not move.

Nica slipped abovewater next to him. "I always wanted to see one of your tree islands—with creatures jumping and swimming in the air. It sounded magical. This isn't one of them, is it?"

Jonnat shook his head, his face grim. "Those communities were full of life. This thing has none. It reeks of death."

He scanned the voluntary border that had raised itself in their seas. "And as I feared, they aren't islands. These land masses are joined. If we can't find a passage through the water-breaks, we may need to travel over them. Even the relays haven't been able to penetrate these barriers."

She rotated, trying to make sense of the fractured scape. "How could this happen—is our world broken forever? Will the Deep ever return to normal?"

"I can't say. The Breaking didn't destroy our world, it changed it. Like any other storm, it came, and then it passed. But in the end, Water will always have its way."

"Let's gear up." He jerked his head down to their base site. "Don't want to stay abovewater too much."

Nica dove after him, gratefully refilling her lungs.

"Do you want to take the first tour? I'll finish setting things up while you take a quick look and get used to moving abovewater." He handed her the kelp coil. "Keep this looped around your ankle and give a tug if you need me."

"A tug?"

"Yes, a tug. Sound won't travel down here from the air." Jonnat shoved the braided kelp at her. "And here's your flask, face cover, blade—"

"Hold up." She backpaddled. "I'm not going to need all that, especially on this trip. Let me get my land legs before you load me up. I'll be back before you can secure our site."

Nica shouldered the coil and slung the flask's strap over her head. Tying the face wrap loosely around her neck, she gave a spin and grin to Jonnat. "Does this meet your approval, instructor Jonnat?"

"Not really, but I guess it will have to do for now. Just, please be careful. Take slow, shallow breaths."

Nica pushed off the alcove they were anchored to, unlooping the cable as she swam for the surface. "I will, don't worry."

"And Nica," Jonnat called after her, mild anxious energy riding the wake of his words, "don't forget to blink."

Nica raised her head above the surface. Her stomach felt as if it were teeming with minnows. It was her first solo foray abovewater—onto the surface that had displaced the Deep. Squinting in the unmuted sunlight, she swam to investigate this new world.

Ugh. The air was thick with rot. It had been moons since the Breaking, and the shoreline was still littered with fish carcasses. She fought the urge to dive and wash away the scent, but she wouldn't give Jonnat the satisfaction. He'd probably tell Kel, and there would be no end to the grief her brother would give her. Netting all her resolve, she took in a last draught and clambered up the embankment.

Rough fingers wrapped around Nica's wrist as she left the surf. Rough, strong, *unwebbed* fingers. Sputtering as she was hauled up, Nica looked from the arm to its owner's face. Not Olomi. But what?

Without warning, an onslaught of noise blared from this surface being. Loud, raucous, and nothing like the informative vibrations exchanged in the Deep. It felt like an attack on her ears and Nica winced, trying to cup her hands over them. The stranger's grasp was unyielding. She stumbled, falling toward him, away from the water.

The rocky surface, sharp as a reef, scraped her skin. *Blood!* Nica fought fiercely, trying to propel herself upward and away. It might have worked in the water, but on the surface, neither her strength nor skill sufficed. She couldn't dive away. Thrashing like a fish in a net, she felt just as helpless.

She had to warn Jonnat. Nica reached for the braid, but the attacker tore the loop off and hoisted her over his shoulder, carrying her from the safety of waves. Writhing with all her strength, her struggles were to no avail. The stranger carried her deeper inland until he dumped her in a clearing.

Nica gasped, her breaths ragged from the exertion and the dehydrating atmosphere. She attempted to right herself, pushing against the dry ground, putting what distance she could between herself and her captor.

She didn't understand this attack or its agent. Her voice, almost unrecognizable out of the water, was barely able to sound the question that consumed her. "Why?"

The—whatever it was—laughed. He stretched his arms wide in a gesture that included all the surrounding area, pointed at her, and then pointed to himself.

REPORT

DELPH-2 — Field Report

Homo sapiens aquan (Genus, species, subspecies)

Aqua Sapien, female, adult

Skin Coloration: Green, variegated

Hair Coloration: Orange

Expedition Commander: Terraformation/Agriculture/Labor

EOR

11

·· TRACKED ··

THE JERK on the cable caught Jonnat by surprise. So soon? He hadn't even started marking the time passed.

He gathered the supplies he had prepared for his expedition: digging tools, storage pouch, water flask, a blade for protection, and husks with a stylus for etching notes. New explorers were typically poor at concealing their scoffs when he shared his recommendations. He ignored them. He'd once been too young and too impatient to bother. It had taken experience to teach him to be prepared. Jonnat pulled at the kelp to let Nica know he was heading up.

The cord offered no resistance, but followed his tug, floating adrift. Jonnat sprang from his perch, targeting the site where Nica had left the water.

Streaming toward the surface, the Olomi deftly navigated the waves breaking on the shore, stepping out of the foam onto the abovewater landing. Not as rough as the dead coral below, the solid surface was still abrasive under his full weight. Closing his eyes to acclimate them to the unshielded light, he pulled a neck wrap woven from the finest fibers and tied the soaked cloth around his head. Cracking open his eyelids as little as possible, Jonnat was thankful for the shade his head covering provided. He scanned the surface and followed the braided kelp inland.

His heart slammed against his chest. Nica's tether lay on the ground, surrounded by signs of combat. Used to reading subtle environmental nuances underwater, the unwashed evidence of a struggle shouted that she was in danger. Jonnat grasped the empty loop and grimly started coiling the line, checking his impulse to dash up the ridge. Nica was strong and resourceful—not easily overpowered. He would have to be cautious.

Though he was an adept tracker, Jonnat had not expected to use this skill abovewater. Still, his experienced eye followed their wake without difficulty. No attempt had been made to hide the trail. This allowed him to focus on scouting and stealth. The lack of blood combined with evidence of struggles along the path told him Nica was still alive and had not been mortally wounded. But what type of adversary would overpower Nica, but not kill her on the spot? Beasts didn't take captives.

The rocks revealed little, but eventually gave way to fine gravel and dirt. Jonnat's jaw set as the terrain began to reveal tracks. Biped. Too deep and large to be Nica's, they confirmed his worst fears. She had not been taken by an animal.

What madness caused this? Had an Olomi been stranded abovewater and lost their mind to exposure? An unlikely possibility, but he could think of no other reason for an attack from one of their own.

Jonnat advanced up the rough slope, ignoring the stones that scraped and gouged his feet, moving as silently as possible. Limited to linear advancement, he was relieved when the path leveled. It was easier to move through air than water, but the absence of buoyancy sapped his strength. Fighting the arid climate and blinding sunlight, he stopped to soak his tunic and neck wrap. It was hard to tell how far behind he was, but he surmised that since Nica's captor had not yet done so, he did not intend to kill her. It was vital to maintain the element of surprise.

Inspecting some disturbed moss, Jonnat compared it against patches of lichen he had noticed at lower levels. It was surprising to see growth on the barren formations. More pertinent to the situation at hand, this moss had been separated from its host recently. Nica and her abductor were not too far ahead. Jonnat forged on, following the signs that marked their progress.

The sun was beginning to sink, and there was not even a sliver of the moon present. Jonnat moved quickly, before the way was fully obscured. He stumbled once, and again, cursing his lack of foresight. He couldn't track here without illumination. But which lumens from the deep would survive abovewater? It didn't help that the cataclysm hadn't been limited to reshaping the planet's contours. The upper atmosphere still reeled from the onslaught above and upheaval below. Clouds of ash blanketed the skies and light from the stars couldn't pierce the gray.

Unable to continue lest he lose Nica's trail completely, Jonnat yielded to the encroaching darkness. He would resume his pursuit at sunbreak.

12

FEAR battered down any thoughts of escape that arose in Nica's mind. *Can't break free. Can't dart, can barely tread . . . weak as a molted crab.* Hope slipped away as her reality sank in.

Every breath caused pain, ravaging the desiccated membranes that lined her lungs. *Slow and shallow, Nica. Slow and shallow.* She replayed Jonnat's words like a silent incantation, but it wasn't enough to stop the violent fits of coughing after each suck of air.

The stranger smirked at her wheezing and crackling. *Did he anticipate her difficult acclimation?* She had to escape—get back to the water. Her eyes darted back, wondering how far they'd come. As if the air carried some scent of her thoughts, the stranger bound her hands and jerked her to her feet.

He stabbed his finger toward the peak of the rock, saying something in angry grunting sounds. She didn't understand the words that left his mouth, but his jerk on the lead communicated clearly.

They seemed to follow the sun, winding up the mount's dark crags while it traversed the sky. Her captor kept the rope taut, ready to throw Nica to her knees if she lagged. She gnawed at the bindings, but they were tougher than dried kelp and the pace too fast to make any progress. Then she smelled water nearby. She prepared to dive at the first chance. The path approached a channel, and she bolted for the safety of a stream. Her captor jerked again at the cord, stopping her just short of the edge. His brows, bereft of receptor cells, drew together. She didn't need the communion of the Deep to feel his contempt.

They continued the ascent. Nica stumbled repeatedly, slowing their progress to a crawl. She was exhausted, her shoulders ached from the constant tugging of the rope, and her arms felt as if they were being ripped from their sockets. They'd covered almost one-third of the distance to the peak and Nica wondered what their destination would be.

The sun began to sink—taking much longer abovewater than it did in the Deep. Its rays changed color, as the reflections slowly made their way down the landmount surfaces. Almost blinded by prolonged exposure to the unfiltered brightness of the sun, as well as the harshness of the desiccating air, Nica welcomed its absence. But even as relief from its searing heat washed over her, she began to shiver from cold. Olomi had never been forced to endure these extremes before. The water had always insulated its people, and Nica wasn't prepared for extended exposure on the outer crust.

Without warning, her captor stopped. He swung the pack slung across his torso forward, pulled something out, and threw it at her feet. Nica flinched. He shrugged and turned away, returning to dig through the contents of his pack. Crouching warily, she reached down, searching with her hand as she kept an eye on the stranger. Sea pods. Weak from the journey and exposure, she trembled as she bit into the liquid-filled pods. After she sucked out the briny fluid, she chewed the husks until they were spent. She even chewed the stems, hoping to be nourished, though they had no flavor. Despite the circumstance, her body received the refreshment and was strengthened. When he saw she was done, the stranger secured her tether to an outcropping and pointed toward the small cavity it created.

She didn't understand his words, but the demand was clear. Berating herself for submitting to this harsh master's rule, but fearful of the unknowns into which she'd been thrust, Nica crawled into the small rock cranny, curling into as protective a ball as she could. She'd never slept on a hard surface, or any surface before, and this was as far from a net of kelp as she could ever imagine. But exhausted, bloodied, and beaten, Nica wept herself to sleep.

Jonnat woke with a start—his heart pounding fiercely. Sleep had not been restful or refreshing. His teeth hurt from grinding, and the hollow ache in his throat threatened to consume him. Fear resonated from his fingers, along his arms to his shoulders, and then down his back again. Every fiber within ached from grief.

The expedition, born out of hope, had disintegrated into a nightmare. They hadn't found Rissa, and now Nica was lost as well. It was one thing to have their world fractured by an unknown event, but this new danger had intent in its design. He had to find her. He had to bring Nica home. And he had to warn their people.

13

PAIN filled Nica's night, accompanied by confusion and fear. If she were in the Deep, Nica could silence her body signs and disappear into the darkness. Here, trapped on the surface, the jarring acoustics of airborne sound distilled her anxiety into terror. Shrieks of unknown creatures pierced the darkness, stabbing into her dreams and tearing her out of what sleep she seized. Would it ever end?

She clung to the shadows, fearful of what the new sun would bring. *Exposure. To the elements, and to him.* She squeezed her eyes tight against the silhouette of her captor, blocking the entrance to the hollow that was her prison. This new tide was to be avoided.

Movement on the rocky terrain was as grating on her body as the sounds were on her ears. The forced climb up the abrasive surface had been painful enough, but every shift throughout the night felt like coral raking her flesh. Her captor spent the night with his back toward her, blocking the opening of the den. She could not tell if he were sleeping or awake, only that he did not move.

The sun began to rise, and Nica scanned the floor for any means of escape its rays might reveal. A loose rock, half the size of her fist, might be helpful to saw her bindings. At any rate, it was all that was at hand. *Just a stumble away . . .*

As if he knew her every waking moment would be devoted to escape, the stranger suddenly stood and yanked her out of the crevice. Propelling herself to fall toward the goal, Nica grabbed the small stone, tucked it in her waist wrapping, and made a show of regaining her footing.

With a jerk of the lead, her captor began to stride up the hill. Nica dared not fall behind. One tumble and her tool, crude as it was, might be lost. She did her best to keep up, trying to understand what kind of being he was.

Unwebbed. She hadn't thought much about creatures unsuited for life in the water, about as much as she hadn't prepared for life above it. No sensory lines that she could see, just as there were no sensory cues to pick up.

No variation in coloring—not spots or stripes, bands, or patches—his skin was just one hue, like dead kelp or, she grimaced at her hands and knees, dried blood.

His clothing clung to his form, unlike the loose wraps her people wore, exposing nothing but his hands and face. Even his feet were covered. The fibers looked strong, undamaged by any of their struggling or the terrain, but not woven from any material she recognized. They might have been hides, but seemed too thin for that. The sheen reminded her of some of the iridescent creatures she'd tended when she was a juvie, and if there was stitching, it was too fine to make out.

Surface respiration didn't seem to be a challenge for him. In fact, he'd greeted sunup by taking in large draughts. No squinting either. *How can he bear that unfiltered light?* There was little grace in his bearing, though any fluid movement was hard to imagine on this linear surface. Instead, he plowed through the terrain as if it were a bed of seagrass, taking on inclines and navigating hurdles without breaking stride. In every move, he seemed to exert his will over the surroundings.

It was clear that he was not Olomi, but if not, what? And if he was not a water-dweller, where had he come from? Before the Breaking, only tree islands interrupted the surface, and she had never heard of them being inhabited.

She slipped the stone from her waistband, sawing at the bindings around her wrist as they walked. By sunpeak, when her shadow's cast was shortest, she had worn halfway through. The ground swam and her head ached from the incessant beating of the naked sun. Just for a moment, she closed her eyes to regain her bearings—and nearly walked into her captor's back. He'd stopped to rummage through his satchel. Pointing at her to sit, he tossed a few more sea pods at her feet before bringing out a thin, gray plank.

Grateful for the respite, yet afraid to be found out, she squatted with her back to him, tucking the stone under her wrap once again. She cradled the fuzzy pods, amazed they had retained their structure this far removed from the Deep. Nipping the end, she took a tiny sip. The briny fluid, not enough to hydrate her lungs, did more for her soul than body, imparting an essence of home. Her gaze drifted back, reviewing the route she had been forced to climb. Water sparkled in the distance, far below their site, as elusive as any hope she had to return to its embrace.

Does anyone know of my fate? What of Jonnat? And was Rissa . . . Suddenly, something struck Nica's thoughts. *Had Rissa been taken captive as well?* It was the only thing that made sense. *Perhaps I am being taken to the same place!*

Odd hope sprang in her heart. She might still find her sister! Draining the last of the sea pods, she spat out what was left of the husks.

A pebble skipped toward her, catching her eye. Another bounced after it, up the rough path. *Up the path?* Nica risked a glance at her captor. He was occupied, etching on his plank. She traced the unnatural course of the pebbles. They were coming from behind a rock just a few lengths back. And in a moment, Nica's eyes connected with Jonnat's. She stifled a gasp but couldn't stop the moisture that broke from her eyes.

Her heart beat wildly, and she smoothed the tiny streams of water marking her face. He waggled three fingers at her with a raised brow. She replied by raising one. She lifted her bound hands with hitched shoulders and a head tilt. Jonnat mimed a strong jerk, pointing at the landwalker. Silently, they devised a plan. Jonnat would track in parallel, keeping out of sight. Just like he had taught her.

He ducked out of sight before Nica even heard the stranger stir. She watched, wary, as the stranger stood, replaced the plank, and pulled on her lead. Hurrying to avoid being jerked along, she followed.

She caught a glimpse of Jonnat out of the corner of her eye, amazed at his ability to stay hidden. If she hadn't known he was there . . . Forcing her eyes forward, she studied their opponent. Jonnat would spring when she made her move. She slowed, allowing slack to be taken up, watching and waiting for an opportune moment.

The landwalker raised his foot to step over a small ledge. This was it. Nica anchored herself and jerked back on the massive landwalker, throwing him off balance. Pain shot through her body, from her arms, through her shoulders, then coursing down her spine, but she held her ground.

Her captor clawed at the air in vain. He fell back, but rolled into a crouch. With a snarl, he pounced at Nica, but Jonnat intercepted, armed with a blade in one hand and a fist-sized rock in the other.

Jonnat brought the rock down on the landwalker's head with a sickening *thud*, but it was not enough to stop the larger male. Roaring in anger, Nica's captor twisted to grapple Jonnat, grabbing at hair and clothing as they rolled on the ground. Nica sprang onto his back, looping her restraints around his neck as she locked her legs about his torso. Though surprised and outnumbered, the landwalker was clearly in his element, possessing advantages of strength and size. His hands encircled Jonnat's throat, squeezing relentlessly as he threw his head back into Nica's face. *Crack.* Nica's field of vision spun as the ground rushed up to meet her.

Blood and sweat dripped from the landwalker. He grinned with malice, continuing to choke life out of Jonnat, who brought his blade around and drove it deep into the stranger's side. He roared in pain and his grip loosened, allowing the wiry Olomi to twist free. Jonnat charged at the stranger again—but was met with his own blade. Staggering, Jonnat gripped the blood-slicked hilt, his hands slipping as he tried to remove the weapon from his stomach. Then Nica's captor hoisted Jonnat over his head.

Blood dripped, bright red, from the blue Olomi, splashing onto the reddish-brown face of their opponent. He walked to the end of the precipice, Jonnat still writhing above him.

Nica dragged herself to the edge and wrapped her arms around her captor's legs. He kicked her in the ribs, and with a loud, guttural sound, he hurled Jonnat off the cliff. An eternity seemed to pass as she watched Jonnat tumble through the air, his hands still grasping the embedded dagger.

His body hit the beach far below. Sea foam surged forward and licked his still form before retreating with the surf, and the roar of a thousand waves washed over and through Nica. Struggling to her feet, she lunged at their opponent, but his backhand sent her spinning against the rock wall.

Her eyes rolled back, and in a mind-numbing cascade, Nica's world turned black.

REPORT

DELPH-2 — FIELD REPORT

HOMO SAPIENS AQUAN (GENUS, SPECIES, SUBSPECIES)

AQUA SAPIEN, FEMALE, ADULT

ATHLETIC BUILD, SOME SKILL IN GRAPPLING, ARMED PARTNER, AQUA SAPIEN, MALE, ADULT (DISPATCHED)

FEMALE STILL RESISTANT. COMPLIANCE IMMINENT.

EXPEDITION COMMANDER: TERRAFORMATION/AGRICULTURE/LABOR

EOR

14

·· SURRENDER ··

NICA'S head bobbed, tugging at her dorsals as soft currents brushed past her. Her chin thumped against a padded, yet unyielding, surface. The pressure behind her eyes confused her attempts to orient. Her head had never felt so full. Awareness emerged with consciousness and the currents that carried her evaporated. A searing gasp brought her back to reality—she was surrounded by air.

And Jonnat was lost.

Images of him plunging to his death broke over Nica again. A ball of grief forced its way through her lungs until it lodged in her throat, where it sat and swelled, choking her.

Resistance met her attempts to open her eyes. Like barnacles on whaleback, they refused to part. She moved to rub them but her shoulders spasmed. Her hands, joined at the wrists, were immobilized.

How am I in motion? She forced her eyes open to the iridescent gray of her captor's back, realizing that she was draped over his shoulder. Nica stiffened. At that, he grunted and heaved her onto the ground.

Unable to break her fall, Nica landed, hard, on her side. She played octopus for a moment, curling into herself.

The stranger shoved her with his foot and a gasp escaped before Nica could stop it. He jerked her to her feet and pointed to a structure at the top of the rise. His words were strange, but the meaning was clear. Her head swam, throbbing as she readjusted to being vertical. She staggered behind, numb.

How long was I out?

The shadows stretched out more than half a length ahead of her, and the air baked her chest with every breath she drew in. These were not morning shadows, but late afternoon, with the tide's accumulated heat lashing at her before it sank with the sun. She swayed, fighting to remain on her feet.

Pink rings of raw flesh stood out against the green of her wrists, glistening as more moisture left her body. But even where the bindings didn't rub, her skin was beginning to flake and peel off. Her webbing was chapped, and her eyes burned whether opened or closed. Desperate for water, need gave her a voice.

"*Omi*," she croaked. "*Mo nilo omi.*"

The landwalker spewed meaningless sounds at her.

"Omi," she pleaded, gesturing at her mouth and throat. "Omi."

He pulled out a container, held it high, and tipped it, pouring precious fluid into his mouth. Nica stared, unable to look away from the life-giving water. He dragged the back of his hand across his mouth, flinging the excess moisture into the air, then extended the container toward her with a cocked eyebrow. Was he offering?

Once again, he spoke, but Nica could only hope to understand the sounds through his gestures. "Omi!" She nodded, lifting her hands to take the flask.

He snatched it back.

"Omi!" she begged, reaching out.

He shook his head and squatted in front of her, pouring some water into the cap. "Waah-ter." He enunciated slowly as he held out the cap. "Waah-ter."

She drew her brows together, focusing as she followed the sounds his mouth made. "Waaa-duu."

He raised his eyebrows and brought the drink almost within her reach, then tossed it aside. Taking a swig, he poured another capful.

Once again, he held the filled cap in front of her. "Waa-terr."

She chewed her lower lip, focusing on the capful of liquid. "Whaa-tt, whaah-terr."

With a nod, he put the cap to her lips.

Nica sucked the splash of water out quickly, holding it in her mouth.

He asked a question, tapping the cap with the flask.

She nodded, repeating, "Whaa-terrr," and reached for another sip.

The stranger rebuffed her with a wagging finger and a headshake. This time he pointed to himself. "Ee-see-tahl." He repeated the motion and said again, "Ee-see-tal." Then, he pointed at her.

Gesturing to herself with bound hands, she said, "Nica."

His hand flashed, striking her across the face. He thundered at her, jabbing his finger hard against her breastbone. He brought his face close to hers. "Tahl-eh-tah!"

She tried to scoot back, but he stepped on the cord and squatted close to her. With a malicious grin, he said again, "Ee-see-tal."

He grabbed her hands and pointed them at himself.

"Eee-sssee tah-uhl?" she stammered, full of fear.

He then reoriented her hands to point at herself, asking a question in his strange tongue.

"Ni—"

Again, his palm met her head with lightning speed. She tried to shrink back, but the tether anchored her.

He jabbed her hands repeatedly against her chest, saying the strange words over and over. "Tahl-eh-tah! Tal-eh-tah!"

Cringing under the shadow of his upraised hand, Nica whispered back, "Tahl-eh-tah?"

He pointed again, demanding her response, his hand still hovering over her head.

Nica pointed a trembling finger at him. "Ee-see-tahl," she uttered with a shaking voice.

Pointing back at herself, she complied. "Tahl-eh-tah."

Her captor poured another capful of water and offered it to her, his grin wide as she received the drink with trembling hands.

It took most of the afternoon for Nica to 'earn' a handful of water, and her hatred for Ee-see-tal grew as her education continued. She learned to obey the commands of her captor like a pet squid. Words like 'down' and 'up', 'stop' and 'run', 'yes' and 'no', 'bow' and 'kneel'. The new words tasted sour on her tongue, and twisted in her stomach, but pain and survival were good teachers. She didn't know who her heart burned against more—Ee-see-tal, for subjugating her, or herself for capitulating to his demands.

She needed to escape, if only to warn her people. Escape would only be possible if she could stay alive. And she still needed to find Rissa. Jonnat's death and her captor's lessons schooled Nica quickly in the futility of resistance. Her only hope was to survive. Too weak to die, Nica stopped fighting and chose life on the landwalker's terms, and she hated them both for it.

REPORT

DELPH-2 – Field Report

Homo sapiens aquan (Genus,
species, subspecies)

Aqua Sapien, female, adult

Begin conditioning immediately

Possible candidate for enhanced
adaption.

Expedition Commander:
Terraformation/Agriculture/Labor

EOR

15

SUNSINK progressed slowly abovewater, as long and laborious as their trudge up the landmount. In the Deep, she'd surfaced to watch the sinking sun, and it wasn't but a few draughts before the last of the orange glow plunged beneath the far away waves. Here, streams of red, orange, and pink meandered down land surfaces until they seeped away, leaving the world cold and purple and blue. Nica wondered if the landlocked trickles of water and light felt as battered and bruised as she did.

A gray wall four times her captor's height loomed ahead. Smoother than the polished stone it resembled, its shining gray planks joined seamlessly, topped with spines that glinted as they reflected the last rays of the sinking sun. Looking sharper than those on the fiercest shark, the sight sent shivers down Nica's dorsals.

The landwalker, Ee-see-tal, approached the gate and opened a small compartment. Reaching inside, he pushed at the panel until it emitted a tone. An underlying hum she hadn't noticed ceased and two panels swung open. Uncertain whether the design's intent was to keep others in or out, Nica had to acknowledge that the barricade was sufficient for either task. *If this isn't a fortress, it's certainly a prison.*

The gates creaked open, shoving aside what appeared to be remains—a mute testimony to the barricade's effectiveness. Nica shuddered as Ee-see-tal towed her over the threshold, forcing her to wade through the bones and bodies. A nearby body, still more flesh than bones, caught her eye—the foot was still webbed. Her stomach convulsed, but she quelled it forcibly. She didn't have much control over her life right now, but she would exercise control over her body.

A small but silent flurry of activity greeted Ee-see-tal upon his arrival. Two Olomi approached. A gray male retrieved Ee-see-tal's travel pack, and an older, light blue female, carrying a tray with food and drink. Neither Olomi met her gaze nor made a sound.

Their hides were faded, scarred, and flaked. *How long had they been removed from the water? How long until I can return?* But the gate scraped shut, sealing her fate.

"Tal-alph," her captor bellowed. A third Olomi approached. Not cowed like the others, the well-muscled female strode to Ee-see-tal, knelt briskly, and then took Nica's lead from his hand. Giving it a sharp flick, the faded, yellow-hued female led Nica to a small stone pedestal in the center of the compound.

"Kneel," the yellow commanded in Olomi, as if she were also a captor.

Nica stared with incredulity. *Does this sister of the water really expect me to kneel?* A retort formed, but before it came out, the Olomi snapped the lead and brought Nica to her knees. In an instant, her wrist bindings were secured to a small hook in the middle of the pedestal.

Ee-see-tal strode to the center and nodded toward two Olomi flanking a large disk. At his signal, they picked up two large clubs and began to beat it.

The reverberations shuddered throughout the compound, like distance-sendings in the Deep. Olomi streamed into the clearing and assembled around the pedestal where Nica stood, eyes down, her hands locked together.

"Tal-aquans! Who am I?"

In unison, the Olomi answered, "Ee-see-tal."

"Who are you?"

Again, with one voice, the Olomi answered, "Tal-aquan."

Nica swayed on her knees, lacking the strength to remain upright. Dehydration, exposure, and exhaustion overwhelmed her. Only the clasp anchoring her wrists prevented her from collapse.

Ee-see-tal fixed his gaze on her. "Who am I?"

"Ee-see-tal."

"Who are you?"

Trained to respond to this simple inquiry with desperate compliance, Nica still hesitated before the assembled Olomi.

His brows drew together as he leaned over, daring her to trigger his hand.

Nica. She dared not say it out loud.

Eyes closed in resignation, she breathed out, "Tal-eh-tah," realizing as she spoke that it was not even a name, but a designation.

"TAL-eta—" He continued with words she did not understand.

As if this was anticipated, the yellow stepped forward from the queue and addressed Nica in Olomi. Her words sounded thin, contorted, and weightless here, above the water, but at least Nica could understand them.

"TAL-eta, I am TAL-alph. I have been given permission to speak the language of you water people, who are referred to as aquans by Expedition Commander TAL. Do not respond in that language unless you wish to suffer severe consequences. Do you understand?"

Afraid to say anything, Nica nodded.

"Do you understand?" the yellow Olomi prompted with a low growl.

"Ye-yes," Nica stammered in the landwalker's tongue.

Satisfied at the correct response, Ee-see-tal nodded at his translator to continue.

"EC-TAL wishes to know if you want him to release you."

Confused, Nica again answered, "Yes?"

He spoke, and TAL-alph translated, "What have you done to earn this?"

Nica looked from one to the other, bewildered. EC-TAL growled more words and TAL-alph swiped at her with the coiled whip. She shrank from the blow as the yellow Olomi translated, "Look at me, not my tool!"

Nica winced and trained her eyes on her captor as the translator continued.

"Nothing is free. Do you wish to earn your release?"

"Y-yes." Nica's voice cracked.

EC-TAL placed his open hand on the table next to the clasp that anchored her bound hands. He waited as TAL-alph translated. "Then you must give me your hands."

She didn't understand this new request, but dared not make him wait.

"TAL-eta. Hands." The EC's quiet words did not sound any less menacing.

Quivering fingers complied, her green-webbed hands dwarfed by his dark and calloused palms. He gripped them firmly with one hand and brought out a knife with the other. She pulled frantically as the knife descended but couldn't break free. The blade landed, but only her restraints were cut. Nica trembled, relieved, though her hands were still imprisoned by his grasp.

"By this act, you have earned release from your former life. You have relinquished your place in the water. You now belong to the land, and you belong to me."

Horrified, Nica barely grasped the words of the translator as EC-TAL pinned her palms to the pedestal and cut the webbing between her fingers. Horror eclipsed thought as her life in the water was hewed off before her eyes. She had given it over without a fight.

16

A SLENDER CRESCENT shimmered in the darkness, sprinkling flecks of moonshine through the woven strips of bamboo that covered the agri-pod quarters. Nica cradled the motes floating in its gentle illumination, careful not to disturb her sleeping podmates. Once, she'd danced in the lunar light on dappled sea floors, but now, that life below the surface felt like a distant memory. How long had it been since she'd been saturated, since she'd been satiated, since she'd filled her lungs with a woosh and not a rattle. Had it been only one lunar passage? And yet, some of the landed Olomi seemed unaffected by the desiccation that plagued others. The yellow alpha, always ready to enforce their captor's will, showed no signs of water deprivation. Well, none but the fading that washed away their bright Olomi colors.

In the weak glow of the nascent moon she could almost forget, or more easily ignore, the scars—if she held her hands just right. She rotated her wrists, squinting at the disfigured tissue. The skin that once spanned her fingers, now fused, lumpy, and brown against the green of her knuckles, didn't stand out as much in the shifting streams of moonlight. And they were finally beginning to heal. The pod-leader had given her hand-wraps, so they wouldn't tear while she worked the dirt. At the time, she'd thought he was being kind. A scoff escaped, quickly followed by a stifled cough and a wheeze. Turned out to be merely expedient, as the brown-striped male drove the pod without mercy.

Raising food was a battle and EC-TAL warred with the land, demanding total compliance from his labor force. Any deviation from his protocol was punished. Harshly. Harsher than that of causing injury to another worker. The seedlings held more value than their tenders and, the pod-leader made it clear, *aquans* were easier to replace.

Nothing but the raspy breathing of her podmates broke the silence of the night. Though their mats were rough, oceans away from kelp-lined slings and soft hammocks, a long day of labor exposed to the elements ensured that their sleep was sound.

It was time. Nica rolled onto the ground with care, cringing at the creak and crackle of the weave.

Treading between the occupied mats with care, she crept out of the sleeping quarters. Her heart pounded and she stopped to slow its wild thumping before anyone . . . She cocked an eyebrow and shook her head. There was no need to conceal signals here, there was no communion to give her away. Her fingers brushed the line of sensors running from temple to jaw. She closed her eyes and shook off the memories. Regret served no useful purpose here. She would have to forge new channels to adapt to the ways of the land. Would this venture do?

Though the compound was empty, shards of moonbeams drove Nica into the shadows. She padded along the walls, through the food-pod grounds, slipping back to the waste mound. Giving a last look around, she poked through the scraps left by food-prep. She allowed a quiet scoff. They should have just served these straight up. By the time what she'd harvested was served, it was almost unrecognizable. Just bland chunks and pastes in tepid broths that did little to fill or nourish her.

Lack lodged like a rock in her stomach and her body had already begun to consume its stored fats. Nets of tiny squid and eel swarmed in her thoughts. She chased them away. Now was not the time for reminiscing. She hadn't risked this trip just to be caught sea-dreaming, logging about like some juvie whale.

There wasn't much, just peelings and husks, and a bit of rotted vegetation here or there, but it would be sufficient. It would have to be. She folded the scraps into the corner of her tunic and crept back to her quarters.

She lay again on her mat, trying to settle her thoughts and signals. Sunup would usher in another abovewater tide and Nica would need strength to meet it. But visions of *Ìyá's* dining bowl still taunted her. Food in the Deep had been fresh, full of life, and readily available. But her heart hungered more for communion. To know and be known. This was the hardest adaption to the surface. Instead, she was expected to school with her pod without shared signals, where landlocked Olomi vied against each other for favor, and sometimes survival. Those granted any measure of power didn't hesitate to buttress their positions by turning in their fellows. The people who had been one now strove against each other. Maybe she could help—make a difference that others could notice—even appreciate.

With a wary glance, Nica untucked the corner of her tunic and spilled its contents into the soil. *Ìyá's* gardens had always flourished and this was one of her habits—turning in the scraps and leftovers. She said it fed the plants. Nica smiled at the memory. Her *ìyá's* gardens were both beautiful and beneficial.

The blow landed just as Nica heard the baton *whoosh* behind her.

"What do you think you're doing?" The agri-pod supervisor hissed, pointing at the mound before her.

"Yes. What are you doing?"

Fear struck Nica at the sound of TAL-alph unfurling her whip.

Muttering arose as the yellow advanced. Flicking her gaze at the grumbling podmates, TAL-alph prodded Nica with the butt of her whip. "I asked you a question."

"I . . . I thought it might hel—"

"You thought?" The yellow smirked, her eyes dark and dangerous. She raised her voice to address the entire work-pod. "Did anyone here give this aquan permission to think?" She rotated slowly, arm outstretched, pointing her whip before resting her sights on the supervisor.

"No . . . No, TAL-alph. No permission granted." The white

between the supervisor's brown stripes nearly disappeared as he shrank from the alpha's glare.

"Hmm. I can see you weren't encouraging the newcomer, but then, who?" The yellow leveled her grip at the Olomi nearest Nica.

"You . . . you . . . you . . . you . . . and you." Each podmate stiffened as they were selected to stand before the yellow. "Which of you encouraged this green to think?"

No one said a word, but kept their gazes anchored on the dirt at their feet.

"Are you suggesting that I am mistaken?"

Nica could read panic in the shallow gasps they emitted. Cold fear ran through her as the yellow smirked at the same tells.

"I didn't think so."

Five Olomi. Five stripes. The first to receive punishment for Nica's transgression did not exclaim until the third lash. The fourth cried out when TAL-alph turned her attention to him. The last bore his stripes with white knuckles and a stoic grimace.

Nica tried to look away, but the pod supervisor dug his fingers into her shoulders, forcing her to face her punishment, warning, "Close your eyes, and she will select more."

TAL-alph turned to her. Nica presented her back, ready to accept her punishment, but the yellow merely said, "Look at me."

Nica trembled as she turned, her dread palpable.

"I trust you've learned your lesson. They should have instructed you better." Her tone was almost sweet, but deadly. "You are not here to think. You are here to serve. Do not forget."

17

·· MARKED ··

I T WAS the *hum* that got her attention. Or its absence. The pervasive ambient *hum* that filled her waking moments and invaded her dreams. Other than when she had been dragged into the landwalker's compound, the *hum* of captivity had been as present as communion had been in the Deep. Until now.

Morning's light had just breached the walls, and firstmeal had not yet been served. With a quick glance behind, Nica stole past the buildings near the outskirts of the compound. Thankful for what cover twilight provided, she approached the entrance, afraid to breathe, afraid to hope. She peeked from behind a storage shelter. *Open!* Her heart leapt. Crouched and ready to bolt, she scouted the area. In an instant, disappointment rose. She staggered back with a stifled cry. All strength was lost as hope evaporated. Sliding down the wall, Nica buried her face in her hands.

The yellow enforcer secured the compound gates behind EC-TAL. His departure could have provided an opportunity to flee, had the yellow overseer not proven her loyalties lay with their oppressor. What made TAL-alph choose against her own people? Was there any hope of swaying her? There had to be. Despite her actions, the yellow Olomi was still of the water. Surely, there was some way to remind her.

The gong sounded after firstmeal, calling all aquans to assemble.

If EC-TAL is gone, who is sending the call?

She dared not ask, but schooled with the others to the courtyard. A figure emerged from beyond TAL's buildings. Female, and not Olomi, like TAL, she was unwebbed, and her skin, a single hue. Neither tinged nor tanned, she was whiter than any underbelly Nica had seen. A massive, gray, scarred Olomi male stood by her— his dark, muscular form in sharp relief to her lean paleness. He swaggered through the crowds, leering at the fearful Olomi. His pale eyes, full of menace, dared anyone to meet his gaze. None did.

Head down and eyes on the ground, Nica whispered to a nearby podmate, "Who is that?"

"That's MO-ASHE, Medical Officer. She commands with EC-TAL. Do not–" The Olomi looked away abruptly as the gray alpha drew near.

Fear tightened Nica's muscles to stay as motionless as possible. The overseers were harsh, but this one felt like a predator.

"ASHE-alph. TAL-alph. I require two mated pairs."

Medical Officer-ASHE did not raise her voice, but she didn't need to. There was no less authority in her voice than TAL's, and the assembled Olomi were still before her.

The alphas walked through the ranks, tapping couples, and presenting them to the pale MO. Of those, she selected two older couples. A male with black and tan sinuous markings and his mate, orange down her dorsals with ventrals presenting white. The other couple, a stooped male with thin yellow stripes barely visible against his light base, and his mate, her pinks faded, almost gray. The selected pairs were directed to a holding pen at the edge of the courtyard containing a pillar and a brazier.

The light pink female fought being herded into the pen. Gasps rippled through the crowd. Some shook their heads, mouthing, "No," as she struggled. Nica didn't know what to expect, but it was clear, many did.

"Release the female."

A chill overtook Nica when she saw how the female landwalker smiled at the resistant Olomi. With narrowed eyes, she nodded to her alpha. His whip whistled through the air and landed with a *CRACK!* The Olomi's partner fell to his knees, howling in pain. Again and again, the whip landed on his back, until she stumbled into the enclosure.

MO-ASHE paced around the weeping female, languid and deliberate, like a shark circling prey. She came to a stop at the pillar and nodded at her. "You may help him stand."

The woman helped her husband to his feet with quivering hands.

"You will serve this Delphim faithfully, yes?" MO-ASHE addressed the broken couple.

Trembling, they both nodded.

MO-ASHE raised her eyebrows and glanced at her alpha.

Cracking the whip again over his back, ASHE-alph growled. "You will answer Medical Officer-ASHE."

"You will serve this Delphim faithfully, yes?" She repeated the challenge.

"Yes," the female replied as her husband gasped, "Ye-yes."

"Yes . . . what?" MO-ASHE replied, her tone even more dangerous.

"I will serve this Delphim faithfully."

"Aquan, embrace my pillar as you embrace my service."

The woman approached the pillar and placed her shaking arms around the pillar.

"And you, embrace your female."

The man lurched to the pillar, almost collapsing as his arms encircled both the pillar and his wife.

"Secure them."

The alpha bound the Olomi male's hands so that his embrace fastened them both to the pillar. Then MO-ASHE removed a rod from the brazier, and Nica felt a sickening knot form in her stomach.

"Do you wish to receive my mark on your arm or on your back?"

The striped Olomi moaned in response, and MO-ASHE drew closer, holding the glowing metal next to his cheek. His wife whimpered, unsuccessful in her attempts to pull away, her white hair writhing and shrinking where the red-hot rod brushed it.

"I will not ask again. Pay heed to your response."

Gasping, he replied through gritted teeth, "I wish . . . to . . . receive . . . your mark . . . on . . . my . . . back."

"Very good. You are ASHE-mu."

At that, MO-ASHE landed the glowing brand on the already beaten back, cauterizing some of the wounds as it burned deep into his hide. He howled and screamed in his wife's ear, crushing her against the pillar as he writhed in pain. She sobbed and screamed until he collapsed, senseless, still pinning her to the column.

MO-ASHE replaced the brand on the brazier and repeated her prompt to the female. "Do you wish to receive my mark on your arm or on your back?"

Through her sobs, she said, "I wish to receive your mark on my back."

Pulling the reheated brand out of the fire, MO-ASHE hissed, "You made your choice when you resisted, ASHE-nu," and plunged the glowing iron onto her cheek.

The gathered Olomi remained silent as the large gray alpha freed ASHE-mu's hands. His senseless body crumpled, crushing his wife underneath his still-unconscious form.

Nica's stomach writhed at the smell of burning flesh. What malice prompted MO-ASHE to abuse the Olomi in this manner?

It became clear as the second couple approached. Offering no resistance, both embraced the pillar stoically to pledge their loyalty and receive MO-ASHE'S brand on their backs.

18

·· CHOSEN ··

"**A**QUANAS."

A chill traveled down Nica's dorsal, but she joined her sisters as they lined up without a sound. The older Olomi women were dismissed, as were any with observable disabilities, aside from the ubiquitous scarred knuckles. Nica noticed that the yellow enforcer, TAL-alph, was also exempt from this selection.

MO-ASHE led the queue into a complex deeper inside TAL'S compound—or did they share this domain? Nica gaped at the structure as they entered. Olomi quarters, not much more than land-caverns cobbled together from scraps and sticks, were designed more to contain than shelter their occupants.

This structure's walls gleamed like the outer gates. Appearing more solid than stone, the unnatural material was seamless, smooth as skin. Nica brushed her fingers against the surface as she passed. No give, no warmth, no evidence that life had been or ever would be supported by this stoneskin. She suppressed a shudder. In the Deep, even long dead coral retained an imprint of the life that once resided in it.

She shuffled through another seamless corridor, unable to break from the shoal. Rising fear clawed at her throat, but she could not escape the vortex. Inside, the air was cooler, devoid of moisture, and its scent burned the inner membranes of her nasal passages.

Nica hadn't even known this section existed. Other than for meals, she hadn't ventured past the agri-pod's grounds. She'd had no desire to explore EC-TAL's property. She glanced over her shoulder at the gray alpha following them. He caught her eye and a vicious grin spread across his face, daring her to run. There to ensure no one lagged or slipped away—it was clear he'd love to see someone try.

Nica squeezed to the middle of the huddle, hoping to hide from the hungry leer in the safety of a crowd. One of the Olomi, with orange and blue markings and a thick orange braid, looked close to her age. Nica brushed by her, murmuring, "Why we are here?"

Brilliant, silver-blue eyes widened, and she stammered, "I . . . I don't know anything. Why are you talking to me?" She veered to the edge of their cluster, as far from Nica as she could, only to be culled from the group when they reached the end of the corridor. Her braid, hanging down past her waist, was the last Nica could see of her before she disappeared around the bend.

Nica's stomach sank. She shouldn't have approached her. There was no safety. Not in whispers. Not in pods. Not in crowds. Not anywhere. And once again, someone else paid the price because of her. She couldn't live like this. No—she *shouldn't* live like this. No one should. There had to be something she could do.

The harsh, almost blinding light in the new room drove any musings away. MO-ASHE directed the queue through channels for various physical examinations. Some women were eliminated after cursory physical exams, others after an endurance test. Those who passed were herded to the next round to have blood taken.

More Olomi were dismissed, and Nica sidled over to join the shuffling procession toward the exit. She had almost made it back to the beginning of the corridor when her way was blocked by ASHE-alph. How someone that large could move without stirring currents, even abovewater, both mystified and terrified her. Grabbing her by the upper arm, he hauled her back to MO-ASHE and tossed her at the feet of his mistress.

"This one tried to squirm away."

"That won't do." The Delphim circled Nica, poking and prodding with a hard rod. "You're new. We always keep the new ones back."

Tipping Nica's chin up with the rod, her eyes glinted. "Yes.

TAL mentioned a new green. Looks healthy enough. We'll see how healthy."

She turned and headed down the corridor.

"Bring her."

The gray beast hauled Nica off the floor, dragged her down the hall, and tossed her into a small room. Nica ran for the door, only to have him grin and slam it shut. She felt the bolt sliding into place scrape at her soul. There would be no escape. She was without hope and at the mercy of her captors.

"ASHE-alph." The icy tone of the mistress froze Nica.

"Yes, MO-ASHE." Was that apprehension in the massive Olomi's voice?

Nica couldn't believe her suspicions, but . . .

"You slammed my door."

The MO did not increase her volume, but her displeasure was clear.

The double thud and the muffled sound of the alpha's voice begging her pardon told Nica that the beast must have dropped to his knees.

"This will not happen again." MO-ASHE's voice would strike fear in anyone's heart.

"Yes, MO-ASHE, it wo—"

His groveling ended abruptly, replaced by guttural gasps.

Nica didn't dare move. Just as she realized she'd been holding her breath, the gasps were replaced by groaning. Eventually, only uneven footfalls and staggered thuds against the wall disturbed the silence of the corridor. Nica listened, uneasy, as the sounds died off in the distance.

If this was how the Delphim treated her alpha . . . Nica scuttled away from the door until her back met the furthest wall. There was nothing in the room except a stoneskin table. Nothing to give any indication of what her fate might be.

Her legs ached and her back grew cold, but Nica refused to leave the shelter of the wall. She had no way to estimate how much time passed, but raised her head at the sound of the bolt grating

76   SOPHIA L. HANSEN

along its slot. The door creaked open, revealing one of MO-ASHE's Olomi enforcers. The last had been dark, dull, and gray—fearsome and imposing. This one was even darker, so dark that he shone. His inky base was marked with radiating lines of blue that almost glowed, and his eyes, also impossibly black, bore through her.

"TAL-eta?" he inquired, glancing at a pad.

Nica nodded.

"Sit." He pointed to the gray table.

She complied.

He handed her a small cup. "Drink."

Putting the cup to her lips, Nica hesitated. *What is this? What will it do? But if I don't . . .*

She drank. The room swirled around her, and then faded. The last thing Nica remembered was his dark hands, scarred and striped with deep blues, catching her.

Her eyelids felt like they were tied to stones as Nica struggled to open them. She tried to rub the weighted feeling away, but her arms stopped short, inches from her body. Panicked to discover her feet were also in fetters, she thrashed, trying to free herself.

"Stop!" A voice outside her cell warned her. The guard who'd given her the drink unlocked the door and slipped in. "*Duro,*" he whispered in Olomi, repeating the admonishment. "*You must lie still. Do not fight.*"

Without another word, he returned to his post, locking the cell door behind him.

Tears began to trickle down Nica's cheeks, dropping onto the hard surface she was secured to. It had been so long since she had heard her language, and it had been as long since she had been shown any kindness. To receive a warning, rather than a beating, was the only compassion that she'd experienced since being taken.

"Is the green awake yet?" Nica heard the female Delphim's voice drawing near and stilled her sobs.

"Yes, MO-ASHE."

The latch slid once again in its setting, and the door swung open for TAL's partner and her alpha.

"TAL-eta. You have been reassigned to food preparation. You will have one additional meal ration before your sleep period. Speak to no one about this. If you do, the consequences will be severe."

The gray alpha placed a note in Nica's hand as MO-ASHE continued. "Give this to TAL-zeta, the kitchen supervisor."

Nica nodded, barely daring to breathe as the MO ran a critical eye over her before she turned abruptly to the door.

"Release her."

19

·· L E S S O N S ··

T HE SUN hadn't peaked when Nica was first herded into
MO-ASHE's enclosure, but she emerged into the cool darkness
of eventide. Last meal was surely over, and she didn't want to disturb
the kitchen supervisor this late, but the medical officer's instructions
were clear.

She slipped toward the food-pod, avoiding eye contact with any
other Olomi. Hesitating at the curtain that hung from the deadwood
partition to the supervisor's quarters, she took in a breath, then tapped
on the frame. Gentle clattering rose from the strings of wooden beads as
a flaked and faded hand of mottled blue pulled them back. It was the old
Olomi woman who'd brought TAL the tray of food when she first . . . Nica
closed her eyes briefly, shaking away the memories.

"TAL-zeta?"

The elder's creased brow concentrated her blues with grays,
hooding the rheumy eyes that glared up at her. "What do you want?"

Nica thrust the note at her wrinkled hands, noting the faded but
familiar scarring.

Glancing at the marking, the supervisor eyed Nica sharply, and
then sighed. What looked like sadness washed over her face, but the
guarded weariness returned in an instant.

"Sit." She nodded toward a bench. "Wait."

Bustling about the hearth, the old woman added some water to the
large pot suspended over a stone fire circle and stirred. Grabbing two
bowls, she ladled the soupy mass and placed one in front of Nica, and
the other across from her.

"You join me, Ìyágba?" Nica risked using the respectful Olomi title.

A bitter laugh escaped the elder. "No snack."

Nica's brow furrowed. "Snack?"

TAL-zeta cast a wary look around before she drew close and whispered, "Snack—*ipanu*." Then, without another word, she returned to her work.

Before Nica swallowed her second mouthful, the beads rattled again, announcing another arrival.

Nica dropped her spoon. "It's you?!" She blinked rapidly, uncertain of her words. "You're . . . unhurt?"

"You! You're here?" The orange and blue Olomi was equally flustered. She had no note, but it was clear she was expected.

"Yes, yes. You're here and you're here." TAL-zeta waved a hand at each of the girls. "Now, finish your food"—she pointed to the bowl across from Nica—"so I can be out of here!" She stomped off, huffing and muttering about extra meals.

The two ate in silence, exchanging furtive glances over their mouthfuls.

Nica felt like she would burst. "I'm so—"

At the same time, the striped Olomi blurted, "Why are—"

They both stopped, and then dissolved into nervous giggles.

"TAL-eta! TAL-kap!" The kitchen supervisor stomped in, brandishing a large wooden stirrer. "Are you trying to bring the guards down on us?"

The two covered their mouths and TAL-zeta threw her hands in the air, puffing threats under her breath as she bustled back to the inner room.

Nica finally managed to choke out her apology, sobering as she continued. "I thought I got you in trouble, when they took you from the group."

"No." TAL-kap shook her head. "I'd been through the first exams already. I was taken straight to the cells to wait for MO-ASHE." She wrinkled her nose and gave a shudder. "She's so scary."

Nica could only nod vigorously in reply.

"I'm sorry I got so upset at you earlier." TAL-kap smiled at her sadly. "I thought you were . . . testing. Trying to trap me."

Nica's head drooped. "I'm sorry I even asked. I should have known it could get you in trouble."

TAL-kap nodded at Nica wryly. "It was kind of . . . *omugo*."

Nica's eyes bolted open at the insult, and she pressed her lips tight to stop from bursting into more giggling.

TAL-kap rounded her eyes. "What?" she said innocently. "I don't know *omugo* here."

Silent laughter overtook them both. It felt wonderful.

TAL-zeta growled from her back room, "The word is *stupid*. Like, if you stupid girls bring the guards here, I'll beat you myself!"

Glancing her direction, then back, Nica pointed at herself, whispering, *"Nica."*

TAL-kap's dolphin-shaped eyes glistened back under the frame of her heavy braid. *"Pescha,"* she whispered.

They exchanged a tiny smile at this moment of solidarity.

"Do you know what happened?" Nica hoped Pescha might have answers that she lacked.

Her new friend's brow wrinkled. "It was like before the last moon. I drank from the cup, slept, then awoke to MO-ASHE and was sent here." She rested her fingertips lightly on Nica's forearm, bright blue and orange striping bright against the green striations. Her smile didn't reach her eyes, but then, it didn't make it all the way across her lips. "But then I was alone."

After a full moon of working in agri-pod, Nica welcomed the transfer to food-pod. Careful to follow TAL-zeta's instructions, she fell in with the rest of the workers, finding her duties far less arduous than working the land. She learned to hull, soak, and dry the pods she'd previously harvested. Pescha showed her how to pour the dried beans into the trough between the large stone wheels, each larger than either of the Olomi. Too fast and they clogged at the entry, spilling out over the sides. Too slow and the beans were so sparse that the stones would touch and grind against each other. Thankful she hadn't been assigned to the harnesses propelling the great stones, she and Pescha collected the meal and brought it back to food-pod to pound into fine powder.

Nica didn't miss the constant bending and back-aching labor of the agri-pod, and after a few tides' respite from constant exposure to the baking sun, her cracked skin could begin to heal. More than that, there was comfort in the camaraderie she shared with Pescha. Both of them were no longer alone.

TAL's gong sounded. Waves of sound and motion pulsed through the compound as Olomi stopped and lifted their heads. Its deep resonance traveled abovewater almost like sound did in the Deep, but no underwater tone ever elicited the fear that this signal did.

The first time she heard the gong, it had marked the end of her life in the water. The second time, the sound of the gong had ushered in a tide of terror. Nica trembled and her stomach lurched at this new sounding.

EC-TAL entered the courtyard, carrying a small Olomi. Behind them trailed an adult, untethered, and obviously its *iyá*—the fry's dark blue primary markings were almost identical, despite its immature translucence.

Neither appeared to be damaged, and there was no sign of struggle. There had been no need. EC-TAL merely secured the fry, and its *iyá* obeyed his slightest command.

The Olomi assembled, and TAL-alph had the blue kneel and secured to the pedestal. Nica tried to suppress the shudder that ran down her dorsal. She wished she could shout a warning. She wished someone had warned her.

MO-ASHE's alpha emerged from the passage between TAL's buildings and knelt before the EC. With a bow of his head, the gray took the fry and returned to MO-ASHE's area, deaf to the wails of *iyá* and spawn.

Nica could not bear to watch but dared not turn her head as a new aquan was initiated into TAL's service. She saw the same confused glimmer of hope as the blue gave her hand to TAL. The same shock as her webbing was cut, and the same despair as TAL-rho was prompted to publicly declare her designation.

EC-TAL headed toward his quarters as his alpha prodded the broken-hearted Olomi with the butt of her whip. By the time the agri-pod overseer took over, half dragging, half kicking the blue to their quarters, most of the assembly had returned to their assignments in silence. Nica wished she could offer the new captive comfort, but the risk to her own safety outweighed any compassion she held for the grieving mother, and she slunk back to her pod.

Sunsink. It was time to serve first shift their eventide meal. Agri-pod came through, silent as usual, the new blue looking lost and miserable. Nica remembered that feeling well, and gently shouldered the newcomer into the food queue.

"Here, eat these." She ladled some of the less-cooked portions onto TAL-rho's platter. "They'll go down a little easier."

She did not tell her that her body would adapt. Or that tubers and protein cubes, dry as they were, would sustain her better in the long run. That she would soon guard these meals for herself, lest an Olomi squatting next to her steal it. Or that she would fight for it. Nobody needed to know how much their life, or their desires, would change—not just yet.

"*Kini eyi?*" TAL-rho asked what the abovewater food was.

"*Jẹun.* Eat," Nica replied in a brusque whisper, turning away from her sharply.

Nica already regretted revealing weakness in this company. All it would take was a sharp ear and spiteful tongue to turn two Olomi words to her painful disadvantage.

TAL-rho would also learn, but how many beatings would it take?

20

·· ADAPTATION ··

THE NIGHT sky, its twinkling lights brilliant in the moon's absence, had not been this clear since before the Breaking. What a gift to look up rather than scuff her toes in the dirt while she waited for Pescha. Though much had changed about her world, the stars had not.

The constellations beamed down on her: the Great Tortoise, the mythic Mermaid, and of course, the mischievous Dolphins—always chasing and never caught. Ìyágba's stories about the Deep's heroes and myths had always entranced her, transforming their family pool into a magical realm. Rissa may have inherited their grandmother's musical talent, but Nica shared her love of story.

Nica wondered if her sister could see the sky tonight, if they both swam in the same pool of memories. Maybe—

A dorsal bump sent her stumbling.

"Pe–TAL-kap!" She whirled to face her podmate. "What was that for?"

"It's not safe to be looking to above," Pescha replied. "You never know what's swimming beneath you."

"Or behind me, I guess," Nica grumbled, but she could only sulk for a few moments. "Do you see?" She pointed to the dolphins in the sky, arced high above them. "It's ẹja!"

"What are you thinking?" Pescha hissed. She grabbed Nica by the arm and dragged her across the compound, all the way back to their pod. She did not speak until they were safely inside Zeta's kitchen, but the blues around her sensory lines were dark. "Were you trying to get us both beaten?"

"It was just so beautiful. I . . . I didn't know the abovewater name of those stars."

Pescha's eyes shot wide, and she blinked several times before she could do more than sputter. "Well, at least no one heard you . . . this time."

"What do you mean, 'No one heard you?'" Zeta plonked down two bowls for their extra ration. She scowled at Nica, fists planted on her hips like barnacles on a whale. "Well?" Her head swiveled from one to the other, blue brow lines darkening as her frown deepened.

Nica mumbled, "It was nothing, TAL-zeta. I was just looking at the stars."

"Just because you're not in the Deep doesn't mean you should forget. Olomi shouldn't be looking above." Zeta waggled her finger at her. "You never know what's swimming beneath."

"Told you," Pescha muttered into her soup.

"*Ma binu,*" Nica apologized.

"*Dariji.*" Pescha's forgiveness was quiet, but accompanied with a smile.

Nica smiled back, thankful to be on good terms once again. "So, how did your exam go?"

The orange shrugged. "It was the same. But they took the new blue in without the first tests. That was unusual."

"Yes, I didn't understand that either. Not like anyone wants alone time with MO-ASHE."

Pescha gave a little snort.

"At least this time I didn't panic." Nica's mouth twitched up. "Thanks for the reminder." She patted Pescha's hand. "I paused to breathe."

"That blue though, TAL-rho? She was practically drafting the guard's wake." Nica shook her head. "Looking up and down every corridor while we were being taken to the cells. I don't know what she was thinking. Like we get any breaks for going belly-up."

"Don't judge her harshly." This time it was Pescha who reached out to Nica. "It was the last place she saw her fry. An *iyá* will do anything for her spawn."

Nica's dorsal quivered. She tried to put the memory out of her mind.

MO-ASHE leaving her cell.

The dark guard releasing her.

The creak of another cell door opening.

Rho crying out for her child, "Ọmọ mi! Ọmọ mi!"

The unmistakable crack of hand against flesh.

She shook her head. "It didn't gain her anything in the end."

They ate in silence, each lost in their own eddies.

A rap at the entrance frame made them both start. It was TAL-rho, handing a small scroll to the kitchen supervisor. With an exasperated exhale, TAL-zeta doled out a third bowl of soup, nearly slamming it on the table next to Nica. Both girls jumped, and then greeted the young mother warmly.

She whispered, pointing to herself, *"Nica."* She then pointed across to Pescha. *"Pesch—"*

"No!" The blue erupted, clasping her hands over her ears. She shot up from the bench, her eyes darting from Nica to Pescha. "Guar—"

Nica pulled the panicked female back down hard and clapped her hand over the blue's mouth.

"No," she said quickly. "TAL-eta. TAL-eta!"

Pescha came on the other side, helping Nica restrain her.

"TAL-kap!" the orange whispered, desperate to quiet TAL-rho.

Nica, emboldened now that Pescha had sided with her, grabbed the blue Olomi by the hair on the back of her head, and growled in her face. "Stop!"

The blue thrashed but could not break free. With a whimper of protest, she raised her palms in surrender, beginning to weep.

Nica released her hold as if her hands were burned.

She had threatened harm to a sister of the water. How could she?

TAL-rho was not the only one who had learned the rules of this land. Nica threw her arms around the heartbroken Olomi and collapsed into tears with her. Drawing Pescha into their huddle, the three girls cried until the old woman roughly shooed them out of her kitchen.

21

SCRITCH scritch scritch.
Tap tap tap. Tap.

Pescha tilted her head toward the chute, her eyes widening as she mouthed Nica's signal.

"O se?"

Nica gave the barest smile with a nod.

Their captors had removed them from the Deep, but could not eradicate the Deep from them. The signals used to communicate over long distances in the depths could also send messages along solid surfaces abovewater.

Pescha glanced around, then messaged Nica from the far end of the meal-chute.

Scritch tap scritch. Scritch scritch scritch.
Scritch. Scritch scritch scritch. Tap scritch scritch tap. Tap.

It was Nica's turn to reply, mouthing, *"Ko t'ope."*

Pescha's eyes sparkled.

It was a small thing. But this most basic exchange in the language of their home was exhilarating, healing, and a little terrifying. If they were caught, the consequences would be severe, but if this was the only connection they had to their true selves, it was worth it.

They guarded their smiles, scritching and tapping out new words across the trough, all the time trying to keep the beans flowing to the millstones. The sooner they finished, the sooner they could head back to the safety of the food-pod. TAL-zeta was a stern but fair overseer. That couldn't be said for the other pods.

Nica's patterns reverted to random scratching when the

millstone overseer turned their way. Pescha took to drumming her fingers whenever TAL-rho came to fetch their output for food-pod.

Pescha's drumming ceased, but TAL-rho was still too far off to hear their messaging. One look at Pescha told Nica something was wrong. All the colors had drained from her face. Her hands gripped the trough, but that was the only thing keeping her upright.

"TAL-rho! Bring TAL-zeta!"

Nica scurried, reaching the other end of the meal-chute, and her podmate, as Pescha began to slip to the ground. She propped her up next to a handcart.

"*Pe–*TAL-kap!" She shook her gently.

"*Omi,*" Pescha whispered.

"Work! Not rest!" Fury twisted the mill supervisor's expression into a fearsome scowl. He stomped over to them from the other side of the grindstones, brandishing a rod. Nica did not know the abovewater word for "sick," but didn't dare speak Olomi. Her heart pounded when she spied Zeta. Only their own pod-leader's presence could protect them from the mill supervisor.

"TAL-zeta! Help!"

"These are mine," she barked at the miller. "You keep to your crew."

"If we fall behind, I'll report you. It's not going to drag on me." He kicked at the dirt and headed back to his station, muttering threats at his crew.

"You finish." TAL-zeta pushed Nica to the collection chute, crouching at her charge's side.

Despite her brusque demeanor, the supervisor handled Pescha with tenderness, daubing at her face with a damp rag and dripping tiny sips of water into her mouth until the Olomi was able to be walked back to food-pod quarters.

The workers harnessed to the millstones, having received the brunt of their overseer's frustration, were not concerned. The grumbling got louder and the glares more hostile.

Nica doubled her efforts, trying to stave off rising tempers. She poured the beans into the hopper but choked the intake chute in her haste. Half the beans overflowed onto the ground. She scrambled to pick them up and grimaced. They would need to be rinsed and dried again. Would she ever learn to work here? *Don't cry. Too many eyes.*

Raking the scattered beans with her fingers was less efficient than she expected. She cast about, looking for a tool of any kind to speed the process, when a spotted blue and black foot with lava-tinged webbing pushed the far-flung bits to her pile. Bringing her bucket close, the Olomi stooped to help her gather them without a word, his sensory lines reflecting the blue of the shallows. His sand-colored face twisted into a bit of a smile, and he tapped the ground when they were done, leaving marks in the dust.

· _ _ · _ *"wà"*

_ · · _ *"ní"*

·_ ·_·· ·_ ·_ ··_· ·· · _ *"àlàáfìà"*

Be at peace? Here? It was too much to expect, but as Nica's eyes lingered on the impressions, the aching lump in her chest eased a bit more, even after his foot passed over the message, erasing every trace with a touch. He nodded as he left, leaving encouragement and questions in his silent wake.

Had he heard us? What if someone else did? How many would dare to communicate? How could she find other like-minded Olomi?

Nica lugged the bucket back to her pod. She didn't want to be around when TAL-zeta learned they would need to be rewashed, but needed to check on Pescha. Finding her sitting in the shade of Zeta's shelter, peeling husks, Nica was relieved to see her friend's striped complexion had returned to its characteristic orange and blues.

Nica scooted next to her, wishing she knew the abovewater word for sick. "Are you . . . *ṣe aisan*?"

Pescha nodded, holding her hand to her stomach and forehead with a grimace. Nica grabbed a couple of pods to help strip fibers, but the orange jumped up without warning and ran behind the structure.

Nica followed her friend and found her, retching in a corner, miserable and afraid. "TAL-kap," she whispered. "You must return to work. If the guards see—"

"I know!" Pescha wailed. "But I can't!"

Zeta stomped out, raising clouds of dust behind her. There was no shelter, but Nica tried to shield Pescha, holding the bucket of half-stripped beans before them. Their supervisor took in the situation as she wiped her hands on a cloth, then called for a guard.

"But . . . TAL-zeta. She is . . . *ais*—"

Zeta pushed Nica aside at the guard's approach. "Take this orange to MO-ASHE."

After he left, she motioned for Nica to come close. "To say "*şe aisan*" here, the word is sick. It's important to know, and you must not lapse into Olomi around the guards."

Shadows stretched, then began to shrink, and Nica kept searching the path that led to the medical quarter. She feared for her friend. How could Zeta turn her over to MO-ASHE? Failure was punished, and Pescha was weak already. *How long would she be held? How sick was she?* Thoughts spun through her head, distracting and accusing without mercy. *I should have protected her. But what could I have done? A Guardian protects. Anything would have been better than nothing. You're no Guardian.*

Relief flooded over her when she saw Pescha heading back to the pod. Scrutinizing her gait, Nica observed no limp or wincing in pain. In fact, there was no indication of any tears or trauma when she squatted to rejoin the crew. Waiting for an opportunity to investigate, Nica made careful inquiry when they were alone.

"What did MO-ASHE do?" she asked in Olomi.

"She took more blood." Pescha shrugged. *"And then gave me a syrup."*

"And? Did she threaten you?"

"No. I was afraid for a beating. She wrote on her pad but appeared . . . pleased?"

"Well, I am glad she did not punish you."

"Bẹẹni." Pescha agreed. *"I am as well."*

The two returned to their tasks, grateful to be spared. What a twisted tide.

22

·· P R E S S U R E ··

U NSATISFACTORY.
Again.

The outer corner of MO-ASHE's eyelid twitched.

How many lunar cycles had they been here? The moons had come and gone, and EC-TAL was supposed to provide her with viable specimens.

Her forefinger bounced, stopping just short of the counter's surface. The tension, unexpressed, would force its way out via the digit if it could. She clenched her fist, throttling the restless energy.

Every month he brought back more aquans, but while most of them were added to the work force, few were of any value as test subjects. Instead, they required training, conditioning, and monitoring to ensure they would not disrupt the mission.

The lab assistant approached.

If I had more samples to work with . . .

"The latest test results." The dull-colored aquana held out a vial. "One match."

"Only one?" MO-ASHE snatched it out of her hand, avoiding any actual contact. "Does this include the samples from those who were previously culled?"

There were alternative collection methods, but after much debate, TAL agreed, for the sake of her research, that the mass acquisition techniques risked damaging an excessive percentage of the samples. She was starting to rethink that theory. A high percentage damaged still left her with some specimens to work with. And for the most part, what TAL had brought in was not suitable. *We got lucky with that blue, but he'd better turn up with more viable specimens. Three does not leave much room for failure.*

"The only match."

MO-ASHE's finger started to pulse again, and her temples along with it. Who needed a centrifuge with this kind of agitation? She spoke, keeping her tone calm. "And you are certain this blue understands the consequences of failing to comply in any way? No language. No names. No infractions whatsoever."

"Yes, mistress, she will not risk complete loss of her—" There was a hasty correction at the MO's icy glare. "Er, the child."

"Well, that certainly makes my job easier, coming in with built-in entanglements."

Her gloves came off with a double *SNAP* and she flicked them at the aquana. She hated these primitive work facilities. She hated the limited resources. She hated the specimens she was forced to work with. She hated being surrounded by this flaking and peeling subspecies. She hated that her—no, everyone's future, was dependent on her to ensure that everything invested in their journey was not lost. She hated needing the EC to provide her with adequate specimens. She hated that he was failing to do so.

She had chosen to partner with TAL, expecting him to provide her with the greatest chance of success. A predator by design, his hunting skills were as advanced as their scientists could engineer. Still, those skills had never been put to a test, not a real test. And now the future of their race depended on them.

Her fists clenched again, still agitated. The grayish brown aquana edged closer to the door. *Well, there is that,* MO-ASHE observed. It felt good to put a little fear in their mud-sucking hearts.

She flexed her fingers, kneading the joints and palms. A martial session would do her some good. Maybe some time with the bo staff. Focusing on this promise of discharging stress, she released the vial containing the latest test results to the tray, rather than against the wall.

"ASHE-pi!"

The aquana froze, eyes wide.

"I need a new opponent for my bo workout. The last one wasn't fast enough. This one better be an improvement, or I'll take you on the mat."

Her aquana gulped.

MO-ASHE allowed herself a smile as she turned back to her work. Sparring would be something to look forward to.

23

·· SHIFT ··

T HE PERVASIVE hum ceased, its absence twisting Nica's thoughts in alarm. TAL had returned. She wondered how many Olomi would he have in custody. What if it was someone she knew? A spasm gripped her heart.

Pescha paused from stirring the giant stone pot, drawing a rag across her brow. Her eyes darted at Nica—the call to assemble hadn't sounded. Nica tilted her head at the delay, but could offer little more than a shrug. Ears were everywhere, and they had learned it was dangerous to speculate.

Just before sunpeak, a guard pushed his way through the food queue to TAL-zeta.

"EC-TAL requires your presence."

Zeta answered him with a brisk nod as she bustled past, directing the pod and monitoring service.

"I said, Expedition Commander TAL requires your presence, now."

"Do you not see I am busy? Am I expected to drop everything in the middle of this tide?"

The guard's eyes narrowed as he tapped his baton in the palm of his hand.

Nica blanched. Was he threatening their supervisor?

Zeta glared at the yellow and green Olomi. It didn't take long. The guard dropped his gaze to the ground.

"Hmph." She whisked the cloth off her shoulder and wadded it up, throwing it at Nica. "Keep the pod going while I'm busy." She cast another baleful look at the scowling guard. "I'll be back soon."

Nica stared after the two as they traipsed out of the food-pod.

One tall and broad shouldered, his yellow and green sheen vibrant under the guard's vest, the other short and slightly bowed, faded blues barely discernable against the worn brown of her tunic. Still, it looked like TAL-zeta was hustling the guard along. Nica blinked and looked again. Yes, Zeta was prodding the guard to move faster. Shaking her head in disbelief, she twisted the bit of rag in her hands. Now what was she supposed to do?

Despite Zeta's assertions, the sun was halfway down to sinking before she returned. Nica almost cried with relief to see her unharmed.

"You'll stop hugging me when you know what's rising," Zeta grumbled. "Are you an octopus?" She extricated herself from Nica's embrace, whispering, "Do not broadcast your affections, or we will both suffer."

Nica's arms dropped as quickly as her smile.

Zeta grabbed a wooden stirrer and banged on a large kettle. All eyes turned to her as she raised her voice. "The pods will be inspected."

Nica murmured to Pescha, "What does that mean?"

"It means," Zeta announced, "they will be looking for anything that falls short of EC-TAL's expectations. There will be no corner left untouched. Our pod must operate at peak efficiency and prove the value of its contribution to the strong functioning of this compound."

Nica muttered under her breath, "I don't know how our contribution can be dismissed—everyone needs to eat."

"There will be no room for insubordination or indolence. Watch your language and actions. Any deviation reflects on your pod, and consequences will be dispensed accordingly." Zeta sighed heavily. "Now, back to work."

"Move!" The agri-pod worker barked at Nica and Pescha as they adjusted the litter on their shoulders.

Nica flinched, and the load of meal began to slide, threatening the balance she and Pescha had achieved. The litter she'd fashioned carried a load several times more than either could manage alone, but it also required them to work in sync.

"This will save us trips," she'd coaxed.

Pescha had been skeptical, but when the weight rested on her shoulders instead of in her hands, she'd agreed to the change. Now her eyes, whites wide and rimmed with red, betrayed her panic. Her worst fears were about to be realized.

Nica stooped and bounced the yoke up with her shoulder, redistributing the shifted pile of milled beans.

A squeak escaped Pescha's lips as she staggered to maintain her balance. "Nic–TAL-eta, we were instructed to increase production–we can't lose this load."

"We'll lose more than this load if anyone hears the wrong word," Nica whispered.

Overseers strode the grounds, and the pod supervisors were looking over their shoulders. New guards hovered over their old pods, eager to prove themselves on the backs of the ranks they'd recently risen from. TAL was everywhere, reminding guards and supervisors that they were easily replaced. Even MO-ASHE stalked the area outside her quadrant, interrupting TAL often, leaving him more volatile than ever.

Everyone was on edge.

"Let's head straight to the courtyard–fewer turns that way." Nica gave the yoke's bar one last bump to stabilize the mound.

The new route added distance, but avoided weaving through agri-pod's many plots, as well as the extra guards stationed at each patch. The new ones were quickest to lose their temper. Though they ensured the compliance their former supervisor demanded, it didn't look like he appreciated their presence any more than Zeta did. Some of them hadn't even been abovewater for more than a moon, but their bodies and attitudes seemed fully acclimated to the new world.

Instead, the path through the courtyard took them past the front of the compound and its deadly gates. There, Olomi were assigned to scrubbing and buffing the stoneskin walls until they shone. TAL-alph drove the grounds-pod at the entrance, whipping those reluctant to approach the gates surrounded by scattered and crushed bones.

"If I say they're not active"—the yellow alpha grabbed one of the resistant laborers and threw him against the gates—"they're not."

Pescha and Nica gasped. The only time Olomi were thrown upon the gates was to make them an example. A permanent one.

TAL-alph whipped about, fixing her eyes on them. "What do you think you're doing, skulking around? Perhaps I should test the gates' effectiveness on you?" She lunged at Pescha, laughing when she shied away.

"Perhaps *you* should focus on your assignment if you want to keep your position." MO-ASHE stepped around the corner into view, her voice dripping with venom. "Or do you need a reminder?" She reached into her garment and withdrew a slim stoneskin object.

TAL's alpha froze at the sight, her yellow fading to nearly white. She trembled, falling to her knees. "I . . . I have always been faithful to—"

"—yourself. Always, only, yourself." MO-ASHE grabbed TAL-alph's chin, hissing the words into her face. "You may not touch my subjects or threaten my work in any way. Am I clear?"

"Ye-yes, MO-ASHE."

Nica leaned into the yoke, trying to nudge Pescha into motion before the MO decided to turn her attention to them.

As if she could read her mind, MO-ASHE slid her gaze over to them. "Hold."

They froze.

"Why are you carrying this?"

"TAL ordered more—"

"TAL-zeta assigned—"

Their words tumbled over each other as they attempted to appease her.

"You." MO-ASHE glared at TAL-alph. "Find another and transport this cargo to TAL's cook."

Then she redirected her attention to Nica and Pescha. "You will serve the cook until I say otherwise, but you will not carry heavy loads."

She turned away, but the yellow alpha whispered to her as she rose from the ground.

"Ah, yes. Take care of it." MO-ASHE waved a hand at the gate and TAL-alph accessed the panel as she had whenever EC-TAL passed through the gates.

And the hum that had been absent returned.

24

·· SWITCHBAIT ··

THE LAST bit of the current moon wavered, a sliver of its former glory, only visible now that the sun had fully sunk.

Nica nudged Pescha as it glimmered high above them. "I think we may float a little easier once this moon has left us."

Her podmate raised a brow but did not speak.

"It's almost time for TAL—"

"—to hunt," Pescha finished, her words barely audible.

The two sat in silence, stripping down beaten stalks, strand by strand. The pile tripled in volume as they transformed it into fiber, but not another word passed between them. They gathered the threads, careful not to let them tangle, and twisted them into textile loops. The cords they would be woven into were not dissimilar to strands of braided kelp.

Jonnat's face flashed before Nica. The memory of him looping cords before they launched from the Deep formed a painful knot in her chest, expanding more than the fibers they were separating. She shut her eyes against the tears that refused to stay in, and the vision would not be put out.

"What if—" Speaking was more painful than taking breath. She tried again. "What if . . . he comes back with someone . . ."

"Someone we know?" Pescha's voice was gentle. "How do we measure family here? In or out of the Deep, are we not all children of the water?"

"I think some of our people have forgotten."

"But those who try to forget—the guards and even the alphas—their pain runs even deeper than ours. We can only forget so much."

Nica tilted her head at her friend. "When did you become Ìyágba, oh wise one?" At Pescha's quick smile, she added, "The sun that follows will be better with TAL gone."

"And we will not dwell on what may come," answered Pescha.

Nica woke early, her sleep restless from last night's musings. She needed to do something—anything to distract her from TAL's activities. It wouldn't hurt to get an early start on this sun, since much of it was likely to be lost to the MO's cells.

"TAL-zeta, is there anything you need me to—" She stared at the pack on the table. The one TAL had when he first captured her. The one that he carried each time he returned with a new captive.

Beads rattled as the supervisor backed through the entry-curtain, grappling a large cook-pot. "Hmph! Never seen you up this early, TAL-eta, but since you are . . ."

"Why is that here?"

Zeta shrugged. "TAL-beta usually picks it up by now. It's not for me to second-guess." She leveled a stern look at Nica. "It's not for you to sort out either."

A chill ran down Nica's dorsals. If she had a choice, she'd have nothing to do with that bag.

Nothing proceeded as it had in previous moons. By sunpeak, TAL's bag remained on the ledge in Zeta's station, and MO-ASHE had yet to call the Olomi to assemble. Nica didn't know what to think of the changes, but she dared to hope.

She whispered to Pescha as they hulled the beans, "Do you think TAL has taken enough Olomi?"

"It is nice to hope that is true, but that one always wants more." Pescha shook her head. "Perhaps this moon, no one else will be added to our number."

One of the MO's guards, the dark one with blue markings,

pushed through TAL-zeta's beaded entry. Nica edged to the wall, trying to catch a drift of their conversation.

". . . don't know how she expects me to reproduce what I do not know."

The dark guard spoke in low, measured tones, but she couldn't hear his words.

"Good tide, ASHE-tau."

TAL-zeta's tone was icier than they had ever heard. Nica scuttled back to Pescha's side before the guard strode out of Zeta's station. It wasn't until he cleared the food-pod boundary markers that either of them breathed freely. Only then did Nica peek in.

"TAL-zeta?" Her eyes darted to the counter. EC-TAL's pack had been removed. "Is there something I can do for you?"

Zeta's smile was distant, and a little sad. Finally, she met Nica's eyes. "There is little we can do for each other, but what we can, we must."

She handed Nica some shells. "Grind these. We're running low on pain salve, and I think we're going to need more."

"All surfaces are to be immaculate. Food without blemish will be stored at my station." TAL-zeta paused her address to her pod. "All aquans are to be showered after midmeal. Fresh tunics will be issued according to pod."

Nica's eyes lit up and she nudged Pescha. "Do you thi—"

"There will be no idle conversations during assignments. Pod supervisors are to report infractions to the nearest guard." TAL-zeta cleared her throat before she continued, throwing a quick frown in Nica's direction. "The shower area will be adjacent to food-pod, and we are scheduled to shower after this meal is served."

Access to water had been limited to only the most basic needs for the Olomi, and the promise of bathing stirred up uncommon anticipation. The first group, agri-pod, sped through their meal, jostling for their place before the designated shower time. Ever-present and efficient, the guards established order quickly.

Nica eyed the queue with envy, almost wishing she were still assigned to agri-pod. They were still serving the second pod when a commotion broke out inside the stalls. Only a few Olomi had entered, but the sound of whipping and outcries of pain revealed a guard presence within the stalls.

The jockeying for position reverted to backing up and withdrawing, eliciting even more threats and force from those guarding outside.

When the first group to enter the showers exited, she understood the cause of the disruption.

Yes, they'd received a shower, enough to exfoliate their flaking skin, but not before each of them, male and female alike, had their heads completely shaved. As the newly shorn emerged, those still queued renewed their attempts to escape the line. The guards were clearly prepared for this reaction and reacted accordingly.

The two most fierce protesters were tackled and cudgeled, and their hair yanked and hacked off rather than shaved. Nica gripped the table, clenching her mouth shut. If she said anything, she could join them.

The insurgents were staged at the entrance, bound, bleeding, and bruised, as warning to those who entered. Order was restored.

25

THE GONG sounded. Nica looked to Zeta, hesitant
to voice any questions, but unable to deny them. The fresh
moon was just one-quarter filled, with each tide more demanding
than the previous. EC-TAL and MO-ASHE inspected the pods
and Olomi daily, observing their practices and scrutinizing their
products. What more could he expect . . . or want?

"Each pod will choose an aquan of each gender, strong,
knowledgeable, and skilled, who will present a sample of work from
their pod. Anything less than the best will result in consequences
for the entire pod."

"Why does TAL need a sample of the work he demands from
us?" Nica whispered.

Pescha narrowed her eyes at her podmate, jerking her head
back to their pod.

The green rose in Nica's cheeks. When would she learn to keep
her mouth shut? She grimaced an apology, turning to follow Zeta
back to food-pod when MO-ASHE's large, gray alpha captured her
by the arm.

"Not so fast. Food-pod needs to represent." His smile was
as frightening as ever. "You and your friends have a special
appointment." He seized Pescha with the other hand, and TAL-
alph grabbed TAL-rho by the back of her neck.

Had he heard her? But why punish Pescha and Rho? "I . . . I'm
sor–" She broke off when Pescha shook her head tightly, eyes wide
with fear.

The alphas escorted the three to the center to stand before

EC-TAL and MO-ASHE. Both poked and prodded the confused Olomi, examining their eyes, mouth, skin, and muscle tone. They argued about "viability" and "replication" as they assessed the three young women. Finally, MO-ASHE's argument for "separation" and "conditioning" ended the discussion. Her alpha took TAL-rho by the forearm and, without a word, bound her to the other selected Olomi.

"Prime these."

At her command, the ten were herded, still bound, back to the shower area.

"You are dismissed to your pods."

An apprehensive glance passed between the Olomi as they passed the showers, but Nica and Pescha were relieved to be released from the combined scrutiny of both Delphim. However, when they returned to TAL-zeta, she was in a foul mood.

"TAL-rho?" The pod supervisor looked around them to see if the blue female was lagging.

The girls both shook their heads and pointed toward the shower area.

"Pr-prime?" Nica offered. She didn't know what the word meant, but perhaps TAL-zeta did.

The supervisor spewed both breath and a few unfamiliar words. Between her tongue-clicking and head shaking, all that Nica could pick up were mutterings about "food" and "time."

Just then, agri-pod workers arrived and dumped twice the amount of food as usual. Nica groaned. Now she understood Zeta's frustration. Double the work and short a set of hands to prepare it.

TAL-zeta drove the pod without mercy until the food was ready to be served. Then she instructed them to secure most of it in containers.

"Take these to the courtyard."

Nica was not eager to appear before TAL again, but it was more dangerous to hesitate, especially on this sun's tide. She picked up her containers without a word and followed the others. Each was inspected by TAL before they were given leave to put it down. As they waited, containers with seedlings, packed to travel, were also deposited in the courtyard. Then ASHE-alph and the ten culled Olomi arrived. TAL-rho and the others were coated entirely in white pigment and looked completely terrified.

A horn sounded from outside the barricade, and the gong in the courtyard rang five times.

The call went out. "TAL-aquans! ASHE-aquans!"

Nica had never seen the combined complement of EC-TAL and MO-ASHE's households before.

So many. Her head swam. How long had TAL been capturing Olomi? How could they control them all? From behind MO-ASHE's alpha, the dark guard caught her eye, the one with blue markings who had calmed her when she had first been taken to the exam cells. His gaze rested on her for a moment, a little disquieting, but not terrifying.

TAL-rho also scanned the host of Olomi assembled behind MO-ASHE, but with an air of desperation. As she searched, she started to strain at her bindings. MO-ASHE nodded toward the worried, white-covered female, bringing her activity to TAL's attention. Returning her nod, he signaled his alpha to handle the whitened crew and then ordered the gates to be opened, announcing:

"Delphim brethren. We welcome you!"

26

·· CHALLENGES ··

TWO BEINGS strode through the entrance into the compound. Both were longer than TAL, with hair black as the rocks that grew out of the sea. In form, they appeared like EC-TAL and MO-ASHE, but with skin the color of sun-bleached vegetation. *There were more like TAL?* A small pod of Olomi followed, bound to litters, bearing trunks.

The visiting Delphim strode through the courtyard, sleek and smooth, circling EC-TAL and MO-ASHE and their households. The male paced around the left, eyeing the gifts and workers nearest TAL, while the female prowled the outskirts on the right, assessing the farm and the kitchen. They met in the middle, standing before their hosts, and nodded their heads in the slightest of bows.

"Come and be refreshed." MO-ASHE's invitation sounded more like a demand. "I present these to attend you."

At that, four of the white-washed Olomi approached the guests bearing bowls of water and towels, followed by the remainder, bearing trays of delicacies.

"Your generosity is humbling," the male replied with a smile that put no one at ease.

"It is the least we could do to honor you," TAL intoned.

The female clapped her hands, startling Nica. Ten Olomi, dyed yellow in the same manner that TAL's ten had been painted white, stepped out of the visitors' queue.

"And we present these to serve and entertain you, most gracious EC-TAL."

Nica's heart caught in her throat as the visitors' painted Olomi moved in unison toward EC-TAL and MO-ASHE. It was all she could do to hold her peace. Included with the offered aquans, coated in yellow pigment, was her sister, Rissa.

Chaos ruled this tide. Nica whirled about following orders, desperate to catch a glimpse of Rissa. When the evening meal was served in the courtyard, the female visitor, SA-CaG announced that CaG-tau would sing for them. It was too much for Nica to hope it would be Rissa until she saw her sister emerge from the recesses of the MO's buildings.

Her heart wavered between joy and grief as Rissa's voice floated across the breeze, thinner than Nica remembered hearing it underwater, but clearer in the air. The rhapsodic voicings poured out pure and soulful tones of longing for a home long gone. It was startling to see MO-ASHE's eyes soften and her brow smooth. She was clearly affected by the song. Even TAL appeared to pay attention.

Did EC-TAL and MO-ASHE miss the home they left behind? That possibility hadn't even occurred to Nica. *Could it be that her captors felt as out of place on this mass of land as she did?* Nica doubted it, but the question persisted.

The performance entranced all within hearing. Even the servers stood still, frozen as they held their trays and pitchers. Pouring out her soul via song, Rissa connected with individuals in the audience, her gaze landing here and there. Nica tried to stay out of sight, lest she be recognized mid-song, but it was unavoidable. Rissa's eyes widened and she faltered, her voice catching, but she recovered smoothly. There was no opportunity to contact each other in this setting. Nica could only hope for an opportunity to see her in a meal line.

The pattern repeated for several suns. Elaborate feasts for the visiting Delphim, and exacting service from their Olomi attendants. If the masters and overseers had been harsh dealing with any lapses in private, any trespass in front of their guests was punished even more severely. But as the diplomatic exchanges heated up, the Delphim paid more attention to strategizing, and less to demonstrating dominance over their *Aqua Sapiens*.

After the third sun, the Olomi of both houses breathed a little easier, though they remained wary. Eventide's entertainment was set aside as the Delphim argued over land rights and well-drilling strategies. TRE-CH proposed a partnership between TAL's house and three other major landholders, suggesting that TAL would be better off joining the houses now, rather than being absorbed by an alliance later. The EC's eyes flashed as black as the visitor's hair at the veiled threat.

Olomi attendants passed rumors back and forth as the discussions grew more intense. According to the excavation pod, TRE-CH tried to charm MO-ASHE into advocating for his proposed alliance, but TAL interrupted his attempts. The agricultural crew spread reports that SA-CaG, his partner, was jealous of TRE-CH's attentiveness to MO-ASHE. Even the guards in MO-ASHE's service whispered that she was not pleased at how the yellow-dyed singer caught TAL's eye more than once. Had the Delphim not been vying against each other for power, many an Olomi would have suffered. Instead, they nervously observed the power struggle of the landwalkers.

Nica caught her breath when she saw the yellowed-dyed Olomi join the food queue. Both sisters blinked back tears as they brushed each other's hands under the serving tray. Nica dared nothing that could draw attention. Their connection would be used against them. To know Rissa was alive thrilled her soul, but to know she was a captive broke her heart in a million ways.

On the morning of the full moon, Nica woke with a feeling of dread. Preparations had been made for the guests' departure, and Nica did not think she could bear to lose her sister again. She sped through the morning food preparation, hoping to be available for deliveries to TRE-CH's party and have a chance to see Rissa again.

"TAL-eta!"

Nica lost her balance and almost knocked over the basket of food she had just put away.

"Yes, TAL-zeta?"

"Take this basket of samples to the courtyard. Do not be careless or they will spill."

"Yes, TAL-zeta." Nica grabbed the basket Zeta pointed out and moved as quickly as she dared toward the courtyard and the litters EC-TAL and MO-ASHE were having filled for their guests.

Rissa! Nica's heart leapt at the sight of her sister. Her face, still dyed yellow amidst the sea of varied Olomi tones, was stoic, almost expressionless. Jawbone locked, eyes forward, lips pressed together tight; every muscle was tensed almost to its breaking point. Nica knew that face—her sister's pain was evident, but only to her. She composed her face to mirror Rissa's, and they exchanged imperceptible nods as she passed the queue.

TRE-CH and SA-CaG stood before their company of Olomi, as EC-TAL and MO-ASHE approached with their contingent of personal attendants, each Delphim couple adorned with their fiercest finery. CaG murmured to her alpha, and the ten yellowed aquans were led before the host Delphim. The guest's alpha directed them to bow, foreheads in the dirt, before EC-TAL and MO-ASHE. TAL and ASHE, in turn, nodded to their alphas, who directed the white-dyed Olomi to assume the same position before the guests.

Drawing himself up to his full height, TRE-CH addressed his hosts.

"In gratefulness for your excellent hospitality, I commit these, my skilled and obedient workers, into thy service. Do with them as thou wilt, they are yours, body and soul."

EC-TAL and MO-ASHE nodded in unison and stepped in front of their newly acquired Olomi, declaring, "We accept your generous gift, and in return we honor you with these skilled and productive servants. Do with them as thou wilt, they are yours, body and soul."

The words and meaning of this ceremony were unclear to most of the Olomi, but as the gifted aquans were bound to their new alphas, a wail of protest erupted from the group of white-dyed Olomi.

"*Rara!* No!"

TAL-rho broke from her group and wrapped herself around EC-TAL's feet.

"*O ko le se.* You cannot. I serve good. I obey! *Emi o ru ofin!*"

Enraged at the embarrassing outburst, TAL lifted his hand to strike the disruptive female, but MO-ASHE squeezed his arm. His expression of rage faded to surprise as she whispered in his ear. Looking from his partner to the Olomi at his feet, he grabbed Rho by the neck and dragged her back to the transferred property. Depositing her at the feet of her new master, he glowered but visibly restrained himself.

MO-ASHE bent over in front of the hysterical female and hissed, "One more outburst and the boy will suffer."

Defeated, TAL-rho collapsed into sobs unintelligible to either Olomi or Delphim.

TRE-CH looked down with disdain at the offensive aquan, then at EC-TAL with the same haughty expression.

"What manner of gift is this unseemly mess? It is clear you lack the ability to control your property."

"I admit, the hysterical display is uncalled for, and should be punished, but there is more to this aquan than meets the eye." TAL stepped closer to CaG and TRE-CH, then whispered and gestured toward his MO and the transferred Olomi.

"Are you sure?" TRE-CH exclaimed.

It was MO-ASHE who answered. "Yes. We expect this trial to be even more viable than the first, due to the subject's history."

Now TRE-CH squatted and grabbed Rho's chin, lifting it to examine her closely. "This is a fortunate turn of events and a generous offer indeed."

He stood, clapping the dust off his hands.

"Take it," he directed his alpha, "but by the arm only. This one is not to be harmed. Keep it confined until we reach the compound."

Nica's heart broke for TAL-rho as the gates closed behind TRE-CH and SA-CaG, with the caravan and their new property secured and fixed to the litters. The *iyá* would not see her spawn again.

27

·· CHOICES ··

EVERYWHERE Nica's duties took her, the air was thick with threats. EC-TAL and MO-ASHE's alphas were devoted to maintaining order, and the pod supervisors followed their lead. She lingered by agri-pod's bales, watching to see where the new Olomi were distributed. Rissa was assigned to serve in MO-ASHE's household with the new designation, ASHE-theta.

To be this close to her sister but still separated stung more than Nica expected. Her bitter disappointment was offset only by knowing Rissa would be spared the harsh labor and exposure most of TAL's Olomi were subject to. MO-ASHE's household was sequestered to the interior buildings, most of which remained a mystery to Nica. Other than the alpha, Olomi in MO-ASHE's service were rarely seen outside her complex. Up to this point, Nica had avoided entering MO-ASHE's labyrinth, but now she ached to be assigned there.

It was dangerous to linger much longer. Nica bent down, as if to pick up scatterings from her basket. If she headed back now, it wouldn't be a problem. Or at least it shouldn't be . . . She straightened—and then ducked in a flash. Why was TAL walking with MO-ASHE into her sector? They'd entertained the visiting Delphim together, but other than that, they'd only met after the new moon's hunt. Little of their captors' behavior boded well for Olomi. She'd be better off proving herself industrious rather than nosy.

Nica rolled off her mat and threw on her tunic. She gave a wry smile as she rubbed her scalp. *That's easy enough.* At least Rissa wouldn't complain about her hair being a mess now.

Pescha rubbed her eyes. "Why did you wake me up so early?"

"I didn't wake you. You woke yourself." Nica's eyes smiled at her friend. "I'm just getting started. It's a lot easier with this haircut."

Pescha propped herself up. "Why? What is going on?"

"Nothing. I just want to see if I can choose an assignment instead of getting what's left."

Grumbles and moans began to rise from the other occupants, so Nica edged quietly to the doorway.

"Let me know if they let us choose to sleep in." Pescha yawned and rolled over. "Or better yet, go back to the Deep."

"You go back to sleep. I'll let you know if Zeta has something for you."

She closed her eyes and blew a silent breath. *You're going to have to run deep and still, Nica. No one can know.*

TAL-zeta bustled out of the back room. Only her eyes were visible under a tall stack of baskets in her arms.

"Morning, TAL-zeta."

"Oh!" The supervisor jumped at Nica's greeting. She juggled the wobbling pile. "Didn't expect anyone to be out yet. Agri-pod just dumped a double load of tubers."

"*Ma binu,*" Nica apologized, catching a basket before it tumbled onto the ground. "Would you like me to take those?"

"Language, TAL-eta," Zeta hissed. "And yes"—she shoved the rest of the stack at Nica—"get started on sorting the roots."

The reprimand stung, even though Zeta was right. *But it's not like anyone else is around.* She placed the baskets around the piles of produce and squatted down to sort them. Small, large, medium—dimensions that never made a difference in the Deep but seemed to be critical abovewater. She tossed the roots into the baskets and missed. And missed. And missed again.

She shook her head at herself. Some tides she was surprised by her own ineptitude. And with cooking as bad as her aim, she was no better suited in the kitchen here than she had been in the Deep. *But at least I could judge distance there,* she sighed. What else did she completely lack out of the water?

Communion. The knowing and being known. Life here, on the surface, was so . . . lonely. Although it was to her benefit right now, that no one could read her emotions or pick up on her evasiveness.

By the time her aim had improved enough to clear the piles, a few podmates began to emerge from the sleeping quarters. *No Pescha.* Nica smiled. *That Olomi can sleep!*

She stacked two of the loaded baskets and headed for the cooking area. Without warning, the world began to spin, and she stumbled. She slammed down the baskets. Maintaining a tight grip on the handles, she tried to regain her balance. She took in deep, slow breaths, hoping her head would stop spiraling. It took a moment. Then it took several more. Now was not the time to appear clumsy. Or lazy.

Hoisting the basket onto her shoulder again, Nica headed to the cooking fires, measuring her steps with caution. Pescha had been ill and was unable to keep up with the business of additional company. *I'd better not have what Pescha had.*

Odors from the cooking pits assailed her. She thrust the produce at the nearest worker, then lurched past TAL-zeta to the refuse pile behind the shelter. Retching, she lost what little she had in her stomach, and then continued to heave.

"*Ma binu,*" she apologized, unable to find those words in the new tongue.

TAL-zeta rolled her eyes upward at this offense, but then, just shook her head.

"You go to medical," the old Olomi muttered. "It is time."

Nica's heart sank. Her plan to get an assignment to MO-ASHE's section had failed. *If I'm sick, who knows how long it will be before—*

Her heart jolted. *Medical?* This wasn't her plan, but it was her goal. *I'm coming, Rissa!*

28

·· CHANCES ··

B ITING DOWN on her lip to suppress a smile, Nica scuttled to medical, head down, wishing she still had hair to shield her expression. Her chances of seeing Rissa were scant, but that was better than not at all.

The poured-stone steps leading to the sentry reflected the peaking sun's rays, washing its austere surface with an illusion of warmth. The steps were few, but Nica's stomach roiled with nervous energy. She'd never approached MO-ASHE's main entrance before—had never even gotten near on her own. She'd always been channeled through the queue and shunted into cells. A sentry loomed over her, bluish with mottled greens marking his sensory lines. His scowl compressed the faded blues of his brow into ashen lines of gray as he scrutinized her, pad in hand. She wondered how many of TAL's household entered MO-ASHE's section without an enforced escort.

"Designation?"

"TAL-eta."

"Pod?"

"Food."

"Supervisor's designation?"

"TAL-zeta."

"Destination?"

"Medical."

"State the reason for your presence."

Nica was confused by this question.

He sighed and rephrased. "Why are you requesting entry?"

"Sick. TAL-zeta sent me." *It's a good thing I learned that word.*

He gave a curt nod and indicated the hallway that led to medical. Starting in that direction, she waited until the door closed behind her, then slipped the other way. Moving quickly, she peered into each of the rooms, memorizing the layout. *It would be a bad idea to get lost in here. Much worse than pretending to be lost.*

Stealth above water was easier than in the ocean. No worries about transmitting elevated heart rates or breathing too fast. Hiding up here was simple too. Don't bump into things. Don't stomp when you walk. Don't talk. However, the Deep was big and there were no walls. This building was not. And she was surrounded by barriers.

Tracing her fingertips along the walls, Nica felt for any sign that could alert her to Rissa's presence. The cool stoneskin transmitted some vibrations, but they were difficult to identify. Noise up ahead alerted her, and she looked in vain for a place to hide. The doors she'd tested were not latched as the exam cells had been. They would not open for her. *Time to play stupid . . . or sick . . . or both.*

"What are you doing here?"

"This section is restricted."

These Olomi, draped in the medical quadrant's spotless tunics, didn't seem hostile, but she didn't want to press her luck.

"Medi-cal?" She feigned dizziness and gasped as if in pain. "Sick."

The two rushed to either side to support her.

"Who let her in here?"

"I don't know, but I hope we don't catch anything."

She let the pair drag her, marking the path through half-lidded eyes. *Even their feet are covered?* They stopped at the main entry. *Shells.*

"ASHE-delt!"

The mottled blue sentry came to the door. "Aren't you supposed to be security?"

"I'm not feeling very secure right now. How'd this TAL-quan get into research?"

The sentry sputtered. "Research? I sent her to medical. I showed her the—"

Nica groaned. "Feel sick." She doubled over and started coughing violently.

"Get her out of here now!"

"We need to get back to the lab."

"I need to stay at my post."

"If MO-ASHE finds us off task . . ."

A new, but familiar voice broke in. "What is going on down here?"

Nica didn't dare lift her head to check but could only hope.

"Oh good. ASHE-tau. We found one of your patients wandering around in research."

"Yes. You need to take custody of this one."

"And we need to get back to the lab."

"She's your problem, Tau," the sentry said. "I just check them in."

"Fine. I'll deal with this."

A dark arm slipped under hers, and another scooped up her legs.

"Careful, ASHE-tau. She's pretty sick."

"And she's trouble," the sentry added on his way out.

Nica's heart warmed to see her helpful guard. *At least I know his name now.*

"Not very sick," she whispered once they were out of sight. "I can walk."

He raised an eyebrow, but with a smile, and put her down. "So, what is it?"

"What is what?"

"Your name. Is it TAL-eta, or is it *Wahala*?"

Nica giggled nervously. "Is that what the blue was calling me? Trebel?"

"Close. It's truh-bul, or maybe you are."

"Neither. My true name is Nica."

Her heart stopped for a second. She broke the first rule TAL had laid down. In front of a guard. But this was her friend, wasn't he?

She considered that for a moment in silence. This guard had never used his position to abuse or humiliate her. He had offered wisdom and compassion in the worst of her trials there, encouraging her in ways that made the indignities tolerable. Yes, he was a friend.

"And yours?" she whispered as they reached the now familiar medical cell. "Are you ASHE-tau?"

"That is what I am called," he replied, "but my name is Girac."

Nica did not fight as he secured her to the table, but rested her fingers on his hand as he applied the restraints.

"Do you know the location of ASHE-theta?" she whispered in Olomi, trusting that he would not betray her.

"It's not here." He shook his head. "She attends to MO-ASHE in the living chambers."

"O ṣe," Nica thanked him, and waited for the medi-pod assistants to assess her.

"Report." MO-ASHE's voice echoed down the hallway.

"A male with a leg injury and a female with vomiting," one of the medics replied.

"Which female?" MO-ASHE asked sharply.

"The green one. TAL-eta."

"Test her blood. I will attend to the male first."

The medic came in, bearing a tray of instruments.

"What is your—" Nica corrected herself. "I mean, what are you called here?"

The yellow-faced Olomi looked up from the tray, flushing brightly from the yellow in her cheeks to the green that started behind her ears. "I . . . Here, I am called ASHE-iota."

Nica steeled herself to not flinch when her skin was pierced. "You did well," she assured the medic. "You have skill in this."

Green-backed hands shook as she put the collection vials in their container. "Th-thank you. Patients do not like me. Not what I do."

"How can I not like you"—Nica raised her elbow to align with ASHE-iota's arm, their greens almost blending side by side—"when we are a little alike?"

The medic cast a glance to the door, then lifted one side of her mouth into a crooked wisp of a smile.

Nica searched for the words. "We all do what we must. But we are not what we do."

The medic grasped Nica's hand, still fettered to the table. "Thank you. And do not fear, you are valuable."

Nica wondered at that while ASHE-iota straightened her tray with care, perhaps with more care than that task required.

Just after the medic left, MO-ASHE swept into the cell. "TAL-eta, your -ecorts- -indi-cays- no pre-vus- -uh-crans- of these -sim-toms-, yes?"

Uncertain about the question, Nica opened, then shut her mouth. *No answer is as dangerous as the wrong one.*

MO-ASHE tapped the pad in rapid bursts and gave a loud huff. She pulled the stoneskin device out of her garment, squeezed it, then replaced it and returned to her tapping. A moment later, her alpha entered. "Translate."

The gray enforcer kept his head bowed as MO-ASHE repeated her words. She glared as he translated her question. "Your records indicate no previous occurrence of these symptoms, yes?" adding, "Answer in aquan if you need to."

Was it a trap? "Yes, er, no," Nica stammered. "Not sick like this. Not before."

MO-ASHE squeezed Nica's legs as she inspected them and directed more questions through her alpha. *"Do you have any other symptoms? Fever, swelling, abdominal pain."*

Shaking her head in the negative to each of these, Nica tried to ignore the prodding as gloved fingers poked around her abdomen.

"Take a sip of this liquid when you feel ill and stay out of the sun if you feel faint. You've been assigned to the kitchen, so that shouldn't be difficult."

The vial looked just like the one Pescha had gotten a few weeks ago.

Finally, the alpha translated the same admonition Nica received every moon.

"Speak to no one of this or you will suffer severe consequences."

29

NICA returned to the food-pod, wondering at the strangeness of the last few suns. She shook the vial, and then sniffed the liquid. Had she contracted Pescha's illness? TAL-zeta would not be pleased.

Losing one of her staff to the visiting Delphim, in addition to having one, and now two, of her workers ill, had put their supervisor at a significant disadvantage. The addition of one of TRE-CH's Olomi had not been helpful. Brown ribbed with orange, and dotted with blue freckles, TAL-tau was slow, clumsy, and not trained in their procedures.

The smell of dinner preparations threatened to send her running for the door, so Nica took a tiny sip, and then a capful of the medicine. A few breaths later, she was thankful to discover it was a helpful remedy.

Sunpeak's meal had been served, and Nica stepped into the routine of clearing the waste and cleaning the serving utensils. Not quite up to hustling, she did manage to bustle around a bit and, as she did, was aware of TAL-zeta's eyes following her. Not sure of the cause for the scrutiny, Nica did her best to focus on the jobs at hand. The last thing she needed was to have Zeta fussing at her.

Pescha had fallen behind as well, so they teamed up to tackle the harder tasks. When the heavy cooking pot was ready to be washed, TAL-zeta called the new Olomi over.

"TAL-tau, come help TAL-kap." Hefting the water to rinse the pot, the poor girl stumbled and dumped the whole potful on Pescha.

Nica and Pescha's eyes met, and both girls started to giggle as their orange and brown "helper" stood staring at them, mortified. TAL-zeta paled, and ordered the embarrassed Olomi to fetch a cloth, and shooed Nica and Pescha into her back room.

"You need to dry now!" the old woman whispered urgently.

"O *Ìyàgba*, water no hurt." Nica smiled.

"Are you blind?" Zeta grabbed a spare tunic and pushed it to Pescha.

Nica laughed at how soaked her friend was. Then she gasped. TAL-zeta had not been upset about the water, but what it revealed. As the wet tunic clung to Pescha's body, the roundness of her belly revealed her state.

"Pescha!" Nica exclaimed. "You're . . . *gravid!*"

"I can't be . . ." the sodden girl exclaimed. "I haven't . . ."

"But you are." Nica put her hand on her friend's belly.

TAL-zeta seemed not at all surprised at this discovery.

"She's not the only one, child. You're not far behind."

Nica sank to the floor. What Zeta said was impossible, but as soon as the words left her lips, Nica knew they were true. She didn't know how. Didn't know why. But she had the same symptoms as Pescha. And it was undeniable. Pescha was spawning.

Their words burst out together.

"*How?*"

"*When?*"

The two sat, staring at each other, and at their bellies. Then both turned to TAL-zeta, and their questions cascaded into Olomi.

"*What do we do, Ìyàgba?*"

"*What will happen to us?*"

"*How did you know?*"

"Enough!" The old lady clapped her hands to silence the girls. "You may have some protection right now, but I do not."

"But when, TAL-zeta?" Nica chose her abovewater words carefully. "How?"

Making sure they could not be overheard, Zeta lowered her voice, *"TAL-kap, you are not the first, but you are the first success. It is MO-ASHE's examinations—they are experiments. I think, when they make you sleep, they place a larva in you."*

"But . . . I would know! There was nothing . . ." Pescha sputtered.

"When they were sure of you, they took Nica, and then Rho. And they sent you to me to work, so you can stay healthy and eat without question."

"But why?" Nica persisted.

TAL-zeta looked around once again, and then whispered even more quietly, *"There are no Delphim children here. Who will inherit what EC-TAL builds? If TAL and MO-ASHE are not of the water, where are they from? They came when the heavens broke the water. They must have come from the heavens."*

It was too dangerous to continue speaking in Olomi, and the answers were incomprehensible, even when they understood the words. There was so much they didn't know, but the past few months were starting to make sense. They had to keep this secret. MO-ASHE couldn't find out that they knew.

Fear gave way to wonder that night. Nica lay on her mat, watching stars peek through the gaps in the slatted ceiling. *I am spawning.*

It was more than she could grasp. A few suns before, she thought her life was over. In just a moment, the tide had shifted and now she had everything to live for.

My offspring will not be enslaved.
From the Water I came, to the Water I will return.
Láti inú Omi ni mo ti wá, sínú Omi ni èmi yóò padà.

30

·· TRUST ··

NOTHING had changed—but Nica had. She awoke to the same circumstances, but with a new reality. No longer fearing for her life, Nica longed for it. *Trying to survive in this unforgiving environment, bound by fear, hiding any sign of love—this is not living.* She remembered the water and the life it held. The life she was made for. Freedom, provision, joy, and community. Thoughts shared, as well as bounty. Nica would no longer accept the life of a slave. Not for herself. Not for Rissa. Not for her spawn.

But she couldn't take on this fight alone. Who could be trusted? She sifted encounters where she had lapsed into Olomi. These would be sympathetic to the cause. Also, those who had opportunity to report on their fellows and hadn't. Overlooking any indiscretion that could elevate their status in the power structure that had emerged on land was a costly show of mercy. And she would need to identify Olomi who served in key positions to devise an escape plan that would succeed. *An escape plan! What am I thinking!*

But it didn't matter how impossible it all seemed. She no longer had a choice. Escaping was not an option, it was imperative. *This is for all of us—the enslaved, and those unaware of the dangers waiting abovewater.* Her mind drifted to Jonnat, and fear turned to anger. The last time she'd fought for her freedom, she hadn't known what she was up against. This time, her captors wouldn't.

"Where are you?" Zeta poked her sea-dreaming assistant with a wooden spoon.

Startled out of her thoughts, Nica flushed, returning her attention to the vegetables in her lap. "Ìyá'g—TAL-zeta. May I talk to you later?" Her heartbeat quickened as she contemplated sharing her thoughts for the first time. She hoped the old woman would have wisdom for her.

"Finish your work and make sure we both don't get beaten!"

After the sunbreak and sunpeak meals were served, Zeta assigned Nica to assist her with the pod inventory. It was difficult for the older Olomi to inspect the upper shelves, and there wasn't room for more than two bodies in the storage shelter. Outside the shed walls, the constant clamor of pots and pans being sand-scraped clean provided safe cover for conversation, and Nica burst into Olomi almost as soon as they entered.

"Ìyágba! I have a plan. I am going to escape with Rissa, and whoever else wants to join me. We're going to leave this rock and warn our people to stay away from the land."

Pssh. The old woman shook her head. "That is not a plan. That is a dream. You need to plan on staying out of trouble. Planning is not good for you, it's not good for your baby, and it's certainly not good for me."

Nica shook her head vigorously. *"But this is why I must leave. For my spawn. We were not made for this. We were not made to scrape and bow on the dry land, begging for food, hoping not to be beaten. We are of the Water. We were made for freedom. We were made to share life, not death."*

Zeta's eyes were distant. "It has been a long time since I have missed the Water. I'd forgotten what it like was to remember freedom."

"Will you help me, *Ìyágba*? I don't think I can do this alone."

The old woman took Nica's scarred hands in her own, looking deep into her eyes. "You will not have to. I may not be able to run, but I can help. Now, what do you need? And who is Rissa?"

Not sure where to start, Nica began at the end. The Breaking.

That Rissa had been lost. That many moons had passed before it was safe to approach the land masses. That Jonnat had trained the teams of explorers from their seas in preparation for the water-breaks to be breached. That she had heard her sister's voice echoing through one of the reef barriers. That she and Jonnat had left the next sun in search of Rissa. That TAL had taken her almost immediately. That Jonnat had been killed. That Rissa had been in TRE-CH's party of Olomi and now served in the inner chambers of MO-ASHE's household.

At the end of the telling, Nica felt wrung dry and exhausted. She watched the old Olomi anxiously.

"Well." Zeta took a deep breath. "Let's get you in to see your sister!"

Nica jumped up and threw her arms around the old woman, feeling like someone had poured a bucket of water over her thirsty soul.

"But that has got to stop." Zeta pushed her away and lowered her voice. "I'm serious, Nica. If you are committed to this journey, you must be wary or you will fail, and you will take down anyone who joins you. Any attachment is a weapon that can be brought against you. It is safer to have none."

Nica gulped and steadied her nerves. "You're right, TAL-zeta. I will be careful."

"From now on, there must be no indication of familiarity between us. I cannot show kindness to you. And you cannot speak in the language of our people."

The danger to herself, and anyone who helped her, was sobering. EC-TAL and MO-ASHE did not tolerate dissension within their households and dealt harshly with any who showed a hint of rebellion. Her gaze fell down onto her hands. The hands scarred by her consent.

Satisfied the young Olomi was taking her warning to heart, TAL-zeta instructed Nica in how she would be expected to behave if she wanted to serve in MO-ASHE's household.

"You will have this opportunity once every moon, after TAL has returned from his hunt. They both meet upon his return to discuss the new *aquans* and the state of their households. TAL requires me to prepare his food according to strict specifications, and I need assistance to meet his demands."

Restraining the urge to hug the old Olomi again, Nica instead held her hands together tight and bowed her head. "As you wish, TAL-zeta."

Her supervisor nodded in approval. "This will do."

31

·· O B E Y ··

"WHAT did you do?" Pescha's hoarse whisper was barely audible over the rustle of the dry husks they were sorting. "TAL-zeta's been riding you for suns. You can't send a ripple without her sifting it."

Nica gave a slight shrug, her glance darting to the approaching supervisor. Pescha dropped her gaze, staring at the dust eddies Zeta left in her wake as she tramped past them. Studying the ground seemed to be the safest recourse, and Nica followed her lead.

If Pescha was convinced by Zeta's act, their plan might work after all. Nica didn't like keeping her podmate in the dark, but the less she knew, the safer she'd be. Rissa had been assigned to MO-ASHE's living quarters, but to gain entrance, Nica had to first serve in TAL's residence.

"TAL will ignore you as long as his food arrives when and where he wants it. Serve without being seen or heard. That is how you survive being in his presence." Zeta's words were not comforting.

Dread streamed from Nica's nape to her soles, and stomach-minnows schooled without mercy as she stepped out of the harsh sunlight and over TAL's stoneskin threshold. It was terrifying enough to try and evade his notice in the compound, but another thing entirely to choose to walk into his den.

The dark was oppressive, and alcoves lining the stoneskin walls displayed tools she didn't recognize. She pushed up to Zeta, asking what they were.

"How badly do you want to know?" Zeta didn't even look at her. "Is it worth a beating? Because that's what questions lead to here."

She slowed, falling to the back of the pod, studying the devices. Their design was unfamiliar, but it was clear the intent was violent. Suppressing a shudder, she scurried past the unlit hallways, fearful of what else lay hidden in the dark recesses.

Zeta showed no hesitation as she led her pod, navigating through the darkness as if in the light. Nica tried to adjust her vision, blinking her eyes as if in the Deep.

Remember to blink.

Unbidden, Jonnat's memory pushed itself to her consciousness. Her eyes no longer fought their lids as tears burned at the edges.

How long had she been here? Like Zeta, she'd almost forgotten to remember.

Just how long has Zeta been held here? Had she always been trusted to serve TAL's food? What had she been doing on the surface when she was captured? Nica kept her questions to herself, almost as afraid of answers as she was of breaking the silence.

With a scrape and a long grate, a crack of light widened as Zeta shoved open a door. Light spilled over the three Olomi, and Nica realized that she had been holding her breath in the dark hallway. *Since when are you afraid of the dark, Nica?* But still, she scampered after Pescha, and they both placed their palms on the door to shut out the inkiness. Turning, they collapsed their backs against the door, breaths trembling. They looked at each other, and suddenly neither could stifle their giggles.

"You look like you swallowed a puffer!" Pescha's eyes twinkled.

"Well, you look like you stepped on a stonefish!"

Zeta glowered at them. "You're both going to look like whale carcass if you don't stop."

That sobered them up. But it didn't silence Nica.

"It's hard to live scared all the time, TAL-zeta." Nica fiddled with her tunic, twisting the end in her hands. "It's not . . . it's not living at all."

"It's your only chance of surviving right now." Zeta's frown deepened. "You, and anyone around you."

The green rose once again from Nica's jaw to her temples. She stared, chagrined, at her feet. She had put Pescha and even Zeta at risk, again. It was only luck that no one had caught them.

Nica squared her shoulders and surveyed the workstation. It functioned much like Zeta's kitchen, but nothing was rough-hewn. Rather, the entire station was made of stoneskin, smooth and cold, neatly fitting together so that no space was wasted. It was also designed to accommodate a much smaller staff. So that was why the crew was so small.

"Enough gawking, you two." TAL-zeta pulled items both strange and familiar from a cold storage box. "It's time to get cleaning, chopping, and cooking."

This station allowed for higher temperatures and faster cook times. Nica was grateful to be relegated to preparing the ingredients. Heating foods was not something she understood, and the higher the temperature, the more likely she was to wreck it.

Later, she and Pescha transferred the food onto shining platters, thin but heavy, and clearly, from Zeta's repeated warnings, fragile. Now there was one task left.

"Remember. Do not speak. Do not lift your eyes to the EC's face."

Both girls nodded, realizing how treacherous these waters were.

"Place the platter down gently, but smoothly. Step back two steps until TAL has pushed the plate away. When you clear the dishes, do not turn your back to him. Back away. Any sign of disrespect will lead to you and me being punished, so do not get distracted."

"Yes, TAL-zeta," the girls chorused.

The servers proceeded with their trays, careful to keep all Zeta's rules in mind. This was only the second time either of them would be this close to TAL since their capture. It was nerve-racking for Nica. She was sure it was the same for Pescha. Other than those brought by TRE-CH, all the Olomi here had been trapped and subdued by TAL. And each of them, in turn, had been subject to MO-ASHE's examinations and conditioning. If anyone had told Nica a moon ago that she would be trying to enter both of their lairs, she wouldn't have believed them. But she wouldn't gain her freedom—or anyone else's—hiding in food-pod.

Steeling herself, Nica focused on the task at hand. This was not about currying favor or mollifying her captors. Serving them was a means to an end. An end to her captivity. In her mind, she repeated, *I am of the Water, to the Water I will return. I am of the Water, to the Water I will return.*

Willing herself to calm, Nica refused to yield to the fear telling her to hide or keep her head down, that she would always be enslaved. And as she reminded herself of the truth, she believed.

While serving TAL was an exercise of self-control and overcoming fear, MO-ASHE's household required training in far more formal procedures.

"Food served by MO-ASHE's household is to be separated from EC-TAL's produce. They are always to be presented simultaneously but can never touch each other. When one samples the other's fare, it is to be dished, in a small portion, onto a separate plate."

"What's the difference?" Nica was mystified and a little annoyed at the details. Zeta directed an exasperated look at the squirming trainee.

"MO-ASHE's food is grown inside, in a controlled environment, not on the land. TAL's plants grow outside, under the sun, some from her lab's seeds, but also from our own plants of the water or the tree islands."

Between Zeta's droning, the technological terms, and the lecture on controlled food experiments, it was all Nica could do to stay awake. Stretching her back far less unobtrusively than she intended, she whispered to Pescha, "Their shared meals sound more like a competition."

"They're not exactly swimming in krill and plankton, are they?"

"Neither are we," Nica said.

32

THE WANING moon pulled at Nica's body and soul. The dark night sky warning of TAL's next hunt. Nica grieved the prospect of another Olomi being taken. But that this moon held hope—contact with Rissa—overshadowed almost any other concern. It took all her discipline to present an appropriate demeanor—she had not come this far to fail.

Returning to his pattern, TAL left the morning after the moon's last gleam. He would most likely return by the time the crescent had filled to one-quarter. Later that sun, MO-ASHE inspected the compound's outside complement of workers, as expected. What was not expected was the attendance of a very young, gloved Olomi, devoid of sensory markings, or any patterning on his face. The child was almost as pale as MO-ASHE, and dressed in the clothing of the Delphim, sporting the same close-cropped hairstyle in black that matched the MO.

As each Olomi knelt before MO-ASHE, she and the boy accepted the demonstration of fealty together. Allowing the boy to proceed, MO-ASHE murmured an order to her alpha, then turned to the line. The blue-marked Olomi next in line had not yet knelt before the boy, and MO-ASHE turned to him.

"Mote, my son, what is this standing before you?"

Her voice echoed off the stoneskin walls surrounding the courtyard and its silent Olomi attendees.

"An aquan servant, Mother." The child's voice cut through the silence as well, competing only against a wind that whistled through the buildings.

"And what is required of a servant, most of all, my son?"

"Fear, Mother."

"And is this servant demonstrating fear, child?"

"No, Mother."

"Then teach him."

At that, ASHE-alph, the great gray Olomi, knelt before the child, offering a rod with his head bowed. Nica gasped. It was TAL-rho's son. Taking the rod, the little one pointed it at the blue male, who had knelt in haste, too late. When he touched the rod to the blue's chest, it discharged an electric pulse that set the Olomi writhing in the dirt. The entire courtyard joined Nica in a stunned, silent gasp, holding their collective breath as Mote walked down the line to the next Olomi. It was clear the lesson had been learned, as she knelt without hesitation before this child of the water.

Sobered by the new display of domination, Nica noted the heightened air of servility from MO-ASHE's interior aquans as the females filed into the medical building behind MO-ASHE and her protégé.

It is the fear that they depend on to control us. We outnumber them, and yet we fear.

Nica inspected the scars that had replaced her webbing. *They've taken our heart and replaced it with shame.* Her gaze traveled from ASHE-alph to Mote. *And they've used our own people to ensure that we remain enslaved.*

Lost in her thoughts, Nica almost stumbled as she was directed to the examination cell, but a hand, darker than night and marked with bright blue, caught her. *On a tide like this, it is good to see a friend.* She settled herself before drinking a sip of the liquid the medical attendant handed her, spilling the rest down the front of her tunic.

Then she woke.

"ASHE-tau," she called softly.

"I am here," Girac replied just as quietly. He unlocked the door and slipped in. Worry creased his usually smooth brow. "You are awake much earlier than expected. Are you in pain?"

"No, there is no pain. Should there be?"

"Not yet." His voice was low, but full of concern.

He took her hand, still bound to the table, and held it as he whispered in Olomi, *"I wish you were not here, but I am glad to be near you."*

"Girac, I need your help, but it may put you in danger."

The glow in his eyes and strengthened grip answered before the words that followed. *"I would be honored to serve you—to be with you, Nica, no matter the risk."*

Nica lay motionless after Girac left the room, her limbs still bound to the table and her body simulating rest, but her thoughts were a maelstrom. She had trusted him with her plans, but he had entrusted her with his life. *Girac. She would know so much more if they were in the water. But so would he. He would know she was gravid. If he didn't already.*

Her cheeks flushed again. *Where did the larva come from? Who spawned it? Who would claim it?*

A chill ran through her. What was MO-ASHE's plan for her fry? TAL-rho's spawn had been as blue as his mother when he'd arrived. Now his skin was as devoid of colors as the mistress's.

Her mind flitted from question to question. *How had MO-ASHE removed his color? How had she secured his allegiance? Mote. Not an Olomi name, and not a Delphim-designation, but a name.*

And—gloves? Perhaps to hide the scarring?

How old was the fry when TAL took him from his mother? Three, maybe? He was barely old enough to speak, and already MO-ASHE has taught him the language and the actions of a tyrant. This would not be her spawn's fate.

Enough! Nica shut her thoughts down. This further tyranny of her captors had strengthened her resolve. And a new link had been forged—perhaps something more. Girac had agreed to contact Rissa for her. Just a few more tides.

Even the sound of MO-ASHE's approach could not still the hope pulsing through her. TAL-eta could play the part of the beaten down servant, but Nica was coming back to life. She was returning to the water.

33

"TAL-ETA!" The kitchen supervisor's gruff voice broke into her seadreams. "You're worse than Kap!"

Nica almost dropped the roots she was cleaning. The flush of guilt colored her cheeks. She shook her head to rinse away the errant thoughts and refocused on the job at hand. Pescha's pregnancy was obvious now, but Nica's rounding belly could still be hidden by her loose hanging tunic. They couldn't afford to attract any extra attention, especially given MO-ASHE's repeated threats. More than ever, Nica needed to prove herself industrious if TAL-zeta could justify adding her to the pod serving at the MO's table.

"Efficiency, attention to detail, appropriate personal presentation. This is required." The supervisor cast a speculative eye at Nica.

Nica shrank just a little bit under the withering gaze, though she knew it was mostly for show. Even in the company of the other captives, she was not the most fastidious. This was an arena where her sister would have shone, but now it was dependent on Nica to rein herself in and pay attention to the social conventions she had always ignored. A corner of her mouth went up as she imagined what her mother and sister would have thought of her attention to appearance, posture, and rules of etiquette. *But Rissa may even see it!* Nica's smile grew despite how inappropriate humor seemed right now.

The buzz at the gate signaling TAL's return sobered her as everyone prepared to be called to assemble at his approach. Nica finished prepping the vegetables she had been tasked with, then cleaned her station and self. Through these tides, life depended on her attention to details. And not just her life.

The familiar *GONG* rang through the courtyard, and Nica hurried along with Pescha to join the other Olomi.

Her heart sank as she saw that TAL had returned with not one, but two young males, both barely tinged along their dorsals and temples with the bright colors of their adolescence. Too young to be part of a search team, she imagined they had been looking for an adventure, and stumbled onto more than they had bargained for.

"Those poor juvies will end up in the pits for sure," she whispered to Pescha.

Smaller Olomi were needed to fit into the extreme crevices of the wells TAL continued to order repaired.

Sure enough, their new designations placed them in TAL's household, and they, as unwittingly as she, gave him their hands in exchange for "release." Nica burned with anger as she watched TAL-alph cut the boys' webbing while EC-TAL maintained his grip on both their hands.

The complicity of their own people still cut deepest, knowing the Delphim could not succeed without the aid of traitors. Fear and self-protection were powerful weapons, and their owners wielded them with an expert hand.

Greatly relieved when the ceremony ended quickly, Nica swiped at her cheeks. Pescha's eyes were also red-rimmed, and her lips were colorless as she clamped them tightly. Both Olomi blinked and steeled themselves to push the sorrow aside. It would just make them vulnerable.

By the sunsink, the food had been prepared, and last-minute instructions given to the new servers. TAL-zeta, flanked by TAL-kap and TAL-eta, transported the best of EC-TAL's produce to MO-ASHE's galley and assembled their dishes. At every turn and entry, she searched and listened for any sign of Rissa. There was none. *She's supposed to be here. She has to be here.* She dared not reveal disappointment.

MO-ASHE's living quarters were separate from the scientific and medical building, and Nica was not familiar with the layout. In contrast to the dark foreboding of TAL's dining area, MO-ASHE's glittered with a harsh but unexpected show of opulence. The kitchen galley was as sterile and utilitarian as her medical bays, but the MO's personal spaces were lined from floor to ceiling with lush fabrics accented by gleaming threads and sparkling gemstones.

She and TAL reclined on low cushioned blocks draped with glistening fabrics, with the son of TAL-rho—Mote. MO-ASHE made a show of petting and feeding the Olomi child, preening with him as if he were a pampered pet, calling him "son," and "my child."

Then, as she and Pescha prepared to bring out the second courses, she heard it. Rissa's voice floating through the chamber, sounding as beautiful as Nica remembered, despite the setting. This was how her sister served in the household. Thankful Rissa knew to expect her, Nica followed the team of servers in, focusing on her duty there, not even attempting to catch her sister's eye. There would be time for that later—if she could just survive the service of the meal.

By the end of the third course, Nica's back ached more from maintaining the prescribed posture than it ever had from carrying a heavy load. Rissa had disappeared, and it was all Nica could do to maintain her composure until she made it into the kitchen. With a sigh of relief, she put her tray down and stretched, arching and curving her aching dorsals, twisting from side to side. Closing her eyes, she took a deep breath through her nose, and allowed it to escape slowly, releasing with it the stress of the day.

She opened her eyes to Pescha's almost silent giggle at her discomfort and to another familiar quiet breath of mirth as well. Then Nica was engulfed by the one she had despaired of ever seeing again. Looking fully into her sister's tear-filled eyes, she dared not breathe.

"I thought I would never see . . ."

"We thought you were lost . . ."

Forehead to forehead, faded scarlet and green, the sisters whispered in their first language, oblivious to the danger surrounding them.

"Ìyá? Bàbá?"

"They wait for you . . . Now I suppose they wait for us."

"Jonnat?"

Nica had dreaded this. *"He came with me to find you . . . but TAL was stronger than both of us. He . . . he . . . I'm so sorry."*

Rissa's face paled. She wavered, then slid to the floor clutching her sister.

"I had accepted never seeing him again . . . but not this . . ." She choked back silent sobs.

Nica joined her and the girls clung to each other tightly.

Having given them a moment despite her misgivings, Zeta finally nudged Nica with her foot, shielding the sisters with a basin of dishes.

"You'd best pull yourselves together if you don't want to pay dearly for this reunion."

Nica rose without hesitation and pulled her sister up, soaking in her presence one more time.

She then took the basin from Zeta and headed toward the washing area, beckoning Rissa to follow.

"We don't have long." She spoke quietly under the clamor of cleanup taking place. "Rissa, I am working on a plan to get us out of here."

"That's impossible," Rissa mouthed with fear in her eyes. "They will kill you, or make you wish you were dead."

"They already have," Nica replied, "and this is not living. You were not made for this. I was not made for this."

She took her sister's hand and gently placed it on her shrouded belly. "And neither is my offspring."

Rissa's eyes widened as she felt the larva's presence and realized what was at stake. "I am with you, *Sisẹ. A wá lati'nu Omi.* We come from the Water,"

"*Si inu Omi, awa yóò padà.* To the Water, we will return."

Rissa glanced at the door. "I must go before I am missed. When will I see you again?"

"ASHE-tau is a friend in the guard. He can be trusted. I will get word to you through him."

And at that, Rissa slipped out of the room, leaving Nica with a new wave of hope.

34

"**A**LWAYS present yourself as subservient and unquestioning when I send you out into the compound. Watch your language and give no one reason to suspect you," Zeta cautioned. "And not just the Delphim and their alphas. Any Olomi might see an advantage to be gained by turning you in."

Nica's fists clenched, as if on their own accord. Even though she realized her body was betraying her heart, she could not stop the anger that set every muscle taut. "Those Olomi thrive abovewater," she said. "The ones who used positions and power against our fellows, their brothers and sisters of the Deep. Alphas and the enforcers, supervisors and overseers, they are strong, and they are cruel. Even their acclimation to the land seems faster and more complete—breathing the air and striding about with ease. How could we hope to win against that?"

"We have positions and power of our own—but cultivating those relationships requires caution. Each person you bring into your circle is a risk—not only are they trusting you with their safety, but also that of those they love."

Nica nodded, feeling the weight of Zeta's warning.

"I'm sending you to hydro-processing, where they harvest water and hydro-derivatives. You will work with MO-ASHE's Phi and Mu. They're charged with acquisition and extraction."

Nica's heart stuttered, recalling those designations. "Those were the . . ." Chills streamed down her dorsals as she remembered the first branding she'd witnessed. The smell of burned flesh and the sound of the screams. "Why did MO-ASHE torment them so? And why their wives?"

Puffs of dust rose as Zeta settled down next to the rough bags of produce. She motioned for Nica to come closer and help her sort. She leaned in, dropping her voice to a whisper, "Remember, attachment is a weapon. MO-ASHE needs leverage to secure compliance in certain domains. Hydro-processing is vital to the compound's operation, to its survival. But to maintain dominance, the Delphim must isolate our people from that source." Then she sat upright and raised her voice. "Since agri-pod has successfully established MO-ASHE's legumes outside her labs, we'll be using more. We'll need more of the crystal by-products."

"But what does this have to do with—"

Zeta pierced Nica with a glare, then leaned in and murmured, "ASHE-phi and his wife are trustworthy and have options we do not."

Nica raised an eyebrow.

Zeta continued to look at her sternly, but her voice was soft. "Don't judge hastily. Phi and his wife are adept at hiding their strength. But be cautious if Mu is within earshot. That one is easily swayed."

Nica began to understand the brandings. The ceremonies were rare, but always public to ensure maximum impact. Chastisement for rebellion, or sometimes even just reluctance, was an excuse to make examples of unfortunate Olomi. It had proven effective in squashing similar tendencies in their peers. Mu's wife received facial branding to stigmatize. Those with face-brands were assigned humiliating positions and treated as pariah. Other Olomi would go out of their way to avoid interacting with them, lest they be associated with their shameful status. And then there were the Olomi vying for positions of importance who volunteered to prove their loyalty. MO-ASHE's gray alpha displayed his brand like a badge.

Hydro-processing. Nica's thoughts drifted. What was it like

to harvest water? What wouldn't she give to step into it again, to gather, or even—

"TAL-eta! You're sea-dreaming again." Zeta shook a handful of beans at her. "You can't swim in your dreams yet. You're still grounded on the land, and you'll be buried in it if you don't pay heed."

Attachment is a weapon.

They're trusting you with their lives, and the lives of those they love.

Zeta's admonitions circled her thoughts as Nica set out to pursue the new collaborator.

"Find ASHE-phi in agri-pod or MO-ASHE's hydro-processing section," Zeta now called after her, waving her long, wide bottomed stirring stick in the general direction. "I need those crystals this sun, so if he needs help to harvest it, make yourself useful."

"And I'm supposed to ask about . . . by-products?"

"Yes," Zeta huffed with exasperation, "*and* what type of water is available, *and* what stage the processing is at, *and* cooking recommendations. Remember, MO-ASHE grows her food in water baths, but until the wells succeed, her resources are as limited as TAL's."

"At least I understand that. *Ìyá*'s gardens were amazing."

"I doubt MO-ASHE's enriched nutritive baths or programmed light-spectrum washes resemble anything you knew in the Deep, but that should give you enough cover to discuss your plans with ASHE-phi."

"That's if my tongue doesn't get twisted into a knot just trying to say the words." Nica stretched her tongue and mouth wide after trying to mimic her supervisor's phrases.

Zeta actually chuckled. "You look like a whisker-fish gulping down minnows!"

Nica had to admit she'd never heard words like these before, in any language. Until now, she'd been spared the need to learn technical terms in Delphim. The physical labor involved when serving under TAL was grueling, but working in MO-ASHE's household required grasping meticulous concepts, and strict adherence to her procedures. Since she hoped to survive this temporary assignment, Nica repeated the unfamiliar phrases until she reached the first station ASHE-phi might be assigned to.

Recognizing her, the agricultural supervisor stepped out of his booth, furrowing his black and brown ridged brow.

"Here already for TAL-zeta's pickup? We aren't finished assembling that order."

"Oh no. I am to discuss a matter with ASHE-phi. I was told I might find him here."

"Well, no. He isn't here right now, and I have work to do." If there wasn't an unexpected pressure put on his pod, the supervisor had no interest in Nica's inquiries.

The next stop was the labs. Nica's heart began to beat a little quicker as she headed to MO-ASHE's science and medical building. She didn't know where Girac might be stationed, outside of her scheduled exams, but hoped to see him.

She approached the building and was stopped at the entrance.

"What is your business?" the dull blue sentry asked, pawing through her basket.

"I am required to meet with ASHE-phi."

"What business do you have with ASHE-phi?"

"Specialized preparation techniques for unprocessed and desalinated hydro resources, ASHE-"—she examined the designation on his tunic—"delt."

"Uh, that's fine," the flustered guard replied, his edges greening a bit. "He's in hydro-processing."

Nica walked past him, taking a little amusement in the deepening furrows across his brow. It wasn't often she had the upper hand. That her advantage was fabricated didn't matter. Just that she had one.

At the medical and science hall junction, she peeked down the way toward the exam rooms. There he was. Now it was Nica's turn to have her colors betray her at Girac's smile. She felt her green darkening, and her insides flip-flopped at his approach. She hugged the basket a little tighter. The sparkle in his eyes belied his formal inquiry into her presence, and the hand on her elbow giving the impression that he was detaining her felt more like a caress where skin met skin.

Trying not to stammer, Nica managed to deliver her rehearsed lines, but with far less confidence than before.

"Despite your assignment," Medical Guard ASHE-tau replied with a straight face, "I would be remiss in my duties if I allowed you to wander these hallways unescorted. You will accompany me."

Nica saw a sliver of a smile, like the first light of a moon, tweak at the corner of Girac's mouth as he guided her down the corridor.

How did this happen? she asked herself, mystified at the warmth traveling from that simple contact to deep inside her chest. She didn't dare question it too much, but she didn't know where it would go—where it could go.

Shifting her load, Nica stopped in front of a table in the hallway, as Girac performed a thorough inspection of her basket and the contents. With a quick glance up and down the hallway, he mouthed, "Is this about your plans?"

She nodded. "If you can help." She barely moved her own lips. "I need to speak to ASHE-phi alone. Can you distract Mu for me?"

He flashed a quick grin, nodded in return, then cleared his throat.

"These seem to be in order, TAL-eta, but I will need to escort you to hydro-processing."

They continued down the hallway, impassive expressions fixed on their faces, but his hand never left her elbow until they reached her destination.

"ASHE-phi." Girac addressed a vibrant Olomi, a far cry from the frail and withered one that Nica remembered from the branding. "TAL-zeta has inquiries for you. This aquana is her representative."

He turned to Phi's bright blue co-worker. "ASHE-mu. There are concerns about security safeguards in this sector. You will review them with me now."

"All is set according to MO-ASHE's wishes!" The smaller Olomi's yellow eyebrows creased together. "I'll show you." He led the dark guard down the hallway.

Now that she was alone with ASHE-phi, Nica was terrified to speak. What if this was a terrible mistake? Could she truly trust this Olomi? "TAL-zeta told me I could . . . that I could trust you . . . and that you may be able to help."

The older Olomi cocked a bushy eyebrow and scanned the room as he waited.

"I plan to return to the Deep. I need to leave with my sister, Ris—I mean, ASHE-theta, and my baby." She rested her hand on her stomach. "I'll take who I can with me, but I won't raise my spawn in captivity."

She scrutinized the water-gatherer's lined face. If Zeta was right, he'd be sympathetic to her cause. If not, she'd just put both herself and Rissa in grave danger.

ASHE-phi strode to the doorway and yelled to his partner, "Don't forget to demonstrate the transfer protocol!"

"There," he announced further. "That should give us enough time to sort this out."

Nica shared her situation with Phi—her and Pescha's mysterious pregnancies, the metamorphosis of TAL-rho's appropriated son, and her own reunion with Rissa.

"We have to find a way to escape. There are only two of them, and scores of us. We're held captive more by fear than we are by walls and chains."

"You sound like my wife." Phi smiled gravely. "Yes, our people have believed the lie that we are powerless to fight this enemy because we have never had to fight before. And it might be true. But if we work together, perhaps we can free ourselves and return to the water."

"Then you will help?" Nica almost couldn't believe her ears.

"We have a daughter, Mischa and I. She was gravid before the

Breaking. We would not have our grandchild raised a slave. Yes, we will help. But it will take time and planning, and a little bit of help from outside. I believe we can get a message out. Return in two weeks."

He raised his voice just a little and cleared his throat. "However, to have a full understanding of the process you will need to be familiar with each step of the procedure. Return in two weeks and we will start at step one."

ASHE-phi then turned on his heel and returned to the water testing just as ASHE-mu and Girac returned from the inspection. "ASHE-tau, escort this female to the exit. I must return to my work. ASHE-mu, have you finished your calculations yet?"

Leaving the two to catch up from their interruptions, Girac escorted his charge down the hall.

35

·· REALITY CHECK ··

SIFTING indicators was exhausting abovewater, but not impossible. Nica weighed every nuance she could—inflection, eyebrows, nostrils, eye darts, fingerings—anything that could indicate whether an Olomi might be willing to fight for freedom. Many were not. But was it just because they thought they couldn't?

Until her plans were realized and her larva safe, it was hard to trust anyone.

Pescha's spawn grew, and so did her discomfort. Her feet were swollen, her back was sore, and she struggled to accomplish most of her duties. Zeta arranged for raised seating—called a stool—to be fashioned that allowed the gravid Olomi to serve food but stay off her feet. Even this, the most basic function of life, was overwhelming out of the Deep. Nica wondered if it would be as difficult when she was as far along. She'd seen her *iyá* weather two gestations and didn't remember it being this hard.

Ìyá. Tears threatened and her heart ached. *You'll be with them soon enough!* She took a slow, measured breath and focused on serving the morning meal.

Why is Girac coming this way?

It was rare to see anyone assigned to MO-ASHE's household outside her domain. Even their meals were prepared and served separately from TAL's work force.

"How—" She cleared her throat lest her voice betrayed her. "How may I serve MO-ASHE?"

"MO-ASHE has summoned TAL-kap to medical." He bent

down to inspect the food and said quietly, "but I wish I could accompany you."

Nica flushed a little greener.

With an apologetic bow and smile, ASHE-tau proceeded to escort the very pregnant TAL-kap for his mistress.

How did romance find her in this place of suffering? She'd had no time for it in the Deep. The danger of discovery inherent in the slightest exchange should have deterred them from expressing their feelings, but it didn't. Something real was growing, and she couldn't help but treasure it.

Sunpeak's meal had come and gone, as had sunsink's, and Pescha had not yet returned. Nica kept a lookout for her friend's return, her concern growing as eventide deepened. The skies were inking, and the stars beginning to reveal themselves when Pescha's rounded figure finally entered the food-pod courtyard.

Deftly scooping them both a bowl of watered leftovers from that tide's meals, Nica set them down at the table where she had first started dining with Pescha, many moons earlier, and waited for her friend to sit next to her.

"You look tired."

"I am." Pescha moved the soup around with her spoon, not lifting her eyes from the bowl. "They didn't give medicine to sleep this time. MO-ASHE said I will give birth before two moons have passed and if anything happens to the *baby*, there will be consequences."

She raised her head. "Nica, she wants this fry very badly, but she does not care about us at all. I'm afraid. For us, and for our brood."

She continued to push her soup around the bowl—not bringing the spoon to her lips.

Nica gripped Pescha's hand tightly, and their fingers intertwined where webbing once spanned. "You're not alone."

"But I will be." Pescha's voice was almost a whisper. "I've never been gravid before. I don't know . . . how to spawn . . . I won't know what's . . . right, or if something is wrong." Shuddering gulps forced their way between her words.

Nica wrapped her arms around her friend, trying to soothe her. "I don't want to be here. I don't want to always be afraid." Pescha wept. "I want to go home and be in the Deep with my family."

Nothing Pescha said was alien to Nica. The only reason she didn't suffer the same despair was the hope she kept hidden in her heart. She yearned to tell Pescha of her plans, but couldn't. Not yet. Instead, they rocked together in their sorrow until they were both exhausted.

Long after the others had fallen asleep, Nica pondered the same questions from her pallet. *Will I be alone when it's time for the baby to come? Will I know what to do? Will I still be grounded, locked to this land, separated from everyone and everything that gives life meaning?* She had no tears left to cry. Just an ache in her heart that threatened to consume her.

36

*T*HE SMELL *of kelp and water . . . like home filling the—*
"TAL-eta!" The kitchen supervisor's voice broke into her slumber, jolting Nica into reality.

Shells! She'd slept past sunbreak. She rolled off her pallet and threw on her work tunic. "Coming, TAL-zeta!"

Running her hand over her fuzzy head still gave her pause, but getting ready for the new tide was easier since she'd been shorn. She sloughed off some flaking skin from her arms and face with a rough cloth and applied a bit of ointment Zeta had made to the worst spots, completing the barest necessities for being presentable.

The morning meal was almost ready to be served, and Zeta was not pleased with her tardiness.

"I don't know why I slept late," Nica apologized as she hurried to her station. "It won't happen again!"

"You're not the only one," the old woman groused as she bustled around. "Several of you have left me high and dry this morning!" Zeta practically threw the food service trays at Nica to bring to the tables.

Taking a minute to get her bearings, Nica realized why she had missed the sun's wakeup call.

Instead of floating, white and sparse against the blue, providing little or no relief from the hammering heat of the sun, this morning's clouds were thick and dark, casting a cloak over the sky. She could smell—no, taste—no, she truly *felt* the water around her. As if the air was gravid with rain and about to spawn. Nica raised her eyes and wondered at the swollen clouds. Throughout her time abovewater, her entire captivity, there hadn't been more than a sprinkle here or there, but this tide, the skies promised rain.

"Eta! Kap! You two stay on the serving line! The rest of you, grab anything that will hold water." TAL-zeta bustled through the milling Olomi, trying to focus them despite the imminent downpour.

All over the compound, the flurry of activity was filled with anticipation. Buckets and basins were distributed throughout the pods and across the grounds, with one notable exception. Thin sheets were raised and anchored to shield the crops from the rain and divert the runoff into collectors. It made no sense to Nica that TAL would order such a thing, but she'd long since learned that it was not safe to question any of his practices.

"After all the work we did in agriculture, measuring and maintaining moisture levels for the crops, you'd think they'd appreciate a little help from the sky," she observed to Pescha. "I got such a beating my first moon here, neglecting to soak a row to the border. Nothing makes sense abovewater."

Her friend nodded. "That first moon—it was so hard to keep all the rules! The supervisor threatened to send me to work in the pits if I damaged one more plant. I think I would have been transferred there if MO-ASHE hadn't pulled me. But now"—she glanced at her swollen belly—"I don't know what's going to happen."

Anxiety disrupted the delicate symmetry of her blue and orange markings. "MO-ASHE has ordered me to come in every two weeks now. She seems pleased at the progress down here." She gestured toward her stomach. "But when she looks at me, I feel like a worm she wants to crush."

Nica shot a quick glance around and lowered her voice. "Even if that is all we are to her, she still needs us. We have value. Like one of those bean plants." She grinned at the irony of their station.

"We do for now. But maybe not for long."

They sighed in chorus and returned their attention to the influx of workers from the next pod, stirring the colorless food before them.

It didn't rain through firstmeal, and not by the sunpeak either. But while food-pod prepared to serve at sunsink, the heavens made good their threat and loosed the precious bounty.

It started with a *splat,* leaving a thumbprint-sized imprint in the dust next to Nica's foot. And then another *splat!* This time on her forearm. Nica stopped for a moment, transfixed on the spot of moisture that had landed on her, raising her arm to watch it seep into the tiny crevices of her cracked, dry skin. Then another, and another, and as she stood, the drops become a shower, and the shower, the awaited downpour. Eyes closed and face upturned, Nica received the rain as it washed over her. She didn't need to chase it. The water had come to her.

The deluge brought life to Nica's skin, and then her soul, and as she opened her eyes to sounds of joy, Olomi all around her came to life. Some stood still, receiving with quiet bliss what they had been deprived of for so long. Others, mouths agape, drank in as much nourishment as they could. Some splayed out their arms, spinning with ecstasy in the heaven's abundance. And there were those who became like fry, stomping and splashing in the fast-forming puddles, exuberant and full of glee. TAL had taken them from the water, had withheld their access to it, but he could not hold back the rain.

As Nica watched her people rejoice, a beautiful sight unfolded before her. Colors, long faded, covered with dead and dying skin—colors they had forgotten in their captivity—these glorious vibrant colors of the Olomi people came back to life. Bright greens and blues, yellows, oranges, reds, and blacks, in all varieties of shades and combinations; the true colors of the Olomi were revealed by the water from the heavens.

Joy, that had been absent abovewater, was sweeter than she

remembered it ever had been. Unable to contain her emotions, Nica's eyes overflowed with tears indistinguishable from the rain.

Laughter erupted beside her. Pescha sat awkwardly but delightfully in a puddle, worry and fear no longer etched on her brow. Orange and blue striping shimmered around her ears, traveling down either side of her neck, the freckled lines flowing from her brows and cheekbones, until they disappeared under her tunic.

"Pesch— TAL-kap! You are beautiful!"

"And you are so gorgeous in green!" Pescha clapped her hands with joy.

"Yes, yes. You're green, you're orange, and I'm old!" Zeta groused. "Enjoy it while it lasts, girls. There's always a price attached to joy on the land."

"*Wo, Ìyágba*, even your blue is showing from the water!"

"Heh!" The kitchen supervisor sloughed off a little dry skin from her arm. "There's a little color left in me after all!" A sparkle danced in her aged eyes as she massaged her temples and scalp, revealing new periwinkle ringlets where her hair had begun to regrow. Her mouth twisted into an impish half grin as she admired her reflection in a puddle.

"Now, there's a face I haven't seen in a while." She rapped her cooking stick sharply against a wood frame. "But all good things must come to an end. Food-pod! At your stations! This meal will not serve itself!"

They served in the rain, and no one minded in the slightest that the water danced upon their food. For this tide, they enjoyed what they had.

It rained all night and continued through the next sun. Nica didn't think her heart could rejoice any more, but it skipped a little faster at Girac's approach. Then she remembered what TAL-zeta had said about the price attached to joy. Her fear began to solidify when he avoided her eyes, heading straight for Pescha.

"But I was just there!" Pescha's eyes were full of fear.

"TAL-kap, you must. If you don't, the MO will make an example of you. She is already furious about the weather. Don't give her a reason to vent her anger." Girac continued in a low tone. "I won't force you, but there are other guards, bound more by fear or ambition, who will do what it takes to bring you in."

Pescha surrendered to the guard's persuasion, mouth set and tears covered by the rain. Nica's face matched her friend's, but she knew that Girac was right. Still, her anger flared against the messenger, and she refused to acknowledge his apologetic gaze.

When Pescha returned, just after sunpeak, she was paler, but not melancholy, like she'd been after the last exam. "MO-ASHE was just asking about the rain's effect on me and the baby. She didn't want us to get sick."

Why would MO-ASHE show any concern? Nica hugged her friend, hoping her worry wasn't evident. She thought back to the first branding she'd witnessed. *What purpose did it serve?* The memory came of the Delphim's response to TAL-rho's desperation. And the training the fry had received. *"What is required of an aquan?"* Mote's answer rang in her mind. *"Fear."*

37

A FTER FIVE full suns of rain, life abovewater was far less painful, and it was time to revisit ASHE-phi in hydro-processing.

"Remember," Zeta warned, "this rain is no friend to the Delphim. If anything, it's a threat. Promote the illusion that it's not benefiting you. It'll make it easier to pursue your plans."

"Yes, TAL-zeta." Nica bowed and picked up her basket of sample containers.

She walked across the compound in the rain, completely unsuccessful at hiding her joy. Buoyant at the sight of her brothers and sisters glowing with renewed vitality, she couldn't help but smile, and for once, it was safe to do so in front of them. They had no idea she was planning a permanent return to the water, and not just basking in the temporary reprieve from its deprivation.

TAL-alph was an exception to the colorful state of the Olomi. The yellow followed the example of her EC, who acted as if the rain was a personal attack. Wearing gear that repelled the water and prevented it from reaching her, her colors were especially pale in contrast to the bright hues of the other Olomi.

Agri-pod was bustling with activity. Borders and diverters were assembled in haste around the produce fields. Protective sheets recently erected were failing in the face of the unrelenting downpours, threatening to crush the tender plants under the unexpected accumulation. Nica inwardly scoffed at the irony of TAL's efforts, amused at their futility.

He'll discover that it's just as futile to keep the people of the water contained. The uprising in her heart strengthened her resolve, and she set about her mission with optimism.

"There's a gap here!" A blue-banded Olomi in the agri-pod supervisor's tunic pointed out an inlet. "Hey! Spots!"

A bright orange Olomi struggling with the edge of a cover raised her head.

"Yeah. What's wrong with you? You're missing the diverter! What's it going to take for you to get that right?"

The orange looked back and blanched, her grid of dots paling till they nearly disappeared. Water was pooling short of the collection trough. She froze, torn between fixing that connection or protecting the covered plants from being crushed. Her head swiveled between the far ends of the sheet. The young supervisor strode toward her, fist upraised. Nica dropped her basket and jumped toward the trough.

"*Du*—Wait! I'll fix it!"

As Nica addressed the uncoupled connector, the dotted orange pulled back on the edges to make sure they were taut, and the water diverted to its collector. She grimaced in relief at Nica, before scurrying to the next sheet.

The young supervisor redirected his glare to Nica. "If she can't do her job, I'll just replace her with someone who can."

The agri-worker blanched under the loud threat voiced for her benefit.

"I'm not getting sent to the holes before you are!" He glowered, continuing to berate the shaken Olomi.

"What's your business here?" The angry young supervisor noted the kitchen-pod designation on Nica's tunic.

"Where is Supervisor TAL-gam?" Nica had a sinking feeling in her stomach.

"*Former* supervisor TAL-gam failed to obey EC-TAL. He is being retrained."

"In what way"—Nica squinted at his baggy tunic—"TAL-xi?" She knew from her short stint in the agri-pod that her old supervisor had been very careful to obey all TAL commanded, and he passed down that motivation of fear to the members of his pod.

The Olomi pulled his shoulders back, failing to fill in the oversized agri-pod tunic. "EC-TAL told him to keep accurate records of the crop's water intake. He failed to accomplish this."

"What, the rain? That's why he's been removed?" Nica eyed the blue, suspicious he'd plotted to take TAL-gam's position.

"Yes. TAL didn't want it to affect his data. TAL-gam allowed it to. And now I have the responsibility of ensuring it doesn't happen again. It's not what I wanted, but I'm not getting sent to the holes! Now state your business and stop interfering with mine!"

"TAL-zeta sent me to gather samples from ASHE-phi." Nica huffed as she bent over to pick up the spilled containers and her basket.

"Well, he's not here, and apparently we don't have as much time for *snacks* as you do in the kitchen. Maybe I should stop in between meals after the rain stops." The supervisor's blue banding seemed to brighten as he leered at her. "Maybe do a little *snacking* for myself."

Nica flushed as she realized the rain and the basket made her condition almost as obvious as Pescha's. Shame, anger, and fear roiled about her chest, making it difficult to breathe without trembling. Shifting the basket from her hip to carry it before her with both hands, she glared at the blue. "You should remember where you're from."

"No," he said, turning to his booth with a swagger. "You should remember where you are, *ipanu*. There's no one here to rescue you, greenie—so you'd better learn to mind your own business."

Shaken, Nica gathered what dignity she could, holding her head high and straightening her dorsals as she turned on her heel.

The recently promoted supervisor shouted after her. "Yeah, keep walking, *snack*."

Now it was her turn to be thankful for the cover of rain.

38

RUBBERY legs carried her past the agri-pod barracks, through the courtyard, and beyond the sprawl of TAL's sector. By the time she stood before the entrance to MO-ASHE's science and medical buildings, her legs felt less like the jellyfish that used to play outside her window and more like the dolphin fins she'd once hitched rides on.

She closed her eyes and stilled her thumping heart. She didn't want Girac to see her in this state. Her heart ignored the caution and hammered a little harder at that thought. *I was so cold to him. He was just doing the best he could, like we all are, trying to survive in this world that we don't belong to. None of us belong here—none of us were made to live like this.*

"And that's why I'm here," she murmured to herself as she stepped up to the entrance.

"Were you talking to me?" The blue sentry's brow was furrowed. He twisted around to see if someone was behind him.

Nica merely nodded down at her basket. "I'm here to gather samples from hydro-processing."

"Oh, all right. Like a few weeks ago. Go ahead." He returned to his post, standing outside the door this time, relaxing a bit in the rain.

Entering the main hallway, she glanced down the hall that led to the medical cells. Her shoulders and spirit slumped when she saw no sign of Girac.

What if he knows I'm coming and is avoiding me?

She still felt bad about being angry with him and had hoped to make amends.

You're just imagining the worst, Nica. Don't expect that of him.

Turning the other way, down to the labs, Nica headed to the very last and largest room. She hesitated at the door, uncertain as to whether she should announce herself or wait until someone noticed her.

Realizing that she might have to wait for a very long time, she finally knocked on the doorframe and walked in. ASHE-phi and ASHE-mu were involved in a loud discussion. Hoping to catch Phi's eye, she skirted the perimeter of the room, trying not to bump into anything, or not anything important.

At last, ASHE-phi glanced in her direction. "Are you back again? I told TAL-zeta that we cannot put up with these interruptions. If our work falls behind, we have to answer to MO-ASHE!"

Nica felt the green rising her cheeks. She thought she could trust this Olomi.

ASHE-mu frowned at his partner. "I didn't make any agreement with TAL-zeta. Certainly not one that would impede my production. This is your problem!"

Then the striped Olomi turned on his heel and headed toward whatever important project was on his list. Nica was just thankful he left.

As soon as the door closed, ASHE-phi smiled at her gently. "I hope my little scene didn't upset you."

Relief washed over Nica. "I wasn't sure, but when I saw ASHE-mu scurry out, I started to understand."

"Yes. Our plans are safer if he thinks I am threatened by you."

He took the basket of sample bottles and walked her to the back of the lab and down a set of stairs made of stoneskin bars. She noted the raised Φ that had been burned into his arm and cringed.

"Does it still hurt?"

"No. It really doesn't," he said. "I barely remember the pain anymore. And if that's what it took to work with the water here, I would suffer it again."

Nica stared at him. "How could you say that?"

"I'll show you, just be patient. But first, let's take care of Zeta's list."

He led her to a large flat pan, three times her length, covered with a lid that rolled back and forth with the slightest touch. ASHE-phi reached in with a tool similar to, but smaller than, the hoes they used in agri-pod. Pulling white crystals to the edge, he scraped some into one of her bottles.

"This is where we dry the water and extract salt for flavoring and preserving."

Continuing down to another similar pan, Phi pointed out where it fed from the first.

"Next, we evaporate more liquid and rake up the flaky residue. It's a little bitter, but works best to make your protein blocks."

"This is the source of nigari? Leftovers from salt and water?"

"Not saltwater—seawater. You need more than salt to collect nigari."

"But how do you get seawater on the top of this mountain?"

A twinkle appeared in his eye, and he smiled again. "That's what you're really here to see."

They went down two more flights of stairs and entered a small, dim room.

"This is going to be a little more difficult, but I think we can both fit."

ASHE-phi twisted opened a crossbar latch on the floor and lifted a heavy stoneskin cover. By the light globes swinging from the ceiling, Nica could barely make out rungs that led down into darkness. Seeing nothing but blackness beyond, she started to straighten up and away from the hole, but then she heard—and smelled—something else.

"Is that the Deep?" She could not believe her senses.

ASHE-phi grinned at her. "Yes and no. You'll understand when we climb down, but this is the best source of water for the compound—and the biggest threat to the Delphim."

He handed her a vest with large pockets. "Put your containers in this. You won't be able to carry anything in your hands down here."

He put on a similar vest and pocketed two of the bottles from her basket as well, before wrapping her waist with a belt attached to a lead. Nica recoiled, reminded of when TAL had first led her in captivity.

Realizing her apprehension, Phi placed the lead in her hands. "No, don't worry. This is to ensure your safety. The tunnel is long, and the ladder, steep. If you slip, it could injure or kill both of us." He fastened his lead to the ladder, then leaned back from it, waving his hands above his head. "See? Despite your experience, even something like a lead can save your life, but more than that, it might help you escape to freedom."

39

·· TRUE WATER ··

STEP by step, rung by rung, they descended into darkness, the
light from above fading into a faint glimmer. Robbed of sight,
Nica's other senses waxed, honing in on sound and smell. Her arms
ached, and her hands were almost raw from looping and unlooping
her safety line when Phi stopped. The crash of waves against the
tunnel walls greeted her, and she almost slipped in her eagerness
to reach the bottom.

"It's true water. The purest we have access to. Soak your hands
and arms in that for a bit and you'll feel better."

There was just enough room at the bottom of the pit for both to
stand. Nica felt around the rough walls for the water's entry point.
A thick grating covered the opening, yet every cell in her being
responded to being submerged up to her waist in true water.

"You said you wanted to get a message out. This is the best place
to send it. These bars may be intended to ensure our imprisonment,
but they offer a means to communicate."

Taking one of her sample containers, Nica tested the bars,
knocking on them above the waterline. Then below. "This could
work! Surely there's a relay within range!" She thought for a
minute, then began tapping out a message.

DANGER. DO NOT APPROACH ABOVEWATER MASSES.
HOSTILES. ESCAPE PLANNED. TWO MOONS. NEED
SUPPORT. WAIT FOR SIGNAL. NICA TI DAEVU

"You think they'll get it?"

"They certainly should." Despite the dark, she could sense Phi's
approval.

"Now, here is another help."

Phi grabbed the bars that had been driven deep into the rock and, placing his feet on either side, began to pull at them, pushing in and out, side to side, back and forth.

"I don't have much time when I come down here, but when I do, I work these bars. The increased rain has helped as well. The waves have been wearing more than expected at this point.

"Omi ṣe ọna rẹ," Nica murmured.

"That's right. Water does make its way." Phi chuckled. "My *Ìyágbà* taught me that, as well. I once thought it was a threat to keep me in line, but now it is a hope."

"And it is truth." Nica's heart ached at the possibility.

"Aye. That it is."

They worked the bars in silence, listening to the water lap against the walls of the pit and regaling in its splashing against their skin.

"Well. We'd better head up now. Don't forget your samples!"

The trip back up was surprisingly effortless, and once they reached the top, Nica was surprised to realize that her hands were no longer raw from the trip down.

"Did you know this?" She stared at her hands in amazement when they reached the top.

Phi's eyes twinkled as he nodded. "It doesn't take much exposure to the source. The rain has reminded our people of what it means to be wet, but it is no comparison to stepping into the actual Deep, with all its properties, and not just a distillation. It's no wonder they barely allow us room to move down there. Can you imagine if we could go under?"

It had been so long, and Nica had been so focused on surviving, that it had not occurred to her to go under.

"If it hadn't been raining so much, I wouldn't have considered letting you down. It will be obvious that you've been in the water, but with the rain, there is cover."

She continued to examine her hands, noting that the green along her knuckles and joints was even more pronounced than after the rains. Her ankles and toes had greened up and the ache in her hips and lower back, a constant she'd grown accustomed to, was absent for the first time in months. Turning her back to Phi, she lifted her tunic and examined her swelling belly. Even the angry dark marks of her gravidity were fading and the skin across her ventrals seemed less dehydrated and taut.

If this little bit of time standing in true water could make such a difference, she wondered how different her pregnancy might be if she weren't denied access to the Deep. Sighing once again at what might be, Nica refilled her basket with the samples she'd collected.

"Thank you." She started to bow, but ASHE-phi's scowl caught her off guard.

"That is all the time I can give you, TAL-eta. Tell TAL-zeta that if she needs more samples before two weeks are up, she'd better come and collect them herself! Show yourself out!"

Stammering apologies, an appropriately chastised and cowed Nica scurried out of the room, past ASHE-mu, and down the corridor before she allowed herself to smile.

40

THE MAIN entrance was in sight, and Nica allowed herself a sigh of relief.

"Halt!" The command from behind stopped her in her tracks.

She froze, not sure what had given her away. She glanced at her basket, then her clothing. All was in order. Turning to face her accuser, she almost collapsed in relief upon seeing Girac, but her relief was tinged with shame. She'd been so hard on him.

Forming an apology as he approached, Nica tried to interpret his tone and expression—both presenting as authoritative and hard set. Startled as he pulled her by the elbow around the corner and into a room and wrested the basket from her, she opened her mouth to apologize. But before she knew it, Nica was melting in Girac's embrace, mindful of nothing else. An eternity of bliss passed, and Nica's eyes glowed green as they melted in Girac's blue-flecked, deep black gaze.

"I . . . I was going to apologize," she started to explain.

"Apology accepted." He smiled.

She leaned back and looked at him. "You have to stop doing that."

"Stop doing what?"

"Making my heart skip."

"Not if I can help it." His eyes were tender as he gently pulled her in close again. "The movement within our hearts is something they cannot control."

Nica rested her head and hand on his chest and felt his heart beating through the uniform, breathing him in deeply as she heard him do the same. After a moment, Girac held her at arm's length.

"You've been in true water!" His eyes widened. "I know the rains have revitalized you outdoor Olomi, but this, this is different. You've had access to the Deep!"

"Should I worry?" She half joked, but apprehension flared her nearly dormant sensory pores.

"Not unless someone gets really close." He drew her back into his embrace. "And has committed to memory your every detail."

Nica closed her eyes, imagining the world away for a moment, wishing this moment could last forever. But they didn't have forever, and this lingering already tested the boundaries of wisdom if they didn't want to be discovered. With one last breath, she eased herself away.

Girac released her with reluctance. "I'll escort you to the exit," he murmured into her ear.

"No." Nica gave him a gentle push. "It isn't necessary this time. We're getting close to real change. Return to your station before you're missed, that way we won't have to cover up or risk being found out."

Girac lightly touched her face and headed down to the medical hallway. Nica readjusted the basket of samples and turned the corner to head out the entrance. Smiling at the rain that continued to fall, she stepped out into the world that no longer owned her.

41

K EL surged up, away from the cavern's entrance. He knew better than to disregard these oncoming signatures. His younger—and only accounted for—siblings were rushing the council. It was safest to let them pass.

Pilto dashed through first, skimming between the Guardians stationed on either side of the entry. He bubbled with excitement. "Who found her?"

Chesnae tumbled after, churning in his wake. "Where is she?"

"We felt the news!"

An older Guardian swam after to shoo the pair out. "Hush, minnows, we're investigating now."

The littles split around the old Olomi, dodging over, under, and around the brown and speckled Guardian.

He threw his hands up. "This is not a nursery!" He glared at Kel and surged to the inner chamber.

Kel held his hands out. "They have just as much right to be here. She's their sister too." Now the littles swarmed him.

"How do we know it's Niccy?"

"Because, *tadpole*, the message said so." Pilto ducked the waterstream his sister blew at him. "When do we see her?"

Their questions filled the cavern, whirling in all directions.

Kel herded his young siblings into the meeting chamber where the elders were gathered.

Their bàbá smiled at their arrival. "I'm just about to give the report, and I'm glad you're here to receive it firsthand. A message has been caught, with the stated sender identified as Nica."

"Our Nica, Bàbá?" Pilto bobbed. "She's really back?"

"When can we see her? Does Ìyá know?" Chesnae swam somersaults around her father.

Daevu calmed them to focus on his quiet reply. "Yes, it is our Nica. No, she's not back, and Ìyá doesn't know yet. I'd like to give her something more than shifting tides. The message didn't come from any of the standard relays. We don't even know its origination point."

He cleared his voice to address the cavern. "A transport has been sent to retrieve our injured Guardian. He's almost recovered from his injuries. Perhaps this will help fill the gaps in his memory."

Kel clenched his jaw and kicked off into the center of the meeting bowl, startling the gathered elders. "Olomi have been disappearing since after the Breaking. When are we going to do something?"

"What would you have us do, Kel ti Daevu?" A faded Councillian, almost white with age, spoke. "Anyone who has ventured out of the water has not returned."

"Except one," Kel countered.

"Yes, our most experienced abovewater explorer"—another Councillian, this one bulging and mottled brown and gray, looked pointedly at Kel—"discovered a halfmoon after he left, free-floating, partially gutted, and barely alive."

"He left with another Guardian—"

"Hardly! That Guardian's cords were still green when they left. She had no real experience. He was a fool to take her above."

"No one else had any experience abovewater before the Breaking. And you wouldn't call him a fool to his face."

"It wouldn't matter if I had," the Councillian muttered under his breath. "He remembers nothing."

Daevu rose to hover above the meeting. "Councillians, Guardians, we all know that in the moons since the Breaking, many of our missing have not been found. And the reports of Olomi continuing to disappear after the Breaking are confirmed, with more as each moon passes. This steady attrition of our population had been unheard of before the Breaking, but no one has brought back a report of what we face. Until now. This communication, which we will assume is from Nica, a trained and sworn Guardian"–Daevu glanced sideways at the portly Councillian–"refers to a presence with hostile intent on the surface–but one that may be thwarted."

Guardians circled the bowl, pounding their staves on the rock in agreement.

"We have been forewarned," he declared, "and we must be forearmed. The water may have been divided, but the people of the water will not be. It is not our way to seek violence, but we will defend our brothers and sisters. We will find them, and we will bring them home."

The thunderous crescendo of drumming staves surged throughout the Deep. It was the sound of hope.

The dolphins were much faster than the tortoise litter he was accustomed to. The rush of current against his face was invigorating. But this reclining–chauffeured in a litter, no less–was agitating. He itched to travel freely.

"How long since you been in Foneesh?"

"Don't know." The moons had bled together. How long had he been in the healing shelter? He wouldn't know his own name if the healers hadn't told him. It hadn't even been a full moon since he had regained his voice.

They said he'd lost much blood, and most of his bones had been broken. But he only had the word of the healers on that. They'd kept him sedated while his body had mended. Whatever he had been told of his condition, it was clear from their emanations that he hadn't been expected to survive. Whispers of terrible trauma rippled in. Trauma attested to by nightmares that their strongest sedatives could not dull. They gave up trying to keep him from thrashing in his sleep. Any constraints sent him into a frenzy.

He hated this weakness of not being able to control his fear. He despaired at the hope in strangers' eyes when they visited him. And he felt helpless being asked about the Olomi he didn't remember.

A scarred but muscular Olomi with patches of auburn hair swam up, followed by a younger male with the same coloring, but without the scars. He pushed off, grateful to see them wait outside the litter. At least he was allowed to exit the transport in his own strength.

"Son, I am Daevu." The elder Olomi grasped him by the forearm. "You don't know how good it is to see you swimming on your own."

"I don't seem to know much, sir, but I have to agree."

"I'm Kel." The younger Olomi also clasped his arm. "I was, and hope to be, your second."

Jonnat allowed a faint smile to emerge. "That's the best offer I've had this tide."

... Not ready ... what does he hope to gain ... remind ... failure ... Nica ... lost ...

Whispered fragments drifted past Jonnat, bits of flotsam of doubt and fear. He knew he was the focus of their concern, but had no solid memory to provide an anchor. Except Kel. There was something ... *Do I truly remember him? Or do I just want to?* He was tired of trying to remember, but just as tired of giving up.

Without thinking, he surged up at an oncoming rush. Not a threat response, but definitely instinctive.

"Jonnat, it's you!"

"Jonn, are you here 'cause of Niccy?

"We missed you!"

The fry circled, darting at and around as they tossed their

questions at him. A little Olomi settled on his shoulder and played with his hair, while her brother tugged at his hand. Were they twins?

"Chesnae! Pilto! That's enough." The green elder called them into order. "You fry get home and clean up a little. Jonnat will join us for dinner."

Daevu? Do I know him? Those scars. How did he . . . Hints of heat and fear writhed under his conscious. Jonnat tried to catch them, but they slipped away like eels before he could grab hold. *Gone.* And now this Daevru was talking at him.

". . . right, you know. You have been missed."

Jonnat tried to focus on the words. If not that, the speaker. "Son?"

It was clear he was failing. "I beg forgiveness, Master Guardian. I must have . . ."

"Yes, your thoughts are elsewhere, and creating turmoil." The elder Guardian's gaze drifted to his clenched fists.

Embarrassed, Jonnat flexed his hands, blues deepening at the tension he'd revealed. "I'm not yet myself." *As if I know who that is.*

"Healing takes time, son, but trust me, it will come."

42

·· RESERVATIONS AND REVERSALS ··

DAEVU'S gaze lingered after Jonnat's wake.
"If Nica sent a message, why are we waiting?" Kel flashed
throughout the cavern, surging at the walls, banking furiously. His
frustration was almost overwhelming in the close quarters.

"We don't have a location yet." Daevu voiced calm tones,
despite his own inner tensions. "The message said there is a plan,
and to wait."

"But—but there must be something we can do." Kel's sputtering
propelled a flurry of bubbles.

"We can prepare. If this threat is what attacked Jonnat and
took Nica, it is not one we can take on without caution. Jonn was
one of our strongest, and he was most adapted to abovewater
environments. We need to be prepared to engage this threat on
solid ground. I need you to renew the training."

"I'd like to take Jonn."

"Do you think he can handle it?"

"I don't know, but he was once the best we had," Kel attested.

"Maybe this will remind him." Daevu's expression was sober.

Jonnat didn't know what to think. He didn't really remember this
Kel, but both the elder and the younger green Olomi said they
needed him. That he was an expert and knew the abovewater
regions better than anyone. Jonnat didn't know about any of this,

but if it would get him out of the recovery bay, he was all for it. He was crawling out of his skin like a molting crab.

He followed Kel to the edge of the water. Without a thought, Jonnat grabbed for his—

"Here." Kel handed him a strip of woven kelp fibers.

Jonnat frowned at the cloth. *This feels right.* "How did you know?"

"It's the first thing you taught me about abovewater exploration." Kel grinned. "And Jonn, don't forget to—"

"—blink." Jonnat finished, suddenly blinking involuntarily. "Why do I remember this?" He dipped the facewrap in the sea before winding it around his face.

"Probably because you drilled it into our heads incessantly." Kel wrapped his weave on the same way. "Ready to step out?"

The two emerged onto black and barren dry land. Jonnat stopped and searched the grounds, and then the surrounding area for any sign of activity.

"It's empty," Kel said. "I swam the perimeter a few times. Whatever these abovewater hostiles do, this doesn't seem to suit their purpose."

Jonnat looked around again. "There's not much to hide behind here. Everything is low." He stopped. Fragments were becoming whole again. "He carried her far from the water before he put her down."

"Who?" Kel asked.

"I followed until the sun sank fully." Jonnat stood perfectly still, gazing at the rocky surface. Words came back, as hesitantly as the memories. "After sunup, I followed again, and caught up with her by its peak. She was bound at the hands . . . jerked along on a tether. They stopped. That's when I signaled. We made a plan. It almost worked. But he was too strong. I—I failed her. I failed them."

Jonnat crushed the facewrap in his hands. His eyes flicked briefly to Kel's face. The greens, like the Head Guardian's, but also like . . . like . . . He snapped his head up. "Her name was Nica."

Kel's eyes widened and he nodded for Jonnat to continue.

"She . . . was trying to find . . ." Jonnat paced the black sands, brow furrowed in concentration. "Trying to find . . ." He stopped again. "Rissa. My dearheart." His eyes stung. "It's all come back. Nica. Rissa. Daevu—the lava, the burns. And the landwalker."

Kel burst out, "Who is this landwalker? What Olomi could do this?"

Jonnat grabbed Kel. "No. The landwalker wasn't Olomi—almost, but something else. No webbing. His color was solid, with no variegation. No gradation. Just a flat, dark sand color. Almost red." He closed his eyes, keeping his grip firm on Kel's arms, fighting to keep hold of the memory. "Tall. He was much taller than either of us. And strong. It was nothing to him to climb the landmount. He took us both on and relished it. He knew he would win, and he enjoyed besting us both."

Jonnat's eyes went to Kel's sheathed dagger. "I tried to help Nica escape and had to stab him. But then he turned the blade on me . . . I remember falling." Jonnat raised his gaze to meet Kel's eye. "Air flows so fast. Faster than any dive."

Kel scuffed at the black sand. Even out of the Deep, his anger was palpable.

"I failed you, Kel. I failed you and your family. Twice over I've failed you all."

"No!" Kel's striations were darker than the deepest green. He sank onto his haunches and buried his face in his hands. "No, Jonnat. You didn't fail. I did. I should have gone with her. With both of you. She knew there was something more. I wouldn't believe her. If I had . . . maybe it would have ended differently. Maybe we wouldn't have lost her too."

"How long?"

Kel raised his face, his brow knotted with pain and confusion.

Jonnat repeated, "How long has it been? Since I left—or since I was found?"

"Close to ten moons. They didn't think you would ever wake."

Jonnat crouched down next to Kel. "That's how long Nica has been captive. If we've received word from her, then there may be hope for Rissa too." He scooped up a handful of sand. "We need to prepare to fight here. To build our strength on dry land. They took the fight for our seas out of the water, but we will win it on the land."

43

NICA hugged the basket, wishing the rain wasn't so heavy. The essence of true water dissipated with every step. Heading back, she hesitated at the edge of the agri-pod. A chill rode her dorsal and she shook her head. *No. Not going that way. Not this tide.*

The long way around, skirting the perimeter of the grounds, was neither scenic nor expeditious, but if she was going to avoid the conflict she'd encountered that morning . . . At least that was the plan. As she followed the path, it wound near the front gates, and the sound of a whip and an outcry of pain greeted her.

TAL-alph, covered in clothing that shielded her from the rain, was cracking her whip over the back of an Olomi near the barrier.

"Clear. The. Gate!" TAL's enforcer punctuated each word with a strike.

Nica was horrified but could not tear her gaze away. The tides of rain had soaked the remains that TAL kept at the entrance to his compound. Electricity was arcing from the top of the fence to the bottom, where Olomi bodies and bones were piled against the gate.

The dark, spotted worker hesitated before the heap, despite the alpha's bullying. The remains included a new body, and the heap sputtered and crackled. It was clear that he did not want to suffer the same fate.

"Either clear the pile, or you will join it!"

Clearly desperate, the Olomi searched for something to move the soaked bodies and bones from the lethal entryway. His gaze landed on an old femur bone that scavengers had picked clean.

Separated from the main pile of sparking debris, he kicked it further away, and tapped it gingerly. Relieved to not be flung into convulsions, he grasped the femur and began poking at the pile. Tentative at first, but then with more confidence, and despite his lashed back, he began pushing remains at the edges away from the mass touching the gate. Little by little, the sparking and crackling died down, until he separated the last soaked pile of body parts from the electric barrier with a final *pop.*

Ashen-faced despite the soaking rain, the Olomi turned to TAL-alph to be directed to his next job. A groan came from the pile. It was the new body, apparently still alive.

"May I take TAL-nu to medical?"

"He's still alive? I suppose so. Drop him there and get back to your pod."

Trying to hoist his unconscious podmate over his shoulders, the smaller Olomi struggled toward the medical buildings. Nica realized she had already tarried too long. Though she had some protection due to her condition, TAL-alph had a vindictive streak. Luckily, the alpha appeared to be busy inspecting the gates, making sure the remains no longer posed a threat to security, and Nica ducked away from the entrance.

"TAL-eta!"

Not lucky enough. Nica set her face and turned. "Yes, TAL-alph?"

"You have time to waste?"

"Yes, I mean, no. I am sorry."

"Assist TAL-iota."

The spotted, inky-black Olomi shot Nica an apologetic but thankful look. His co-worker, all tan and black and blue markings, was much taller than he, and nothing but dead weight right now. Iota slid his co-worker's body off his back, draping a limp arm across his own shoulders. Nica took the other arm and stretched it over hers. The rain-soaked body was difficult to keep a hold on, and with a jolt, Nica realized that she hadn't used her denticles since before her capture. She flexed her palm, and just as she'd done in the Deep, dermal projections rose, allowing her a firm grasp on the Olomi's slick hide.

She nudged the body to get TAL-iota's attention. "Flex your palms," she whispered.

A sheepish look came to his face as he did so. "I can't believe I didn't think of that."

"I'd forgotten as well. I think we have forgotten a lot."

It was a little cumbersome to manage both the body and the basket with samples, but she hooked the handles through her other arm and used it for balance as they headed back to the medical building. As they half dragged, half carried TAL-nu, Nica probed for information.

"Why was TAL-alph willing to risk losing you workers to clear the gate?"

TAL-iota glanced around before answering. "Because she was worried about losing them all."

"All? How?"

"The rain has been causing problems with the gate. If it stops shocking—killing anyone who touches it—how many of our people do you think would try and escape?"

Trying not to sound too hopeful, Nica dared ask, "Do you think it could have? Broken the gate?"

"I'm sure TAL-alph thought it would, and she only takes her orders from EC-TAL. So, you tell me."

Interesting, Nica thought. She was starting to pant from the exertion. "How did you avoid getting knocked out, like Nu?"

"TAL-nu was too afraid of TAL-alph, and not afraid enough for himself. One crack of her whip and he grabbed for the closest body." The Olomi stopped to catch his breath. "As it turns out, he became the closest body."

They shifted the dead weight draped across their backs, refreshing their latch on his dorsal and arms, before they continued toward the medical building.

Nica grunted despite the repositioning. "He's lucky he's still alive."

"I guess so. I don't know how lucky any of us are here. But while there is life, there's still hope, I figure."

"I like that, Iota. I think you're right, and I think TAL-nu will be thankful."

Iota huffed, but his mouth curved as he hoisted TAL-nu up to MO-ASHE's main entrance. ASHE-delt, the blue sentry, was still there, soaking in the rain.

"Back again?" He peered at Nica.

"Yes," she said, struggling to keep up her hold on TAL-nu. "He's had an accident by the electrified gate, and TAL-alph sent us."

"You're a regular here?" Iota sounded surprised. "This place gives me bad feelings."

"It's a long story, but you aren't wrong."

They headed right, down the hall for the exam cells, and Nica slipped a smile at Girac. Appearing to be all business, he still snuck in a wink as he assumed her part of the weight.

"You will accompany us until MO-ASHE or I dismiss you."

The Olomi carried their fallen brother further down the hallway than Nica's usual destination. As they took TAL-nu to a back room, Nica, thankful for her Guardian training, kept track of the details, adding them to her mental map. The shape of a crab on its back came to mind, with the legs being hallways, and the body the lower hydro-processing area.

I think I'd prefer the smell of a dead crab to these hallways. But it could be worse, I could be the crab.

Noting the sections seemed to mirror each other, she was able to complete the map pieces in her memory.

Once the unconscious Olomi was settled, they waited in silence. Nica wondered if she had missed the midmeal. Rain clouds continued to hide the sun, making it difficult to gauge the passage of time, but Nica's stomach began to make it clear that she had not eaten. Her discomfort grew, and her stomach began to rumble at random.

"I think I need to go back to my pod," she said. "Does MO-ASHE really need me to stay here?"

"Does MO-ASHE really need who to stay?"

Fear flashed across their faces at the Medical Officer's sharp tone, and they all straightened and stood at attention.

Her silent approach unnerved them all, as did the probing expression turned on each one of them.

"ASHE-tau. Report."

Girac, standing tall, with his eyes forward, delivered his succinct understanding of the situation.

"The patient was electrocuted but removed from the wall. TAL-alph ordered TAL-iota and TAL-eta to bring him here."

"TAL-alph ordered one of my subjects to carry this?" MO-ASHE's pale eyes glittered icily. She turned to Nica. "Did you inform her that you are not to be engaging in any risk-taking activity?"

Nica quailed under MO-ASHE's harsh scrutiny. "Er, no, I haven't received any instructions about that. But if I hadn't obeyed . . ."

Nica's voice trailed as the clear implication of TAL-alph's retribution didn't need to be voiced. Her stomach, on the other hand, having no respect for its audience, let loose with another loud, gurgling rumble. All strength and color drained from Nica as her body betrayed her.

"And how long has it been since your last meal?"

What should have been an innocuous inquiry made her knees quake. She knew MO-ASHE would be further angered at the answer.

"Since first meal, MO-ASHE."

Crack!

The MO slammed the pad in her hand against the stoneskin table, startling everyone in the room, except the still-unconscious patient.

She hissed to her guard through clenched teeth. "Take her to the OB exam room. I will finish here."

"And bring her a meal ration!" MO-ASHE shouted after them as Girac guided his charge out of the door. It wasn't until they were past the hallway and had turned down toward the exam section, that Nica took in a slow shuddering breath.

Grasping Girac's arm, she stopped him. "Please."

"Can you stand?" His voice and eyes were full of concern.

"Yes. I just need a moment to breathe."

Closing her eyes and taking a few deep breaths, Nica felt her heart slow down a little. "Okay. I'm better."

"Should I carry you?" Girac's face was still marked with concern.

"No, that's not necessary. I just needed a moment."

They continued down the hallway, and Girac left her in the company of one of the medical attendants as he went in search of food. He had no sooner returned, when MO-ASHE entered behind him, noting that her orders had been followed. Dismissing him with a nod, she turned to the attendant who was preparing the sleeping medicine.

"That won't be necessary."

"But Mistress MO-ASHE, she is not yet seda—"

MO-ASHE's hand flashed, and the medic crumpled to the floor. "Any other objections?"

The Olomi whimpered, shaking her head as she scooted out of reach.

Turning back, MO-ASHE addressed her patient coolly. "I assume you are not an idiot, although I can't say the same for all of your species. You do realize by now that you are pregnant, correct?"

"Yes, MO-ASHE."

The MO drew closer. "The safety of this embryo is of utmost importance. Nothing can compromise this. Am I clear?"

"Yes, MO-ASHE."

"You will not skip meals and you will not carry unreasonable weights." She came even nearer, her voice increasingly quiet, yet menacing, as her eyes bore into Nica.

"Yes, MO-ASHE."

"If you fail to safeguard this child, there will be severe consequences."

"Yes, MO-ASHE." It took every bit of self-control Nica could muster to remain still as she stared at her own reflection in the pupils of the medical officer's unblinking eyes.

"Log." MO-ASHE held her hand out to the side, her gaze still locked on Nica.

Uncertain of the expected response, Nica flicked her eyes to the instrument tray, catching sight of the Olomi medic scrambling to deliver the pad into her mistress's hand.

"Now, what is your account of the incident that brought TAL"—she glanced at her notes—"TAL-nu here?"

"He was not conscious when I passed. TAL-iota was instructed to clear the debris from the barrier, and when he finished, we heard TAL-nu groaning."

"It was correct that TAL-alph sent him to me—aquans this strong are difficult to replace. However, she should not have pressed you into service." Her lips formed a thin, compressed line, and she inhaled sharply through her nose. "I will address this. Return in two weeks. Dismissed."

Nica understood now why Pescha had been so upset after her visit. It was clear that, while MO-ASHE was highly invested in the welfare of the offspring, her own life was of little value if anything went wrong.

How do you separate the life of a mother from that of her fry? How can she prize one so highly, and threaten the other in the same breath?

How odd to have the same goal as MO-ASHE—to protect her spawn. But it was one she could live with, for now.

Settling her basket on her hip, Nica headed back for the kitchen-pod, this time avoiding both the agri-pod area and the entrance. She had missed her shift to serve TAL's meal, but did not mind avoiding TAL-alph for now. She had much to process, and the continuing rain was a comfort. She would sleep well tonight.

44

·· FALLOUT ··

*S*LAM!

The sound reverberated along the halls of EC-TAL's work sanctum. He strode out of his office in time to see the mud-colored, and blessedly mute, aquana who'd been scrubbing near his entryway, holding tightly to her bucket. Her eyes widened as its sloshed contents oozed along the floor, joining the new puddle forming at his threshold.

"Where is she?" MO-ASHE stood in his entryway, dripping from head to toe.

His beta, whose duty it was to answer the door, was motionless, clearly unequipped to man his post in the face of this fury. *But then, he clearly isn't a man.* EC-TAL allowed a twist on one side of his mouth.

Wind-blown and rain-soaked, with a tangle of black hair surrounding her face, MO-ASHE vented her fury at the aquans.

"Where . . ." Her soaked raincap hit the door with a *splat* and slid down till it puddled on the hard floor.

"Is . . ." MO-ASHE shrugged off her cloak, dropping it to the ground.

"She?" Foot gear flew off in the direction of the housekeeper, still frozen at her bucket.

The two exchanged panicked looks. TAL-beta stammered, "W-w-where is who, MO-ASHE?"

"Slimy uncivilized fools." She grit the words through her teeth. She stormed past EC-TAL and into his office, leaving soggy footprints from one sock that had gotten soaked.

"What is the problem?" EC-TAL leaned against the doorframe, watching in casual indifference.

"It's bad enough to be stuck here on this cesspool of a planet, with no weather control whatsoever, let alone proper transportation, forced to conduct research as if our lives depend on it, which, for your information, it does"–MO-ASHE paused long enough to glare at him, then continued with her tirade–"with these moronic *Aqua Sapiens* for assistants, *and* inadequate equipment. And you haven't exactly been showering me with viable subjects, leaving me forced to work with subpar specimens, let alone we have no backup plan whatsoever, so that if for any reason our experiment fails, we are lost and stuck here." She refueled with a breath. "But I actually manage to pull off a miracle and get something to work and we have a chance of actually not going extinct in the Back End of Nowhere despite the ridiculous hostility from these savages who should appreciate the fact that they no longer have to live in their own urine and have a chance to progress as a real civilization." Punctuating with yet another sharp intake of air, MO-ASHE went on, "but your slimy, yellow assistant, who parades around as if she were one of us, had the audacity to put one of my subjects at risk, one out of two, mind you, that we have a chance to ensure the future of what's left of our species, and your alpha dared to put it to labor that might have caused a miscarriage and set me back months, *and* that's only if I could find another viable candidate. That"–she took one last breath to finish–"is the problem."

"Oh. I thought it had something to do with me." EC-TAL cocked one eyebrow at his counterpart as he leisurely straightened. "I'll send the alpha over and you can deal with it. Just don't do any permanent damage. It took me months to train properly. I'd hate to have to start over."

He pushed a button on his desk, summoning his beta. As if it were standing just outside the door, the aquan entered, edging around MO-ASHE to bow before TAL.

"Fetch TAL-alph, immediately."

"Yes, EC-TAL." The gray and silver ribbed aquan bowed once again, hurrying out.

EC-TAL busied himself at his desk, ignoring the still-dripping fury that was MO-ASHE.

Beta must have run, and pressed TAL-alph to do the same, because both were out of breath when they returned.

The yellow aquana bowed before him. "How may I serve you, Master?"

"MO-ASHE has business to discuss with you." With that, he left the room.

"Yes, Mistress?" TAL-alph bowed uncertainly.

"Your whip, aquan." MO-ASHE held out her hand.

The yellow aquana maintained her bow, presenting the whip with both hands.

"You put a subject of mine at risk, presuming to exercise authority over her."

The alpha's hands, still extended, began to tremble. "But MO-ASHE, I would not dare to interfere with any members of your household." She fell to the floor, forehead to the ground before MO-ASHE. "Am I to be replaced?"

"No," MO-ASHE released her words slowly, "but you will not forget."

TAL-alph's proximity to MO-ASHE's feet was tempting, and her leg twitched. She wanted to kick the yellow square in the face—but checked herself. Instead, she shook out the whip, cracked it in the air with expertise, and began to flay the yellow aquana.

"All," *crack* "medical," *crack* "subjects," *crack* "are," *crack* "under," *crack* "my," *crack* "jurisdiction," *crack* "no," *crack* "matter," *crack* "what," *crack* "their," *crack* "designation!"

Turning over the gasping aquana with her foot, MO-ASHE re-coiled the whip and lowered onto her haunches. She pushed the alpha's cheek with the handle until its eyes met hers. "I trust I have made myself clear."

She stood and tossed the whip on the aquana's face muttering, "Be thankful I'm not wearing boots."

EC-TAL strode out of the room, enraged that MO-ASHE had disturbed his workplace over something that an aquan had done. He refused, however, to give her the satisfaction of knowing how furious he was. But somebody was going to pay.

Opening his door to a curtain of pelting rain did nothing to improve the Delphim's temper. Slamming it shut, TAL bellowed, *"Beta!"*

The silver and gray household attendant was already in motion. Anticipating TAL's needs, Beta had waterproof gear in hand to protect him from the rain he despised so much.

"When is this cursed rain going to stop? I've half a mind to put all our resources toward weather satellites," EC-TAL groused as he put on the gear. His aquan knew better than to offer any opinion or recommendation unless specifically directed to speak. There were others, less wary, who'd lost their tongues that way. Sufficiently shielded from precipitation, TAL stormed out, turning toward the fields.

A haphazard array of poles, tarps, and ropes greeted him. The tangled mess appeared to be an attempt to shield his plants, but swollen pockets of collected water threatened to collapse the entire rigging. He glared at the nearest worker. "What exactly do you think you are doing here? Who is responsible for this?"

"I-I'll get him." The flustered worker stammered before he scurried off to fetch the supervisor.

A blue-banded aquan hurried out. "Expedition Commander TAL! What a surprise. Let me show the improvements I've made since replacing the last supervisor."

TAL stalked around the perimeter of his covered fields until he found a weakness in the defenses. Unaccounted-for water was making its way to the tender shoots. Grabbing the soon-to-be ex-supervisor by the neck, he shoved the aquan's face at the offending connector, dripping from an overlap onto a vibrant plant.

"How are we supposed to measure the amount of water this plant is receiving?" TAL growled. "If you can't handle this job, I'll find someone who will!"

Maintaining his hold on the squirming aquan, TAL strode out of the agricultural sector, dragging the blue-banded aquan through the mud until he arrived at the gates. The constant wind and rains had continued to deposit debris along the gate, triggering connections that buzzed and fizzled along the perimeter of the fence.

"Do you think you will be able to handle these plants?" Throwing him down near the base of the fence, TAL grinned at the aquan's expression as he scrabbled back from the fence, flinching at every random spark. *Let the rain be a problem for them for once.*

"I want this fence cleared of all debris or you will be part of it." He glared down at the fearful aquan. "There is no room for more failure."

45

·· CONSEQUENCES ··

"STOP stepping on my heels!" Nica whispered. "Please excuse TAL-tau. Dark makes it . . ."

"Impossible?" Nica was exasperated at the transfer. She felt a little bad about how often the brown and orange ribbed Olomi got on her nerves, and it wasn't the Olomi's fault that the Delphim that had first taken her spoke a different dialect, but—

"Ow! For such a short Olomi, you pack a lot of power into your step," Nica said, wincing as she rubbed her well-trodden heel.

She tried to reset her attitude inside the kitchen. Her embarrassed podmate was ribbed in three colors now instead of just the two.

"Hey!" Nica banked into a counter, barely avoiding another collision. "Watch where you're going! It's not even dark here!" *This would be so much easier with Pescha. But TAL is so out of sorts, the last thing we need is her huffing and wincing. It's no wonder TRE-CH traded this one to EC-TAL.*

"Am I going to have to separate you two?" Zeta grumbled as she started organizing the team's efforts in TAL's kitchen.

"No, ma'am," both Olomi chorused with embarrassment.

"The plan is to get in and out with as little tension as possible. Understand?"

They nodded. Quiet, eyes down, hands folded as she lined them up. Chloe, then Nica.

Not the soup. Not the soup. Don't give her the soup.

TAL-zeta hefted the steaming soup tureen and raised her eyebrow at Nica's gasp. "Is there a problem, TAL-eta?"

Now Nica could feel her own color rising. "No, ma'am."

"Then mind your own business." Her tone squelched any muttering. "TAL-tau, take the bread. TAL-eta, vegetables."

Chastened, Nica focused on her own trayful of vegetables, careful to keep the sauce from slopping out of their bowls.

"Apologies. So much." TAL-tau twisted to face her, worry creasing her brow. "Please forgive."

"Fine. Forgiven." Nica hissed. "Just watch where you're going."

The team entered the dining room, TAL-zeta in the lead. Nica held her breath as Chloe held her tray before TAL, releasing it with relief once the rookie server passed behind the EC.

Chloe turned to flash a smile of triumph. Time seemed to slow down to a trickle as Nica watched in horror.

Chloe's tunic catching the back of TAL's chair. Chloe reaching to free it with one hand.

Her tray, mostly but not completely empty, tipping.

The platter sliding off.

The vain attempt to stop it from falling. Knocking the dish toward the table. The bread platter landing on the edge of TAL's soup bowl.

A roar erupted as TAL shoved back from the table, too late to avoid the searing liquid that doused him from chest to knees.

Towering over the trembling Olomi, TAL raised his arm in a position Nica knew too well. She cried out as he loosed his rage against Chloe, gasping as his backhand drove the brown-and-orange Olomi into the wall.

Frozen in place, Nica's eyes followed Chloe as she crumpled against the stoneskin wall, a red smear following her head as she slowly slid down.

TAL roared again, "*Beta!* Clothes!" then stormed out of the room.

Released from paralysis by TAL's exit, Nica and Zeta rushed to Chloe's side. Her eyes stared past them, and her hands lay limp in theirs. A sound escaped. Nica put her ear close to the dying Olomi's mouth.

"Master . . . TRE-CH . . . wrong . . . TAL . . . hit . . . hard . . . er."

46

"WHAT ..." The words lodged in Nica's throat, swelling, threatening to choke her. "What do we . . ."

Zeta massaged her knuckles, kneading the scarred webbing in silence. Her gaze landed on Nica, but its focus was fixed elsewhere.

I've seen this before. Nica swallowed her panic.

"What do we do with her?" It was almost a whisper. She was measuring the elder Olomi as best she could abovewater, noting her breath-spacing and color. *Please, Zeta, I can't lose you. Not like this—not like Ìyá.*

Several slow breaths passed before Zeta's eyes moved to meet Nica's. "This is the first loss . . . death . . . in my pod."

Her voice faltered, but her grip on Nica's hands was firm. "If TAL returns, go into the kitchen and stay there. There's little you can do for our sister at this point. I'll see about something to wrap her in."

Nica sat by Chloe, listening for Zeta or TAL. She wanted to smooth her hair, but there was so much blood.

I shouldn't have been impatient with you. If I hadn't nagged you about following on my heels . . . Maybe I could've gone first. Maybe you wouldn't have turned. Maybe you might still be alive . . .

Tears trickled down Nica's face, dropping onto the lifeless hand she cradled. Saline drops hydrated blue freckles scattered across strips of orange as Chloe's last minutes flickered across Nica's thoughts, dancing like shadows filtered by ever-moving waves. Sorrow racked her body and she couldn't bear to breathe.

Zeta's face darkened when she saw her. "You need to calm

yourself. This isn't good for you or for the baby. And if TAL returns and sees you in this state, who knows what he'll do. Please," she implored, "get a hold of yourself."

"It's all . . . my fault. If I hadn't been so frustrated . . . maybe she wou–" Nica could hardly get the words out.

Zeta grabbed Nica and looked into her eyes. "You stop right now. You didn't cause this, and there's nothing you could have done. We are living under great evil and do what we must to survive, but you are not responsible for this terrible thing."

Nica took great gulping breaths to stop the stream. Finally, wrapped in Zeta's arms, the shudders eased into hiccups, and then deep slow breaths as Nica closed her eyes and tried to accept the truth of Zeta's words.

By the time her crying stopped, TAL-mu, the housekeeper, had wrapped Chloe's body in a large cloth and was almost done cleaning up the blood.

"I'm so sorry. I should have . . . I wasn't any help." Waves of self-recrimination threatened to overwhelm her once again.

The tan Olomi just shook her speckled head and waved her off, continuing to scrub. She gestured at Zeta, then frowned, jerking her head in the direction of the kitchen.

"Yes, you're right," TAL-zeta said. "We'll clear out. Be safe."

The housekeeper nodded and went back to work, glancing at the door frequently, wary of TAL's return. Silent as their tongueless sister, Zeta and Nica hefted the bundle containing Chloe and made their way through the kitchen exit.

Zeta addressed the food-pod as they gathered around Chloe. "We are limited in how we can honor our sister here on land. At home, we could release her to the Deep, where she would become one with the water, and with us. But here, there is no release. And if we do not take care of her ourselves, we know that her life will not be honored by our captors. This is the furthest thing from our traditions, but we are just as far removed from them.

"We will burn our sister's body and scatter her ashes to the wind. Perhaps she will find her way back to the water. Perhaps she will find her way home." Despite scattered gasps and muffled sobs, no one protested. TAL-zeta laid her hands on the wrapped body and blessed it. "Our dear sister TAL-tau, from the Water you have come, to the Water may you return."

The pod gathered around her murmured, "From the Water you have come. To the Water, may you return." Once the Olomi paid their respects, Chloe's wrapped body was added to the great waste-fire outside the food-pod, to burn until no trace was left.

47

·· G R O U N D E D ··

"**T**AL-ETA!"
Zeta's stick landed on Nica's mat with a startling *crack!*
Nica's head bobbed up—eyes wide.

"Those beans look done." Zeta grimaced at the pasty mess radiating from the stone basin.

Thousands of barbs seemed to shoot through her legs when Nica released the rough-hewn vessel in her lap. She scooted back to survey the damage. Bean pieces and paste were strewn across her mat.

"Mash a little less . . . vigorously," Zeta muttered. "More will stay in the bowl."

She'd failed again. "Do you desire me to clean this up now, or after I've finished preparing this batch?" She could not hide the quaver in her voice.

"What I desire"—Zeta dumped a fresh supply of shelled beans onto the spattered mat and whispered—"is for you to pull yourself together. You cannot afford to appear unstable."

She knew Zeta's words were true, but Nica's heart continued to ache. Her soul was desperate for a holdfast, but found none. There was no relief, no respite. Only shame, swirling with guilt that threatened to engulf her.

What if she hadn't made such a big deal about Chloe being clumsy?
Why had she been unkind?
What if Chloe hadn't gone first?
What if . . .
Nica looked down. The beans were pulverized—again.

Zeta sighed and gently pried the pestle from her grasp. "Perhaps you need a different task. The new crop at agri-pod—"

Blanching at the thought of facing that supervisor, Nica shook her head.

"Well, you're not due for a medical appointment"—she hobbled to the storage area, beckoning Nica to follow—"and TAL doesn't leave until tomorrow."

Lashed shelves towered over Zeta's slight form. The bindings squeaked and creaked as she shuffled between them. She rummaged through the supplies, tipping this basket and pulling out another from the lower levels. Nica trailed behind, still hugging the rough bowl against her growing belly.

Zeta knelt, then pulled herself up with a groan.

"Here." She produced several containers from the bottom shelf and shoved them at Nica.

"Go to hydro-processing and fetch some more nigari. We need to increase production. All this rain has increased appetites, even if it's just for those grainy protein cubes."

Nica gave a tremulous nod.

"Now go clean yourself up. You can't be seen in such a state."

"Ẹ ṣe, Ìyágba."

"You can thank me by bringing the nigari, child. And watch your language."

Skirting the perimeter of the compound allowed Nica to avoid the agri-pod. Alert for any sign of TAL or his alpha, she slipped past the gates and excavation sites they frequently inspected. Wielding her basket as a shield, she shifted it from side to side, trying to block the visual inquiries directed her way. Wary, especially as she approached MO-ASHE's entry, Nica kept her eyes trained on the basket and its contents, hoping the guard would not be bothered to hassle her as she requested entrance.

Unable to resist, she paused inside the doors and shot a hopeful glance toward medical. Swallowing disappointment, she headed the other way to hydro-processing. ASHE-phi's warm greeting both comforted and surprised Nica. "Is Mu around?" she whispered, glancing around the room.

"No. We're clear, but to what do I owe this unexpected visit?"

"Zeta sent me to fetch more nigari, but I think she wanted to get me out of the pod." Nica began to share the news of Chloe's death.

ASHE-phi listened in silence while she poured out her heart, the lines in his face deepening as she explained how her actions and attitude contributed to it. His face was grave, the usual emanations of peace and compassion absent. "You must listen. There was nothing you could have done. None of this was your fault. This is the evil of our captors. Do not let their actions tie you in knots."

"But, what if I—"

"No! Stop." He put out his hand. "Do you think I wanted my wife to be taken? To be branded? Don't you think I ask myself a thousand times why I chose to travel to the shore that sun? Was it my fault that TAL trapped us? That he nearly killed me?"

His voice gentled. "I would give anything to not have her here, to not have her suffer as a slave, to not have her threatened by the likes of EC-TAL and MO-ASHE, and worse, even our own. I would give my life for her to be freed, but my death won't accomplish that. At least not yet. We are not responsible for the evil that others do, but we will not be subject to them forever. Because of you, we are making plans to leave this prison. Do not forget this."

Nica took in a shaky breath. "I will try."

"Now what is the excuse that Zeta had for you?"

Nica sniffled and wiped the last of the tears from her eyes. "I almost forgot! She wants more nigari."

"Well, let's take care of that!"

They worked the sediment. Long, smooth-handled rakes pulling at the slurry, separating the minerals present, leaving that which was to come. Only the sound of wooden teeth skritching softly across mineral interrupted the silence. Nica etched patterns in the wide drying pan, the process washing over her thoughts, soothing the turmoil within her. After they had gathered what was needed, Nica looked around, conscious of who might be near—of who might hear.

"ASHE-phi, what do you know about TAL-iota?"

48

M UD cushioned Nica's steps, soft and warm, caressing her feet as the moist earth clung to her. Memories of harvesting grass for the gentle manatees floated forward in her thoughts, gently guiding her to the deepest puddles. She paused a moment, closing her eyes, reluctant to surrender the tenuous connection. But this extracted bit of contentment dissipated as she approached the well. There should have been at least three workers at the crank. The landing was deserted.

Her basket creaked under the increasing pressure of her grip, due not to the absence of Olomi at their post, but the echoes of laughter drifting up from the well.

At the sound, her pores flared, alert for threat signals that were not present to wash over her. Surely no one was foolish enough to attract attention in this treacherous domain—but that laughter was sure to do it.

She edged to the opening and peered in. "Is anyone in there?"

She heard splashing, and then loud shushing.

"*Wo*," she called again softly. "Are you safe down there?" No answer. She tried again. "You'd better swim straight before TAL-alph catches you fooling around."

A voice snickered, "I don't think that alpha is going to catch anyone for a while."

Splashing echoed up the walls, and a brown-striped worker clambered up the knotted rope. Pulling on the winch, he swung his legs over the mouth of the stone wall and perched there.

"Sister, you need to take care of yourself. We be fine down here, and nobody need to mind our business. The rain is keeping our well full, and we are inspecting it thoroughly." He gave a wink and a grin.

"What about TAL-alph?" Nica persisted.

"Oh—she's not going to be climbing down here." He laughed and then swung himself down on the rope faster than she could blink.

Must be nice. Nica left, shaking her head. She worried at the foolish bravado of the well-diggers. A shudder ran down her dorsal at the thought of TAL or his alpha catching them.

An example would be made, just like . . . Chloe. But Chloe was different. She made a mistake and was just . . . Did TAL even know which one of us he killed? Did it matter to him? Do any of our lives matter to EC-TAL or MO-ASHE?

Revulsion churned in her chest at the memory of Chloe's eyes dimming, the blood following her down the wall, the smell of her pyre. Nica's stomach roiled, and she ducked behind a building, retching violently. Sliding to the ground, she buried her head in her lap. With no one to threaten, console, or reason with her, she was free to pour out her despair—shielded and comforted by the falling rain. She lifted her eyes to the clouds, receiving the steady downpour as it washed away the evidence of her grief.

"Thank you," she whispered, strengthened by the water's embrace. *One more moon.*

Rising to her feet, Nica shook off the debris clinging to her wrappings and moved to her next destination, focused on her purpose. Still keeping an eye out for TAL or his alpha, Nica walked the perimeter of the compound, until she reached the gate. She scanned the crew clearing it.

"TAL-iota!"

The spotted, black Olomi waved cheerfully at her. Giving a few words to his crew, he dropped the stick he'd been using and headed over.

"What brings you here?"

"I had a couple questions and wondered if you could take your meal later this tide."

"Is it about Nu? Have you heard anything? We haven't gotten any word from medical."

"No. I haven't heard anything, but I have some things to discuss with you."

"Sounds interesting. I'll come with last shift."

"Thank you."

Nica was grateful that he didn't have more questions that she'd have to avoid in front of others.

"*Ipanu!*" A familiar voice jeered from the crew at the wall.

Nica froze.

He's not supposed to be here.

She'd avoided agri-pod areas throughout this sun. Why Xi? Why did that supervisor have to cross her path here?

Don't react.

For once, she was glad to be out of the Deep. Here, the shame she felt was private, hers alone to feel and bear.

Ignore him.

She kept her eyes on the path and her back to the gates, and walked away, trying to slow the green rising in her cheeks.

Iota's voice cut through the rushing in her ears. "You're not in charge of agri-pod anymore. You're not in charge of anything. Here, we show respect. Do you understand?"

TAL-xi's answer was barely a grunt.

"I didn't hear you," TAL-iota pressed.

"Yes, supervisor."

Nica's steps became a little more buoyant.

49

ZETA bustled past. The crew with her was small, but Nica was in no shape to serve at TAL's table. Just the thought of entering that building churned up the visions she'd tried to scrub from her mind.

Blood and brown hair mingled, trailing down the wall. The bewildered look in Chloe's eyes before their light faded. Orange ribbing fading against the brown scars on her hand as death released her grip.

She gripped the serving frame to steady herself and clung to the anonymity afforded by the thin, gaseous atmosphere. She had grown adept at hiding fear and hope alike.

It was almost eventide. Her hands darted about her station, preparing for the first wave of weary Olomi, grateful for the mindlessness of the serving line. Scooping food onto platters required no mental energy and wouldn't distract her from the coalescing plans. Pescha, who shared volumes with a fleeting look and unspoken camaraderie, was absent, directing replenishment from inside Zeta's station where she could be comfortable. But Nica had no time for whispered confidences. She had less than two moons to sort out how and with whom she could plan an—

Dusty hands grabbed at a platter.

Without a thought, she slapped the culprit's wrist, mid-trespass. "*Wobi!* Look here, we're not serving yet. There are rules. You come with your pod."

"Not me . . . TAL-alph . . . requires . . . broth." The young Olomi could barely stammer out the words.

Her heart dropped. Once again, she had lashed out against an Olomi. It was one of the new captures. The poor fry hadn't even been grounded a full moon and his bright blues had drained to almost gray—except for the angry welt that crossed his face from temple to lip. It was clear that TAL-alph had chosen to make an impression on the boy, dispatching him with more than just her usual bullying and threats.

How could we abuse our own people—especially a juvenile. She swallowed at the thought of her own quick wrist slap.

Yet, she couldn't help but wonder what it would be like for TAL-alph to be afraid for her life. To cower at the hands of an Olomi.

But TAL-alph is not her true name. It's just the designation our oppressors have put upon her. How completely has this Olomi embraced the lie as her identity?

"Here." Nica placed a cooled tuber in his hand. "Don't worry, I will help. What does TAL-alph require aside from the broth?"

"That juvie'd best slow down." Nica waddled after him as he dashed ahead, picking her way through the puddles.

He looked and ran back when he saw she was lagging. "Please . . . faster . . ."

"You're not the one carrying the food. I cannot move more quickly."

"But TAL-alph is already very angry." He grabbed hold of her tunic, trying to pull her along.

Exasperated, she stopped. "And what will her mood be if I spill her meal?"

Any remaining vestige of color left his face at her reproach. He let go of the cloth and trudged forward until he stopped at the agri-pod supervisor building.

Makes sense her quarters are here. Agri-pod is TAL's primary focus. He'd want TAL-alph's attention on it.

Hesitating at the entrance, the fry put a hand on the door. "You need to be quiet. She doesn't want any noise." His eyes darted to her face. "And it's dark. Real dark in there. You need to be careful. If you drop something—she'll get mad. Real mad."

"You get the door, and I'll take it from there."

Tilting her head for one last spray from the heavens, Nica went in.

It *was* dark. But no more so than TAL's hallways. She waited for her eyes to adjust as she had in TAL's quarters.

The first door had agri-pod's symbol carved on the post. She paused, considering who occupied that room now. Across the hall, excavation was etched on the door. Who might be their pod supervisor? That brown Olomi with the white stripes? What was the symbol on his tunic? *You're just stalling now, Nica.*

A few paces further, at the end of the narrow hallway, was the last door, marked *Alpha*.

Steeling herself, Nica knocked softly.

"Enter."

The alpha's voice sounded raspier than usual. Nica pushed the door open and stepped in.

"You."

Nica faltered, wondering how to proceed. "Where would you like me to serve your meal?"

"As if . . . you haven't"—*wheeze*—"done enough." TAL-alph's voice trembled, full of venom, even as she labored to speak. "Bring it . . . to the table."

Squinting, Nica made out the small table next to a raised pallet frame. She lowered her tray onto it and began to ladle out the broth. As she set down the bowl, TAL-alph grabbed her, digging into her forearm with bony, yellowed fingers.

"You won't be carrying a child forever." Her rasping voice crackled into a cough. "Then what protection will you have?"

The hand used to wield a whip with terrifying force dropped weakly back onto the bed.

"Leave. Send in the boy."

Nica scrambled back, stumbling to the exit.

"She—she's ready for you."

The boy gulped and scuttled around her, keeping his gaze fixed to the ground. Nica shivered in the warm rain, clutching her arms about her waist as she watched him enter the darkness.

50

·· WEAVING WATER ··

NICA trod heavily away from the structure, TAL-alph's threat driving her without mercy. *Why does she hate me?*

Rain beat down, the fat drops of water hitting against the lashed-together shelters that served as housing for TAL's Olomi workers. Even in this deluge, she couldn't breathe as she wondered what she had ever done to the alpha.

She had to avoid direct paths—routes between pod stations were heavily trafficked, and she couldn't risk being caught in this state.

"I need you, *Ìyá*," she cried to the clouds.

The clouds didn't answer, but the rain continued to pour.

Her gaze followed the drops as they splashed at her feet. *If Ìyá was here, she'd tell me to find a focus, to breathe.* Nica stared at her toes—webbed and planted in a puddle—and her own face looked back up at her. She rubbed the scalp, feeling the new crop of curls. Obedient to the memory, she closed her eyes, took in a deep breath, held it, then released it to stop the waves of panic from overwhelming her.

Phi was still waiting on a response. What if no one heard the message? What if EC-TAL or MO-ASHE caught wave of their plans? How would they find a way out? Who could she trust? There were too many streams to track. She felt her heart begin to race and forced herself to stay calm.

She had to think. Who could she count on? Who could be trusted? She moved a little deeper into the shadow of the wall.

Rissa. That's one. She tapped her thumb against her smallest fingerpad. She would keep her promise. For *Bàbá*, *Ìyá*, and Jonnat.

Zeta. She moved her thumb to the next fingerpad. Nica didn't even want to imagine where she would be without the elder Olomi's protection and wisdom.

ASHE-phi and his wife. She tapped her middle and first fingerpads. What a comfort and resource he'd been. The pounding in her temples began to decrease. She blinked her eyes wide in the rain, pulling strength into her core and willing it to spread through her dorsals and lats.

Girac. A smile hooked the corner of her mouth as the count reached her thumb, but she couldn't linger on him. There were still others to draw in.

Those poor juvies—I have to make sure they return to the water, but it would be the height of folly to include them in any planning. We need a way to notify the rest of our people when we break. Another stream to weave into the plan.

Iota. Her thumb rested on the middle pad again, dermal teeth barely catching as she rubbed them. He was a new factor, and one shown to be sympathetic to their people. But could he be trusted with this plan, given the risk and lives of others involved? So much was at stake, and she had little time.

The yellow alpha already hated her for the protection pregnancy afforded. If TAL-alph ever caught drift of their plans to escape . . . There was no room for failure.

51

T HE SECOND pod shift finished their pass at the meal line and third shift was beginning to queue. Scooting behind the serving frames, Nica did not dare join in the high spirits of the evacuation pod, but their lightheartedness and energy were infectious. No one could know what she did—why they hadn't seen TAL's alpha.

What isn't clear, she pondered, *is how TAL-alph ended up in that state.* She searched the line of jostling Olomi.

There—that brown-striped Olomi from the well landing. She checked the symbol on his tunic. "Hey, Lam."

The young Olomi broke from his crew, eyes dancing as he drew closer. "Sister."

"I could use some help if you have a moment."

"As long as you promise to save me some supper." He grinned as he accompanied her into the kitchen.

Once they were out of the crews' earshot, Nica lowered her voice. "I saw TAL-alph—she doesn't look good. Do you know what happened?"

A soft whistle escaped his lips. "You saw her? She hasn't checked on us for two suns. Rumor has it that MO-ASHE was pretty roiled at her."

"That's odd." Nica stacked some of the baskets, intentionally banging them against the storage walls noisily. "The alphas are cleared for most anything. And I've never seen TAL or MO-ASHE interfere with the other's enforcer."

Lam nodded slowly. "Yes, I know. Whatever happened, both

Delphim came out in the rain. I half expected to see someone on the gate by the sinking of that sun."

Nica's breath stopped for a moment.

Before the first moon of her captivity had waned, TAL had summoned his workforce to the gate, where her initial assumption was revealed to be incorrect. The bones and bodies strewn about the entrance of TAL's compound didn't belong to Olomi who'd failed while attempting to escape. A digger, forced to report the collapse of a well excavation, was dragged to the entrance and thrown against the gate. It was the first time she'd witnessed an execution. The sight, the sounds, even the smell, of the hapless Olomi writhing in the grip of the deadly field were indelibly carved into her memory, and that was the intent. This was made clear when TAL-alph redirected Nica's attempt to look away with a swift blow from her whip handle.

Later warnings and threats to follow revealed this was not a surprising outcome for those who delivered news of failure to TAL.

"But you don't know what happened to TAL-alph?"

"No." TAL-lam shook his head. "I have no idea. I don't like to hear about any of us being hurt, but Water always returns to its source."

Nica nodded, wondering still at the plight of her oppressor. As much as she hated the alpha's treatment of their people, she was ashamed at the part of herself that wanted the yellow to suffer. The part inside that said she deserved it.

"You have to admit," TAL-lam added, "it's nice not having to look over our shoulders constantly."

"Yes," Nica agreed. "But don't get too used to it," she warned. "TAL-zeta says there's always a price attached to joy on the land."

Grimacing, he hefted the load she had been piling on the tray. "How about we head back out before my diggers are done eating."

"I think you're safe. I gave them the tough tubers."

TAL-iota nodded at each member of his pod as they joined the line. Unfortunately, that included TAL-xi. Nica avoided eye contact with the unpleasant blue-band as she plopped his portion onto his tray. *Though it wouldn't upset me much to accidentally hit him in the face with his food.*

She almost missed his mumbled, "thk," as he moved on from her station.

"Excuse me?" A kick from Iota clarified the prompt as the formerly new, more-recently-demoted, ex-agri-pod supervisor turned to face Nica once again.

"Thank you, TAL-eta," he said, his voice clear and formal. "I apologize for my rude behavior earlier."

Iota grinned.

Nica gave a cool nod. "I accept your apology."

Once the pods had all passed through the line, Nica got a tray for herself and sat alone near the trash chutes. She caught Iota's eye and he walked over and joined her.

"We're going to serious lengths for this discussion, eh?" He warily watched the insects buzzing around the odorous trash bins.

"Well, it's a pretty serious discussion." Nica kept her voice low. "You said earlier that where there is life, there is hope."

His brow wrinkled as he waited for her to continue.

Nica toyed with her food while one of the agri-pod crew passed by to dump his waste.

"Well, there is life, and there is life." She gestured discreetly to her stomach. "And sometimes we need to work out hope."

She paused for another trash run. "What do you hope for, TAL-iota?"

He raised his eyebrows, but replied quietly, "I hope I don't die here."

She toyed with her food again, before meeting his eyes. "My

hope is that my spawn doesn't live here. And I am now working on that."

A long, slow breath left Iota's lips. He pushed back from the table, his gaze flicking momentarily to her belly.

"Well . . ." he said. "There are some things worth working for. How can I help?"

52

"IT'S ALMOST time for the new moon," Nica whispered in the stillness.

Pescha nodded, focused on the water planet's lesser light—hidden, but still felt. Its invisible drag was far more tangible to the Olomi than the first visible sliver of its appearance. "It pulls at me . . . body and soul."

Framed by shadow and structure, the two crouched out of sight, pressing their backs against the slatted storeroom wall. Nica, too, felt the Deep shift in her blood as they watched darkness fully claim the cloud-covered sky. Wave-swept memories flooded her. "We have been removed for so long, but the tide still knows us, still calls us its own."

"It's not that, Nica." Tension strained Pescha's hushed voice. "It's not what we've lost, it's what's coming. I don't . . . I can't do this."

Nica pulled her water-sister close, wishing her pain was merely the familiar lunar pull dredging up longing for their past life. But they didn't require water to commune. She knew this fear that emanated from Pescha, primal and steeped in despair.

"How can we . . ." Pescha choked out the words. "How can we bring life when we are separated from all that nurtures us? How can our captors require us to bring life on this foreign land?"

What would *Ìyá* say? Nica ached for her mother's wisdom. *Ìyá* would tell Pescha that she was made for this, that Olomi women had been bearing children from the beginning, that it was as constant as the waves. But there was no comfort to be found here, for nothing was as it had been since the Breaking. Nothing abovewater was as it had been in the Deep.

"I can't even move without carrying this weight." Pescha cradled the larva growing within, her waifish frame accenting the disparity against her distended abdomen. "Our tides of spawning have always been supported by the water. This is not the place to usher in new life."

Her bright orange and blues were ashen, her eyes sunken, as the encircling rings deepened. Nica wondered when her friend had last slept and mourned the dearth from which they both approached motherhood, even as life grew within them.

A quiet murmur began to stir at the appearance of the smooth-faced gray Olomi. TAL-beta was rarely seen outside the residence, but Nica knew why he was tasked with delivering TAL's supply list to the kitchen-pod. She kept that to herself. Neither TAL nor MO-ASHE had left their quarters much in half a moon, and it had been almost as long since TAL-alph had made an appearance.

Rumors swirled. Would EC-TAL hunt in the rain? Some whispered that they wouldn't have been taken if they'd encountered TAL under more favorable conditions. Others speculated on why his alpha was conspicuously absent. Nica added nothing to the wondering. While she didn't know how, she knew why TAL-alph hadn't been seen lately. She also knew if any reports were traced to her, it would not go well.

Zeta had been informed that TAL-eta was not to bring meals to TAL-alph's quarters, but the other pod members who served her that week were as tight-lipped as Nica.

"I think I can live with that disappointment," Nica said when Zeta informed her of TAL-alph's demand.

Zeta grabbed her arm. "Don't be so dismissive." The frown

she wore perpetually deepened into a scowl. "If TAL-alph has set herself against you, she can cause you serious problems."

"TAL-alph seeks to cause problems regardless of reason. It's how she stays in . . . *agbara—*"

"Language, TAL-eta," Zeta hissed. "Realize what it will cost you—what it will cost all of us if you are caught speaking Olomi."

Nica's green deepened. "I didn't know the word."

The old woman sighed. "The word is power, but that will not be enough to satisfy TAL-alph if she feels threatened by you. She will not stop until she destroys you."

As her mind raced, Nica kept her head low. She couldn't let hope make her careless.

"Iota, help clear these trays." TAL-zeta's tone brooked no discussion.

The white dots sprinkled across TAL-iota's brow nearly melded into a line at her order, but the food-pod supervisor outranked him. He threw a warning to his crew. "Clear out before she presses us all into service. You've already worked your shifts."

The dark Olomi kept his glare trained on TAL-zeta as he ambled over to the stacked cooking pots, but she ignored him, turning her attention to the other needs in her pod. His team took their leave, hastily mumbling thanks as they made their exit.

The scowl remained in place until he and Nica reached the cleaning shelter. Free from observation, both relaxed. Nica took the bowls and started scraping noisily to cover their conversation.

"You said the electric force might weaken with the rains, but for how long?"

"Once TAL leaves, we can test the charge. It should have killed Nu to be in contact for that long. I've tested it with a few 'brushes' since." He ran his hand against the fresh shock of white hair, standing bright against his dark scalp. "It would be better to have someone standing by—just in case."

Blanching at the possibility, Nica steadied herself against the shelter. "Should we be taking risks like that?"

"Not if we want to survive," he shrugged. "But if we intend to live, we don't have the luxury of playing it safe.

"Then tomorrow night, after meal cleanup. Who knows how long MO-ASHE will keep Pescha and me in medical."

"Yes, or when TAL-alph will return."

53

·· WET MOON ··

E C-TAL emerged from his quarters, equipped with supplies and additional rain gear. Soon after, a murmur arose, traveling among the clusters of Olomi. Nica turned her head to find the source of the distraction. Clad in the rain-protection trappings of EC-TAL, the unmistakable figure of TAL-alph emerged from the agri-pod buildings, her whip grasped in her left hand as her right arm hung, oddly limp, at her side.

As she walked past them, Olomi tried to avoid staring, uncertain as to what the safest reaction might be. Nica and TAL-iota focused their gaze on the ground.

Taking her usual position at TAL's departure, the alpha supervised the closing of the gate behind him. No one lingered long within her sight.

There was no general call to gather in the courtyard later that morning, but ASHE-alph collected the females and brought them straight to the medical center for examinations. The enforcer was swift and ruthless as ever in serving his mistress.

Pescha and Nica exchanged apprehensive glances as they were herded directly to the examination cells. A feeble smile was the best Nica could do to encourage her Olomi sister before they disappeared behind their respective doors. Her stomach wrenched when the door closed with a harsh clang. The grate of the bolt, securing the door, further underscored her impotence.

This is not my fate. I will not fear. This is not my fate. I will not fear.

Nica repeated the mantra under her breath, closing her eyes as she sat on the cold table. Refraining from reacting when she heard the bolt grate open, Nica exhaled with a slow breath before she opened her eyes. The smile she received that warmed her heart was more than she expected. It was the white Olomi with bright orange hair who had attended to her a few moons ago.

"Ara—Sister!" Nica stopped herself before she completed the word in Olomi, but she couldn't hide the joy that sprang from her heart. *I don't even know her name.*

"Sister, *Arabinrin*," came the medic's soft reply. "You need not fear. We are both *ti Omi.*"

"Yes," Nica responded with relief. "We are both of the Water."

"I need to take your blood again." The medic's voice was as light as the touch of a crab eddy. "This is how we first met." She wrapped the band around Nica's arm, but dropped her volume as she drew close to pierce the skin. "I have learned much about you since that last meeting." She smiled. *"Emi ni Mischa."*

Nica's eyes widened. *ASHE-phi's wife!*

"Our time is limited, so we must make the most of it. I am thankful that you no longer require sedation, but I am sorry for what you may endure. Please cooperate so that it will go easier for you." The medic grasped Nica's hand with a firm yet gentle touch, binding it to the table.

"MO-ASHE will not risk unfettered gestational patients. *Ma binu,*" the Olomi apologized again as she finished binding her feet and hands.

"Mo dariji ẹ," Nica forgave Phi's wife, knowing she only did what was required.

"Kolas anticipated that I would be able to deliver a message to you," the medic continued.

"Kolas?"

"My husband, called ASHE-phi." Mischa uttered the designation her husband had been given with disdain. "He wanted me to tell you that he received a response to your message. They understand the danger and await your signal.

"Kolas said there is more, but he needs to meet with you. Be still, MO-ASHE approaches."

The new, weekly appointments with MO-ASHE were harrowing, but provided Nica opportunities to see Girac. These stolen moments were strategic to planning the escape, but also soothed her heart. Security rounds were a perfect cover. Not just for staying in touch with Kolas, who communicated with the free Olomi, but also to keep an eye on Rissa.

Lingering outside the cell door as Mischa performed the preliminary exam, Girac spoke just loud enough for her to hear. "She doesn't look good, your sister."

Nica gripped the edge of the cold stoneskin table. "What do you mean, is she ill?"

"Not ill, but . . ." He hesitated as footsteps echoed at the other end of the hallway. "She isn't well. She's always sad."

"Please, tell her to not lose heart. I will see her soon, at TAL's return."

"I hope so. She is not always present when MO-ASHE dines. I will encourage her to be ready for your visit."

Girac came to Nica, and she rested in his embrace for a fleeting moment as Mischa stood watch. She'd volunteered, taking a risk that neither of them dared request.

"If she gets caught . . . if you get caught . . ." Nica faltered at the memory of the branding ceremony. "I don't think I could bear it if one of you were discovered."

Girac's arms tightened around her. "I'll make sure that doesn't happen."

"I never want this to end." She looked up at him. "But no one can know what we share."

He kissed her brow. "But soon, we will live, not fear."

"Soon," Nica repeated, promising to herself as much as to him.

54

·· B O U N D A R I E S ··

DARKNESS hid Nica's movement as she crept from the food-pod. Cloaked by the steady rain and armed with a wooden stirrer Zeta had slipped her, she scurried to the outer walls, slipping behind the sleeping quarters and excavation site, until she came to the gate.

TAL-iota waited there, working in plain sight under the guise of needing to inspect the grounds around the gate after its last opening.

"Listen," he said as she approached.

"For what?"

"The snaps."

The snaps that warned of the charge that ran through the only known exit in their prison. The snaps that exploded into a flurry of activity whenever a large object, or body, was brought into contact with the gates.

"I figure if TAL and the Alpha are so concerned about keeping these piles away from the gate, then maybe we need to investigate it."

Nica couldn't argue with that logic and listened as Iota counted off the space of time between them.

"Now help me throw these piles against the gate. But remember"—he instructed as she began to pick up brush from the recently cleared pile—"throw, don't place. You can't be in contact when it hits the gate."

Nica took a deep breath, stepped further away from the fence, and began to help undo Iota's work. With each toss, the piled debris crackled a little, and when she stopped to listen, the *snaps* were less frequent. She tried to ignore the bones and body parts added to the pile, but continued with the gruesome task, regardless.

"Stand back," Iota warned. "You don't want to be touched by this eddy."

Uncovering a cart, he tipped out a barrel of water near the pile. A renewed flurry of *crackles* and *snaps* emanated from the soaked pile leaning against the gate.

"Now, listen again."

Snap . . .

. . . Snap . . .

. . . Snap . . .

Nica grinned at him. "They're coming more slowly!"

"That's what I was hoping would happen. Now, let's see how much of a difference it makes. I need to test its force. Knock me free after the count."

Iota cautiously brought his hand near some brush touching the fence. Nica stood ready, with the stirring stick raised.

"One . . . Two . . . Three!" Nica knocked the wet brush out of his hand.

"Whew!" Iota rubbed his hand through his hair. "I don't know that I want to try that again anytime soon, but . . ."

"But what?" Nica was relieved that he was still talking, but anxious for a plan.

"But it wasn't as bad as it's been before."

"How many times have you done this?"

Nica had a hard time believing that anyone would plan to get shocked like that on purpose, at least not more than once, or unless they were trying to plan an escape.

"Well"—he ran his hand through his now-standing-straight-up hair—"it's why I started wondering if we might be able to figure out how this thing works."

At Nica's confusion, he went on, "Nu should have died. I've never seen anyone survive contact with the gate before. But since the rains have started, the gates are weaker. They're even weaker now than they were when Nu got hit. We need to find out what's making the difference. Listen."

He tilted his ear toward the gate again. "It's even slower now."

Nica closed her eyes and listened intently.

Her eyes widened. "You're right!"

The *snaps* were coming even further apart.

"Now give me your stick."

Nica handed it over. Iota tapped the gate quickly, experimentally. He tried wedging it where the gate doors met. As he pried, the humming surged and then dropped, as if it were fighting his efforts to open the doors.

"Can I help?"

"No. Not in your condition. I wouldn't want to explain to MO-ASHE if anything went wrong."

Nica hurriedly stepped back.

A renewed hum interrupted the stillness, an echo of something new connecting reverberated through the fence.

"That's not a good sound." Iota's face paled and he pushed Nica further back.

As if the current knew its attacker, the pile they had pushed against the gate started to crackle with renewed vigor. The snapping also increased in frequency, confirming the presence of deadly consequences for transgressors.

Testing the pile, Iota began to separate the pieces on the edge from the main body with the stirring stick.

He threw the stick on the ground in frustration. "It won't work."

"What happened?"

"There's a backup. Draining this one won't be enough. We need to find that power source. But we need to find it fast—the rains won't last forever."

And neither will my pregnancy. She would not let her voice tremble. "Now what?"

"Now you get back to your pod."

Iota retrieved the stick and returned it to her. "Don't worry. We'll figure this out. *A wá lati Omi.*"

Nica repeated, "We come from the Water."

Iota prompted, again in Olomi, *"Si inu Omi, awa yóò padà."*

"To the Water, we will return."

55

·· B R E E C H I N G ··

NICA ducked behind the post, trying to cover her grin as Pescha supported her belly with the edge of the basket.

She choked back a chuckle. "You look like you could use some help. Unless you're trying to push the larva out—but that's the wrong direction."

"Just you wait. It will be your turn soon," Pescha snapped. "Then you won't think it's so funny," she said with a grimace.

"Don't be angry. Let me help you."

Pescha twisted away. "Don't!" she hissed, blocking Nica. "They're watching."

Nica craned her neck to see the agri-pod crew dumping their loads of pods. Most were heading back to the field, but a few loitered, mimicking a very pregnant Pescha, exaggerating her waddles. They made no attempt to contain the guffaws, and her ears turned bright orange at their jeering.

"Help me—I can't work," a tall, striped Olomi mocked, his broad bands of yellow and black intersecting as he crossed his hands over his chest.

"I'm sooooo tired," came from a speckled blue and green fellow. A stout, sand-colored worker chimed in, "How about a snack!"

"Yeah, I wouldn't mind a little *ipanu!*" the banded one leered.

Nica was almost shaking with fury. "Just ignore them. Please, let me help you."

Pescha shook her head mutely, walking as tall as possible, still supporting her swollen abdomen with the basket. Glaring at the agri-pod workers, Nica picked up her load and followed her friend to the back of their pod.

How long have we been isolated? Away from the water? No Olomi would treat another with such coarse disrespect in the Deep. Communion saw to that. Everyone within the currents would feel the reverberations—and the pain emanating from the victim.

The water kept us kind.

The water kept us one.

Pescha gasped and dropped her basket. Her color drained and she grabbed the corner post of the nearest shelter. She held on, motionless, barely able to breathe.

Nica's basket landed on the ground alongside Pescha's as she caught her friend. "TAL-zeta! Help!"

The supervisor whisked around the corner just as Nica lowered Pescha to the ground.

"Don't hold your breath. That's it, breathe. There you are. You're all right." Zeta rubbed the younger Olomi's back, speaking quiet words of reassurance, but locked her eyes on Nica's and mouthed, "Get help. Now!"

Nica froze for a split second, then dashed to the medical building as fast as she could. Taking the narrow passage between the agri-pod fields and storage building, she emerged on the far side of TAL's work building and started calling out as she approached MO-ASHE's main entrance.

"Help! Help! We need help!" As Nica rounded the bend yelling, the blue at the entrance grabbed her arm as she tried to pass through.

"Hold up, greenie. What's your business?"

"We need medical at food-pod! Pe—TAL-kap cannot walk. She has severe pain!"

"And your name?" ASHE-delt busied himself getting out a pad.

"There's no time for this!" Nica tried to jerk away. "Medic! Help!"

"You can't just barge in and—"

Girac burst on the scene, thundering. "Release her!"

Even Nica startled at his vehemence.

"Release her," Girac repeated, at a lower volume but with just as much threat in his tone. "Or you will answer to me."

"More specifically," a quieter but more menacing voice silenced them all, "you will answer to me."

"MO-ASHE," Nica bowed, "TAL-kap is in great pain—TAL-zeta sent me to get help." Nica was barely able to get the words out.

"Tau, get a stretcher and take Delt here to help."

Nica turned to head back out the door but was stopped by MO-ASHE's icy grasp.

"No. You report to the examination rooms."

"But—" The vise on Nica's arm tightened.

"Are you arguing with me?"

The ice in MO-ASHE's tone eclipsed that of her grip, racing up Nica's arm and down her dorsal, converting her panic to terror. She couldn't move, or even speak.

MO-ASHE reached into the folds of her robe and pulled out her controller, glaring at Nica as she squeezed it.

A gust rushed into the entryway as the door from the medical section burst open. Nica winced, anticipating its impact against the wall, but MO-ASHE's burly alpha kept his fist tightly on the handle and checked the swing.

"Yes, MO-ASHE." He released the door with a bow, his eyes straying to the device in her hand.

"Take this one to the exam rooms. She doesn't leave until I've seen her."

With a nod, he grabbed Nica and began to tow her back down the hallway.

"And don't damage her!"

The enforcer huffed but slowed his exit. Nica submitted without a word, allowing herself to be propelled down the hall.

The cell door clanged shut, the bolt grating as it slid into place. Confined. Again.

She stared at the door, afraid to approach it. Wishing Girac was on the other side. But he'd been dispatched to retrieve Pescha. Instead, the great, gray brute, ASHE-alph, was posted there.

Nica paced the room, fidgeting with the scars on her knuckles. *Did they get to her in time?* How would she know, locked up in here? *If one of the medics came in, I could ask them.* She'd even welcome one of their tests right now, just to get an update.

At the sound of the bolt sliding, she took in a deep breath. *Finally, an answer.*

MO-ASHE stepped inside the cell. Nica's breath refused to move. Even her thoughts froze, and the room began to spin.

"Don't even think about passing out." MO-ASHE pointed to the table.

Blinking rapidly, Nica slowly backed up to the table, trying to manage her fear. MO-ASHE advanced, as if toward prey, lips pursed and eyes piercing.

A scream erupted from nearby and Nica jumped. *Pescha!*

MO-ASHE's gaze didn't waver. "Do I need to sedate you, or will you control yourself?"

Her nails dug into Nica's shoulders as she maneuvered her patient on the table. "You'd think none of you had ever given birth before."

"I'm sorry, MO-ASHE. I'll be still." The last thing Nica wanted was to be drugged again, unaware of what was being done to her and to her spawn.

There were no more words as MO-ASHE continued her examination. She measured, poked, and prodded in silence, pausing only to make notes on her pad.

With a sniff, she snapped off her gloves. "That's all for now. Return in a week. I am needed elsewhere."

Nica reported to Zeta what little she could about Pescha's condition.

"The screaming was awful, but MO-ASHE did not seem to be at all concerned about it. I tried to see her, but wasn't permitted." She paused uncertain about how to continue. "TAL-zeta . . ."

"Spit it out, girl! What's worrying you?"

"Has anyone else ever spawned here? I've seen my mother gravid, twice. This . . . Kap's is different. I don't remember it being this hard."

"I wish I could tell you what you want to hear," the elder Olomi shook her head, "but I haven't heard of a successful spawn yet." She rushed to finish at Nica's stricken expression. "But I've never seen one last as long as you or TAL-kap's either."

Her hand rested on top of Nica's, wrinkled light blue stripes atop the faded green striations, both scarred where webbing once bridged. She had no words of comfort, but her quiet presence gave the younger strength.

The elder Olomi broke the silence. "One way or another, this gestation will end. You need to get out while you can."

56

·· GENERATION ··

S HIFTING her basket from one side to the other, Nica fidgeted as ASHE-delt logged her in. She longed to check on Pescha, but it would be asking for trouble.

"Is this necessary?" Nica sighed, impatient at the blue guard's attitude.

"As a matter of fact, it is."

The officious doorkeeper evidently didn't appreciate the pressure put on him earlier, taking pains to put her in her place.

"Designation?"

"TAL-eta."

"Pod?"

"Really? You can see on the tunic!"

"Pod."

"Food."

"Supervisor?"

"This is ridiculous!"

"Supervisor!"

"Zeta."

"Is that TAL-zeta or ASHE-zeta?"

"Are you serious? You know food-pod is under TAL's oversight."

"State your supervisor's full designation."

Sigh. "TAL-zeta."

"Destination?"

"Hydro-processing."

"What is the nature of your business?"

"You really need to know?"

"State the reason for your presence." ASHE-delt tapped his stylus impatiently.

"You're going to write this all down?"

"Yes."

"Okay." Nica took a deep breath. "My assignment is to investigate specialized food preparation techniques with unprocessed and desalinated hydro resources and their subsequent by-products. Did you get it all?"

He glared, stylus poised above his pad, lips tight as Nica waited for him to finish writing.

"You don't need me to repeat that, do you?" she asked lightly.

"Proceed," the blue-hued guard muttered as he slammed the pad on its shelf.

It was all Nica could do to keep her laughter under wraps until she was out of sight. But the encounter sobered her, as well. *How can we hope to overcome our oppressors, when we so readily seek to undercut each other?*

And how do we survive, without betraying those who would betray us?

Nica filed the turmoil flooding her thoughts away. She'd sort it out later, whenever that might be.

"What are you here for?" ASHE-mu scowled at her as she entered the station he shared with Kolas.

"TAL-zeta sent me to collect—"

"I don't even want to know—this is Phi's problem, not mine! I have enough to manage without you and TAL-zeta adding to it."

With that, Mu stormed out, nearly colliding with his partner as Kolas walked in.

"Was it something you said?" the older Olomi asked with a twinkle in his eye.

"It could be anything I said," Nica admitted ruefully. "That Olomi is never happy to see me in his pool.

"You mustn't blame him," Kolas said with gentleness. "His life abovewater has been significantly more wretched than most of ours, and that's saying something."

Nica's mind shuddered as she recalled that branding ceremony from almost a year ago. It was not the only branding she'd seen, but it was the most traumatic one.

"Let's discuss the matter at hand." Kolas changed the subject with a smile. "Mischa enjoyed her little visit with you."

"Yes, I didn't realize who she was when we met before. She is very kind."

"She is, as long as you stay on her good side." Kolas's smile broadened, and Nica couldn't help but giggle.

"She said you received word back from the message we sent out?"

"Yes. It wasn't much, but it is safest to keep our communication brief." Kolas beckoned for her to follow him to the back stairs that led to the hatch.

"Last night, I was working late and something strange happened. The energy that powers the labs was interrupted without warning. We were operating at half power for part of the night. This building's lights were dim, and the atmospheric control was offline, until we were back to full power. The mistress was furious and had me follow the path that leads to the reef generator, but nothing was found."

Nica's heart skipped a beat. "When did this happen?"

"A few hours after dark." Kolas eyed her. "Did you have something to do with this?"

"Perhaps." She went on to describe TAL-iota's experiments of the previous evening.

Kolas immediately began to pace back and forth across the tiny hatch room, rubbing his hands together furiously. "This is it. This has got to be it! If we can . . . but how . . . Perhaps if we could . . ."

He stopped, muttering to himself even less coherently.

Then, "Yes!"

Nica nearly jumped out of her skin. "Yes what?"

Kolas's gaze landed on her as if she had just appeared. "Oh, er . . . um. Yes. I believe I understand what happened last night, and more importantly, what needs to happen the next time your friend wants to drain the gates."

He ran his fingers through his already messy, gray hair. "It's the reef generators. They power this section—the medical and science labs, atmospheric controls, all MO-ASHE's buildings. But, when your friend drained the outer gates, power was diverted from here to there."

Nica's brow was furrowed as she tried to follow Kolas's explanation.

"Don't you understand? If we can disable the reef generators, there will be no backup power for the gates!"

Her eyes widened. That was what Iota was trying to figure out. "How do we disable them? Where are they?"

"We don't. That's the trick." Kolas folded his arms and nodded in triumph. "They are deep in the foundation of this mass. We have no access, but . . ."

"But?"

"But the free Olomi can—*If* we can coordinate the timing and explain what needs to be done. We need to contact Daevu—he sent the message—and have him investigate the reef generators, then we can plan the break."

Nica grabbed the edge of the stoneskin table behind her.

Kolas paused at Nica's expression. "What is it? Do you know this Daevu?"

"All my life."

57

"**TAL-ETA!**" A harsh whisper broke in on her slumber. Nica opened one eye with difficulty, and then the other, but neither shed light on her morning intruder.

"TAL-eta!" The voice shuffled closer and was punctuated by a hand shaking her to fuller consciousness.

Sitting up, she blinked. "TAL-zeta? What? Why is it so dark?"

"No time for that!" the supervisor whispered. "And don't make a commotion here! Come to my station immediately. And stay quiet!"

Adrenaline banished any remaining stupor. Throwing on her shift, then tunic, she fastened her leggings about the waist and ankles. Splashing through the mud, she stopped short at the sight of Girac outside Zeta's station, his face ashen and marked with concern.

"It's TAL-kap." He led her into Zeta's station. "She needs you!"

Nica rushed to the makeshift cot and took Pescha's hand. The Olomi was pale, and her breathing shallow. Feeling for her pulse, she looked up at TAL-zeta. "Too fast!"

Zeta bustled over, pushing down on their patient's abdomen. "Fever?"

Nica placed one hand on the forehead, and another in the hollow under her arm. "I don't think so, and both sites seem to be consistent."

"Good. Now, massage here." She moved over so that Nica could take over. "Don't be afraid. Knead deeply."

Zeta bristled at Girac, still standing in the doorway. "What about the fry? What happened to it? Why did you bring this poor girl here?"

He flushed bluer and tried to move out of the way. "I didn't see the spawn—but I did hear a cry, long past sunsink."

Zeta sighed with relief as she shoved him to the side.

"It was the middle of the night, and I was directed to transport TAL-kap here. MO-ASHE determined that she no longer needed to be held in the medical wing."

"Eta, start the fire." Zeta started scraping together a soup from the previous evening's meal. She squeezed past Girac again, pushing him back toward the shelves. "Are you helping or leaving, ASHE-tau? I have no room for spectators."

The blues on his brow and cheekbones deepened even more. "I wish I could stay, but I've already exceeded what MO-ASHE would allow. There will be consequences if I do not return soon."

"Wait, Girac." Nica lifted her head. "Can you get to ASHE-phi?" She looked hopefully at Zeta. "If we had true water . . ."

TAL-zeta nodded. "That could make a difference." She turned to Girac. "Do you think you can arrange to bring some back?"

"If I can't, I'll send word. Just be careful, we're too close to risk carelessness right now. There's much at stake." He surveyed the food-yard, then headed out of the shelter.

Pescha began to open her eyes, moaning as she stirred. *"Ọmọ mi!"*

Nica looked helplessly to TAL-zeta, uncertain how to respond. Their supervisor shuffled over and sat on the edge of the cot, holding Pescha's hand.

"Your spawn is healthy. You need to rest."

"No." Pescha shook her head, wildly refusing to be comforted. *"Ọmọ mi,* they took my fry."

Her orange-rimmed eyes were wide as they landed on Nica. The slight Olomi grabbed Nica's tunic with surprising strength. "Don't let . . . don't let MO-ASHE . . . take your spawn, you can't . . ."

Pescha's grip slackened as she faded from consciousness, but her words lodged in Nica's heart.

Zeta tended to Pescha in her quarters while Nica directed the morning meal. As much as she wanted to be by Pescha's side, she was thankful for Zeta's skills in midwifery, despite being limited to abovewater resources. The tubers were almost ready for the porridge when TAL-iota and TAL-nu approached with a delivery from agri-pod.

"Did you get demoted?" she asked as she surveyed the requests on TAL-zeta's pad.

"Not really." Iota smirked as he pushed the pad aside. He lowered his voice and tapped on the sacks. "You're not going to find this on your list." The sacks jiggled. "Special delivery from hydro-processing."

Girac and Kolas had succeeded!

Nica swallowed her relief as she led them to the back of Zeta's quarters, but tears of joy stung her eyes. Delivery completed, she helped fold the borrowed sacks and filled Iota in on her meeting with Kolas.

"Reef generators? Are you sure?"

She nodded. "We're making arrangements to disable them, but we need to figure out the timing. We'll only get one chance to spring this surprise."

"And we need to make our move before the rains end. We have maybe one more moon."

"There's so much to get right, and so much that could go wrong." Nica bit her lip. "But there's more to lose if I stay much longer. I can't have my baby here."

"You won't. We'll make this work." Iota tucked the bags under his arm and rescued what was left of the first pod's breakfast from TAL-nu.

"Sorry." He grinned. "Waking Nu early appears to make him hungry."

"Take more, you've earned it." Nica smiled. "I don't know how to thank you."

Being down two workers made for a busy morning. All three shifts had to be served and the sunpeak meal prepped before Nica could attend to Pescha. *She needs something more than that starchy porridge.* She scoured the stores for anything that would add value. Fresh sprouts, protein squares, fermented beans . . . *If only we had kelp, it would be so good for her.* She combined the ingredients in what she hoped was a soothing stew. *Will the true water be sufficient?*

Pescha's pale face swam in front of Nica. The warning echoed in her ears, triggering a cascade of fear.

You'll see Rissa soon, Nica comforted herself. In a few tides, she'd be able to let her sister know about the escape plan. She'd keep her promise to Bàbá and bring Rissa back.

Who else should she tell? How many could they leave with? Their small band was secure, but was it fair to leave others—or any—behind? She had no answers.

She sent another broadcast out, indicating where she and Jonnat had landed when they first ventured abovewater. They'd informed the free Olomi of the reef generators, including a rough description and location. She hoped it was enough. It had to be enough. It was all they had.

The alert sounded from the front gates. It could mean only one thing. TAL was back early, and if he was back this soon, he would not be alone. Her heart sank at the thought of another captive, even as she began planning for the limited pool of time she would have with Rissa. Sorrow and hope crashed over and against each other as she joined the other Olomi, waiting for the call to witness another surrender.

But the call didn't come. TAL's servants milled in confusion, knowing what was expected of them, but uncertain, absent the call.

As TAL-alph reached to key in the gate code, TAL's staff waited in the recesses of his doorway for their cue. But there was no cue or call. There was no TAL.

58

·· RETURN ··

TRE-CH stood in the gateway, his black locks parted by the driving rain. Rivulets traveled like spears from crown to toe, coursing down the folds of his mud-spattered coverings. The Delphim arrived without entourage or fanfare, but he looked no less dangerous, glaring as he waited for the doors to part.

TAL-alph keyed open the gate to allow TRE-CH entrance. Moaning followed the scowling Delphim but did not come from him.

"Ọmọ mi. Ọmọ mi. Ọmọ mi."

TRE-CH yanked on a lead wrapped tightly round his fist. Tethered to it was TAL-rho, crying incessantly for her baby. "Ọmọ mi. Ọmọ mi."

TAL-alph bowed deeply. "How may we serve you, TRE-CH?"

"I'm not dealing with you, mud-sucker. Where is TAL?"

"We beg pardon, but EC-TAL is not present."

"Well, then get MO-ASHE out here!" he roared with exasperation. "Better yet, take me to her. Why are you keeping me in this rain?"

"Yes. Yes." TAL-alph wavered just a bit as she gestured, turning to keep her strong side toward the visiting Delphim. "Please, this way."

TRE-CH ignored the yellow Olomi as he wrangled the blue he had in tow.

"Ọmọ mi. Ọmọ mi. Ọmọ mi. Ọmọ mi."

"Will you shut up!" He jerked again on TAL-rho's cord as they headed to MO-ASHE's buildings.

"*Ọmọ mi. Ọmọ mi. Ọmọ mi. Ọmọ mi.*"

Nica leaned around Zeta and tried to get TAL-rho's attention, but the blue didn't seem to be aware of her surroundings. She just kept crying out.

By now, the unusual cluster had drawn a fair amount of attention. TAL-alph, hobbling as quickly as her limp would allow, followed by the visiting Delphim trying to avoid the numerous puddles, and the disheveled blue, wailing and pulling back against TRE-CH with each step.

As they approached MO-ASHE's buildings, TAL-rho's cries escalated. She bolted through the main entrance. "*Ọmọ mi! Ọmọ mi!*"

Apparently, TRE-CH hadn't expected the aquan he'd been dragging to suddenly advance, and was jerked off balance. ASHE-delt, unaware of the commotion until it crossed the threshold he guarded, was also caught unprepared. With uncharacteristic swiftness, the blue guard launched from his post and tackled the frenzied Olomi. They landed in a muddy pile just inside MO-ASHE's entrance, the female's dark blue limbs writhing under the solid weight of the guard.

"*Ọmọ mi, Soto. Ọmọ mi!*"

Soto? Was that the true name of her son? Nica dared not wonder aloud.

The blue sobbed and called out, ignoring the Delphim still holding her lead and the guard struggling to subdue her.

"With your permission." TAL-alph stepped forward with a grim curve of her lips, whip readied in her undamaged hand.

"I am done with this one!" TRE-CH swore violently. "It is worse than useless."

"What is this?" MO-ASHE's cold fury cut through the air like a blade.

TAL's alpha hesitated, then withdrew, bowing to MO-ASHE and TRE-CH.

TRE-CH kicked at the Olomi on the ground before him. "I am

returning this aquan. It is worse now than when you dumped it on us. This is not what I agreed to."

MO-ASHE flicked a calculated glance at Nica's midsection, and then at the blue female, still struggling despite being pinned by the guard, Delt. "Was there a child?"

"Yes, barely. It came early, and there is no guarantee it will survive." TRE-CH glared at MO-ASHE. "I was promised a worker and a child. The one worthless, and the infant may be as well. I left you good stock and demand recompense."

MO-ASHE's eyes darkened, but her tone took on a sweeter edge. "You must be exhausted from your journey. Let us discuss this once you have rested."

She linked her arm through TRE-CH's. "Leave your aquan to TAL-alph. That one is . . . adept at curbing troublemakers."

She nodded at the yellow enforcer before she led her guest down the hall. "Delt, release the blue to TAL-alph, and send word to TAL-zeta. I require a proper meal befitting our guest."

The sight of TAL-alph readying her whip was sufficient motivation for Nica to leave. But not before their eyes met, and the whip was leveled in her direction. She didn't need communion to know what fate TAL-alph had in mind once her usefulness to MO-ASHE was over.

59

DESPITE the warm rain, icy drops of sweat slithered down Nica's dorsal. Trembling, she headed toward the food-pod. *She means to kill me.*

She hesitated at the entrance to Zeta's station, fingering the beads that hung in the doorway. Pescha was still there. *I can't let her see me like this.* She backed around the structure till she was out of sight. Sliding to the ground against a support pole, Nica buried her head in her hands. *I don't know what MO-ASHE did, but TAL-alph blames me. She's going to kill me.*

But Bàbá is coming. But what if he can't find the reef generators? What if he gets caught?

The thought of TAL beating her father the way he had beaten so many others pierced her heart.

He wouldn't get caught. But TAL killed Jonnat. He'll kill my father. And TAL-alph will kill me.

Two hands grasped her, diving into the maelstrom of her anxious thoughts and pulling her out of its murky depths.

"Girac!" Tears began to fall.

The guard gently pulled her up. Guiding her into a hidden recess in the storeroom, he put his arms around Nica, hushing her weeping.

"Nica, Nica. What brought this on?" He tilted her face up.

"It-it's TAL-alph." Almost incoherent, she pushed the words past shuddering breaths. "She is b-beating TAL-rho right now. And as s-soon as I have this baby, she will kill me."

"Shh." Girac cradled her against his chest. "You're going to be okay. We're not staying to find out what she will do."

She drew back, refusing to be mollified. "But why? Why does she hate me so much? What h-happened to make her so"—land words failed her, and Nica grappled for them in Olomi—"*ibi?* Yes, evil. Our people are not *buru*. We do not commit this kind of wickedness against each other."

"Shh, dearheart, what you say is true, but I will do everything in my power to keep you safe. As to the why, I have some understanding."

She looked at him questioningly.

"Were it not for Mischa, it could have happened to me. I could have become like TAL-alph."

Nica stared, incredulous. "How can you even say that? You would never, ever harm an Olomi or abuse your position. You have never been anything but kind and gentle."

"But only because Mischa warned me about the dangers of the boost."

"What is boost?"

"Boost is a treatment they use to make us stronger. It is only given to those who are designated guards or chosen to serve as an Alpha. Some supervisors may also receive it—if strength is needed to enforce their authority."

"What is the problem if it makes you stronger? Not that you are lacking in that area." She sniffled and squeezed his bicep, attempting half a smile. "Wouldn't it give you an advantage?"

"That's what I thought," he said gravely. "But Mischa knew better."

He peeked outside the door. "We don't have time, but I'll try to explain. I've known Mischa since I was a fry. She was a healer in the waters I come from. She and Kolas were not happy to discover I had been taken, but they were quick to warn me of many dangers here.

"Taking boost enhances lung adaption and increases land strength, but there were also other changes—effects initially unknown to Olomi. Strength, irrationality, and violence. These all increase together as the treatments continue. But our bodies cannot sustain that level of elevation. Olomi have died after prolonged treatment, and some grow more aggressive, even toward our own. Mischa didn't want me to be swept up in that current. She encouraged me to be a guard, but warned me before I started the treatments. She thought in med-pod, she could help me avoid it."

"Why would she encourage you to become a guard if this enhancement was required?"

"Because it could keep me safe from beatings, and only she and I would know the truth."

"How long has TAL-alph been taking these treatments? Wouldn't someone realize the danger after seeing the bad reactions?"

"Boost not only gives strength, but it makes you feel powerful . . . and good. Once started, missing a treatment is painful. It can be crippling, to the limbs as well as the mind. Mischa helped me avoid some of the early sessions, but not all." Girac's gaze was fixed on the ground.

"You were able to resist—even after you received a treatment?"

Girac's voice was low. "I almost didn't. I had to remind myself that the power rush was a lie, but it didn't feel like one. If Mischa hadn't practically raised me, I might have turned her in. In fact"—his blues flushed almost as dark as his black stripes—"I'm ashamed to say, I nearly did."

He looked down at her hands resting in his, subdued in his remorse. "So, you see, it would not have taken much for me to turn into a brute."

Nica squeezed his hands and raised a smile to him. "I am grateful for who you are. Girac, dear to my heart."

He raised her fingers and kissed the tips. "You are, and always will be okan mi, my heart. And now that we have stopped the tears, I need to deliver MO-ASHE's order and hurry back. Even guards are not invulnerable to her temper."

Nica blanched at the thought of MO-ASHE turning her rage on Girac.

"Tell TAL-zeta that MO-ASHE requires a feast tonight for the visiting Delphim. You should try to be there." He smiled at her. "Rissa is to perform."

60

ZETA sprang into action at MO-ASHE's order, issuing her own orders in every direction. "Pi, Omi, and Epsi! Flow with the current—we're still down workers.

"Nica, get Pescha out of the way, back in the sleeping quarters— No!" Zeta shook her head furiously. "Not by yourself—get some help!" She scowled and huffed in a show of exasperation but slipped Nica a veiled smile.

The respite was welcome, but Nica couldn't relax until she'd gotten Pescha to take a few sips of broth. She applied rags soaked in true water along the Olomi's sensory lines as Zeta had instructed, exchanging them as the healing moisture was absorbed and checking for any sign of fever.

Her patient slept in fits and starts, but Nica took the opportunity to consider escape options. They could wait for the next moon, when TAL would be gone, or they could leave as soon as the reef generators were disabled. The rain hadn't let up, but there was no telling how long it would continue, and it was a factor that could not be taken for granted.

She patted her belly. *I don't know when you're coming, little one, but I promise you, we will be gone before that happens.*

Pescha's breathing began to slow and deepen as she slipped into peaceful slumber. Nica tiptoed out to help Zeta before she took her crew to MO-ASHE's residence.

The supervisor was still barking out orders. "Don't forget the fermented paste. MO-ASHE will be pleased to have something new to impress her guest. It gives her an advantage."

"Why do you worry so much about making her happy—or look good, for that matter? You're the one doing the work, Zeta, and she gets the credit?"

"Child, do you think I care about the opinion of one Delphim or another? No, but I do care that my staff is viewed as valuable and worth safeguarding. If MO-ASHE is pleased with our service, it goes well for us. So I serve and wish her well." Zeta gave a little shrug. "And I hope for peace."

Is it wisdom or waste? It made sense, a little, when Nica considered the logical benefits of serving the MO well. But it went against every fiber of her being. Still, for this tide, she would follow the wisdom of her elder. Until she made the break—until she was free.

There were no surprises in MO-ASHE's kitchen. Painfully bright, like all the MO's workspaces, it was designed to maximize utility.

Peel . . . Clean . . . Chop. Steps that weren't alien to her in this abovewater environment. Ingredient preparation was neither stressful nor taxing. It was difficult to fail here—even for Nica. Cooking, on the other hand, confounded her, and Nica was content to stay out of the way while Zeta and her counterpart handled the final seasoning and food preparations.

Serving the meal in her living space required a different sort of preparation. The display of opulence was overwhelming. Cushions and lights of all sizes were scattered throughout the room. Glittering fabrics of every color hung from ceiling to floor. Smoking pots of incense perfumed the air. It was almost an assault on the senses.

Nica much preferred the comparatively ill-equipped Olomi food-pod. The hearth, wide and open from all sides, was a rough source of cooking heat, with vats of soups and porridges rotated in stages of preparation for the next meal. The few eating surfaces scattered throughout the pod's serving area were supplemented by odd left-over containers for seating, leaving circles where most of the workers, whether by choice or by default, squatted as they shared a meal.

Some of the Olomi wove discarded branches, as they had once with kelp, to provide shade or decorations around the common eating area. Others had taken a try at beating stalks into fibers suitable for braiding or weaving into a more delicate material which could be dyed.

Nica loved these works that reminded her of kelp weavers and their tapestries that decorated the walls and doorways of Olomi homes. It didn't make their prison feel like a home, but that was not the purpose. It was their stand. Forced to dwell in captivity, outside of their element, deprived of their language—these Olomi would not be assimilated to become mindless drones under this hostile rule. They would leave their mark, reclaiming their culture and identity. Their bodies might be imprisoned, but not their hearts and minds.

We come from Water, and to Water we will return.

We come from Water, and Water always—

A touch on her shoulder broke into Nica's thoughts. *Caught drifting again.* She felt the heat travel up her face and knew a flush of green was betraying her. Hanging her head, she formed an apology as she turned to accept the reprimand.

"I'm sorry, TAL-zeta, but I am nearly—" Nica gasped, then threw her arms around her sister.

They held each other tightly over Nica's protruding belly. Nica felt Rissa shaking. "*Mi o le şe . . .*" her sister choked.

"Shh. You can't what?" Nica loosened her hold to assess Rissa's state. "Gir—ASHE-tau was right, you don't look well. You barely show any pink, let alone your beautiful scarlet, and you are far too thin." She tried to calm Rissa. "There's no fever, now let me hear you breathe."

"No, no." Rissa gently pushed her away, resisting the attempted examination. "I'm not ill. But I suppose your friend is right, I'm not well, I can't . . ." She broke down.

"Shh, shh." Nica cradled her sister, rocking her like their mother had so long ago. Eventually Rissa took a shuddering breath and wiped her tears with her sleeve.

"I'm so sorry, Nica. I didn't intend to fall apart on you like this. It's been so long since I last saw you, but it seemed ages before TRE-CH brought me here. I almost think it would have been easier if he hadn't."

Nica's heart fell a little at her sister's words. "What do you mean? I'd been searching for you since the Breaking."

"Do you think I wanted to discover that you were enslaved like me? You don't know how hard it's been finding out that Jonnat was dead. And that *Ìyá* and *Bàbá* are broken." Rissa shook her head, refusing to meet Nica's eyes. "Captivity was survivable when it was mine to bear alone. I cannot live with the knowledge of my whole family suffering, and most of you suffering because of me."

Nica looked at her in shock. "What do you mean, because of you? We suffer because the—"

"You, *Ìyá*, *Bàbá*, all suffer because I was lost. It was me you and Jonnat came looking for. If you hadn't, Jonnat would still . . ." Rissa's tears fell afresh. She took Nica's hand. "I could have endured this life if I knew you were spared this fate. I could have found comfort knowing that Jonnat would rebuild his life, and that *Ìyá* and *Bàbá* had the rest of you. But these weeks, all I can think is that I have nothing to comfort me, and no one to be happy for."

"No, Rissa." Nica tried to reason with her sister. "It is not all what you think." She brushed Rissa's tears away. "You must calm yourself, because what I have to tell you is for your ears alone."

At Rissa's questioning gaze, Nica poured out all that had transpired since their last visit.

Rissa grabbed her arm. "*Bàbá?*" she breathed. "He is well?"

"Yes. Well enough to lead in the Guardians again. But he doesn't know how we are—yet."

"And you have a way to leave? Truly?"

"Yes. It will need to be by next moon, if not sooner. I cannot risk spawning here. MO-ASHE will take it, like Pescha's was taken."

Rissa's eyes filled with alarm. "They brought an infant to MO-ASHE's quarters earlier, then moved Mote from the chamber adjoining hers." Her face grew taut. "I don't like that fry. He is cruel and his rages are terrifying. I don't even know what he is, but it is not right for a fry to be that cruel." She shook her head. "He is always gloved and I don't know why. MO-ASHE dotes on him, then torments him, and it makes him crueler still. He hates us more than she does!"

"He is Olomi, Rissa, the same as you and me, but taken from his mother when he was very young," Nica told her. "TAL and MO-ASHE have been molding him. I hate to think of what she will do with an infant in her possession."

"Well, she's not going to get her hands on yours. You must make sure that doesn't happen, no matter what it takes."

"I don't intend to, *Sisi*." She took Rissa's hand. "And you must come with me."

"I don't know, Nica." Her reply was hesitant. "What is there left for me with Jonnat gone? To miss him here, where we are each isolated from each other, is one thing, but to enter the water, and still not feel his presence? I don't know if I could bear that."

"We don't have much time Rissa, but you must," Nica pleaded. "I cannot—I will not—return without you. Jonnat would hate for you to live like this if you had the choice to be free. You do no honor to his memory or his love by punishing yourself. It is not a disgrace to survive."

Zeta peeked her head around the corner. "You two better pull yourselves together. MO-ASHE isn't having much luck placating TRE-CH. He's pushing to trade back." She pointed at Rissa. "You for Rho."

Nica's heart stopped. If MO-ASHE traded her sister back . . .

Zeta regarded them with a worried frown. "If you want to stay together, you need to convince MO-ASHE that keeping you is worth the bother."

61

·· R E A S O N ··

"WHAT is that?" TRE-CH drew back as Mote, unnaturally pale and gloved, was escorted to a cushioned seat across from him and next to MO-ASHE.

Despite the visiting Delphim's exclamation, Nica noticed the bows and lowered eyes MO-ASHE's household displayed before the altered Olomi spawn. She would have to follow their example.

The combined efforts of Zeta's pod and MO-ASHE's crew had produced an impressive dinner, accented by Rissa's voice and an Olomi who plucked on strings attached to a frame. The melded tones transfixed Nica, wafting currents weaving around and through her, transporting her home, into the Deep. A swift elbow in the laterals grounded her.

Zeta fumed. "Attend to the Delphim."

Serving slowly, Nica moved with care, storing snatches of conversations that both illuminated and alarmed her.

". . . acquired early . . . retraining . . . successful response . . . conditioning . . ."

Nica hovered a little closer.

"Are you . . . biologically it's . . ." TRE-CH's incredulous expression could have been considered comical to an onlooker if the topic of discussion were not a fry who had been taken from his mother.

". . . visit . . . opportunity . . . test . . . conditioning . . ."

As the servers headed back for the second course, MO-ASHE called Mote over, whispered in his ear, then pushed him toward their guest.

The child squirmed and turned to her with a pout. "Why do I have to bow?"

Nica froze at Mote's petulance.

"Because I require it. And because TRE-CH is Delphim."

"But so am I," he argued.

"My child, you are becoming, but you must know and show respect to your betters." Her tone lost any of its previous sweetness as her eyes narrowed. "Bow."

"Yes, MamMam."

What kind of retraining did they mean? Were they physical enhancements like boost? It did seem TRE-CH's visit provided opportunity to test Mote's conditioning. She understood that much.

By the time the servers prepared to bring the next course, Mote was in his seat, glowering at TRE-CH, who was inspecting a squalling fry. Pescha's. The newspawn's shuddering cries pierced her heart, and Nica's stomach knotted as the Delphim examined the fry, turning it over and back like a piece of produce.

Returning the spawn as abruptly as they had removed it from the attendant's arms, the two Delphim returned to negotiating. MO-ASHE's expression of triumph fell away as TRE-CH's gestures grew more energetic. Then she directed her alpha to the cluster of servers. Nica's muscles tensed as he streamed straight to her, calling another Olomi to take her tray. She froze and locked uncertain eyes with Rissa as her forearm was grabbed and she was escorted to their table.

"This subject was in the same sample group, so yours should still be carrying." MO-ASHE gestured to Nica's very swollen abdomen. "I won't be held responsible for your inability to maintain the pregnancy. I gave you a proven viable carrier, my only subject with previous success."

TAL-rho's baby came too early and might not survive. What if my little one . . .

MO-ASHE struck a sweeter tone. "Just because it was birthed small, doesn't mean it's worthless. Let me send you a wet nurse. This will solve a problem for me as well as provide a remedy for you. The blue is neither physically nor mentally stable, but we can put it to use here."

"My intention is to take back the musician." TRE-CH stabbed his utensil in Rissa's direction. "I don't need another worker right now, but CaG wants entertainment when we have guests. She has been disappointed with what we've had during this rainy season."

Zeta was right. He did want Rissa back.

"If the infant is to remain viable, it will need therapeutic nutrition. I have a wet nurse who will be available to travel in three days, sooner if you use a litter. Take it or leave it. We can consider a trade later. That infant is our future. The red, merely ambiance."

Nica held her breath. She understood the term wet nurse. That had to be Pescha. She could barely walk across the room, and MO-ASHE expected her to travel in three suns? Farther away from her spawn. Nica swallowed the lump in her throat.

MO-ASHE gestured at Nica, with a curt nod to her alpha.

This time, Nica was grateful for his grip as the gray returned her to the serving station. Her legs were traitorously weak. She served numbly as her mind raced. She couldn't wait for the next moon, too much could go wrong. Implications began to overwhelm her. She stumbled back to the kitchen and nearly dropped her tray.

Zeta eyed her sharply, then herded her to the back corner. "You're done. Rest, eat, and breathe. I will send you to medical if you don't calm down."

Nica leaned against the wall, weak as a molted crab. "But, what if—"

"I don't have time to argue. Stay, or I'll put a guard on you."

62

N ICA was still trembling when it was time to head back to the pod.

"You need to go to medical," Zeta groused.

Nica tried to slow her breathing. "I need to talk to Rissa." She understood Zeta's concern, but she needed information that only her sister or TAL-rho had.

"Language, TAL-eta!" Her supervisor's tone was sharp.

Nica flinched at the reprimand, but Zeta was right. There was danger enough these tides without broadcasting a request for it. But she had to warn Zeta about Pescha. "TAL-zeta," she whispered.

"What is it, child?" Zeta leaned into her.

"TAL-kap is in danger," she managed.

"Danger? How?" The supervisor looked about to see if there was a present threat.

"No. Not here. MO-ASHE means to send her with TRE-CH. Three suns. I am," she gulped, "I am afraid for her." Her words stuttered out, breathy and uneven.

Glancing around at the other workers, Zeta moved with a grumble, and handed her a cup. "Here, drink this. It should settle your breathing." She muttered to herself, but in that muttering, her words were clear as she leaned in again to Nica. "Thank you for the warning. I will do what I can to prepare her."

Nica cradled the steaming mug in her hands, her icy fingers absorbing its warmth. She sipped, tracing the comforting fluid as it traveled down her throat. Her muscles began to relax, like anemones letting down their guard in still waters.

Fragrant steam transported her to the hot pools of her youth, and the healing warmth that would envelop her before she moved into a cooler slipstream. The mist soothed her lungs as much as the aroma calmed her heart and quieted her thoughts.

Rissa slipped in, trying to avoid the attention of MO-ASHE's household, but looking at Nica with concern. "TAL-zeta said you needed to see me. Are you all right?"

"Thank you, Rissa. I'm better now. I am taking a chance, but I had to. I promise this won't take long. I need to know how long the journey is from here to TRE-CH's compound. And the route or any markers you might remember."

"Why? What possible reason would you—"

"Please, Rissa, we don't have time." Nica looked around to make sure no one was in earshot.

Her sister gave a hesitant nod. "I must think. Well, when we traveled here with TRE-CH and SA-CaG, we walked for about four suns. But that was with a large group, and several litters. Olomi not bound to the litters were bound to each other, to prevent any from escaping. Then, for part of the journey, we were penned in a large container and put to sleep. When we awoke, we walked in this manner for three more suns before we arrived at this compound.

"You know I'm not good with directions like you are," she said apologetically. She closed her eyes for a moment, in concentration, then opened them. "I do remember that the sun was behind us in the mornings for the first part of our journey, and then we traveled with it on our left side after we were released from the container." She gave a wan smile. "I remember this because when we arrived, the Olomi who were not painted like I had been, looked striped on their left side, because of the sun.

"Oh, and another thing," Rissa added. "TRE-CH's compound is atop a steep barren climb, like TAL's."

"This will help." Nica said gratefully. "We will need to leave in the next two weeks. I'll get word to you. TRE-CH wants to take you back, but MO-ASHE has put him off for a bit. If you stay, though, he intends to reclaim his property."

Zeta approached the shielded corner, placing a cooking vessel near them with needless shuffling and clanging to cover her words. "ASHE-theta, go now, before someone notices you've lingered. TAL-eta, get to medi-pod."

Girac's presence, even with Mischa in the room, was precious. Nica rested her head on his chest. Each moment they had was stolen, and none were guaranteed.

"We need to leave soon, before the next moon," she told him. "TAL-rho's spawn came early and is in grave danger. I can't risk being here much longer."

Girac looked at Mischa. "Will it be safe for Nica and the larva to travel right now?"

"It's not going to get safer, or easier before I spawn," Nica said, "but it will be too late afterward."

"She's right. I'll be with you to help, but the sooner we leave, the better." Mischa started to assess Nica. "Tau, you'd best be at your post. MO-ASHE will be arriving soon." She began to fasten the fetters. "I hate doing this, but the mistress cannot suspect anything is different."

"I understand, and I am grateful for all you have done." Nica patted Mischa's hand. "For me and my baby, and for Girac." Her voice caught. "He told me how you warned him about the boost treatments. How you helped him stay himself." She squeezed the hand tightly. "I can never thank you enough."

Mischa blinked rapidly. "Enough of that, you'll get me crying and then we will have a lot of explaining to do."

A double tap on the door warned them of MO-ASHE's approach.

This time, MO-ASHE's exam was far more extensive. She even brought her alpha in to translate, leaving no uncertainty about what she required. Together, they grilled Nica in detail about her symptoms and activities, ending with an extended list of prohibitions.

Nica quelled the instinct to squirm away as MO-ASHE dug her fingers into her arm. The gray alpha loomed from the other side, conveying equal menace as he translated. "You will do nothing to compromise complete gestation and a successful delivery. If any action on your part leads to a poor outcome, you will suffer the most severe consequences."

Even his look of contempt matched that of the Delphim's.

But once I have served their purpose, they will toss me aside. She was just a vessel. The journey ahead for Pescha, unimaginable given her condition, revealed the worth MO-ASHE accorded her aquans.

Examination complete and instructions delivered, MO-ASHE and her alpha left for the next patient. The door to the next cell creaked opened, allowing TAL-rho's cries to echo down the hallway, followed by the sound of promised punishment being meted out.

Nica's eyes widened, and Mischa closed the door, muffling the sound of threats and pain. Moving to her side, the Olomi nurse loosened the fetters and took her in her arms. She murmured in Nica's ear, "You will soon be free. Don't let fear control you—its guidance leads to destruction. Believe in hope, and it will lead you to freedom."

Nica inhaled deeply, thankful for Mischa's steadying presence. Easing off the table, she hugged the white Olomi, fondly tracing the orange splashes on her arms. "It will be soon, this week or next, and we will be swimming. From Water we have come . . ."

Mischa's green eyes sparkled. ". . . to Water we shall return."

63

"WHAT *am* I allowed to do?" Nica thrust the list of proscribed duties into TAL-zeta's hand.

Zeta rubbed her temples, focusing bleary eyes on the sheet. "There'll be no more serving tables, that's for sure." She scoffed at Nica's complaint. "Be grateful you were able to serve last night at MO-ASHE's table."

"That is true. I wouldn't have been able to see Rissa, even after TAL returned. But why all the restrictions? Pe–TAL-kap was serving until she spawned, and now MO-ASHE intends for her to walk for several suns while she is still so weak."

"TAL-rho's early delivery has made MO-ASHE hypervigilant. She's had one successful outcome, but the fry born into TRE-CH's household may not survive. Rest and gain strength while you can, little one. You'll need it."

Zeta pulled together some dried and fermented ingredients and handed them to her. "In fact, what would be best is for you to help TAL-kap regain her strength. I will try to prepare both of you for your journeys."

Nica nodded, grateful for any opportunity to help Pescha. "Thank you, TAL-ze–."

Bam! The doorpost shuddered, sending bits of dust and plant matter swirling.

"What ha–"

"*Shh.*" Zeta waved her back as she approached the doorway.

Nica crept behind, trying to sort out the commotion.

"Stop fighting, it will not go well . . ." came a warning.

"That sounds like Gir–ASHE-tau," Nica whispered.

"No. No! *Soto!*" an Olomi wailed.

"And that's TAL-rho . . . or whatever her new designation is," Zeta muttered.

They peeked around and almost burst out laughing. Girac, gleaming dark with his bright blue markings, was struggling to control a much smaller, blue-striped Rho.

"I don't wish to—Hey! No biting!" The frustrated guard held his writhing charge firmly, but at arm's length. "TAL-zeta, can you do something?" The desperation in Girac's voice matched the pleading in his eyes. He enclosed the blue between her seat and the table. "Please!"

Zeta shook her head with the slightest hint of a smile. "TAL-eta, heat some water." She sat by the distraught blue, murmuring in soothing tones and stroking her hand.

Such foolishness—heating water, Nica thought impatiently. But she watched until the liquid began to bubble.

Once it was ready, Zeta switched with Nica and poured the water over some dried vegetation. Sprinkling a bit of powder into the hot liquid, she stirred it in and brought the cup to Rho's lips. "Drink this, child. It will help."

"No! *Ọmọ mi, Ọmọ mi.*" Rho shook her head violently.

"I'm sorry, but we'll have to restrain you if you don't calm down." Zeta sighed as she examined the stripes TAL-alph had left on Rho's back. "And we have to dress those wounds. I need you to drink this. If you don't, you'll get sent back to MO-ASHE."

The unwilling patient quailed, yielding enough to drink from the cup TAL-zeta held to her lips. By the time it was emptied, she stopped resisting, and Girac was able to release his rock-solid grip on her.

"Her designation is TRE-sichi—and must remain so for her stay here. MO-ASHE is intent on sending her back with TRE-CH." He breathed heavily as he ran his fingers through his hair. "This transition was unexpectedly strenuous. I hope I didn't hurt her, but . . ." He looked at the impressions her teeth left on his forearm. "She was . . . difficult."

"Her wounds at TAL-alph's hands are far more significant. I'm afraid we'll have to restrain her to help the healing process." TAL-zeta sighed. "Other guards will not be as forgiving."

Nica started to move to TAL-rho's side, but Zeta blocked her. "This is activity that you are restricted from. No lifting. At all. Carry her back here, ASHE-tau." The aged supervisor directed her new orderly into the sectioned-off area where Pescha lay. She watched them wearily. "Just when did my pod become an infirmary?"

She searched through her stores. "TAL-eta, move your mat in here so that you can better attend to these two, and rest when they are still." Zeta turned. "Roll her onto the ventrals so I can dress those wounds. Where's the numbing salve? There!" She pulled a small container from the lowest shelf and examined the contents. "This will do the trick. Best put the restraint bars under the mat first, so we can constrain her."

Nica's heart was sore as she slowly bound the blue's hands and feet to the bars. "I'm sorry," she whispered. Now she understood why Mischa apologized whenever Nica was to be bound. To allow TAL-rho, or, TRE-sichi, to go free would only bring more suffering on her, but it was painful to be the agent of captivity. "Do you think she will forgive me, when she is herself?"

"I don't know, child." Zeta shook her head, her expression tinged with sorrow. "Her heart has been broken more than most. We can't see where her path will lead."

Nica smoothed on the salve as directed and Zeta left to fetch more broth for her patients. She tried to work in silence, but as the worst of her wounds were treated, Rho's groans disturbed Pescha on the adjoining mat. The blue pulled against the bindings, her feeble protests wrenching Nica. Pivoting between the mats, she tried to attend to her podmates, but Rho renewed her cries for her stolen fry and Pescha refused the spoon Nica brought to her lips.

"Leave me." Pescha pushed it away. "Let me be."

"You need your strength, sister, or they will harm you more."

Pescha's eyes flashed. "What more could they do? I've served their purpose, and they have no use for me. Why do you bother nursing me when I should be nursing my fry?"

Nica seized on Pescha's one expressed desire, but she had to speak truthfully. "Your spawn is healthy, but they will keep you from it, even as they did TAL-rho. Her fry is weak and will not survive without a mother's milk. This is the plan they have for you."

Silence hung between the Olomi, as Pescha regarded her through her tears. Looking past Nica to the new occupant in their tiny quarters, she blinked at the sight of their former podmate. "TAL-rho?"

"Yes, although, her current designation is TRE-sichi. She arrived earlier this tide, with TRE-CH."

"But her larva . . . it wasn't time."

"The spawn came early and is not expected to survive. MO-ASHE intends to send you back with TRE-CH to nurse the fry until it is stronger."

"But you said mine is healthy?"

"Yes. MO-ASHE is pleased with herself about the fry you bore." The irony burned like bile in Nica's throat. "She is sending you in three suns, and it is a long journey. You need to regain your strength."

"But I will never see . . ."

Nica set a soft hand on her friend's arm. "You know MO-ASHE, she never let TAL-rho, that is TRE-sichi, near her child here, and she will torture you in the same way. This way you can care for one of our children. Let this soothe your soul." But even in speaking, she herself could not bear the thought of such a separation.

"Please, TAL-kap. I beg you." Rho's hoarse voice broke into their conversation. "Don't let my baby die."

Nica whispered, "You do not have a choice in going, sister. Your only choice is in surviving, and if you do, her baby may survive as well."

"It's not fair."

Nica nodded but persisted. "What about our life here is fair?

But we don't need fair to do good. And this is a good that only you can do."

Pescha closed her eyes for a long moment, then opened them to look at Nica. "As you said, I don't have a choice." She took a deep breath. "But I *can* choose to give our sister's child a chance."

"*O ṣe . . . o ṣe.*" The blue Olomi thanked her pod-sisters repeatedly, tears staining the mat.

Nica moved over and stroked Rho's dark, almost-black hair. "Shh. Your baby will live, and so must you."

Under Nica's care, the patients convalesced steadily. She kept her pallet between the two to ease alternating care from one to the other, and rested when they slept, as Zeta directed. The pod supervisor was scarce during much of this time, tasked with supplementing the feasts for MO-ASHE and her guest. But by the third sun, TRE-sichi's wounds were closing and infection free, and Pescha could walk for short distances. All of them, however, were anxious.

"Soon it will be time for TAL-kap to travel," Zeta remarked.

Nica was fretful. "I don't think she is ready for a journey."

"You know as well as I, it matters not what we think," the elder Olomi chided. "Learn to find peace in what you can affect and let go of what is beyond your control."

"I know, Zeta, but it doesn't change how I feel."

"Only you can manage your emo—"

The unmistakable sound of the barrier powering down cut off Zeta's words and Nica's breath. TAL was back.

64

·· R E S T A R T ··

C AUTIOUS whispers circulated in the wake of EC-TAL's entrance.

"He returned alone."

"He's empty-handed."

The tidings were received with discreet elation—and a measure of fear. An unsuccessful hunting trip would put TAL in a foul mood, but Olomi hearts were grateful that another had not been added to their number.

Perhaps the warning we sent out helped some avoid capture. Nica's spirits rose when she realized there would be no ceremony to mark another victim of TAL's cruelty, and she smiled at their mutual relief.

TAL-zeta paused and pulled her cooking pot out of the full heat. "I don't know what is causing you joy right now, but you need to swallow it. On this tide, it is dangerous to smile." She replaced the pot on the flame without a change in expression and returned to separating the prepared ingredients.

Nica accepted the reproof without argument and tried to change the subject. "Do you think TAL will receive the news of the visitor well? He wasn't happy about the first visit, and this time TRE-CH came with complaints."

"That's hard to tell. I suppose it depends on how well MO-ASHE smoothed things over with the Delphim. But there is one bit of good news in all this." Zeta tested the broth, stirring in some more of the fermented paste before helping Nica bring it in for their patients.

"What?" Nica was hard put to imagine any good about TAL's return.

"It's not likely that TRE-CH will depart as planned, given TAL's arrival, and that means—"

Nica almost danced. "That means Pescha doesn't have to leave on this tide!"

She returned to the pod, smiling as she smoothed the bright orange tendrils framing her friend's face and brought a spoonful of broth to the ashen blue lips. Pescha was still so pale in the wake of her ordeal. "You have another sun. You do not have to leave with TRE-CH yet."

Grimacing as she sat up, Pescha took the bowl. "If only a sun's reprieve would allow me to see my fry," she sighed. Then she looked up to Zeta. "Will there be a meal tonight, in MO-ASHE's chambers?"

Zeta's eyes widened as she realized what Pescha was asking. "Child, you still need to heal," she warned. "You can barely stand."

"Strength I can muster if you give me something for the pain. Just let me help in the kitchen. MO-ASHE will be sure to present my baby to EC-TAL."

"Aye, she will, that's for sure." Zeta shook her head.

"Please, TAL-zeta," Pescha pleaded. "I may never see my child again."

"I wish I could say you were wrong." She grimaced as she pushed herself up from the stool. "But I won't deny you this chance. Let me find something to ease the pain."

As Zeta turned away, Pescha clutched Nica's arm and hissed in her ear, "Get out before you spawn! You must escape while you can!"

Eyes wide in fear, "How did you—who spoke of—" Nica fumbled in vain for words to protect her plan.

"Don't worry." It was Pescha's turn to reassure her friend. "Your secret is safe with me."

"But how did you know?"

"You stopped crying out in your sleep." Pescha paused. "And

you stopped worrying about survival. It's clear, you are preparing to live."

Zeta took the crew to prepare and serve at MO-ASHE's table, leaving Nica to direct food-pod. And if the supervisor left a little earlier, walked a bit slower, or had a larger crew, no one noticed.

Checking on her former podmate, still lightly restrained as per TAL-alph's orders, Nica applied another layer of the healing salve Zeta had prepared. When Iota's pod began to filter in, Nica joined the servers before the inky-black Olomi went through the line.

"TAL-iota. Our pod is split between serving both households. TAL-zeta directs you to assist after your pod has finished their meal."

"If it is necessary, I suppose I must," he replied with a slight bow.

When the meal had finished, Nica directed the pod members to finish clearing the kitchen and service area, then checked on TRE-sichi oncè again. The blue was resting well, and her back was much better than expected, despite TAL-alph's brutal lesson. Still, Nica shivered as she inspected the wounds, tracing in the air above them.

A sound in the doorway roused her attention, as TAL-iota tapped lightly.

"We are finished, TAL-eta. If you still require assistance, I am available now."

Taking care to not disturb her patient, Nica moved with soft footsteps to TAL-zeta's storage room, making sure that the other pod members had finished their duties. Closing the door behind her, she demanded, in full voice, that the grounds-pod supervisor move several of the larger bags of vegetables to the back of the storeroom. Amid his complaining she divulged the plan in bits and whispers.

"We must be ready to leave soon, in less than two weeks."

"How many loads do you need me to move?!"

"Free Olomi are locating and preparing to disable the reef generators."

"Oof! What do you have in these sacks?"

"They can give us one sun's warning. We must be prepared to drain and force the gates."

"I'm serious! I have to work in the morning!"

"Stay in contact with ASHE-tau."

"I'm done here!"

Mouthing a silent *ę şe* to thank him, Nica replied curtly, "I will inform TAL-zeta of your assistance."

As the white-spotted Olomi headed out, Nica glanced around. Her sensors were on edge, and she had the sensation of being watched, but there was no one visible in the light of the full moon. *Stop acting like an anemone, Nica.* She shook her head, chiding herself for being foolish, and headed back to check on TRE-sichi.

Nica turned in to their sleeping area and gave a yelp of surprise to see her charge standing, just inside the doorway. Glancing at the empty restraints on her pallet, she murmured, "I guess they were a bit too loose."

The blue Olomi put a hand back. "They were designed to tighten when I struggled—but slackened when I was calm."

"Please know, TRE-sichi, that I wish you no harm. But if you roam unrestrained or lose control, as before, TAL-alph will take pleasure in making an example of you, once again."

"Auryn."

"What?" Nica was confused at the quiet word.

"Auryn," TRE-sichi repeated. "My name was . . . is Auryn."

"Oh." Nica had had no clue of her podmate's true name when they spent almost every waking and sleeping moment within two paces of each other. She smiled. "It is a beautiful name. But why . . ." her voice trailed off.

"Why am I telling you now?" TAL-rho—TRE-sichi—Auryn stood tall. "Because, for every tide since my . . . since our capture, I have obeyed. I did everything they told me to, without hesitation, in the hopes that I would be able to be near my son." She twisted the hem of her tunic. "Now they have stripped me of my spawn, not just once, which was devastating enough, but twice. I was not even allowed to put the larva I carried to my breast." Her voice caught. "They attached me to a machine that suctioned out what milk I had until there was nothing left to take."

She took Nica by both arms. "There is nothing you can do to stop them, TAL-eta. The Delphim will take what they want and leave you for dead. If you have a chance to flee, you must. But when you do, take me and my son with you. If you don't, I will inform TAL-alph of your plans."

A chill ran through Nica, and she broke away, staring at the blue. *How could she . . .*

The blue's deep violet eyes drilled into her. "You must take us when you go, or you and your spawn will never leave this place. *Soto* cannot stay."

"*Soto*? Mote? He can't . . . he won't go. You don't understand. He's become one of them."

The desperate mother shook her head vigorously. "He must go. You will take him with you," she stated, "or you will not go."

In an instant, her defiance drained away, and she collapsed at Nica's feet, lifting her head. "Please, TAL-eta, please," she begged. "We can't . . . I can't . . ."

Still aghast at her podmate's threat, Nica hesitated for a moment. Then she sank to the floor and embraced Auryn, stroking her black hair as the grieving mother sobbed in her lap.

65

·· R E V E L A T I O N ··

E VEN BEFORE the fog of sleep fully retreated, Nica's heart
pounded, flooding her with the knowledge that something was
wrong. She bolted up from the pallet, eyes wide.

Her gaze pivoted to TAL-rho—TRE-sich—Auryn. *If she knows
about our plans—everything is at risk.*

Pescha's tunic hung alone on the pegs. Nica looked down and
shook her head. She hadn't removed hers last night. She didn't even
remember lying down. Groggy and sore, she ran her fingers through
her curls and tried to jog her memory. As her roommates began to
stir, so did some impressions of the past evening. Smoothing the
creases on her tunic as fast as she could, she set out to find TAL-
zeta. Hurrying wasn't the same in her ungainly state. "TAL-zeta! I
don't remember how I got to my pallet last night, but—"

"You don't remember because you and TRE-sichi fell asleep
sitting up. I don't know what happened here while I served
MO-ASHE and TAL, but she was unrestrained, and you both
looked like you cried most the night. I had to pull you onto your
mat. Hrmph." The old Olomi sounded annoyed.

"Oh, TAL-zeta! It was terrible! TAL-rho, er, oh, you know who
I mean. Actually, her name is," Nica's voice dropped to a whisper,
"Auryn, and she must have heard something while we were
unloading the produce—"

"Wait," the supervisor interrupted. "Don't tell me you were
lifting these heavy—"

"Oh no! TAL-iota did the lifting, but I really called him in to
discuss the escape plans, and I think TAL-rho must have overheard

because she told me I had to leave, because they would take my baby, and she said it was good to leave, but then she said we had to take her and *Soto*, that's her son, Mote, or she would tell TAL-alph everything and I don't know what to do." Nica's tone was close to a wail by the time she ceased her torrent.

"Well," TAL-zeta said, her expression grim. "That is a lot to digest."

She handed Nica the stirring stick as she headed into the back. "Start the porridge while I find seasonings. I need to think."

Heading dutifully to the large pot that contained breakfast for the Olomi, Nica plunged the stirrer into the sandy-colored potage. Grasping the paddle with two hands, she pulled from the outer edges to the middle, circling around the rim to make sure the whole mess was evenly blended.

She stirred methodically, and almost put herself to sleep. The rest of the pod was beginning to come to life, with Olomi stepping into their positions throughout the compound, when Nica realized she'd nearly drifted off. She dragged the stirrer across the bottom, hoping it hadn't scorched. She craned her neck, looking for Zeta. It wouldn't be long before the first shifts made their way to the serving lines, and conversation would be difficult.

Just as she began to fret, the supervisor came out with a small load of seasoning. Salt, as always, to enhance the flavor, but fermented paste as well, now that it was ready, bringing the filling gruel from tasteless to satisfying, and even making it a bit more nutritious.

"I've been thinking about the proposal your blue friend made, and I think it is reasonable, even though she is not."

"But Zeta, the child is a—"

"The fry is hers, and if your positions were switched, you would do the same."

The supervisor's tone was firm, and Nica had to admit she was right.

"But he will not go willingly . . ."

"Do you remember the tea I made his mother?" Zeta tilted her head in the direction of their sleeping quarters. "It may be helpful for him as well. We just need to be able to administer it." She checked the porridge. "I'll get someone else to serve. You go check on your patients."

The bowls rattled as Nica carried the tray to their sleeping section. Despite her best attempts, she was unable to still her hands, and her heart. If only there was a draught or powder that could erase last night from Auryn's memory. But there was not. Taking a deep breath to calm her defiant nerves, she pushed aside the hanging reeds that served as a makeshift partition and forced the worry from her face as she greeted her patients.

TRE-sichi was awake, sitting despite the restraints that secured her.

"Is this necessary?" The blue held out her fetters.

Nica shrugged, placing the tray down between the Olomi's mats. "You tell me. If you are unfettered, will you cooperate? If not, the consequences will be swift, severe, and not limited to you."

She handed a bowl to Pescha before fixing her gaze onto the newly returned member of their pod. "If I free you, the responsibility for your behavior will be on my back, and TAL-alph is already eager to lay into it."

"I give you my word, there will be no trouble from me." Auryn attempted again to hold her bound hands up to Nica. "I have only one goal, and you have already given me a chance to realize it."

With a sigh of resignation, Nica loosened the bindings and passed the bowl to her. "First, you must prepare TAL-kap for the journey."

Auryn's retelling of the journey to and back from TRE-CH's compound confirmed much of Nica's sister's account, with more specific information of the approach between the two points. Although distraught when she had been given over to the new Delphim household, she was intent on returning to her son, and had attended to the details on her journey.

Applying her memory of the roughly mapped land extrusions that Jonnat had prepared so long ago, Nica was able to get a better picture of the route and, of greater importance, opportunities to access the water along the way.

Nica reached to clear the bowls but stopped short as she realized Pescha's remained untouched. "Pe–TAL-kap, you need to eat. Have you not been paying attention to the journey that lies ahead? The food will help you regain your strength."

Tears rolled down the Olomi's pale, orange-striped cheeks, tracing the fluorescent blue contours of her jaw. She shook her head mutely at Nica's efforts to feed her, staring at nothing, and saying nothing.

"Pescha, please. What is wrong? Are you in pain?"

At that, the postpartum Olomi focused her eyes on Nica, and began to form a response, but stopped. Not knowing what to do, Nica sat on the mat and held her friend. Eventually, the shudders that shook the orange's frame slowed enough for Pescha to squeeze out some words.

"I saw . . . ọmọ mi!"

The last two words were a wail as the bereaved mother unleashed her sorrow. *So like TAL-rho.*

She had served, hidden in MO-ASHE's kitchen, until the Delphim ordered the baby to be brought forth. Pescha watched from behind the doorway as MO-ASHE displayed her success to TAL and TRE-CH. When the MO realized she was present, she ordered Pescha to be brought out as well.

"I'd hoped that she would allow me to hold my spawn, but she had a different plan. She held my fry in her lap with a knife to its throat"–her eyes squeezed shut–"and commanded me to cut the webbing. I couldn't do it. Until her blade broke the skin, and my fry started screaming. It was the first time my spawn looked on my face . . ." Her eyes opened, tragic and despondent. Her voice was a whisper. "I cut its webbing."

Nica was in shock, horrified.

Pescha took a breath and continued, her body rigid. "As the fry screamed in pain, that alpha held me directly in front. My face was all it could see. Then they brought a numbing salve, which

MO-ASHE applied after she turned the baby to look at her. As soon as the crying stopped, she gave it something sweet to drink, and my little one fell asleep, comforted, in *her* arms. MO-ASHE warned me that every time I trespassed into what was now her child's world, I would be the source of pain, and she would be the source of comfort."

She lifted her eyes, rimmed red and underscored by dark circles. "I don't even know if I have a son or a daughter."

It seemed like all they did was weep in this horrid place. This time it was Auryn who put her arms around the two of them and held them tight. "This is their way." She turned her head slightly to Nica, their faces only a couple of inches apart. "You must leave. You must leave soon. Do you understand now? And you must take us with you."

66

T HE SUMMONS came before the first pods had finished their morning meal when TAL-alph, shoving aside any Olomi in her path, came to fetch Pescha. The yellow enforcer looked stronger than she had just a few suns ago, and the glint in her eye matched the fervor with which she wielded her whip.

She descended on the three Olomi huddled under the woven fringe, smirking at Pescha. "Your presence is required, TAL-kap, but not here."

A cry of dismay escaped them all, and the girls tried to hug, but the alpha laid her whip with expertise across the backs of her blue and orange victims, grazing Nica's arm in the process. Gasping in pain, they separated, Auryn, writhing from the reopened wound on her back, and Nica gingerly touching a burn-like mark on her arm.

"The sooner you're gone, the better." The yellow enforcer dug her fingers into Pescha's upper arm. "You breeders think you're immune because MO-ASHE protects you, but you're fools. She protects only the babies, then you're all fair game."

"O ṣe, Pescha," Auryn cried out as TAL-alph callously dragged the wailing mother away. "O ṣe." Her voice dropped to a whisper as Pescha's crying faded from the courtyard. "Yours may be the only love my baby ever knows." She turned to Nica, her lower lip beginning to tremble. "We have to leave before it is too late."

There was no fanfare when TRE-CH left with TAL-kap in tow. Only her few friends watched as the gates opened and shut for the single Delphim and his exchanged property. Pescha offered no resistance. Her heart was already broken, and there was no hope left for her in TAL's household.

Do I dare visit Kolas again? How will I get word to Rissa? Will Iota be prepared to disable the gate? How will we give Mote the sleeping draught?

Nica's thoughts tumbled over each other, one after the other vying for an answer, only to be shoved aside by the next.

Calm yourself, Nica. You cannot panic. You'll worry yourself sick. But maybe it is the perfect time to be . . . "TAL-zeta!"

Nica rushed out to the food lines as fast as she could waddle, her hands supporting her abdomen. Speed seemed to be more of an impossibility with each passing tide, but she was learning to compensate.

"What is the problem now, child?" The supervisor didn't even lift her head. She just kept dishing out food and made space for Nica to help. "Bah, you can't even refill these trays, stay here and keep the line moving while I fetch enough for the last pod."

"But . . . I . . ."

"No excuses, I'll be right back."

Nica sighed as she automatically dished out the gruel as the last pods made their way through the line.

"I don't suppose you have something a little more edible back in the kitchen?"

Preparing a sharp response, she raised her head. "Iota! You had me for a second."

"I'm serious!" the white-freckled Olomi protested. "Those bags were heavy. I don't know how I'm going to be able to keep up at the gates. The least you could do is sweeten the deal. Or maybe my meal?"

His grin was so infectious that she couldn't help but return it. "Well, I'd hate to leave you ill-prepared for your workload. You just might need to work well into the night if you fall behind."

"You don't say." The dark creases deepened under the spattered white dots. He cocked his head.

Nica nodded slowly, maintaining eye contact. "I do say. In fact, it's looking like we're going to have a busy week, so eat up!"

The grounds supervisor returned her nod and took his tray without another word.

"Zeta, I need to visit the medic," Nica whispered as the supervisor came back to the line.

"What, are you feeling ill?" She lifted her hand to Nica's brow.

"No, but I need to—or at least look the part. Can you help with that?"

"Come back after this line finishes, and I have something that will safely send you to medical." She flashed a grim smile.

Zeta's solution did the trick—a poultice to give Nica a terrible rash, and some leaves to induce vomiting that would be safe for the baby. Armed with a hidden stash of sleeping tea, she set off on what she hoped would be her last examination by MO-ASHE. She stowed one of the nauseating leaves inside her cheek and started chewing on it as she approached the entrance.

ASHE-delt, surly as usual, blanched at the rash that covered her neck and arms. He started scratching his own arms as he searched for his pad to register her visit, but she didn't let him get that far.

Lurching forward and grabbing at the blue guard's arm for balance, Nica emptied her stomach all over his pad and the table. She also left a layer of paste from the poultice on his arms as she fumbled to regain her balance.

"Go!" he begged, stepping back from the disaster she had left at his station. "Just get some medicine!"

She headed down the familiar, over-bright and artificially lit hallway that led to the exam rooms, when she bumped into Girac.

Lighting up at the sight of him, she faltered for a moment at the horrified look on his face. "Don't worry," she assured him. "I'm fine. I'll explain later."

His expression changed to one of relief, and he took the apparent illness as an excuse to help her to the room as she relayed her message. "We leave as soon as the reef generators go down, but we need to take Mote with us." She slipped Girac the bundle of sedating tea leaves as he helped her onto the table. "We must give this to the boy so he will not fight us. It is TRE-sichi's demand, or she will expose us."

"I'll get it to Mischa. She or Rissa can handle that."

"Iota has been keeping the gates drained, it won't take much to disable them. Tell Mischa and Rissa to be ready." She gazed into his eyes. "It won't be long."

He kissed her cheek. "You are braver than any of us, okan mi. Because you dared to hope, we can too."

67

·· DISPATCH ··

T HE CALL came.
Kolas was sequestered deep in the hydro-processing tunnels. The post was designed to remind the aquans who it was that controlled access to the water. Water the Delphim had violated to adapt this world to their needs. They required the Olomi to convey water from the depths but barred them from immersion. The Delphim never expected this would prove their undoing.

Percussing through the Deep, unrestricted by the grating, the looped message was simple: REEF GENERATORS LOCATED. DISABLE AFTER NEXT SUN.

He tapped out "RECEIVED," filled his containers, and listened for the reply. There was none, but the loop stopped.

Tomorrow, Mischa. Tomorrow night.

So little time—these trembling hands will give me away. Mischa attended her duties, trying to maintain a calm demeanor.

Girac handed her a tray. "This requires cleaning, ASHE-xi. See that a thorough job is done this time."

Mischa glanced around furtively before whispering, *"Tomorrow night."*

The guard coughed loudly and cleared his throat to cover his whispered, *"The tea is for Mote. Tell Theta."*

"Fine, I'll rewash it. But next time keep your hands off." She stomped off to the kitchen, muttering, "These guards make more work for me than anyone."

Girac surveyed the sentry station. "ASHE-delt! You'd better be careful cleaning up that mess."

"That pregnant greenie vomited all over my station, and now I have a rash, as well."

Girac backed away, throwing in an exaggerated grimace for good measure. "I wouldn't be touching any of that. Maybe you should call for grounds-pod. They're responsible for exterior maintenance."

"That's a good thought, Tau! But I can't leave my post till after the evening meal. Could you send one my way?"

"I'll head out and take care of that now."

Girac walked briskly to the gates. He took note of the rubble piles just inside the perimeter. The piles TAL-iota moved against the fence every night, only to remove them before the sun rose. *We couldn't do this without him.*

Iota straightened up as Girac approached. "What do you need from me?" he asked with a scowl.

"There's a mess at MO-ASHE's sentry station that needs attending to. That falls under your pod's responsibilities." He closed the distance and loomed over the shorter Olomi.

"I'll get to it as soon as I can," TAL-iota blustered. "You don't need to be an alpha about it."

"See that it gets done immediately!" Girac glowered in Iota's face and poked him in the chest. "MO-ASHE's household doesn't need to be low on your list."

He brought his face nearer. *"Tomorrow night. Be ready. Tell TAL-eta."*

Iota hung back, waiting for his pod to file though the serving line. He glanced around before he approached. Clinking his tray against the serving frame, he whispered, *"Tomorrow night."*

Nica was speechless. It was really happening.

"Be ready."

Finally, she managed to choke out, *"Remember the juvies."*

Iota nodded, knowing the green Olomi's heart for the youngest captives under TAL's control. He would get word to TAL-phi and TAL-psi, the young blue and green, as well as TAL-lam, the brown-stripe in the well-pod. These were all who could be safely informed. It was going to be a busy night, but it might also be the last one he spent abovewater.

Nica's gaze followed the grounds supervisor as he rejoined his pod. She needed to let TAL-zeta and Auryn know. Tomorrow she could inform a few others, but they risked exposure if too many found out. They would spread the word tomorrow night, after the break started. All would quickly realize the opportunity.

She waited for a moment to speak with Zeta alone. The rain beat on the woven canopy, covering their whispered conversation. Nica filled her in on the plans for the next night.

Her friend and confidante patted her hand, saying only, "We'll discuss this tonight."

Puzzled at the subdued reaction, Nica tried to press Zeta, but the old Olomi turned from her and headed out to direct her pod.

She pondered this reaction as she headed to the back room

that she still shared with Auryn. The space felt empty without Pescha, but TAL-zeta wanted Nica to remain there while she was still gravid.

TAL-rho—Auryn had not yet been released into the general population and was supposed to be restrained or sedated. The hope of reclaiming her son had tempered her distraught behavior so far. Nica hoped it would be sufficient for one more sun.

She searched for the correct designation before addressing her former podmate out loud. They were too close to freedom to risk any missteps. "TRE-sichi. Are you feeling well enough to assist with cleaning?"

The blue lifted her brows at Nica. "Since when does how I feel factor into what I must do?"

"According to Zeta, our orders were to keep you sedated or restrained," Nica replied. "However, if you display the ability to participate in pod duties, you need not be subject to those conditions."

"There is little advantage for me either way," the Olomi said. "But it would be nice to stretch a little." She held out her hands for Nica to remove the restraints.

As she bent over to free Auryn's wrists, Nica whispered, *"We leave tomorrow night. Rissa has been given something to sedate your son so that he will not fight us when we leave. But you must stay in control, or you put us all at risk."*

The blue nodded as she rubbed her wrists. *"O şe."*

68

"ZETA?" Nica stood outside the supervisor's station, long after the last of the pods and workers had melted into the darkness.

"Come in, child, I suppose this can wait no longer."

TAL-zeta settled herself on a mat and patted the one next to her. Nica carefully lowered herself onto it, then turned to face her mentor and friend. "What is it, *Ìyágba*? What is wrong?"

Zeta took Nica's hand and turned it over in her palm, the bright green of youth cupped in her deep and faded blues. Nica's scars still stood out prominently, while Zeta's were more difficult to see. She gave a deep sigh.

"It has been close to twenty moons since the Breaking changed our world and our lives forever. And I have lived here under TAL's authority for all but two of those moons. He has the one who is designated Alph, but I was the first to serve in TAL's household."

The thought of her old friend suffering the abuse so many of them had when taken squeezed Nica's chest. She clung to Zeta's hand. "It hurts to think of what you had to endure being taken captive."

"But it wasn't like that, child. You see, when TAL happened upon me on that abovewater seamount, I had already left the Deep"—she paused as if reluctant to speak—"to die."

A chill washed over Nica as the aged Olomi's words sank in. "But . . . ?" She struggled to find words. "But why?"

"The first wave of destruction that reached the depths found my home. All were trapped. My husband. My child. My grandchildren.

I was returning from a visit to a friend when the heavens hurled stones into the sea. I rushed home to help, but the lava flows made any approach impossible. There was nothing to be done. All I could do was listen to their screams and cries of terror and of agony . . . and then the silence as they were swallowed by the lava."

Nica's heart seized at the despairing horror. *Oh, Zeta!*

"I alone was spared that agonizing death," Zeta said. "I alone was cursed to remember and relive their torment. I alone was left . . . to live."

The two sat in silence, clasping each other's hands.

Nica groped for words, uncertain how to begin. "I am honored you have shared this with me, Zeta. But I do not understand why it is now."

"Because, my child, I will not be joining you when you return to the Deep."

Nica stared at her, stunned. "You won't? But why? Why not?"

"There's nothing left for me in the Deep. Only pain, and an aching void. To be immersed and surrounded with other people's life and love . . . it was too much to bear then, and I don't want to return to it."

"But why would you stay here? Always to be treated like a slave."

"To be needed? To be useful? To care for those who have lost hope? If I leave with you, who will watch for TAL-kap when she returns? Who will protect the heartbroken, like TAL-rho? Who will warn the unwary of the alphas' tempers? Who will make a poultice for those who have been whipped?"

"But *Ìyágba*, I can't leave you here." Nica's voice broke. "I won't."

"Hush, child. You can, and you will. My choice is not yours to make."

Nica stared into the black night. Her heart should have held nothing but compassion for Zeta, the one who had been by her side and supported her, but she struggled. TAL-zeta had provided the means to take an unwilling Olomi by force, back to the Deep, yet she herself was unwilling to return.

But she didn't belong here. How could she stay?

We were meant to be community, in the Deep. We could be her family . . . She had never pictured leaving Zeta behind. Eventually, Nica gave up fighting for reason and against her feelings of loss and betrayal, and surrendered instead to a troubled sleep.

69

·· B U R N E D ··

A WAVE TOSSED by tempests would be more stable than Nica's heart. She slipped into the kitchen, avoiding TAL-zeta, unwilling to risk breaking down in front of any others. Only when Zeta directed her to fetch supplies from the storage area was she forced to confront the pain.

"TAL-eta." The older Olomi cornered her while the rest of the pod was serving. "You cannot avoid me throughout this tide, and we will not have forever."

"I know, I'm sorry. I just didn't want to start . . . crying . . . in front of everyone."

But the tears started, and then there was no stopping them. Zeta gathered Nica into her arms until they ceased.

"Are you done?" Zeta offered the corner of her tunic to Nica.

"I'm sorry, but I will miss you so much it hurts my heart . . . I was trying so hard not to."

"You needed to let that out. Now I can wish you well, and you can go—"

The gong interrupted them, calling all to assemble. They looked at each other. The call only came when TAL returned from his expeditions, and he had already returned, empty-handed.

Not daring to hesitate, they hurried out. TAL-zeta shooed her pod along with other confused Olomi out to the courtyard where TAL would be waiting.

Moving as fast as her rounded belly would allow, Nica splashed out to the courtyard several paces behind the rest of the pods. She was not eager to see TAL's display of control, which was what his assemblies usually were. Reluctant to push, she waited behind the outer ring of onlookers. When the crowds parted for a moment, her legs nearly gave out and she grabbed onto Zeta.

It was TAL-iota on his knees, trussed to a beam across his shoulders, flanked by TAL and his alpha, each wielding their whip.

"It has been brought to my attention"–*crack!* TAL brought the whip across Iota's back–"that there is a conspiracy"–*crack!* TAL-alph's whip laid into his back at her master's nod–"among you."

TAL swept the whip handle in a circle, pointing at the gathered Olomi before bringing it down again.

"We have not yet convinced your accomplice"–TAL nodded again to his alpha, *crack!*–"to divulge the details or collaborators in this scheme"–*crack!*–"but be assured, they will be revealed."

"There . . . is . . . no . . . plot." The white-spotted Olomi managed to shake his head as blood and rain streamed down his dorsal.

Nica was nauseous. She started to move toward Iota, but Zeta held her back.

"He's shaking his head for you," Zeta whispered. "Don't make his pain for nothing!"

TAL and his alpha continued to whip Iota, but he continued to shake his head, denying the existence of any scheme, until he collapsed into a puddle of reddened mud. Nica turned to hide her face from the sight when a smirk caught her eye. Straightening, she looked again. It was Xi, who'd been demoted from agri-pod supervisor to Iota's grounds crew. He was enjoying watching Iota suffer. Nica narrowed her eyes.

He was wearing Iota's supervisor tunic.

Her temples and cheeks flushed green with fury as her tormentor smiled through Iota's beating.

Grabbing the beam, TAL dragged Iota through the crowd until he stood him before the gates. Nica's hand flew up to her mouth as the assembled Olomi gasped as one.

"This is your last chance, mud-sucker. Give me a name."

Iota groaned as he stood before the gates surrounded by piles of Olomi remains. "There is no plot. I have no name."

With that, TAL hurled the bloodied Olomi into the gate, and gave a twisted smile of satisfaction at the sound of his victim screaming as the charge reached out and met him. Even TAL-xi blanched as Iota convulsed violently and then was still. The assembly stood petrified, some silent, others weeping.

TAL turned his back on the body of his latest victim and glared at the mourners. "Don't ever forget. You belong to me."

TAL-alph dismissed the gathered Olomi after TAL left, scrutinizing their individual reactions to their comrade's demise. Nica didn't resist Zeta's grip on her arm, silent and insistent, as they made their way back to the kitchen. She barely noticed when they reached the back room and were safely ensconced behind the bags of produce and canisters of meal. And she stayed in place, unmoving, once Zeta released her arm, moving to her hands, flexing and rubbing her knuckles. She stood, swaying slightly between the shelves, emptied and lost.

"TAL-eta." Zeta's words staggered to her, broken and distorted, like currents interrupted by a seaslide. She cupped Nica's head in her hands and tried to capture her gaze, but Nica couldn't meet her eyes.

When Nica did speak, her voice was not her own, but sounded like an echo from a memory. "I have only caused more pain. More death. Iota lost everything–because of me. Chloe is dead because of me. Jonnat died because of me." She stared past TAL-zeta. "It's always because of me."

"Child," Zeta said firmly. "What happened this morning was tragic, and senseless, and evil. But you didn't kill Iota, or Chloe, or your friend, Jonnat. TAL did that. It can't be undone, but it can't be for nothing. You can mourn for him another sun, but for this tide, you need to focus on the plan. For Iota, so his death would not be in vain. For Rissa, who has almost given up hope. For your spawn, who deserves a better life. For your family that waits for you."

Nica stared at the dust settling around her feet. "I can't, Zeta. I can't bear this anymore." She buried her face in her hands.

TAL-zeta took Nica's hands and gently pulled them from her

face. "You can." She moved the young Olomi's hands onto her expanded stomach. "And you must."

Nica closed her eyes, took in a deep breath, and then let it out. "But how?"

Zeta's eyes seemed to focus on something far behind the storage shed walls. Then she shifted and turned her gaze back to Nica. "Where we are from?"

"Food-pod?"

"Silly child, *nibo ni a ti wa?*"

"Oh. *A wá lati Omi,* we come from Water . . ." Nica picked at a loose fiber from her tunic before she could trust her voice to continue. "But what chance do we have against the ones who have broken the water?"

"Have they?"

Nica's thoughts churned until she finally loosed the words. "There are water-breaks throughout our world. Our communication is blocked. And every time I think there is a chance to move toward freedom, it gets dashed against immovable rocks."

"And yet you got a message out."

"But what good is a message when—"

"And who says the rocks won't move?"

"Zeta, they are solid. And the Delphim planted them in our waters. They broke the Deep and fenced it in. How can we fight this?"

Zeta shook her head. "Child, the Deep cannot be tamed. Nor can it be curbed or contained. Some may place obstacles to direct or influence the flow, but water will not be stopped. It will go over, under, and around those obstacles, eroding what is rock-solid, until those obstacles are reduced to sand." She patted Nica on the knee. "In the end, Water makes its way."

Nica cradled her belly with one hand and rested the other over Zeta's. "*Ẹ ṣe.* I don't know what I would do without you."

"You can thank me by getting back to work," Zeta said, wiping a tear from Nica's face. And then, one from her own.

70

·· R I S K ··

OOD-POD was thrown into mass confusion. All of the
pods had descended on their serving area at the same time.
There was not enough time to feed each grouping separately, and
there was not enough food to feed all at once. TAL-zeta divided
her staff into three teams, directing each team to the queued pods
for a light meal. It was an imperfect solution, but better than none.

The third shift pods were eating closer to their normal time
than the other two. Still, they complained about the small portions.
Nica wanted to throw the food in their faces and tell them that a
little hunger was better than dead. But she didn't. She just served
them in silence.

The lines had finally petered out when Nica noticed TAL-xi
hanging back, somewhat out of sight. Her jaw clenched as she
glared at the one who was most likely responsible and had profited
from Iota's death.

He jerked his head at her in the direction of the trash bins, but
Nica continued to glare at him. He repeated the silent request with
urgent hand gesturing. Nica started to turn her back, but before she
could, the blue-banded Olomi mouthed, *Jọwọ.*

TAL-xi had never used the word "please" with her.

Checking to make sure no one would notice or miss her, Nica
collected some refuse and headed to the back of the trash piles.

"What do you want?" she hissed. "You have a lot of nerve,
showing up in Iota's tunic and demanding I come back here. I
know it's your fault he's dead. I know you're the one who fed TAL
some story about a plot. Now that you've replaced two of your

supervisors, you'd better watch your back. These things have a way of washing back on you."

To her surprise, the blue Olomi didn't threaten her or defend himself. In fact, he looked as miserable as she thought he deserved to be. This was not going as she'd expected.

"I'm sorry. I didn't know—I just thought he would get sent to the holes." Xi's voice wavered. He took a breath. "If I could change anything, I would. But I need to deliver a message."

Xi looked around quickly, then said quietly, "Iota is still alive."

"You cannot trick me. I will not fall into whatever trap you are setting. I saw him die."

"Please, I tell you the truth. He told me to tell you, 'Remember Nu.'"

Nica stared at him in disbelief. But her mind was reeling. *Had Iota's plan worked? Had the gate been drained enough for him to survive? If the free Olomi were able to disable the reef generators . . .*

Xi continued now that he had her attention.

"After everyone left, I had no stomach for food, and it was quiet, other than the rain. I wanted to apologize, even if it was just to his body. I couldn't live with myself." He took a gulping breath. "As I got closer, I heard groaning. I couldn't believe it, but Iota was still alive! He told me to pull the beam from the wall, but leave him there, and tell only you."

Nica studied him for a long moment. "You know what will happen if anyone is caught helping him. The consequences will be even more severe."

"More severe than death?"

"Yes," Nica snapped. "There are worse fates than death, and our keepers are fully capable of visiting them on us."

He blanched under Nica's scorn. "I'm sorry, I really am. And if there's anything I can do . . . I can't undo this, but let me do something to help. Anything."

Nica considered their possibilities and relented. "Stay out of sight until I return. I know of something that will help."

She hurried back to her station, bringing the serving utensils and platters to be cleaned. Slipping into Zeta's storeroom, she searched the shelves for the numbing salve they had used on TAL-rho.

Once she returned, she started tossing scraps into the waste-fire and began speaking without looking at him. "Act as if you are moving his body." She dropped a packet of salve from under her tunic. "Apply this to any open wounds."

When she turned her back to the fire, she had a small blade from the kitchen hidden in her palm. "Cut him free from the beam but tell him not move from it." She hesitated, then rested her hand on his arm. "Thank you."

His eyes turned bright, and he began to blink them rapidly. Hers were beginning to sting. She needed to focus.

"Return the blade as soon as possible. You can't be caught with it."

71

·· REDEMPTION ··

"TAL-ZETA." Nica leaned against the wall, grateful for its support. She shifted her basket, filled with empty hydro-processing containers. "We're low on nigari. Should I fetch some from ASHE-phi?"

"Are you sure?" Zeta didn't look up from her work.

Nica moved closer to her and whispered, *"Iota is still alive. We need to protect him until sunsink."*

With rising blues at her temples, Zeta gripped her hand. Barely audible, she urged Nica, "Go quickly, little one!"

Careful to maintain a neutral posture and expression, Nica made her way to hydro-processing with little interruption. ASHE-delt was eager to hurry her along, lest she make more of a mess than she had last tide.

A quick glance down the hall toward medical confirmed that Girac was at his post, but she just shook her head. They had agreed to minimize contact until they could make their break, and reduce the chance of discovery. Still, her heart warmed at the sight of him, and she closed her eyes for just a second, thankful that he was part of her world.

Hurrying down to Kolas's station, Nica shifted the basket from one side to the other, trying to alleviate the bumping against her belly. A twinge of heartache surprised her. *Oh, Pescha, I miss you.* Steadying her mind and body with a deep breath, she moved the basket under her abdomen, the way Pescha had. *This actually helps.* Nica allowed a hint of a smile past the lump in her throat. *O şe, dear friend.*

"Oh!" ASHE-mu nearly collided with her as she entered their workroom. Looking paler than usual, the Olomi's gray striping was barely discernable in the bright lighting.

He glared up from the pad that occupied his attention. "What do you—" His eyes landed on the basket, then traveled up to her belly and he scoffed, "Oh, you. Go pester Phi. I have enough to worry about."

"But TAL-zeta requires these samples immedia—"

His bushy gray brows drew together as he shook his head. "Tell TAL-zeta that she's not my problem! And neither are you!" He marched out the door.

Kolas was watching, arms crossed, shaking his head at her. "You really shouldn't tease him like that." His sheen was bright, and the whorls covering him, vibrant, in sharp contrast to his co-worker. "Can't you see he's under enough stress?" He winked and took her basket.

"More samples?" He took out the containers and shook them next to his ear.

"I need true water," Nica whispered. "TAL-iota has been severely injured."

His teasing expression was immediately all business. "Injured? I thought . . ."

"I'll explain later, right now we need—"

"Wait here—I'm faster alone."

One, two, three, four . . . Nica counted her steps as she paced the floor. *Sixteen, seventeen, eighteen* . . . She wished Girac was waiting with her. *Thirty-one, thirty-two, thirty-three* . . . *Sigh.* They wouldn't have long, but . . . *Fifty-three, fifty-four, fifty—*She jumped as Kolas emerged from the doorway. She hadn't even heard him clambering up the steps.

He smiled and refilled her basket. "Here. Go safely."

Nica threw a quick glance at the door, then whispered, "Does Mischa have the tea? We need to make sure that Mote gets it tonight after dinner."

"Yes, yes. She gave it to your sister. After the baby arrived, Mote was moved further down the hall, closer to Theta's room. We'll get the boy. You take care of Iota and be ready for our move. When the generators go down, you may not notice it right away, but I will."

72

S ILENCE was the signal.
The instant the generators stopped, Kolas felt it deep in his gut.

This silence, followed by darkness, marked the advent of their freedom.

To those ignorant of the plans, stillness eroded the comfort of what they knew. Confinement had provided a structure they'd learned to live with. Absent the familiar sounds of captivity, the unknown was terrifying.

To Kolas and Mischa, it was the signal to move. They retraced the rehearsed path through MO-ASHE's hallways to Rissa's door. Girac was waiting there, shouldering a large bundle. Stopping only when they lagged, their guard led them safely out.

Once they emerged from MO-ASHE's household, Rissa broke off to alert Lam. Minutes later, he emerged from the darkness with two young Olomi. Moving from shadow to shadow, they hastened to the gates.

Rissa took charge. "Lam, help us." She looked over the blue and green juvies at his side. "You two help Iota stand."

There was movement and the trio gawked.

"But . . . but . . . he was . . . you were . . ." the youths stammered. The others were equally astounded, yet hit by a wave of what could only be called joy. Even in this place.

"Stop yammering and give Lam a hand." Iota himself waved off their attempts to support him.

"The name's *Osiah*." The lanky young Olomi brushed aside a

lock of hair almost indistinguishable from his darker striping. He straightened. "I don't answer to Lam anymore."

"You'll have to answer to an awful lot if we can't get this gate open soon." Iota tipped the beam that he had been bound to toward Osiah. "You can probably wield this with a little more strength than I can right now." Taking a smaller stick, he flipped part of a pile at the gate, noting the *crackle* that sounded when it hit. "All of you, pile the debris against the gate, but don't maintain contact when it touches."

The boys grabbed at smaller chunks from the piles, eager to toss them. Then they realized what they were handling.

"A foot!"

"Is this a leg?"

"I'm just glad that's not pieces of me you're shoving right now," Iota said with a grimace. His eyes grew sorrowful.

Upon listening to the snaps and crackles grow softer and further apart, Iota nodded at the tallest member of the trio. "It's time, Lam—Osiah. Start prying that gate apart."

"I'm glad to put these abovewater-muscles to good use!" Osiah planted his feet firmly and wedged the beam deep between the gates. Shaking off the buzz that briefly traveled over his skin, the Olomi began to push and pull, back and forth, prying at the obstacle that had been so formidable that morning.

"Come, juvies, add your strength!"

They scampered to his side, adding their weight to the lever, quickly joined by Girac.

Mischa and Kolas held hands, watching with glimmering eyes as the gate inched open. Nica and Rissa joined in a wordless hug, while TAL-rho—Auryn—cradled the bundle Girac had transferred to her, crooning softly. *"Ọmọ mi, Soto. Ọmọ mi."*

Kolas turned to Nica, his eyes bright even in the darkness. "Look, child. Look at what you've done."

Nica blinked back her tears as the juvies slipped through the gates. She whispered urgently through the gap, "Run! Don't stop till you reach the water! Our people will be waiting for you!"

Blessing the rain that strengthened them and the bit of moon that slipped through the thinning clouds to light their way, she watched as these first captives left the confines of TAL's compound. Phi's blue melting quickly into the darkness, then Psi, his light green visible for a bit longer. Girac and Osiah widened the opening to let Rissa, Mischa, and Kolas through. Muscles straining, they forced the beam between the gates until it was wedged wide-open.

Helping Nica over the beam, Girac grasped one hand and Rissa took the other as she stepped into freedom. "Go, my love!" Girac bade her. "I'll catch up!"

Nica hesitated for a moment, then waddled down the path, Rissa by her side.

Girac held his breath as the sisters disappeared into the dark. "Iota, you're next."

As he held his hand out, sounds of commotion reached them. Cries arose throughout the compound as word of the escape spread and guards were stirred to action.

"TAL-iota!" The wounded Olomi was halfway through the opening. It was TAL-xi.

Girac swung around to block the informant, but Iota stopped him. "He's no longer against us."

"Ma binu." The dark and light blue banded Olomi apologized to the brother he had betrayed. *"Dariji mi?"*

Iota closed his eyes and bowed his head. "Forgiven." He looked into his antagonist's eyes. "Tell our people there is freedom—if they have the courage to pursue it. Then follow me."

Xi bowed to the one he had hated and darted back to spread the word.

Iota stepped completely through the gate. Turning his head back, he grinned at Girac. "She did it. She really did." Then he followed their path, winding out of sight.

Osiah reached for Auryn's fry from the other side. At first, the mother shook her head, clutching him tightly, but it was clear she couldn't make it through carrying him. With a kiss, she passed Soto to the Olomi on the other side, then nearly leapt through to reclaim her son. Kissing him again, still bundled, she bustled down the path that had twice been death to her.

Girac heard a new cry arise from within the compound. It was Xi, keeping his word.

"*Ominira!* Freedom!"

"*Eniyan Omi!* People of the Water!"

"*Pada si ibu omi!* Return to the Deep!"

Xi bolted out, well ahead of the new ranks of Olomi streaming for the gates. The sounds of whips piercing the night followed him, accompanied by the bellowing of TAL and his Alpha.

"Get back!" *Crack!*

"Stay away from the gate!" *Crack!*

"*Ominira!*"

"You will pay!"

"*Pada si Jin!*"

"Guards!"

73

THE AQUANS following Xi made it to the gate, spilling through and scattering before the guards knew what was happening.

Fuming at the mayhem, TAL shouted, "TAL-alph! Close the gates!"

The yellow alpha's fingers flew over the controls, but she paled as he approached. "It won't move. There's no power!"

The alpha was right, he fumed. It was completely drained. "Then why aren't the backups working?" he bellowed.

"Backups? I only know what you charge me with." The aquan trembled, shrinking away from him.

He snarled as the remaining pockets of aquans attempted to get past him. "Gather MO-ASHE's elite—the strongest guards!"

Planted in front of the passage, he cracked his whip at anyone who came within reach. "Get back to your quarters, or I will make examples of you all!"

But MO-ASHE was already storming through the courtyard, alphas in tow.

He glared at her. "What happened to your backup generators?"

"My generators? You're in charge of containment. It's your system that went down."

"Give me your controller and the guards attached to it." He thrust his hand at her. "You maintain order here with my alpha."

Her eyes narrowed as she drew the device out from under her cloak.

"Hurry! They're getting away! And get a count while I hunt the runaways down."

TAL grabbed her controller and slapped his into the gray's hand. "Lead these guards, I'll take the others. Get the escapees. And don't fail!"

"I will not, EC-TAL."

The sound of MO-ASHE and TAL-alph wielding their whips followed TAL as he charged through the open gates. He was going to track down every single one of those runaways. He was going to catch them and make them pay.

74

"WE DON'T have much of a head start," Nica fretted. A look over her shoulder as the compound walls began to shrink, did little to reassure. She was too slow. "I'm dragging you back."

"Maybe the confusion in our wake will slow their response."

Girac was using his reassuring voice. It wasn't helping.

Rissa tried next. "We're taking the route TRE-CH used. It might not be the first one TAL checks."

"At least it's still raining." Nica was too winded to argue with her encouragers.

She doubted it would slow any Olomi guards still loyal to the Delphim. More than likely, the ones pursuing them would not hesitate to loose their fury. She had seen more than one of the guards explode with rage at a fellow Olomi with little or no provocation. Sometimes it seemed like they were waiting for an excuse to strike out. *How does this so-called enhancement twist our people so?* It was a mystery to her. She put her hand through Girac's arm, thankful that he was by her side.

"Are you all right? Do we need to stop?"

"No." She tried to keep her panting hidden, blowing air out of compressed lips as if she were buzzing on a reed. "We need to keep going."

She hefted her belly and its precious cargo. "Rissa, you go ahead," she urged.

"No. We have been separated for too long, I'm not leaving you now." Her sister was firm.

"Well, then, I guess I'd better pick up my pace," Nica said wryly.

Rissa leaned in and whispered in her ear, "I'm happy for you, Nica. Girac is a good Olomi."

Nica smiled at her sister, but then let out a soft grunt that surprised even her.

"What was that?" Girac couldn't keep the concern out of his voice.

"I'm not sure, but this is not a time to slow down."

Rissa and Girac exchanged concerned glances.

"Let's keep this run moving," Nica pressed.

Rissa caught Girac's eye and raised her free palm and flexed it. He gave a quick nod, and they both slipped supporting hands under Nica's tunic. Using the gifts of the deep, they latched on to her dorsal layer with a strengthened grip.

Rissa smiled. "I guess it's time to remember where we came from."

"Give me your son." Osiah supported Auryn as they fumbled through the dark. "We could go much faster."

"I can't. It's been so many moons. He hasn't even seen me yet."

"You will not keep him if you are caught." The lanky, brown Olomi was sober in stating his concern.

"But . . ." She had no further argument. With reluctance, she allowed him to hoist her son over his shoulder.

"Now, let's go!" Osiah started through the darkness, homing in on the landmarks that had been shared with him. "Take hold of my tunic and keep up!"

Soon they were out of Nica's sight.

Xi caught up with her group next. "Is there anything I can do to help?"

"You can keep going. We have this." Girac's face was set like stone.

Nica groaned through her nose—lips pressed tight to prevent any outcry.

"Do you need to stop?" Rissa put Nica's arm over her shoulders, supporting her sister around the waist.

Nica shook her head, biting onto her lips as she waddled as fast as the larva growing inside her would allow.

Girac looked at Rissa and let out an explosive breath. "I give up. Xi, you take over for Rissa. Rissa, you go ahead of us. We can follow you faster than you can help your sister along."

The darkness hid Xi's skin tones, but Nica could feel him flush as he assumed Rissa's position.

"I need to apologize to you as well, TAL-eta. *Ma binu.* My words were cruel, and my behavior unforgivable." TAL-xi's voice was filled with chagrin. "You were right, I had forgotten where I come from."

"You must call me Nica—and we all needed to remember who we truly are. But if it helps, *o dariji rę*, of course you are forgiven."

He pressed his lips together with a furtive glance, then took a breath. "If you could . . . I mean, if you choose, would you call me Salu? I'll need to get used to my true name if I'm returning to the water."

With *Salu* and Girac practically carrying her, and Rissa leading the way, their little pod made better speed toward their goal. The sounds of others making their way through the wilderness came at them from all sides, but it was difficult to tell whether what they heard was their pursuers, or others being pursued. It made little difference. They moved as quietly as they could.

With time, the sounds of others faded. The sun began to make its presence known, and the group continued their escape in silence. The path began to descend, and Nica could see the sun's rays reflecting on the surface of the deep, far off in the distance. *Almost there*, her heart sang. *Almost home.*

She stopped short and doubled over. "Oh!" She gasped. "I can't . . . I don't think . . ." A moan escaped her.

They stopped and waited as she panted for a few minutes, Rissa and Salu kept a look out for the guards, while Girac helped Nica to stand.

"Okay. I think I can go now," she gasped.

Her trio of guardians took up their positions and began to head down the steep path again. They made their way down a bit, but the pangs started again . . . and again. The realization hit that she would not be able to go much farther.

"I . . . need someplace . . . to hide." She gripped Girac's arm. "This fry is coming."

75

·· REALITY CHECK ··

GIRAC'S eyes went wide. "It's not time! You can't spawn yet!" He cast a frenzied look to Rissa. "Tell her she can't have the fry yet. It's not supposed to come until after the next moon."

Nica leveled a hooded gaze at him. Lips pursed and teeth clenched, she muttered, "I don't think the larva knows the schedule." She gasped again. "We need to find someplace . . . to hide."

Usually calm and composed, Girac floundered in this uncharted territory. "Rissa and Salu, scout ahead and find a safe spot. I will follow with Nica at whatever speed we can manage."

Rissa hesitated for a heartbeat, but as Nica turned pale with another moan, she headed out with Salu in tow. "I remember a shelter along the way. I hope TAL doesn't know about it." The sound of her voice trailed off as they hurried ahead.

Nica looked to Girac. "I'm sorry, I—I don't mean to be—"

His smile was tender. "I'm beyond thankful to be with you for this spawning. That would have been forbidden."

She smiled back. "It is more than . . . I could have hoped for: to have you by my side."

They made haste as best they could, stopping when the pangs made it impossible to continue. The sun had made its presence known, even behind the clouds, by the time Salu doubled back for them.

"We found it. Rissa is preparing for you."

Girac grunted his approval, as he was now carrying Nica through the worst of her pain. She buried her head in his shoulder, doing her best not to cry out. His face blanched with each spasm. "Quickly!"

They joined hands and carried her between them as they navigated down the path. It was farther than expected, but at least some progress was being made. Veering off the planned route, Salu led them around a large pile of rocks and into a small cave, its entrance hidden by the angle of approach.

Rissa greeted them as they ducked into the cavern, urging them to the back where she'd laid out some leafy branches. She took Nica's tunic and put her hand out for Girac's and Salu's as well.

"You aren't going to need these anymore," she said as she laid them out over the branches, "and I have a better use for them here."

"There," she straightened up, "that's much better."

Nica groaned.

"Here, be gentle. And we need more branches." She helped settle Nica on the improvised bedding. "I need a short stick—the thickness of two fingers."

Girac and Salu exchanged confused expressions.

"I'll explain later, just get it."

Mystified, but not convinced he wanted to understand, Salu ducked out of the cavern, with Girac close on his heels.

"Don't worry, little sister, I actually know a thing or two about babies. I was there for your entrance into the world, as well as Kel and the littles." Rissa smiled as she held Nica's hand.

"But you haven't seen a birth abovewater," Nica protested faintly.

"Wrong again." Rissa informed her. "I was present for TRE-sichi's labor and delivery as well. TRE-CH and SA-CaG weren't exactly up to the task, and I was one of the few Olomi with any birth knowledge."

She gave one of her brilliant smiles that lit up any room she was in. "So you see, little sister, you are being attended by the foremost seasoned professional in the pool of Olomi abovewater spawning."

Nica laughed weakly at Rissa's proclamation and held onto her hand. "Professional or not, I'm glad to have you here." Her voice trembled. "I missed you so, Rissa. I thought—I thought I would never see you again."

"But you were wrong." Rissa stroked her hair. "And I was wrong to give up. I have so much to live for. I will never stop loving Jonnat, but I can continue in the knowledge of that love."

Nica gasped again, then cried out. "It's . . . getting . . . worse." She clenched her teeth.

"Don't hold your breath! Let it out slowly, one little stream of bubbles at a time."

Nica followed her instructions, pushing out a strong but thin stream of air.

"Yes, good," Rissa encouraged. "Now, give slow, steady breaths. Like you are blowing away a little seahorse from Ìyá's plants."

Nica complied again, pursing her lips to blow away the imaginary pests. She clung to Rissa's arm. "Girac?"

"Don't worry, he'll be back soon. I sent him to get something to help you."

There was little light inside the cave, and the only sound that reached them was the rain, drumming outside the entrance. Focused on coaching Nica to breathe, Rissa almost missed the quiet footsteps.

"Here." Salu handed her a short, thick branch, while Girac laid his armful of leafy branches on the ground next to Nica.

"I don't suppose either of you have any sort of blade." Rissa started peeling the stick with her teeth, spitting out strips of bark to the side.

They looked at each other. "No."

Rissa sighed. "Well, could you find a very sharp rock, or anything sharp I can hold in one hand? I need something that can cut."

They looked uncertain about the request, but weren't reluctant to leave when the next contraction hit. Nica's pangs were increasing in frequency and intensity.

Rissa lifted Nica's head and placed the stick she had peeled between her sister's teeth. "Here—bite down on this." She again stroked the auburn curls. "That should help a little. At least for now."

It didn't take long for them to return, but their faces were grave.

"We need to keep it down for a bit," Salu said. "One of TAL's teams is nearby. I don't think they will find us this far off the path, but if they hear something, they may decide to investigate."

"No rocks?" Rissa's mind was only on one thing.

"I didn't say that! Here."

Both produced an assortment of rocks for her to choose from.

She tried to inspect them, but the meager light was insufficient. Hefting them, she judged how they felt in her hand. "No. Not this one either. That one is too huge." She looked at them. "I need something that will fit firmly in my hand, but with a sharp edge."

"Let me try something." Girac took one of the larger rocks and started chipping at a smaller one.

Soon Rissa was rotating the improvised tool in her hand. "Not bad. This'll do nicely."

Nica groaned again, biting down hard on the stick between her teeth.

"Girac and Salu, stand near the entrance. Keep an ear out for trouble." She turned back to her sister. "It's not going to be very long."

Nica writhed as the next contraction unleashed its full force on her. Clenching the stick, she managed to force more air than noise out of her lungs, even as her pain intensified.

"Pssst, I think someone is getting close," Salu whispered.

Rissa nodded and focused her attention on Nica. "Honey, I need you to be quiet and deliver this baby. It's coming now, but you have to be quiet, or they'll find us."

Nica's eyes were wide, but she nodded.

"I'll show you how to breathe through this. It's just like Ìyá did, but abovewater."

She smoothed the hair out of Nica's eyes again. "You can do this. I know it's harder here than in the Deep, but it's not impossible."

"You are so strong, dearheart." Girac came alongside and took Nica's hand. "Rissa is right. I know you can do this."

Nica nodded—keeping her eyes fixed on him.

"They're getting closer!" Salu whispered.

Nica gripped the black-and-blue-striped hand that engulfed hers.

"You're doing great!" Rissa mouthed. Miming deep breaths and blowing out small streams, she gestured with a whispered, "Now push!"

"*Shh.* They're still within earshot," Salu warned.

Rissa's eyes never broke contact as Nica fought every instinct to scream and pushed through the pain. "Keep breathing," she whispered. "You can do this." She patted Nica's hand as hers wrapped around Girac's.

"That's right—you keep squeezing. He can take it!" Girac winced, and Rissa grimaced a silent apology.

Within moments, Rissa's face lit up. "Oh! That's perfect!" she whispered. "The head is out! Now one more push. Big push."

Nica pushed again—her face contorted in agony.

"They're almost gone," Salu whispered.

Rissa beamed at Nica. "It's a girl!" She mouthed, laying the baby on Nica's chest. Then, the impromptu midwife rubbed the baby's back to help clear its lungs and was rewarded with a squeak and a cough from the tiny Olomi.

Nica looked exhausted but elated. She tenderly cradled her fry. "She's so small," she marveled.

After a few precious moments, she relinquished the spawn to Rissa, who cleaned her and prepared Nica for nursing. Soon nuzzling her mother, the fry was quickly rewarded and began to feed.

"Enjoy this, Nica," Rissa said softly. "TRE-sichi never had this chance."

"Neither did Pescha," Nica's whisper of wonder as the translucent spawn nursed, was subdued. "Auryn."

"Who?"

"TRE-sichi. Her true name is Auryn. Her son's true name is So—" In an instant, Nica's face drained of all color. Even the darkest of her striations faded from their seaweed green into whiteness. "S-s-s-so c-c-cold."

"Oh, Sise! Your teeth are chattering!"

"Take . . . her—"

Rissa took the fry and hurriedly laid it in Girac's hands. Blood was pooling beneath the bed of branches. "Salu, she needs water, now. True water would be better, but there isn't any nearby. How far are the search parties?"

"We're clear for now." He still stood at the edge of the cave. "I don't think any will come this far off the path now that they've come and gone."

Rissa began ripping the tunics that were under Nica, forming wadding to try and stem the bleeding. She handed the bloodied tunic to Salu. "Rinse this and return it. Quickly."

Salu's stripes disappeared as the color drained from his blue-striped face almost as fast as it had from Nica's. He immediately left to follow Rissa's instructions.

Rissa did what she could. She tried to warm Nica and staunch the bleeding, but there was little to work with in that barren cave. The baby began to squirm and cry in Girac's arms.

"Girac! Come sit behind Nica and prop her up."

The burly guard moved to comply, but didn't know what to do with the tiny bundle in his arms.

"Give her to me and wrap your arms around Nica. That will warm her."

Rissa cooed at her niece as Girac settled into place. "You are a precious little one, aren't you?"

She played with the baby's fingers and toes, rubbing the little extremities to help increase circulation.

"Perfect in every wa—" Rissa's voice caught as she examined the baby's fingers, and then her toes. "You are going to be just fine, baby girl." She laid the baby on Nica's chest. "You're perfect, just the way you are."

Wrapping Nica's arms around the baby, she then moved Girac's arms to cradle Nica's. "You need to help her hold the baby so she can nurse. That should help both mother and fry."

Throughout the tide, Girac supported Nica, while they cradled the baby. Nursing and sleeping, she lay content on her mother, rising and falling with her breaths. Salu came in and out, bringing water, rinsing rags, and keeping an eye out for searchers, while Rissa tended to her sister.

Nica faded in and out of consciousness, her green faded to almost gray. Sometimes she shook so badly that Girac couldn't keep her still.

Murmuring and moaning in her unconscious state, Nica cried out "Ìyá!" as Rissa hovered over her. Her eyes fluttered as they lit on her sister, unfocused and confused. She spoke again in her semiconscious state, "Ìyá, o wa nibi."

She thinks I'm Ìyá.

Rissa kissed Nica on the forehead, resting her rosette-marked hand on her sister's cheek.

"Yes, Ọmọ mi. Ìyá's here."

76

S OU N D S of rustling caught Rissa's ear. It was approaching their refuge. Squinting in the dark, she and Salu moved to either side of the cave's entrance, armed with the extra rocks. Girac shrank against the back wall, holding Nica and the baby close.

Salu motioned for quiet as the sounds of footfalls converged. Poised at the opening, the sentries loomed, rocks at the ready.

A soft call broke the tension. "Wo. It's me, Osiah."

The rocks fell to the ground with a spattering of thuds.

"What are you doing here?"

"How did you find us?"

"Shhh," the brown-striped Olomi whispered. "You're all in danger."

The little pod of escapees froze in stunned silence.

"We've been keeping a lookout. All who fled with us are accounted for—except you." He cocked his ear to the opening for a moment, then motioned everyone to come further inside the cave. "We overheard one of the searchers say there was movement in this area. They're going to return in force at first light."

Rissa cast a worried eye at Girac and Nica. "She's in no condition to move, let alone run."

Girac nodded in sober agreement.

"But if you don't leave, you will be taken," Osiah warned.

A groan rose from Nica. "You must . . ."

"Must what?" Rissa drew closer to hear her sister's words.

"You must go." Nica's voice grew stronger. "And you must take Ayla."

"Ayla?" Girac repeated with confusion.

"Ayla." Nica kissed her daughter's forehead tenderly, then turned to Rissa. "Take her to the water. Take her to Ìyá and Bàbá. Teach her to chase the minnows and tease the grumpy morays and dance with the jellies."

Rissa's eyes glistened.

"Promise me she will know the ways of our people, in the Deep. She will know what it is to share emotions, feel another's pain, and pursue healing. Promise me, Rissa, that she will not live a life of fear. Promise me that she will know and be known."

"But . . . I can't," her sister objected.

"You must," Nica said with all the strength she could muster. "*I* can't."

"If the rest of us run for the water," Osiah cleared his throat, "we might make it. They won't think anyone would stay behind. But we have to leave now—the sun's not far from rising."

"I'm not leaving," Girac declared softly, his arms remaining clasped around Nica. "If this is where I die, so be it. But I will not leave you here alone.

"Rissa," he continued. "You take the baby and run with Salu and Osiah, and don't look back. Do you understand? If you look back, they will know we're here. So run . . . go to your bàbá."

Rissa started to speak, but found no words that would make a difference. She had no choice. Taking the last of the tunics, she bound Ayla to her chest, kissed her sister, and turned to Girac. "You're a good Olomi. My sister is fortunate to love one such as you, just as I was, once."

Both sisters wept silently as Rissa ducked out after Osiah and followed the blue form of Salu.

Sounds of the trio distanced just as another group sounded an alert. As cries of confusion and frustration joined in, it was clear that the escaping Olomi were well on their way, and ahead of their pursuers.

Nica and Girac could do nothing but wait.

77

·· RETURN ··

THE HEAD Guardian watched from the water. Olomi
returned, not as a wave, but in drips and drabs scattered
along the shore where the sea lapped the edge of land.

First two youngsters, barely juvies. They'd run for the Deep,
but strangely lacking adolescent bravado, froze once they reached
the water.

Daevu's team was prepared to ensure their people reached the
water, but it was clear these needed more than that. They would
require an escort until they could be delivered to their families.
His Guardians exchanged uncertain looks as they transported the
young blue and green. What had they survived?

The waiting was maddening. A handful had come and gone, and
though Daevu was thankful to have any retrieved, these were not
who he longed to see.

The ridges, punctuated with crops of larger rocks and pockets
of waist-high plant life, were devoid of movement while the shadow
of the sun crept higher, moving from one overflowing cloud to the
next. The sensation of water impacting his body one drop at a time
was unusual for the guardian, especially for an extended period.
Mildly unsettling, it served as a reminder of the air's coolness
rather than an insulator from it.

A lone Olomi—black with white spotting—limped to the water.
His back was scored with open wounds, raw and oozing through
what was left of a tunic. He reached the waves, and collapsed, his
tears mingling with the spray that rose to meet him.

An older couple followed. She approached, iridescent white

from face to feet, while gleaming orange cascaded down her hair and shoulders, and he, covered with meandering brown and white whorls. They waded in, hand in hand, seeming to savor the moment and each other as they returned to the Deep.

Daevu dispatched Guardians to welcome, to arrange transport, and see to their needs. And he watched. And he waited.

Another figure staggered to the beach. This one, large and misshapen. As it drew closer, it was revealed to be one struggling with another. The larger of the two dominated this battle but appeared to be growing weary. Uncertain as to why there was a struggle at all, Daevu dispatched two more Guardians to assist, as he kept a vigilant eye out for Nica.

The Guardians reached the struggling pair, greeted with calls for help from one and frenzied resistance from the smaller. As the fry grew louder, Daevu realized it was not yelling in Olomi, but another tongue. He also realized that those shrieks were not unheard. A flurry of activity further up the rise raised their own call and descended toward the shoreline where Daevu and his forces lay in wait.

Pulling out a conch shell, the Head Guardian sounded a warning. Alerted to the danger, his Guardians moved into action, picking up the smaller combatant, and swiftly aiding the larger blue to the water's edge.

Haspian's charge began to scream and clamber up his back to escape the water. The shrieking fry perched on his assigned Guardian's shoulders, grabbing at the kelp-colored hair to steady himself. Valtos, his partner, was not faring much better as he hefted his charge by the waist into deeper water, despite her attempts to free herself and reach the fry.

"Incoming!" Daevu barked as his head jutted toward the pursuers. With one look, the Guardians grasped both Olomi they were attempting to rescue and dove under the surface.

A few moments later, Haspian broke the surface of the water, further from the shore. The fry in his arms was sputtering and choking. The Guardian shouted, "He's not receiving the water. If I dive, he may drown!"

Watching the opposing force approach, Daevu decided quickly. "Take him out, but not down."

The pursuers reached the water's edge. They were Olomi! *How could this be?*

He called out, "Olomi!" amplifying his voice with the shell to reach the shore.

Those closest to the water hesitated, looking at him, then back to the large Olomi who drove them. Huge and gray, he bellowed as he cracked his whip.

Daevu didn't understand his opponent's words, but the meaning was clear. The pursuers became like statues, still as a dead reef, poised at the shore, but not entering the water. *What would possess an Olomi to stop their own from reaching the water?*

The two forces were at an impasse, facing off at the invisible wall that rose where the surf left the sand. The land force was soon joined by a second team, led by one who was clearly not an Olomi.

A growl rose from Daevu's second, "That's the one."

The Head Guardian did not take his eyes off the approaching group led by the foreign being. "The tall one? Brown, and not Olomi?"

"Yes," Jonnat confirmed. "That's the one who took Nica."

78

TAL stalked the beachhead, assessing the battlefield. He had not expected this much difficulty. Hunt down the runaways, catch them, return. He had superior numbers and conditioned fighters, or so he'd thought. Serious opposition prepared to aid and defend had not been anticipated.

He glowered at the force assembled in the surf. "ASHE-alph! Watch for others en route to the water. They're waiting for someone, so not all the runaways have made it to the water."

One of MO-ASHE's guards, a barrel-chested fellow, light orange in hue and topped with darker brown hair, glanced back as TAL approached. He looked to the water, and back at TAL, then made a sudden break, preparing to dive. In an instant, he dropped in the foam and began to writhe, unable to continue. Without a pause, TAL barked to the gray alpha, "Bring him to me. The rest of you, maintain positions."

Only when MO-ASHE's dark gray enforcer had a grip on the defector did TAL lower the arm holding the controller, releasing his victim from the device's invisible hold.

"Teach him a lesson—by the rocks."

ASHE-alph dragged the aquan to the outcropping at the base of the rise, removed his tunic and top-cover, and began to apply his whip to his victim's back with vigor.

TAL addressed the remaining guards, "No one puts foot in the water, or you will suffer worse. Keep watch for the rest of the escapees. I will increase the boost dosage for anyone who brings me one."

At that, several of the more powerfully built guards licked their lips, eager to earn the reward that TAL had put out there.

"Hey, you. Water creatures!" TAL spat on the ground, realizing they didn't understand his words ". . . ignorant uncivilized beasts . . ."

"ASHE-alph, leave that. Translate!"

Given over to the violence he had been assigned, it took a moment for the alpha to clear his head.

"Yes, EC-TAL."

"Water people, I am Expedition Commander TAL of the Delphim. We require your planet."

"*Enin ara'nu omi . . . Emi ni Expedition Commander TAL ti Delphim . . . A nilo aye yin.*" ASHE-alph translated as TAL continued.

"Your world now belongs to us, and we have adapted it to our needs. You do not have the technology to resist. Your planet has already been conformed to our design, and soon you shall be, as well. If you resist, you will suffer. If you cooperate, you may be granted power and influence. I will not demand the return of those who have fled their posts—they are of little consequence. If, however, you aid any more of those who belong to me in their mutinous attempts, I will punish both them and you. There will be no mercy."

The one who appeared to be their leader moved closer and stood in the waist-high surf, answering the challenge.

"Delphim. We do not fear you. Your greatest advantage is not your technology, which we have already disabled, but our ignorance of your presence. We are no longer ignorant.

"Be assured, land dweller, you have already lost—and you will continue to lose. We will aid any of our people who come to us, and if you continue to capture and enslave our people, we will completely destroy your devices. Do not try me in this. You cannot wash away the Water. It always makes a way."

Infuriated as the answer was translated to him, TAL had no response for this aquan who did not cower at his threats. Turning to his guards, he roared, "Hold this line. If another mudsucker gets through, you will beg for a whipping."

The guards strengthened their resolve, and it was hard to tell what pushed them more, the promise of reward or the threat of punishment. Either way, they would make it difficult for any aquan to make their way to the water.

"We do not wish to fight you, brothers," Daevu appealed in Olomi to the guards, "but this is not right. Since when do Olomi abuse and imprison their own?"

One of the guards near him whispered, "You don't know what it's like abovewater, we had no choice."

"There is always a choice." The Head Guardian then turned to Jonnat. "Ask the escapees how many more we should wait for."

The blue-hued Olomi dove toward the older couple who were being examined by the healers.

"How many more? Hmm. I'm sorry, you have no idea how pleasant it is to be in true water—especially after the tease of limited exposure. It's been so long! Oh yes, who have you received so far?" The older Olomi turned back to his wife. "It is so delightful to commune with you, my dear.

"Well, sir, we don't exactly know who we have, but I can report that besides you and your wife, we have received two adolescent males, six adult females, nine adult males, one who was badly injured, and a mother with a very disturbed fry."

"Ah. I don't know all their names, but I believe the mother's true name is Auryn—very, very sad story. Her son's name is Soto, but he has been reconditioned and will not assimilate well. Still, she wouldn't let us leave without him. And, Iota, poor chap. He was left for dead after TAL punished him, but hard to kill, that fellow is. Hard to kill, indeed. We wouldn't have been able to leave without him! Now this is my dear wife, Mischa. Oh, and I am Kolas—isn't that a lovely sound. Kolas. It's good to say that out loud. So, er, we are still waiting for . . ." The old man began ticking off fingers as he thought on who was left. "Hmm, there's TAL-eta, of course, and her sister, and Girac, that's her young man. Fine boy, fine boy. We've known him since he first emerged from the family pod. The tall skinny one, and, oh that disagreeable fellow, Xi. But he actually came around in the end. So I can't really hold his attitude against him, I suppose. Hmm, so that's"—he held his fingers and started ticking them off again—"and there were more who made it out with Xi when he squeezed through, I'd say another seven or eight of our original pod."

Jonnat thought his brain would explode before the old man finished making his calculations and observations. He practiced the deep calming inhales learned from the healers while Kolas prattled on, thankful to hear that there were more captives. He hoped that Nica had made it out with them.

Healing had been slow, and for a long time uncertain. He had to work hard to earn his way back into the Guardians—even harder to return to Daevu's side and serve as his second—almost as hard as the man he once hoped to call Bàbá fought to recover from his own injuries. And they would both fight just as hard to see their people return from captivity, going back to retrieve them if that was what it took. But for now, they waited for the rest who had escaped.

A cry and a snap in the water alerted Jonnat to yet another approaching the shore. He shot up to join Daevu as they prepared to guide their people home.

Small stones cascaded, clattering as they ricocheted down the incline, broadcasting Salu's descent. Rissa and Osiah stayed hidden behind the boulders, out of TAL's line of sight, while the blue-banded Olomi's attempt to reach the landing raised an alarm. The guards made chase, and Salu scurried for the outermost edge of the inlet. Guardians rose from the water to meet him at the edge, but TAL's enforcers were on him before he reached the waves.

TAL approached, tall and imposing even before he unraveled his whip. His lip curled as he closed the distance. There was no doubt in his anticipation of delivering punishment. The sneer, however, faltered as he met the gaze of his intended victim—steady, unflinching, even triumphant in the face of his fate. This was not the posture of the defeated.

As planned, while the guards chased down Salu, Rissa and Osiah made their silent approach to the water's edge. The tall, brown-striped Olomi safeguarded Rissa's slow and deliberate steps until they reached the surf where Rissa uncovered her head. "Bàbá?"

The elder Guardian was undone. He rushed to her side. "Rissa, my jewel, you live?"

She stopped him before he could embrace her, continuing to unwrap her coverings to reveal Ayla. "Bàbá," she said as tears glistened in her eyes, "this is your granddau—"

Jonnat broke the surface behind her father.

The blood drained from Rissa's face, and with it, her strength. She staggered. Osiah moved in to support her, tightening his hold around her.

"You . . . you were dead. Nica said . . . she said TAL killed you . . ."

Jonnat attempted to grasp the sight before him.

It was too much. He had hoped to see Nica, lost in that struggle against TAL so many moons ago. But it was his love, Rissa, who stood before him, with a baby in her arms, and another Olomi by her side. His heart pounded as his being rejoiced. Lost since the Breaking, his Rissa stood before him. But was she still his? He'd failed her, not just once, but twice. What right had he to claim her?

She moved toward him, raising her hand, slender and accented with scarlet, to touch his face. Tracing the deep blue contours, her trembling hand cupped his cheek. "Is it really you? Jonnat. I had no reason to hope. I thought you were gone—forever."

She moved to embrace him, but he held her at arm's distance.

"I . . ." He forced out the words. "I can't do this. I thought you were lost, forever, as well. We tried, Nica and I. We tried to find you, but we failed. I failed. I am so sorry, Rissa. I can't blame you for going on, for living. And I wish you well, but I can't . . ."

Jonnat turned and dove, heading for the depths before his splintered heart betrayed him.

79

R ISSA stood, her mouth open, staring after the wake Jonnat created. An instant later, she set her mouth, lifting the baby in its wrappings over her head and handing it to Daevu.

"This is Nica's daughter, Ayla. She has not yet been introduced to the Deep." Then Rissa dove.

It was her first dive since she'd been taken captive. The flood of emotions and knowing that rushed over her was overwhelming. Communion. It had been so long. She hadn't realized how isolated she'd been. Letting the waves of presence wash over her, she inhaled the true water and focused her thoughts on Jonnat.

Homing in on his trajectory, she called for a porpoise transport, knowing that her strength was not up to this pursuit. The waves of pain emanating from him stabbed at her heart, but she could not deny her own disbelief and frustration. After all the grieving she had suffered over him.

"Jonnat! Stop!" Rissa sent her call ahead at full force, not caring how far it traveled.

His halt reverberated back to her, as did his bewilderment at her anger. The porpoise allowed her to catch up to him in no time. Sliding off, she briefly met its forehead with hers, and sent it back to Daevu's team. Springing like a torpedo at Jonnat, she ran into him, headfirst, butting him in the stomach.

He gasped, struggling to maintain his stance. It had been a while since he had been suckered like that, and certainly not by Rissa.

"You have some nerve! All this time my thoughts have only been of you—even when I had been told you were dead." The waves of heated frustration coming from the increasingly crimson Olomi matched the verbal assault she launched at him. "How could you think I had 'gone on with my life!?' There was no life to go on with without you!"

"Rissa, what are you saying? You have a fry—and the Olomi with you . . ."

"The fry? You think that's mine?" Although Rissa could see how the mistake could be made, she was still furious at him. "You don't know anything about what I've been through, and what I've survived. That's not my spawn."

"How was I supposed to know?"

"Did it occur to you to ask? Did you even give me a chance to speak to you?" Before he could say a thing, she went on. "I almost didn't even join Nica when she told me she was planning to escape—do you know why?"

Jonnat backpaddled a bit, his bewilderment broadcasted loud and clear.

"Because she told me you had died trying to rescue me! How was I supposed to go on after that?" Unexpectedly, Rissa burst into tears.

Taking a chance at this pause, Jonnat surged forward, took her in his arms, and met her arguments with a kiss.

Unwilling to capitulate completely, the slightly mollified Olomi punched her long-lost fiancé in the chest for good measure before she relaxed in his arms and kissed him back.

"I thought I'd never see you again," he murmured.

She lifted her head. "Jonnat, it's Nica's."

"What's Nica's?" he queried, a little lost at the miracle of Rissa in his arms.

"The fry," Rissa's voice caught. "She insisted we leave her. She lost so much blood after spawning . . . and she told me to take Ayla. We were all sure to be discovered if we stayed. But I left her there . . . she said we had no choice." She buried her face in his chest and sobbed. "And all this happened to her because she came to find me."

Jonnat held his love's face in his hands, heart-stricken at this report. "You saved her spawn. And if I know either of you, there really was no choice." He brought her close again, and swallowed. "I can never thank Nica enough for bringing you back to me. She swore she would, and she did."

Daevu gazed at the wriggling bundle in his arms, speechless.

A granddaughter? Ayla!

"Hello precious. I'm your . . . Bàbáagba."

He was barely able to voice the words, but it mattered not to Ayla. Gold flecked green eyes took him in with the softest of coos.

The world had come to a stop around the Head Guardian, but as Ayla's gaze brought his responsibility to her and their people back to the present, Daevu took in the scenes him. Behind, the sound of struggle as a fry, terrified of the water, continued to scream. Further off, its mother's hysteria reverberated under and above the water's surface. On the shore, TAL vented his frustration on the inert body of an Olomi. No longer content to inflict pain slowly, he had taken to striking him with his fists. Up by the rocks, the guard who had attempted to defect crawled to the water, casting wary glances toward the cluster of guards surrounding TAL. And the brown who had arrived with Rissa stood before him, watching helplessly as a brother of the water was beaten mercilessly.

Daevu directed his attention first to one he could help, addressing the nearest guardian.

"Take this one with you," he indicated Osiah, "and fetch the one by the rocks, quickly."

The two slipped ashore and grabbed the disciplined guard under each arm, half carrying and half dragging him into the water.

"Distance . . . fast," he croaked through swollen lips, "controller has . . . limit."

Osiah understood at once. "We need to get him out to the open sea quickly. Once TAL realizes he's escaped again, he will activate the pain circuits. But the device he uses has a limited range. Get a porpoise, I will ride with him."

The Guardian nodded and called for a porpoise as soon as they reached the water. But as Osiah mounted the transport behind the beaten guard, TAL noticed the activity at the water's edge of the water. He growled, pointing the controller at the pair. The Olomi screamed out in pain, as his body seized. Osiah wrapped his arms tightly around his former oppressor and signaled the porpoise to dive and head for deep water. He hoped they could put enough distance from TAL in time. He didn't know of anyone who had died from this punishment, but no one had ever defied the Delphim in the face of their cruelty quite like this.

"Enough!" Daevu thundered. "You will release our people immediately and you will leave them alone."

The gray brute translated at TAL's request, and then gave his scoffing response.

"You can't win, old man. You don't have the strength and you don't have the technology."

"You have already lost," Daevu declared. "Your only advantage was being hidden. But now you are exposed."

As Daevu spoke, Olomi began to emerge from the water, up and down the surf. The pod of Guardians present outnumbering those with TAL more than three times over. They stood on the shore, dripping, grimly facing down TAL and his guards.

TAL's face darkened. He lifted Xi, unconscious and bleeding, and shouted, "Go back to the sea, you old mud-sucker. You are too late. We Delphim are here to stay. Our technology helps us, but we are prepared to survive without it."

He pointed at Daevu. "We have hundreds of your people in our compounds, and if we catch you on our land, we will destroy them before you." With a grunt, TAL lifted Xi's body to his chest, wrapping his thick forearms around the Olomi's neck and forehead. "This is more mercy than any of you will receive." With a swift move, he twisted Xi's neck and tossed the lifeless body to the side.

A horrified gasp ran through the Guardians.

TAL barked a few words to his guards, spun around, and left with them.

Is this what my daughters have suffered under? Waves of what might be to come if they had to fight against such evil flowed through him.

He wept for his people. Ayla started to squirm and wriggle, and then began to wail.

Her grandfather's focus returned to the world he held in his arms. "Yes, my little one, you have more immediate needs, don't you?" He stroked her head. "Well, if you have strength to fight in you, I suppose I must match it. We all shall. For you, your children, and for your children's children. But first, I must introduce you to the way of water—the Deep."

Then Daevu, the Head Guardian of the Horesh Shallows, turned toward open water with his infant granddaughter and, speaking soft truths into her ear, took her home.

80

·· REST ··

NICA'S eyes fluttered open. "I don't want to die here, removed from the Deep. How far is it to the water?"

Girac's arms held her close. "Less than a sun, according to Rissa and Auryn, but how much less? I don't know."

"Girac . . . do you think they made it safely?"

"They must have." He tried to assure her. "We haven't had any sign of TAL's guards in two tides."

"Are you certain?"

"Yes, love. Now rest."

Every part of Nica's body ached. But the deeper pain of grief swelled within, threatening to crush her as she continued an ongoing fight for consciousness.

"Girac?"

"Yes?" He kissed her brow. She was so cold.

"Will you place me in true water?"

He bent his head and looked into her eyes, resolved. "I'll take you there now."

Girac lifted her with care, apologizing at her gasp. Cradling her against his shoulder, he began their trek down the mount.

Though her bleeding had stopped, Nica had little strength. The path was uneven, and Girac could not avoid the jolts along the way. She pressed her lips tight against the pain whenever they landed heavily, but some small cries escaped. Still, the rain refreshed their spirits as the sun diffused beams through clouds. Soon, maybe, they would reach the Deep.

She rested her head on his shoulder, watching the landscape

swell like waves as he carried her down the mount. "You know, this reminds me of when I was first taken."

"Do you recognize something? A landmark?" Girac rotated with her, taking in the full view.

"No, not that." Her mouth had a wry twist. "Perhaps I should have said the angle was familiar.

"After TAL defeated Jonnat . . . he hit me, I think." Her voice was weak, and she tried to speak loudly enough for Girac to hear. "I remember coming to and seeing the world upside down. He was carrying me over his shoulder, and . . . well, this is much better."

Girac was silent as they continued their descent, but his tightened jaw, elevated heart rate, and raised temperature all belied his emotions. As he carried her, their physical contact provided some semblance of the communion they would have shared in the Deep. Or as much as could be experienced abovewater. They had this small time and space to be together, and she'd managed to ruin it.

"I'm sorry," she whispered. "I shouldn't have said anything."

"You're sorry?" He stopped, looking at her in disbelief. "You have nothing to be sorry for, my love. I hate that TAL found you before I could. And that I stood guard while MO-ASHE experimented on you. And now . . ." His voice broke. "All I can do is hope to reach the water before—"

Nica reached up and gently pulled his head down, stilling his lips with hers. Eyes closed, they left the outer world for a fleeting moment, while a few tears mingled and meandered down their cheeks.

"Well, your fever seems to have gone down a bit," he eventually said with a small smile. "But so has the sun, and the path may become treacherous." He set her down with another kiss. "Rest here. I'll scout ahead."

Settled against a rock, Nica released a sigh. A respite from the unrelenting pain of travel was welcome. She closed her eyes and breathed in the still night air. Her eyes flew open.

"Girac!"

In an instant he was by her side. "Is the pain worse? Are you bleeding again?"

"No." She sniffed strongly. "Do you smell it? Kelp!"

He took a deep whiff and held it. "Brine!"

As they took in the scent of salt and sea life, the distant sound of a low roar reached her ears. She gasped and clutched Girac's arm. "Now I can hear it! The Deep!"

They smiled at each other.

"Surface-waves!"

"We're almost home!"

Signs of struggle—patches of bloodied sand and torn up mats of kelp—greeted them as they approached the shore. Still, the crash of waves and the taste of the ocean welcomed them.

"This is good," Nica said. Her lips brushed his brow lightly. "This is a good place to say goodbye."

"Never," he whispered in her ear. "I'll never say goodbye."

A skittering of rocks drew their attention.

"TAL-eta." The yellow alpha's voice sent a shiver down Nica's dorsal. "MO-ASHE will be interested to learn who has been helping you make a fool of her."

"My name is Nica," she spoke as firmly as she could. "I no longer answer to TAL's designation."

"It doesn't—really—matter." TAL-alph lashed her whip closer and closer to the couple. "Soon you will be unable to answer to anything, or anyone."

"You wouldn't dare," Girac growled. "MO-ASHE will have your hide if you hurt her."

TAL-alph spat onto the sand. "MO-ASHE has already laid into my hide for this grasping opportunist." Her eyes bore through Nica. "But now, your protection is gone. No baby. No problem."

Girac lowered Nica to stand the best she could and stepped in front of her. "You'll have to go through me."

"How romantic," TAL-alph sneered. "But that was the plan." She closed in with a burst of speed, snaking the whip around Girac to tag Nica.

Girac shielded Nica with his body, working to keep between the frenzied alpha and the green Olomi.

"Did you really think—I would let you—ruin everything—I worked for?" The alpha kept flicking the tip at Nica, forcing Girac to circle. "After MO-ASHE tore into me, TAL actually considered you as a candidate for enhancement—after you provided MO-ASHE with her baby, of course. He thought I was 'too damaged' to resume my duties."

Her eyes glittered, darker than Nica had ever seen. "He doesn't even know I'm gone, but when I bring you back, or proof of your fate, EC-TAL will see that I have no damage. It took some extra doses of boost, but right now, no one's going to miss it."

Girac tried to back Nica to the surf, but the whip kept herding them further from freedom. Nica stumbled and stayed down, unable to regain her feet.

TAL-alph advanced, her lashes landing on the dark guard, glistening stripes of red scoring his blue and black.

Girac crouched over Nica. "I'll take her down. You get to the water. Don't try to stand, just crawl or roll."

Nica's heart shattered. "No. I can't . . . I can't lose you. I won't lose you." She clung to him. "Please, Girac. I'm dead already. Don't die for me."

But he charged the yellow with a shout. "Go, Nica!"

Frozen as Girac dove under TAL-alph's arm, all Nica could do was watch. The alpha smirked as she stepped back with lightning speed. Catching his feet with the whip, she sent him flying, face-down into the sand, then stepped over him, straddled his dorsals, and wrapped the whip around his throat as he tried to push up.

The alpha hissed as she twisted the cords. "You'd be surprised at what a little extra boost can do."

Horrified as Girac writhed under TAL-alph, Nica tried to scoot to them.

If I can just get to her, she'll stop. It's me she despises.

"Please, TAL-alph, stop. You don't have to do this."

Girac stopped struggling. Releasing the stranglehold, TAL-alph rose and turned to Nica. "You're right, I don't have to. I'm not even supposed to. But I'm going to enjoy this, and no one can stop me." She kicked the body at her feet, smiling at the agony on Nica's face. "Looks like he's not such a threat after all."

She snapped the whip back and forth, cracking closer and closer to Nica's face. "Did you really think TAL was going to let you go? Did you think you could overcome the Delphim?"

Nica flinched as the whip snapped the air all around her.

"You can give yourself up, and follow me back," TAL-alph told her, eyes glinting, "or you can die. Slowly and painfully."

81

"**TAL-ALPH**! Get your slime-covered hide over here!" EC-TAL didn't bother to hide his rage. His workers had run off. His generators had been sabotaged by the feral aquans. And now his alpha was missing. If that yellow didn't show up soon, he'd have to rein in the remainder himself.

"This is not what I expect from that alpha," he muttered as he tramped through the puddles. "The yellow knows this will cost. No more privilege. No more boost."

He stomped into his quarters and headed for the office. "Beta! Where's the controller?" He'd put it somewhere safe. He swore again.

"Beta!" he bellowed again. He hadn't even needed to use the device with this alpha. It had been eager to please and showed no reluctance in keeping the rest of the aquans in line. In fact, this had been a source of contention when the yellow alpha crossed the line and disciplined one of MO-ASHE's medical subjects. But now everything had been turned upside down. The rain hadn't let up in weeks, he'd had no luck hunting, TRE-CH had tried to renege on their trade, the aquans had organized some kind of break, and his alpha was AWOL.

He started dumping out bins and drawers, frustration growing more with each turn. "Beta!"

"EC-TAL?"

TAL gripped his desk. The gray had appeared silently, without warning. "Where were you?"

"I retrieved your device, Expedition Commander TAL." Beta

trembled as he bowed low, holding the remote device before him with both hands. "It was in your sleeping quarters."

The Delphim snatched his missing equipment from the hands of the cowering aquan. In his rage, the urge to swipe at the weak underling swept across TAL, but he stayed his hand. *This one,* he reminded himself, *has at least been useful. No, I'll save my energy for that feckless yellow.* That one would regret having ever received favor when he let his fury loose.

He turned on the tracker and almost threw the remote. The directional heading was faint. He'd have to head back out immediately to catch up.

"Beta! Provisions! Now!"

The aquan disappeared into the pantry, reappearing with a pack and raingear.

Without a word, TAL grabbed the supplies and slammed the door behind him.

MO-ASHE's alpha was standing guard at the gate.

"No one else gets in or out, or I'll take it out of your hide."

The gray's steel eyes narrowed, but he remained silent as TAL passed through.

Hmph. Smarter than he looks. Might see if MO-ASHE is willing to trade.

Guided by the remote's locator, TAL abandoned the path, hoping to make better time. The target stopped moving. He compared the readings against his map. *Oceanside.* The smirk disappeared and he swore, turning on the proximity alert. He wouldn't be within signal range for hours, even if he doubled his pace. Tightening his grip around the pack straps, he powered ahead, daring anything to get in his way.

After a while, there was a *beep-bee-eep. Beep-bee-eep.* TAL grabbed the remote from his holster and studied the display. He'd made good time, but was just barely within control range. *That'll do.* His smile was grim as he activated the implant.

82

N ICA tried to quell her fear. She lifted a weak hand to the surf just beyond them. "You could join us. You could be free."

"I could never join you," the alpha snapped. "I did what I had to to survive, and I'm going to keep on surviving." She grabbed the Olomi by the hair. "I know what it takes, and right now, that's you."

"I won't return." Nica desperately grabbed onto the beach, clinging to the handfuls of sand as if they were solid.

TAL-alph laughed at her with scornful malice. "You can't even stand." She yanked Nica up to her knees. "Do you have any idea how dearly you will pay for what you've cost us?" The alpha spat at the unmoving Girac next to them. "That one was just a guard, easily replaced with a little muscle and boost. But you," she hissed, crouching at eye level, "you were one of MO-ASHE's successes. And so, I can't quite dispose of you. But I—"

Girding up all her strength, Nica swung at TAL-alph's head, striking her temple with the rock she had been clutching in the sand. Heart racing in her panic, she managed to grab at the yellow's whip and thrust her full weight on the maimed hand's grip. Collapsing and rolling away, she cast the weapon into the surf.

Blood dripped down the alpha's cheek. Her voice was livid. "I've taken more than that, you disgusting slime. You'll need more than a rock to—"

The yellow alpha froze, and then seized, her face contorted in a silent scream. She fell to the ground, convulsing on the sand, her limbs extending in spasms.

Once Nica realized what was happening, she scooted anxiously to Girac. "Girac?" She pulled at his arms, trying to roll him toward her. "Please, Girac." She inched him toward the surf. "We're so close." Adrenaline overtook her own pain, and she dragged him little by little to the surf.

The foam reached her limbs, taunting her with a taste of the Deep before it receded. She kept pulling as the waves continued to lap against them.

"Wake up, Girac," she implored. She could see the alpha's body on the shore, continuing to spasm. "If TAL-alph's pain unit is being activated, TAL can't be far off."

Wake up, Girac. Please. Half-submerged, Nica felt the water erode the sand from underneath. She nearly cried with relief as Girac's body shifted with the ebb. She tugged harder, working with the flow.

"There you are! You traitorous piece of filth!" TAL's voice broke from the rocks. "Did you think you could get away with this?"

Nica's heart almost stopped, but she kept scooting and pulling Girac with the tide. TAL descended onto the beach, venom lacing his furious tirade. But he halted at TAL-alph's twitching frame, continuing to unleash threat after threat.

He hasn't seen us. He doesn't know we're here.

Now submerged up to her shoulders, Nica pushed Girac's upper body completely under the waves. A gasp escaped as he coughed and true water reached his lungs. His eyes widened, and he took in a full draught, the first since he'd been taken abovewater.

Bringing her finger to her lips, Nica tried to shush him before he was alert enough to speak, but the Delphim had spotted them. Roaring with anger, he started toward the surf.

"Move, Girac!" She gave a final tug, and they were both afloat. That was all they needed. Not to dive deep or far, but surrender to the current and follow it to freedom.

83

"**W**E MUST take back our planet!"
"We can't undo what has been done. Can we shovel the lava mountains back under the seabed? Can we hurl these Delphim structures back into space?"

The Councillians had been arguing for tides.

"But they must go!"

"They can't go back, and we have no need of land."

"Then leave it to them, but they may not enter the water!"

"We cannot overpower them abovewater, but we can protect our people."

"We must protect our people."

Daevu looked up from the fray as a presence, long absent, washed across his sensory lines. The ache of longing was palpable as his being resonated with the familiar signal. *This can't be true.* But communion was strongest amongst family. He craned his neck to search past the arguments and posturing of the council. He swam toward the archway, testing the waters that came his way, attending to every trace that washed over his receptors.

His heart began rejoicing before Nica swam into his arms.

"Bàbá!"

"My Nica. Little Nica. Can this be true? Rissa told us . . ." He could not continue.

Nica clung to her father, allowing the currents to carry them. "I was as good as dead, but for the healing in the water." Her voice caught as the words she had despaired of uttering flowed. "I'm home, Bàbá. I'm home."

IPARI

THE END

"**G**OT HER!" Kel's declaration reached their cavern long before he towed his niece into view.

Nica tried to turn toward the signal source, but Rissa held her back with the hank of hair she was braiding. "Don't move." Rissa shook her head. "Your hair is as difficult to tame as you were."

Ìyá hovered nearby, smiling at her son and grandchild's turbulent entrance. "The same could be said of her progeny."

Ayla planted her feet against Kel's side and pushed with all her strength, broadcasting her ire throughout the surrounding waters.

Nica sighed. "She doesn't want to wear the wrap."

"That"—Kel handed the writhing child to Nica— "thank the Deep, isn't my job," he said with a smirk. "And Girac won't be any help. Tall, dark, and broody is working on his vows."

Kel gave the wrap to Ìyá. "You're going to need to keep denticles in play with this one," he warned, kicking off with a grin.

"Ayla," Nica said, "did you forget this is a tide of great importance?" The fry in her arms looked up and finally stopped wriggling.

"At least she's slow as a seahorse." Chesnae looked up from her game of shells. "Makes her easy to catch."

"That's for sure." Pilto hopped his pieces across his sister's and leaned back, triumphant. "They say if she swam any slower, she'd be bait."

Nica reached up to stop Rissa's persistent comb and swiveled to her younger siblings. "Who said she's bait?" she demanded.

"Just some larva," Chessie said in a small voice.

Nica took a deep breath, but Ìyá gathered the two young shell players. "It's your bonding tide, I'll handle this."

"You know," Rissa bent down to whisper in Nica's ear, "you complained about wearing a wrap just like that." Her eyes held a mischievous twinkle. "At least Ayla didn't dart for the kelp."

Nica settled her daughter firmly in her lap and turned around again so Rissa could finish her hair. "However, I *did* wear that wrap," she pointed out, "not too long ago, when you and Jonnat made your bonding vows. And now," she said with a light tap on Ayla's nose, "it is your turn to brave the dreaded drape."

Ayla nestled deeper into her ìyá's embrace.

"In the Deep, ọmọ mi, you are fully known. And you are fully loved. And as for those who think we are slow"—Nica took up Ayla's small hand in hers—"they do not understand that even though we are different, that difference makes us stronger in some ways." She traced the edge of each small finger, from tip to base, then interlocked her scarred fingers with her daughter's unwebbed ones and looked into her eyes.

Ayla's tiny fingers, translucent and tinted green, gripped hers, pulling against the gap separating them. Her eyes, green and glowing, widened as her ìyá's face drew near.

Nica touched her forehead to her daughter's and whispered, "We are of the Deep and cannot be curbed or contained. When obstacles are placed before us, we will wear them down until they become sand. We are of the Water, and Water always makes its way."

REPORT

MO-ASHE: The Aqua Sapien Hybrid project continues to produce viable offspring. Embryonic indicators are positive for Delphim longevity and immunity as well as corrective Aqua Sapien procreativity. Syndactyly has been addressed at the genetic level, with minimal trace webbing projected for future generations. Contributions to this ongoing research are invaluable. We will reclaim a future for our race.

BOOST: Initial doses yielded lung adaption and muscle strength within acceptable parameters, along with expected aggression and mental instability. Increased doses resulted in memory loss, suggestibility, and inducible anxiety. This aids in re-educating landed Aquans, especially if collaboration is incentivized. Aqua Sapien water aversion, and even hydrophobia, is noted.

Indigenous aquans seek to exploit perceived vulnerability. Our encounters along the water's edge have been unsuccessful. However, these reports serve to reinforce the threat the water presents.

This planet is ours. We have come too far to fail.

Expedition Commander:
Terraformation/Agriculture/Labor

EOR

·· PRONUNCIATION GUIDE ··

Nica (nee-**kah**)—a rookie Guardian
Rissa (riss**ah**)—Nica's older sister
Kel (rhymes with fell)—Nica's older brother
Jonnat (jaw-**NAT**)—Rissa's fiancé
Ìyá (ee-**yah**)—mother
Laina (**LAY**-nuh)—Nica's mother
Bàbá (bah-**BAH**)—father
Daevu (**DAY**-voo)—Nica's father
Sisẹ (see-**sheh**)—sister
Sisi (see-see)—fine lady, teasing when addressing a younger sister
Ìyá'gba (**yahg**-bah)—grandmother
Babaagba, B'agba (bah-**baahg**-bah)—grandfather
Pescha (peh-shah)—Nica's best friend while in captivity
Girac (jee-**rock**)—guard in medical section
Auryn (ore-inn)—Olomi mother who was taken captive with her young child
Olomi (Owe-**LOW**-mee)—amphibian people of the water, the inhabitants
of the Deep

·· OLOMI TERMS ··

cords—Braided colored kelp to indicate your area and level of training
in serving the community.
communion—The sharing of physiological information as transmitted
through the water. This includes movement, temperature, vibrations,
and reveals the emotional state of the Olomi as well as their physical
condition. Communion enforces empathy in the Deep.
Councillian—A member of the guiding elders in the Olomi community.
When decisions need to be made on behalf of the community, the
councillians discuss the options and vote. Councillians are guild
leaders, similar to senators.
dorsal—Back.
dulse (**dŭls**)—Rhymes with pulse, a seaweed.
fry—Olomi in their first stage of development, similar to a human toddler.
Guardian—Guardians serve as protectors for Olomi communities.
juveniles (**juvies**)—Adolescent Olomi, not quite adults.
sensory lines—Similar to lateral lines in fish, the arrangement of pores
that receive sensory input.
spawn—Baby (n.), giving birth (v.).

S OPHIA HANSEN is an organic author, using no hormones, antibiotics, or pesticides in her writing, unless absolutely convenient. She's lived on a tiny island in Alaska, and the bustling cities of New York and Boston. Now Sophia resides in the Southeast where she writes and edits between fresh(ish) cups of coffee and slices of crisp bacon. After thirty-plus years of marriage, seven children, and numerous pets, she can still fit into her high school earrings.

·· ACKNOWLEDGMENTS ··

Once upon a time, there was a mom.
A mom with many children.
She was a very busy mom.
One day the pastor's wife asked her to write something for the
Christmas program.
"Why would you ask me?" she replied. "I'm just a mom."
"Because you love words," was the quiet answer.
When the mom heard this, she realized it was true. And so, she
began to write.

The Beginning

STORIES don't grow in a vacuum. Like tending seeds, some
people come into our lives to help plant, some weed or water
alongside us, and some help with the harvest. I am deeply grateful
to those who have walked with me on this writing journey.

Thanks be to God who loved me first and planted this story in
my heart.

To my amazing family, especially my dear husband, Craig—your
steadfast love and unwavering support mean the world to me.

To the Enclave/Oasis family—thank you for believing in and
shepherding my book. Your commitment to bringing the best out
of my story has blown me away.

Kirk DouPonce—your cover brought my imaginary world to life. Thank you for helping me show the world what my mind envisioned.

Sandra Lovelace—when you invited me into your world of authors, who knew what lay in store? *Water's Break* is the result of your invitation.

Author communities that have enfolded me, starting with:

BRMCWC (which is easier to type than Blue Ridge Mountains Christian Writers Conference)—DiAnn and Edie, when I stepped into your conference, I was met with encouragement and a fire hose of equipping. Definitely more than I expected or could handle, but you set me on a path of growth. Cherilynn Bisbano, thanks for pointing me to Realm Makers. And Bob Hostetler, your words continue to spur me on: "God has planted in you a story that no one else can write."

Firsts in Fiction—Aaron, Alton, and Molly, yours was the first writers enclave I joined, a virtual meeting where you freely shared your experience. I'm especially grateful for your words, Aaron Gansky, which God used to encourage me when I wasn't sure I had any business pursuing this dream.

Realm Makers—Scott and Becky's vibrant community for speculative fiction writers has been life-giving. I am so thankful for this space and the souls that occupy it!

Writers Chat—Bethany, Johnnie, Jean, Brandy, Melissa, your welcome, encouragement, and friendship through the years has been so much more than a Zoom hangout.

Havok Publishing—Lisa, Teddi, and Andrew—you encouraged me to submit and then published my first stories and invited me to join the team, er, horde. I've learned so much from writing and editing with you. Thanks for your collective heart of encouragement and excellence.

540—Becky, what can I say. Your vision to serve the author community has been beautifully realized. I'm so thankful for you.

Special mentions:

Kim Thomas, you looked at a busy mom and called out the writer in me.

Tosca Lee, my kimchi sister. Always gracious and welcoming, your sweet spirit infuses encouragement wherever you are present. I've learned so much from your teaching and your example.

Halley Cotton, your enthusiasm is infectious. Thanks for being the most amazing cheerleader!

David Jung, my awesome critique buddy. Thanks for sticking it out as we both learned novel mechanics.

Prayer Warriors: Angela, Charity, Lisa (and clan), Kat, Melissa, and Kim, who have faithfully stormed the gates on my behalf. I'm so blessed to be loved by you.

Finally, Cathy, Lauren, and Brandy: You've been with me through the good, the bad, and the ugly—sharing in my joys and fears, and even tears. Thank you for having my back and helping me to stay the course.

It's been an honor and a privilege to learn from so many beautiful people. I couldn't possibly name each of you, but know that I am deeply grateful for the hands and hearts that have encouraged me on my journey.